The Light in Hades

Olympus Retold Series
Book 1

Elise Nelson

Shattered Glass Press

The Light in Hades

Olympus Retold Series Book 1

Published by Shattered Glass Press in the United States of America.

ISBN: 978-1-7776329-4-6

Book cover art by E.M. Lawrence

Book cover design by Covers and Cupcakes LLC

www.coversandcupcakes.com

Edits by Romance Editor, Nina Fiegl, s.p.

www.ninafiegl.com

First edition printing 2024.

You can stay up-to-date on Elise Nelson's work at www.elisenelsonauthor.com.

CONTENTS

To all those who have suffered mental anguish of any kind.

This is for you.

PROLOGUE

Fire roared in the houses, collapsing them into lumps of ash. The boy's eyes burned, the fire's rising warmth a sinister lick across his face. The god behind him clawed his nails into the boy's skin as he forced him to watch—every crackle of fire and failing roof caving into the homes of wailing gods and goddesses fleeing from the wreckage. The claws sunk deeper, digging their jagged ends into his flesh until the teen could feel the heat of blood trickle down his cheek.

"Watch, *boy*," the deity hissed. A searing pain tore into his chest like the fire singeing his skin. "This is the first night of many. Your future starts now."

CHAPTER ONE

Corre

The air smelled like sunshine. That warm earth around the cottage always smelled faintly of the cocktail of flowers Correlia and her mother carefully grew. But today it was different. *More*, somehow, though the young goddess couldn't place why or how. Maybe it was simply that her powers were getting stronger, growing like the pastel fields around her. The thick blanket of dewy grass stretched its way to the forest entrance beyond her tiny home. She swore it was all she'd looked at for the past week.

But it was worth it.

She stared down at the emerald leaves pouring over her fingers. The bright blush of pink that bloomed at the center created the perfect contrast. "Finally," she breathed, blowing a strand of rose-gold hair from her face and placing her creation into the soil. With one slow wave of her hand, the earth swallowed the stem and roots, branching the velvety plant into the ground beneath.

A smile tugged at her lips for a fraction of a second, but it quickly collapsed when something tightened in her chest. Something threatening to take this small joy away from her. "Not today," she whispered, patting the ground beside her rosy creation, anchoring herself to the present. Today was a day to celebrate. Her plant had been welcomed into the earth, successfully formed. At last.

It took almost two years of serious study, but Correlia—or Corre, as she was most well known—was finally getting the hang of this life she was to lead. These powers she never understood. Her mother had spoken with her extensively about her grand calling since she was old enough to retain the information. Then, as she got older and she approached training age, the discussions became more serious. She'd spoken of Corre's responsibilities and why she and her powers were so necessary. So *important*. "You are Persephone," she'd said. "You are the embodiment of life and light in this world."

No pressure, she'd grumbled to herself.

Corre swallowed hard and planted her gaze firmly on the newly birthed flower draped beside her bent knees. As that sweet, grassy aroma once again filled her senses, a feeling of peace soaked into her skin. The newfound serenity allowed that faint smile on her lips to reform and spread in fullness across her face.

Despite any doubts or anxieties that crept into her mind, she couldn't deny this victory. Up until now, all she could make were rust-colored weeds and wilted flowers that never stuck around or lived beyond their first moment placed in the earth. But today, she managed to bring color into the world. To make something sprout and liven the field around her home, alongside the intricate flowers created by her mother.

The nineteen-year-old had made her first successful creation at last. Not just a replica of whatever her mother had last shown her, which to date had been the only plants to stick around. She created something all her own, and it stuck. Just in time for her coronation.

And it felt pretty good.

Her cheek sunk lazily into her palm as she admired her little sprout. Strands of wavy hair fluttered against her skin, the wind wiggling the leaves and making the blades of grass dance around her. A content sigh escaped her lips as she fell back and stretched against the earth. "Day one of successfully becoming Persephone." *The first of many*, she hoped.

When the wind blew the plant against her toes, and her eyes settled on the clouds swirling drunkenly above her, her smile dropped. *How am I supposed to make a world of these?* Her chest tightened again. That familiar pull tugging just a little harder. The moment her body tensed, something shook beneath her feet. She snapped up, and a gasp shot up her throat. Her beautiful pink and emerald creation shivered violently and began to wilt. "Oh no," she whispered, immediately squeezing her eyes shut. "Breathe, Corre. Breathe."

I don't need to worry, she assured herself, tidying the chaos spiking in her mind. *I'm already off to a good start. I can do this. I can do this.*

Her breaths steadied, and the world around her slowed. Sunlight warmed her freckled skin, and the scent of that new flower wafted through her nose, pooling through her. She opened her eyes and looked at the pastel petals. Her shoulders relaxed. Her fingers slid down one of the plush leaves. "It didn't disappear this time." She closed her eyes again, soaking in the perfect combination of fresh, earthy aromas and warm caresses from the sun.

As soon as Corre had turned eighteen, she'd embarked on the path of study and tutelage to become Persephone. As a "Great One," she was required to train thoroughly for two years in order to take on her given title at age twenty. It was what her adopted mother, Berenice, had readied her for since childhood. She hadn't been allowed to train until then—something about it risking the wellbeing of the planet. So, Berenice taught her as best she could, having received instruction from Zeus himself.

But her twentieth birthday was only a few weeks away, and until today, she'd been no closer to fulfilling her role and prophecy as the goddess Persephone than she'd been when she was a child. Was one plant really something to celebrate?

The loud chirping of a bird made Corre look up. Its feathers were a beautiful mix of cyan and ruby, perfectly paired with the vibrant world around it. She smiled and leaned onto her back, studying the small creature's round puff of a body and the sharpness of its beak. It chirped one more time before flying away. Her eyes followed it until its body became shrouded by the rich fullness of a maple tree a few yards away. Berenice had created that one. She had to learn the ways of creation before Corre did so she could properly teach her, but her powers were limited. Only her daughter could fulfill the job in its entirety.

Her mother was the Goddess of Agriculture, the assigned goddess "Demeter". She had been given that power and title to help her adopted daughter. But all the pressure was on Corre, and she desperately wished it wasn't.

The young goddess groaned, begging herself not to think about it all. But the time to show Zeus her powers was coming soon. She'd have to walk before his throne and show him what she could do.

But what if she wasn't good enough? What would happen? Would she be cast off, too?

Her fist curled around a patch of grass. *Would I become like...him?*

Corre had heard stories of the Underworld for as long as she could remember. About the dangers lurking there, and who would one day be running it. It gave her chills to know that he'd been down there all this time, training to be completely evil, while she was up here training to make the world a brighter, more beautiful place.

Part of Corre didn't believe he existed. He could be a myth for all she knew. Theron. The ruler of the Underworld. The appointed Hades.

"Corre!" Her name pierced through the songs of birds and shimmering plants. She tried to ignore it. "Corre!" She sighed and plastered on a smile, turning to face her mother. The tiny goddess waved at her from the end of the path at the mouth of the cottage. "Come in, child! Supper is ready, and I have something to tell you."

"Coming!" she called, smoothing her starlight-colored dress as she rose. She reveled in the softness of the dirt and grass beneath her feet. Whatever her responsibilities were and whatever was going on around her melted away. It was a gift she'd always possessed: the ability to move forward. To be cheerful, despite anything and everything around her. Her mother often told her she was the sun itself. Which was why her true identity meant so much more than her title as a Great One.

She was Corre. Just Corre.

The moment she walked through the door, the young goddess was hit with the scent of freshly baked cinnamon bread. Every muscle in her body relaxed as they adjusted to the warm, cozy home. Her feet slid against cool tiles, wiping away the dirt as she padded to the wooden table in the middle of the kitchen, which was affixed to both the front entryway and main living quarters of the house. It was a small, snug cottage, but it was home.

"How was it out there?" Berenice asked, sorting through a drawer of silverware. Her hazelnut eyes crinkled as she smiled.

"I finally made something that didn't die, so pretty well, actually." Corre laughed, but Berenice's eyes widened.

"Is that so? See!" she wobbled a spoon at her daughter, "I knew you were almost there!"

"Yeah, yeah," Corre teased, waving a hand back with another laugh. When her mother grinned back at her, Corre couldn't help but wonder if every god and goddess on Olympus was as happy as she was. *Of course they are*, she assured herself as Berenice placed a bundled loaf on the table in front of her. *They have to be.* If an orphan like her could revel in such happiness and love, all the others must have it in spades.

It only made sense.

Theron

Pain splintered through Theron's chest, jerking him awake. His body shook as he lurched forward in bed. With one swift movement, he swept the inky black hair from his face and caught his breath. The slick coolness of sweat was nothing new, but he hated the clammy residue it left on his skin.

He couldn't remember what he'd been dreaming about before panic jostled him awake. Sweat clung to his skin, sticking the dark strands of hair to his face. He sped across his chambers, bending over the small fountain in his bedroom for any sort of relief. In the dim light of the washing room, Theron sighed, splashing cool water against his skin. These dreams—these nightmares—were becoming more frequent, more intense, in a way he didn't understand. Grabbing a ratted towel to dry his face, Theron couldn't help but wonder if it had anything to do with his coronation. Maybe it was finally coming, after all these years.

His destiny may finally come to pass, and he would be Hades, ruler of the Underworld and God of the Dead, after all this time. The ruler of his own kingdom.

A scream echoed through his corner of the labyrinth, but he didn't budge. He hated that he was used to it. The screams, like the nightmares, were his constant companion and were becoming more frequent. It had been hard at first—when he was small and afraid of every creak and snarl that snapped at him—but now the sound was like static in the back of his mind. Just another sound to ignore.

He pulled on a new tunic and wrapped his crow-black cape around his shoulders, clasping it at his throat, when a knock pounded at the door. "What?" he shouted, irritation dripping from the word. Someone mumbled on the other side, but the thick metal was impossible to hear through. Theron growled under his breath and strode to the door, flinging it open and glaring at the hunched creature gawking up at him. "What is it?"

The demon trembled, bowing its long, hollow head. "You're wanted in Master Thanatos's quarters, sir." Even without eyes in its beaked skull, the servant's fear was evident. It, like most other creatures slithering around Tartarus, appeared decayed—this one even more so. Its body was withered, shriveled to little more than bones, making its large, crow-like face even more exaggerated.

Theron raised an eyebrow. What was so urgent that his master needed him so early in the morning? He hadn't requested his pupil's presence for weeks. Thanatos's face flashed through Theron's mind, in a memory from long ago, but he resisted the urge to let it linger. Pain cranked the muscles in the young Hades' chest, and his gloved hand curled into a fist. *Whatever it is, it doesn't matter. I can handle it.*

He swallowed and shot a glare down at the trembling creature. "Why is my presence needed?"

"Something about a new assignment," the demon croaked, raising its head to stare up at its master.

"What?" Theron's eyebrows drew together. *New assignment?* After another moment, he nodded and said, "You may leave now. Tell him I'll be there right away."

The demon nodded and scurried away like a rat down the corridor.

Theron's heart pounded against his chest, but he didn't let the possibilities of what Thanatos might do poke fear into the armor of strength he'd spent all these years constructing.

Without another thought, he took a deep breath and headed toward Thanatos's chambers.

CHAPTER TWO

Corre

C orre smiled, her cheeks full of the iced cinnamon bread freshly pulled from the oven. Her mother snorted and shook her head. "How is it that you can eat an entire loaf in one sitting? Do you have a secret power I don't know about?"

"I don't know. I just love your cooking," she said with a laugh, tearing off another piece of bread and letting her teeth sink into it as she hummed in delight.

Her mother chuckled and sauntered to the stove, where a thick potato chowder was bubbling to a boil. The older goddess stirred the heavy soup absentmindedly, singing softly to herself.

Corre's hands stilled. "What is that? It sounds familiar."

Berenice smiled, still stirring. "I'm surprised you remember it. I haven't sung it for quite some time." She tapped the spoon against the rim of the pot and tasted the tiny drip of soup that stuck to the wooden rim.

Corre looked back at her half-eaten hunk of bread, focusing on the melody. It was a memory like smoke. It was so familiar, but when she searched her mind, racking it for a concrete moment to grab hold of, there was nothing to grasp. Nothing but the vague knowledge that it existed somewhere in her past.

"Did you make it up?"

"No," Berenice said as she plopped the spoon back into the burbling chowder.

"Is it well known?" A stupid question. If it was well known she wouldn't be asking about it. Plus, it seemed strange. Like it was intimate in some way. She supposed it was a valid question after all. Maybe it was a song known only to the humans, and somehow her mother heard about it in her travels while creating the plants and trees in their various lands.

Corre lived a sheltered life. She didn't know a lot about the world, despite all her research and questions. She knew the other gods and goddesses, but the humans seemed to have such rich lives all their own, unlike those of her kind. They seemed to do a lot more than she did, despite the fact that, without her, their world wouldn't grow. Without her and her mother, they would die.

Still, she envied them. Their communities, their songs, the freedom to choose their own destinies.

"No," her mother's voice cracked through her thoughts. "I actually learned it from you."

A lump wedged its way into Corre's throat. "From me?"

The room fell silent, and an unsettling chill snaked down her spine.

"When you came to me," Berenice started, her voice almost reverent, "you sang it every night as you fell asleep. I tried to comfort you, but you wouldn't let me. Not for a year or so. You just wrapped yourself in the comfort of your blanket and sang that melody, sometimes with words I've long forgotten."

Corre shook her head, her rose-gold hair sweeping across her shoulder blades. "Why can't I remember?"

Berenice let go of the spoon and turned to face her daughter. She wrapped her petite arms around Corre, squeezing her tightly against her chest. When her daughter wrapped her arms around her, too, Berenice finally spoke. "Sometimes we lose parts of ourselves when we have to face new lives."

The young goddess frowned, pulling back slightly to look into her mother's chestnut eyes. "But...why did I stop?"

Her mother cupped Corre's face with her slender hands. "Maybe you didn't need it anymore." Berenice's smile widened, but there was something off about the glimmer in her eyes, and Corre couldn't stop thinking about the song. That familiar melody.

She forced a smile. "You're probably right. It's nothing." But something in her stomach turned.

Berenice's hand fell away. "Good. Now, why don't we eat? The chowder should be ready."

Corre nodded, a smile dimpling her cheeks, but she couldn't shake the feeling that accompanied that song.

"Did you leave any bread to have with the soup?" the older goddess asked with a laugh.

Corre's eyes fell to the remainder of the loaf, but her stomach twisted and her ears fogged.

"Corre?"

She looked at her mother and forced another smile. "Yes, there's plenty. Let's eat."

Choking every bite down until supper was over, Corre made sure her true feelings didn't show. A smile stayed plastered on her face as she spent the evening the way she always did—spending time with her mother in their little cottage in the middle of the glen. By the time Berenice brought out a book of Olympus's history to teach Corre more about her place in the world, the young Persephone's cheeks started to ache. But still, she kept smiling, trying her best to ignore the aching for a memory she couldn't grab hold of.

CHAPTER THREE

Theron

Theron trudged into the cavern deep within the belly of the labyrinth. He avoided the eyes of his mentor, whose gaze burned into him as he tapped one long, gnarled talon against the arm of his onyx throne.

"Ah, there you are, my loyal pupil." The gravelly words fell from the deity's mouth like boulders crashing down on his apprentice. Theron quickly stepped to his place at the foot of the throne, kneeling and bowing his head before speaking.

"What do you require of me today, master?" he asked, trying his best to steady the tremble in his voice. He *hated* that, truly detested it. That tremble. That slight tremor in his voice that never went away whenever he had to come before Thanatos like this. It didn't matter how many grueling years he'd spent building resistance against the deity before him—how many missions he'd gone on and how many lives he'd stolen at the River Styx.

Everyone on Mt. Olympus was said to fear him—the dark and powerful Hades—and every wretched soul in the Underworld cowered at his presence. So why was it that no matter how many times he knelt before Thanatos, he trembled like a child?

A long chuckle rolled from Thanatos's throat. Theron flinched, hoping his master didn't notice.

He did.

"Why are you so nervous, boy?"

"I'm not," Theron said, his low voice echoing across the cavernous chamber.

"Then look at me," he hissed.

Swallowing sharply, Theron adjusted his face to show no fear and looked up into his master's eyes. He forced a deep scowl on his long face—a look that apparently appeased his master. For now, at least.

Thanatos sat back. "That's better. Now, the reason you are here. I have a new assignment for you."

His apprentice squared his shoulders and stood up, his cape curling around him like a curtain of shadow. "What is it?" His voice was steady now, but his master eyed him carefully. Theron fixed his eyes back on Thanatos, skeletal and ominous on the throne that would one day be his. The enormous being's crooked, malformed mouth smirked. "You are to go to the world above. Just for today." Theron bristled. His steady breaths faltered. *A-above?*

He'd never been allowed to leave the Underworld. He was brought here at thirteen and hadn't left for twelve years. What would it be like to step back into the sun? "Why?" he tried to sound indifferent, but the surprise was too potent.

Thanatos's eyes narrowed. "I've noticed something disturbing recently," he said, his beady eyes still burning into his apprentice's skull. Theron tried not to look, opting to keep his head bowed instead. "Have you noticed that there has been a lack of human souls as of late?"

On a typical day, they received around two hundred souls. How many had there been lately? "I haven't noticed a sizable decline," he concluded. "There have still been well over a hundred a day."

His master's hand curled against the arm of his throne. The talons on his withered hand scratched against the stone slowly, deliberately, the grating sound scratching against Theron's eardrums. "Yes," Thanatos said through gritted teeth. "But we should be getting twice that at least."

"I understand, master." Theron's gaze flickered up before quickly falling back to the floor.

"So, we need to find out what is happening. I suspect it has something to do with this new round of Great Ones coming of age on Olympus."

Theron looked up. "New round of gods?" Thanatos's mangled face contorted as he pounded a fist against the throne.

"Are you stupid, boy?" he hissed. Theron's eyes darted back to the floor. "You're one too, aren't you? You're twenty-five years old! How do you not know your place?"

The young Hades swallowed hard, summoning any ounce of his powers he could to help his limbs stop shaking. "I know my place," he tried to say firmly, but the words came out weak. "My place is here."

"That's right," the deity hissed. "And just as you are reaching your prophecy's fulfillment, so are your counterparts above." Theron nodded, though he wished he could say what was really on his mind, but he guarded the words in his mind so his master wouldn't know. That he should have been crowned the ruler here five years ago. *I'm sure he has his reasons*, he told himself. *He's looking out for me. As he always does.*

"So you remember that the gods such as Zeus, Demeter, and Poseidon—and many others—had been created by the Titans first, and you and the others your age came from them. Correct?" His words oozed with patronizing disdain. Of course Theron knew the tale. Everyone did. There was a first wave of gods, and from them, more came. Some of these first gods' offspring were Great Ones, and each one was given a prophecy at the appropriate age so they could do what was needed of them when the time came.

When they were twenty. When a Great One came of age, they were to take on their true identity. Theron's, of course, was to be Hades. But he wasn't ready yet. He was behind, so he needed to do everything in his power to catch up. Whatever Thanatos needed of him, he must do.

"Yes, master," he managed to reply, though his own fists curled tightly at his sides.

"Well things are amiss. It makes sense, does it not? Suddenly fewer souls are passing through the River Styx when, coincidentally, many newly coronated gods and goddesses are reaching their full strengths and fulfilling their prophecies?" He shook his bulbous head. Theron watched the oblong shadow cast at the base of the throne. "I don't like it. It leaves a bad taste in my mouth."

"Why?" Theron winced when he realized he'd said the word out loud. "I trust your decision," he quickly added. "I would just like to understand."

Thanatos sighed, drawing it out longer than necessary. "The gods up there are unpredictable. Who's to say Zeus isn't overstepping? He could be trying to reign over the dead now, too."

"How could he do that?" Theron glanced up. "He's not in Tartarus, and he'd be going against what the Titans have prophesied—the way things need to be done." If things went against the prophecies, what would happen to the state of the world?

"He may not be able to work in Tartarus, but he can help the others keep the humans alive longer. He can make things...*difficult* for us."

"Wouldn't it be better for the humans to stay alive as long as possible—"

The deity pounded a fist against his throne again. The sound roared through the room like the breath of a monster. "Have you learned nothing of your role?" he shouted, but this time Theron stood his ground and fixed his stare on his master.

"I've done nothing but prepare to be Hades all these years." He kept his voice strong. "I know my role."

"Then you know you have no jurisdiction over the souls on Earth, just as Zeus has no jurisdiction over their souls once they reach Tartarus?"

"Yes, of course."

"And you don't find it suspicious that fewer souls are making their way here?"

Theron paused. "No, but I will do my duty and investigate. Whatever you think is best."

"Try to keep up, *boy*," he hissed. "And *think* for once. Use that blasted head of yours! Who knows what Zeus could do with his power if he gains control of the humans for longer periods of time?" Theron tried not to shiver at the rising anger in his mentor's voice, but those burns and scarred flesh on his back throbbed.

After a long silence, Thanatos lowered his voice, leaning forward on his throne. "You know I always think of what is in your best interest, right?"

Theron nodded. "Yes, master."

"This is something that will help you become the great leader you were born to be."

"I understand."

"Good." Thanatos's misshapen face cracked into a crooked grin. "Go to Olympus at once. Find out all you can of the new Great Ones. It would be too risky to get information out of Zeus's men. He could spot you, and they would likely report the news back to him anyway, despite any threats or torture you inflict upon them. Go after the gods most likely to threaten us. Any source of light must be examined. Any threat against our rule over the dead. Is that clear?"

"I'll investigate thoroughly and find any possible threats."

"That's my boy," the deity croaked. He started leaning back on his throne when a thought made him stop. "Oh. In particular, look into who will be the goddess Persephone."

"Persephone?" He'd never heard the name before.

"She is your antithesis and is being trained by Demeter to make Earth filled with life. Another goddess who may know her whereabouts is Athena. I've learned she is training her, too, for reasons unknown to me. Check on the young goddess, and anyone who may know her, and tell me what you find."

"Yes, master," he said, soaking up the information and committing it to memory. His heart raced. *I can't screw this up.* He could still feel the burns from the last time he screwed up.

I can't go through that again. Not until the burns heal.

"Good," the deity said again, sitting all the way back on his throne. He turned to the demons standing attention around the room, each one a deformed creature of the night. Unlike those which served Theron, these ones possessed thin, but strong, bodies of pure bone, with blood-red eyes like fiery stones. When the monstrous god's gaze settled back on his apprentice, he said, "Now, go. And do *not* disappoint me."

"Of course." Theron bowed, then quickly turned on his heel and left the room. As soon as his back was turned, he let his face fall and his mind wander. *Above*, he thought, walking deep into the labyrinth. *Finally.*

Chapter Four

Corre

T he market was bustling today, and Corre loved it. She practically lived for the days she could go into the market and show everyone the fresh, plump creations her mother had produced. And soon, she'd be able to sell some of her own, too.

The smells were always divine—one of her favorite parts of it all. As soon as she could see the marketplace, she could breathe in the delightful air of candied fruits and the sporadic waves of earthy aromas from a variety of homemade concoctions. The market was a chance for everyone to get together and show off what they'd been working on. But most of all, it was where everyone could take a break and just *be*.

Today the spirits were especially high. The sounds erupting from the crowd were louder than usual, the mass of bodies denser. Corre smiled and waved at unfamiliar faces, excited to see anyone new. Anyone who wasn't the small handful of people she saw on a regular basis.

"Whoa," she mumbled as a group of teenage goddesses bumped into her, all of which were laughing and huddled together. Beyond them, children held hands and giggled, giving each other hand-crafted necklaces of precious beads and gems, and a husband and wife were adoring each other by a booth of bottled jams. Gods and goddesses all around Mt. Olympus were showing off an array of different rarities. Corre had a hard time deciding which booth to go to first. The market was once every cycle of the moon, and it was getting bigger and better each time, likely because the second wave of gods and goddesses was coming of age.

Corre strolled through a row of booths. Bright fabrics, gems, and hand-painted pottery lined the slick, wooden shelves around her. Symphonic harmonies played by musical goddesses and gods crooned through the air, a delightful undercurrent of laughter bubbling beneath it. Corre *loved* it. All of it. She looked forward to it every new moon.

"Corre!" a familiar voice called out. A tall, slender goddess approached her, crimson hair cascading down her back in strong, rippling curls. Corre always thought of Athena as the perfect combination of grace and strength, and anyone could see it in the way the goddess walked.

"Hello, Athena," she said with a smile, putting her basket down to give the goddess a hug. "How are you? You look radiant, as always."

Athena chuckled and swatted the air, waving off the compliment. "Oh, you're too kind, dear. I'm doing well. How is your mother?"

"She's doing well. She..." her voice trailed off as the jubilance of the crowd behind Athena made an abrupt shift. The air grew heavy, like a prickly blanket had been tossed over the festivities. A small group of gods nearby whispered to each other hastily, and when overhead by passersby, the shocked expressions they wore grew contagious. Soon, almost everyone in the market was either wide-eyed, gasping, or holding a hand to their chests, anxiously twisting the fabric of their colorful robes.

"What's going on?" Corre whispered. Athena's forehead wrinkled as she scanned the scattering crowd. Corre took a step closer, but the people were already rushing out of the market. "I'm sorry, Athena, but I have to go. I hope you have a lovely rest of your day."

Before the older goddess could respond, Corre sped toward the dwindling crowd. When she spotted a plump god she'd never seen before, she grabbed him gently by the elbow. He turned to look at her, muttering something under his breath. She gave him an apologetic smile. "I'm sorry, but I couldn't help but ask what's going on. Why is everyone running away? I've never seen such a fuss here before." *Or anywhere*, she thought, trying to remember a time when she had.

The god's eyes bulged. "You didn't hear?"

"No, what—"

"It's him," he said, his voice ragged. "It's Hades. He's coming."

Corre's blood turned cold. Her hand froze on the god's elbow. "H-Hades? As in Theron of Tartarus?"

"Yes," the god said urgently, tossing her wrist to her side. "Hades. Theron. Whatever you want to call him. He's been spotted coming out of Tartarus. We're all in danger." Before she could ask any more questions, the stout god bolted out of the marketplace.

She didn't even have time to process what was going on before everyone was gone. Every single vendor, musician, and soul was gone, their scattered goods left in disarray. She couldn't believe they'd abandoned such precious materials. These weren't easy items to make. There was a reason they were sold here.

Was Theron truly that terrible? How could one god instill so much fear?

A hand curled over Corre's shoulder. She gasped and turned around swiftly, her heart lodging itself up her throat.

When she saw it was Athena, Corre's muscles relaxed. "Oh. I thought you were—"

"Hades?" the older goddess said, a thin brow rising. Corre nodded, and Athena offered a gentle smile. "Don't worry. They're all afraid of a myth. I'm sure there's nothing to fear." Corre nodded once more, but she wasn't convinced.

Hades. Athena had said his title as if that was all that defined him. Then again, a lot of gods and goddesses chose their titles as their names. Anyone who was appointed as one of the "Great ones" could either embrace the title as their own name or keep their birth name and only call themselves their title when summoned by Zeus or when needed for their duties.

Corre liked her *own* name and had decided long ago to only go by Persephone when absolutely necessary. It was an identity given to her. It wasn't who she really was. She had to be fine with both, though. She'd be called Persephone almost exclusively soon, even if she expressly told the others to only call her Corre. But she couldn't help but wonder if Theron wanted to go by Hades at all. Athena had made a point of doing it, too, as did the other gods. His title defined him to them.

Maybe it made him less real to them. But it just didn't sit right with Corre, though she couldn't figure out why. Perhaps it was because the young goddess wanted to believe that someone couldn't be as bad as Hades. It made more sense that the stories were of a persona. A myth born from the prophecy Theron was appointed to fulfill. Who knew what the legends spoke of the kind of goddess Persephone was? Well, Corre knew the basics, as she was told them backward and forward. But there could be more. There were things that didn't make sense to her. Her duties, for one, were not something that came naturally to her.

And someone who had the strength and power to kill without breaking a sweat? Someone who could drag a soul to the Underworld and doom them for eternity? Surely, these myths about Hades were just that: myths. Theron had to be just a god like everyone else.

But the more she thought of the gods and goddesses fleeing the marketplace with such haste and fright, the more she felt that something was very wrong with Theron. That he was more beast than god. Someone who looked like the demonic creatures that swarmed the Underworld and snapped at the heels of dying humans. That blanket of unease that had fallen upon the once happy, active marketplace couldn't have been brought on by mere tales. Theron must be just as evil and ugly as the stories made him out to be. A decaying skeleton of a man with no heart, soul, or eyes to peer into. A monster.

She gave Athena a tight smile. "I'm sure you're right. I'm sure there's no such Hades. I'm sure the real Theron is nothing to be feared." But the words spilled from her like broken petals, wilting with the fear soaking her lips. Nothing could stop the tightening in her chest. No fake smile or empty sentiment could loosen that knot.

As Corre left the market and sped back home, all she could think about was the god who'd left the Underworld—more *monster* than god—and how she hoped to the Titans that she would never run into him.

CHAPTER FIVE

Theron

The air was different up here. It wasn't muggy or damp. It didn't smell like the inside of some living thing. It was fresh. Open. Theron couldn't place the right word on the sensation; it was just *good*. Relieving. Like he'd been breathing through a mask for twelve years, without realizing it until leaving the Underworld and looking into the light. Breathing in this new atmosphere.

Scanning the area, Theron tried to figure out where to go first. Thanatos had given him very few directions, but he knew which of the gods to target and had a general sense of where to find them. "Head west," he commanded his fleet of demons, each one chomping at its hooked, chiseled bit to get their clutches on any unsuspecting gods or goddesses. Theron turned to look at each one. There were five in total. Perhaps next time Thanatos would give him more. But this time, he'd gotten this handful of lackeys—these gargoyles come to life, taking on a more sinister presence than any mere statue ever could, especially in the light. What was it about the daylight that made them so much more repulsive?

"What are you waiting for?" he barked. "Go!"

The creatures fumbled to attention. "Yes, sire," one cawed, quickly scuttling forward. The others followed. Theron trudged behind them, his cape snapping in the hurried wind. The young Hades resisted the urge to look at the scenery around him. It was nice to get something new to look at. Something not gray, pale, or pitch black. But he knew better than to appreciate this world, especially in front of his servants.

He needed to stay focused.

He rushed by the trees stretching to the blue-gray sky, the blossoming flowers, and the fields of strikingly green grass. Everything was so far from death and decay that it made him uncomfortable. He stared straight ahead, striding through his pack of demons and taking the lead toward the first stop on his trek of Olympus.

"Find me the goddess Athena," he barked, and his demons bowed their heads and fluttered past him. He kept moving, kept staring ahead until they made it onto the outskirts of a village. Maybe they could get some information here that would prove useful. "On second thought," he said, lifting his gloved hand. His demons halted. "Stand behind me. Let's see what these gods have to say."

He strode into the village and scanned the empty cluster of huts. The ground between each straw home was dry and cracked, with only occasional spurts of grass jutting in uneven patches between them and through the middle path through town. "Should we keep moving?" One demon croaked.

"No." There was not a soul to be seen, but several could be felt. They were all around him. He felt their presence. He'd been taught better than to leave his judgment to his eyes and ears. "There," he said, pointing to a hut to his right, following the ebbing sensations inside him. Thanatos had told him that gods and goddesses without special titles were basically humans. They possessed no significant powers other than immortality and maybe something mundane. He could feel that the residents of this village were these types of gods. He felt nothing more than living, breathing, immortal souls.

The town was dusty, the ground obviously frequently trampled upon by busy beings going about whatever purposes they deemed important in their trivial lives. He wondered why they were here, what their purposes were. He had a hard time believing any god would be destined for nothing. But that's what Thanatos had told him, so he'd have to trust him on it.

He kicked open the wooden door of the hut that sat lined up next to identical houses of the same flimsy calibre. As he trudged in, something shuddered down his spine and into the soles of his feet. He staggered back, and a flash of something crossed his mind—something darkly familiar. A splash of crimson. A flash of something black. A cry. An image he couldn't make out.

What the hell...

He shook the thought from his mind and grunted, swiping the tousled black hair off his face and moving his broad body through the gaping mouth of the tiny hut.

The minuscule residence was barely more than a small room one would use to store cloaks. It consisted of a shabby rug that appeared to have once held color, flat, volume-less cushions spread out on the floor on the far back wall, and a wooden board propped up to be used—Theron presumed—as a table. In a place this cramped, he shouldn't have a hard time finding any residents, and he felt their presence here.

Slowly, he moved one boot against the powdered dirt floor, then another, until he spotted a curtain the same color as the wall of one spot he hadn't noticed. He should have, though. The house was cylindrical, and the curtain's placement added a corner and depth that didn't make sense with the rest of the hut.

"Check there," Theron commanded, nodding his head toward the curtain. As if completely starving and just told to eat, the demons swarmed the curtain and ripped it open, revealing a few huddled figures, maybe three or four, crouched together in fear. Theron could only make out the first person, as he was hiding whatever others were behind him. "Take them outside," he said. "Maybe they'll tell us what we need to know."

Whimpers filled his ears as he strode out into the center of town. With every step he took, the whimpers grew louder, putting him on edge. He was used to whimpers of fear. He heard them every time he offered a command or trained for combat with the creatures that lurked in the Underworld. Why did these ones make his stomach turn sour?

"Sire, the villagers," a raspy voice called out behind him. Theron turned to see a family of three. The god he'd seen before was now facing him, standing up with his back slightly bent backward, his arms stretched out to his sides in an effort to shield his family. There was a goddess behind him, huddled over what appeared to be a child.

An odd feeling swirled in his gut, squeezing his soured stomach. What was he to do now? He needed answers. Thanatos expected that of him. If he didn't find the information he needed—if he didn't find Athena or the others—*he*'d be the one made an example of when he returned. Thanatos would take it out on him. Punish him. Rightfully so, he supposed, but still, the thought sent chills crawling down his spine.

He focused on the adult male god and stepped forward. With every slow movement, the trembling god pulled his arms back a little more. As Theron approached and his demons snapped and swirled around him, others in town poked their heads out of their doors and windows. Exactly as Theron had hoped.

The god's dirty face and pale blue eyes stayed on Theron's, never straying from the young Hades' gaze. "State your name," Theron said, his deep voice swelling across the town center. From the corner of his eye, he saw some of the villagers retract into their homes.

"B-Brutus Faire," the god sputtered. "W-we have done nothing wrong, sir. We j—"

"Quiet!" Theron barked. The woman let out a small yelp as she crouched over her child. Theron's servants were unaffected by their master's command and continued circling the small family. "Now," Theron said, bending to meet the male god's eyes more evenly, "tell me. Where can I find the goddess Athena?"

The powerless god's lips sucked in, as if he was forcing himself not to speak. One of Theron's eyebrows flickered. "I am not a patient man," he said. "You will tell me now or deeply regret it."

"I-I don't know," the man said. "H-honest to Zeus, I don't know. We—"

Theron pushed the man aside and looked to the demon on his right. "Take the woman."

"No!" the man cried, but the demon did as he was told and took hold of the goddess's arms, peeling her from the young boy who now stood alone, his head on his tiny kneecaps.

"Please!" The goddess cried, reaching for her son. "He's just a boy. He—"

Theron raised a hand, his gaze shifting to hers. "Quiet! Do not speak unless it is about Athena."

Tears spilled from the woman's eyes, dripping down her cheeks. She couldn't wipe them away because of the demon now holding her by the wrists. Theron's stomach squeezed, but he didn't have time to wonder why. He shifted his eyes to the child and focused on the task at hand.

"Look at me, boy, and tell me what you know." Theron stared at the balled-up child. "Unless any of you can tell me where to find Athena!" he called out to the rest of town.

"I-I don't know, sir," a tiny voice rose to his ears. When Theron looked down, the small boy was peering up at him, his large brown eyes welling with tears. The god froze. Something lurched in his chest, and then he heard something again. A shrill cry. A blazing fire blinded his vision. Houses splintered and broke into clouds of dust in the streets. And for some strange, unknown reason, he was afraid, too.

"I know where she is!" A voice called out from another direction. Theron blinked, and the vision was gone. He turned and saw a woman in tattered clothes, with blond ringlets hanging limply by her shoulders. Her hand clutched the brown bodice of her dress.

"*Where?*"

"Across the valley. She lives in the Twisted Wood, about fifty paces in. Her hut can be seen about thirty paces from the west entrance. She teaches pupils out there. It can't be missed."

Theron nodded, suppressing a satisfied smile.

"No!" the mother of the child cried out. Theron whipped around and saw one of his demons opening a claw above her son. Another odd feeling curdled in his stomach, and he leapt slightly forward.

"Halt!" he yelled, and the demon stopped. Even in its strange, object-like form, he could tell the demon was confused. When the goddess's face matched it, Theron tried to salvage the situation. His reputation needed to stay intact. But as he looked down at the innocent child, he couldn't bear the thought of anything happening to him. A flaw on his part, he presumed. Thanatos would not be happy about it. He needed to think fast. "Th-the child is of no use to us," he said to his servants. "We have what we need." He clenched his fists.

What am I doing? What will Thanatos say?

Panic rose in his throat like bubbling acid. "But if any of you so much as get in my way, I will do what I must!" he yelled at the town and then turned toward its edge to follow the path to the Twisted Wood.

He couldn't bear to look at the child so he kept his face forward, but when the small voice said, "Thank you," he couldn't resist shooting a glance back. When he met the boy's eyes, he heard another cry, but it didn't match the child's mother's or anyone else's in town, as far as he could tell.

Something sunk in his stomach. He looked at the mother and down at her restrained wrists. "Let her go," Theron said, and the demon did as it was told. "Let's go."

They strode away in silence, the god-to-be of the Underworld doing his best to intimidate the crowd on his way out. His demons were confused, but there was nothing he could do about it now. He'd just have to try harder in the next village if he ran into another situation like this. Be more intimidating. More *God-of-Death*-like. He had to make it to Athena and—with his power and skillset—force all the information he needed out of her. It shouldn't be too hard. He just needed to do it right.

When another cry pierced its way through his ears, he jerked back, causing one of his servants to bump into him. Another flash of fire passed through his mind, only this time he could feel the heat—the smoke burning his eyes. He clutched a hand to his head.

What the hell is going on?

He didn't realize his eyes had shut until he tried pushing the confusing feelings away. When he opened them, he saw his subjects staring at him, their sunken eyes agape.

"Put your heads down!" he barked, then strode on as if nothing had happened, his demon army skulking close behind him.

He had a lead and would think about the rest of this later. He just needed to get the job done and hoped the lead was a good one. There wasn't much time. Thanatos was watching the clock.

CHAPTER SIX

Corre

A s if in some hazy dream, Corre passed through all the usual markers that guided the way back to her house, but she didn't see a thing. She couldn't get out of her head. All she saw was a mangled form rising from the shadows. An image she was spawning in her head of this Underworld god. This Theron of Tartarus.

Who is he? The thought pressed deeply into her mind. *What does he want? And why now?*

She played out scenario after scenario but couldn't think of a single reason why he might have come here or what might be going on. As her shoes skidded across the cobblestone path to her front door, she wondered if she should bother her mother with such questions. Should she tell her about his entry—his trespass—onto their land?

She had to. What if Berenice didn't know and happened to get into an altercation with him? What if—

Corre shuddered and opened the door.

Her mother smiled as the young goddess walked into the warm cottage. The smell of firewood tickled Corre's nose, but it didn't comfort her like it usually did. Her mother's smile vanished. "Oh honey, what's wrong?"

"Mother, I..." She couldn't find the words. How could she explain the situation when she barely understood it herself?

After taking a moment to gather her thoughts, Corre looked at her mother. "Theron is coming. Hades. He was spotted leaving the Underworld, and I don't know what to think." She waited for Berenice's face to change—to twist in horror, jaw gaping open. But it didn't so much as twitch.

"Oh," she said, and her face was still steady, though her eyes looked off, pensive. "I see. Well, best be safe then. Stay close." There was no urgency in her voice, but the air in the cottage grew thicker by the second.

The cheerful pastel walls and windowsills bursting with lilies and roses suddenly didn't seem so chipper. But more than anything, Corre was confused. "If I didn't know any better, I would say you weren't afraid of the God of the Underworld," she said, almost scoffing in disbelief.

"I suppose I'm not," Berenice said. She tossed another small log into the fireplace that sat nestled into the lefthand wall of the living room. "Though I probably should be."

"What?" Corre let out a half-laugh. She couldn't believe what she was hearing. "How could—"

"I imagine he's been living a terribly dreadful life down there," Berenice said, cutting Corre off but seeming not to notice. "And I'm sure he's been twisted into a truly monstrous god indeed."

"You're not scared at all," she said, her voice rising in disbelief. "Why?"

But her mother didn't answer. Her eyes stayed in that off place, wherever they were looking. Somewhere far into the distance. Perhaps she didn't fully grasp it herself.

After a long minute or two, Berenice shrugged. "Like I said, I *should* be afraid." She turned to her daughter, her eyes focusing again. It was like her soul had been grabbed and snatched back into the present. "As should you." She took a few steps forward and took hold of Corre's hands. Corre searched her mother's eyes but couldn't make out the feelings behind them, though the small goddess's brows weighed heavy above them. "You *must* stay away from him. Do you understand? He's extremely powerful. He's said to have the power of a thousand gods, and since he has never been here before, he's unpredictable. I'm sure his reason for coming up here is not to smell the freshly grown roses."

Her grasp tightened on Corre's slender fingers. "Stay away from him," she repeated. "Understand?" The young goddess nodded quickly. Berenice's shoulders relaxed, and her grip released. "Good." She puffed out a loud breath. "I'm glad you've been training with Athena. I suppose the combat training might be of good use for the Goddess of Life and Nature after all."

Corre's mouth scrunched to one side, and her stomach dropped. *Phineas.* Corre and her best friend Phineas always practiced combat on this day of the moon cycle. They met for lessons on combat at Athena's cottage almost every other day. As the Ares-to-be, Phineas trained there every day, and he was probably there now.

"I have to go to Athena's," she blurted, and her mother's head jerked back.

"What?"

"Phineas is there. He doesn't know Theron has come. I have to tell him—"

"Whoa, whoa, hang on." Berenice grabbed hold of her daughter's arm before she could run out the door. "What did I just tell you?"

"But—"

"No! Theron is dangerous. Please stay put for now." When Corre opened her mouth to contest, her mother added, "Don't go out looking for trouble." The young goddess snapped her mouth shut and slumped into her chair.

What am I going to do?

She thought of Phineas. Of him waiting for her by Athena's cottage and wondering where she was, and she thought of when she last sparred with him and how he always made her laugh. *If anything happens to him, I don't think I could stand it.* He was a good friend and her favorite training partner. Best of all, he never judged her for *wanting* a combat training partner. She went against the status quo, which was very, *very* taboo to do.

There was a lot about Corre that wasn't typical—at least not for a goddess prophesied to one day be someone like Persephone. She never shied away from a fight. Especially if it meant protecting those she loved. Another good reason she started blowing off steam with Phineas and Athena.

Berenice's eyes narrowed. "Don't worry. I'm sure he will be okay, but you need to stay put." She dug her stare into Corre until the young goddess finally accepted defeat.

"Okay, okay. I get it." She let out an agitated sigh. Her palms were sweating, but she at least stopped her leg from shaking as she added, "He won't come here anyway. Theron, I mean." She laughed nervously. "But I'll go mad if I stay in here for the rest of the evening, so I'll just go out and work in the grass." She got up to head back outside when her mother clapped a hand on her wrist.

"I know you better than that, Corre."

"But I—"

"Stay inside until it's safe to go out."

"I highly doubt Theron will be paying me a visit in our garden."

"It's never unwise to be safe."

Corre sighed. "Fine but I'm not a child. I'd be safe out there, you know." She waited for a retort from her mother, but nothing came. It wasn't like Berenice not to coyly respond. Instead, she let go of her daughter's wrist and shuffled back to the cushioned seats near the fireplace.

After it was clear that her mother was done speaking, Corre decided to camp out in her room. "I'll see you at supper," she said softly, but her mother didn't respond. The slight goddess was silent, still, her body rigid and unmoving. Corre's throat went dry, her mouth chalky. A lump bobbed in her throat as she attempted to swallow. Something was going on. Something her mother wasn't willing to admit. And it was eating Corre alive.

Theron

The smell of pine and rain-soaked dirt nearly knocked Theron over as he was swallowed by a sea of trees. He couldn't tell if the smell was pleasant or revolting. It was strong. So new and unfamiliar. The stench of blood on one of his servants wasn't helping the overstimulation. "I told you not to kill anyone," Theron grumbled.

The demon cackled. "I didn't," it squawked. "It was a mere animal. I saw it twenty paces from here."

The god stopped. He looked at the bony creature. "If you saw that," he hissed, "then you must have seen Athena's house, *correct*?"

The demon shrunk, its hooked lips sewing together. It was the same demon that tried hurting the child. Theron lifted his hand and crushed the air between the two, causing the creature's throat to shrivel, almost to the point of collapse. The power surged through Theron's veins, spilling from his mind with ease and pulsing out his fingertips.

He tossed the creature aside, its body hitting the earth with a loud thud. "Do any of *you* want to stray off track?" He roared at the others. They slumped in fear, shaking their heads emphatically. "Good!" He looked at the demon gasping on the ground. He watched it rake the dirt with its claws, searching for breath until it captured enough air to wobble to its feet. Theron looked at the rest of his servants. "Let's keep moving."

Theron was ready to search for hours. The woods looked expansive and, knowing how enormous and complex his own labyrinth was, he assumed Athena's palace of trees would be the same. But he was thankfully wrong. Maybe it was his booming voice that shook the trees and caused the crows to caw and flee as he treaded through the forest. Or maybe it was the scent of blood still lingering on his limping servant. Whatever the warning signal had been, it made the Goddess of War stand before her own house, ready to fight.

Theron chuckled. "I see you're here to welcome me. How kind."

The goddess didn't move. She stayed locked in a battle stance, her slightly muscular frame firmly set in place as she watched his every movement. Tall for a female god, the red-haired goddess almost came to Theron's chin, which was saying a lot. He'd never met anyone whose stature rivaled his, other than his master.

"Since you know that I'm here, this will make things much easier for me." He lifted his arm and swept it forward, focusing his mind. Everything between them—the wind, the smells, the spores in the air—moved with his command. Her body froze as he restrained her solely with the invisible power he possessed, tying her in place with his mind. It was a piece of cake for him, but she was obviously struggling.

"Not so powerful now, are we?" he spat, stopping a mere few steps away from where she now stood bolted to the ground. She tried moving her face, but the strain quickly took its toll on her. Beads of sweat pilled at her hairline, and a vein bulged at her temple. "Tell me. Where can I find the goddess Persephone?" Strands of crimson hair stuck to her face, but her lips refused to so much as part. Theron's eyebrow flickered in frustration. "This is very little effort for me," he said. "To save some time, why don't you tell me so I can be on my way?"

He loosened his grip on her mind, relaxing some of the muscles in his own, so she could speak. When her face could finally move, she gasped for breath. "You're...wasting your time," she said, struggling to rasp out each word, "I'm not going to tell you a thing."

Theron's face twisted, and he let out a loud, unintelligible yell. "*Where is she?!*" His power pushed deeper into her mind. He felt each movement of thought around invisible fingers. Then he released the grip slightly to give her a chance to speak. She didn't budge.

He didn't want to have to expend the energy to do this, but he had no choice.

He reached further into her mind, passing through the barriers he'd previously left untouched, and searched her memory through any sensation and thought she manifested. He needed to find something. Anything. Any information at all that would lead him to Persephone.

Finally, he saw something. In his own mind, an image formed. The image of a god and goddess. Running. Fighting. They were running through the woods—through these familiar, pungent trees. They shifted from children to adults within his mind. Their skills sharpened. Their power intensified. He had a hard time making out their features. He couldn't see their faces—just their bodies and movements.

He barked out a frustrated growl and kept working through the goddess's mind. She grunted in frustration, futilely trying to resist his power.

He needed more information—who these gods were and where he could find them. *Anything.*

"Tell me who they are!" he yelled, letting go of Athena's mind. She gasped for breath, and he let her fall. Her body collapsed at his feet. "Who are they?!"

"I don't know what you're—"

"You know damn well who I'm talking about!"

Athena's shoulders dropped and rose in long, slow strokes as she struggled to even her breaths. It was clear that this goddess wouldn't give him any information willingly, but he was afraid any additional use of his powers would destroy her.

"Tell me," he repeated.

"No—" she said, but as she said it, he saw something else. With her mind left unguarded, her body working solely to regain its strength, he caught a glimpse of something he knew was a clue. A cottage. A patch of grass. A field of flowers. The head of that young woman running with that god—her golden hair, tinted with pink, half-tied back in a bun at the base of her skull.

He had a lead.

He grinned. "Thank you for your cooperation." He whisked around, his cape rippling above the fallen Goddess of War. His demons scurried around her, examining her body. He gestured for them to follow as he strode out of the woods. "She'll get up soon enough," he said. *But by then it will be too late. I'll have already found her.*

This girl in the flowers.

CHAPTER SEVEN

Corre

S omething wasn't right. A twitch or rogue muscle in her mind was tugging her toward Phineas—toward pain. Her gut coiled, and the blood cooled in her veins. *Did something happen?*

She'd managed to stay in her room for about an hour, genuinely trying to keep the promise she'd made to her mother, but the soft, teal duvet covering her restless body suddenly left her suffocated. Her room was now too small, too confining.

I have to get out of here. I have to get to Phineas.

She pushed the covers away and slipped on a pair of gold-trimmed slippers that matched her shimmering sun-colored nightgown. It might not be the right outfit to fight in if something really was wrong, but there was no time to change. She had to hurry. The feeling was growing. Pain squeezed her chest as she carefully opened the window beside her bed. Hopefully her mother wouldn't check on her.

Corre slid out the window, her dress snaking down the side of the cottage on her way down. As soon as her impractical shoes touched the soft soil below, she took off toward Phineas's house. Following the feeling, she pumped her arms and ran as quickly as her long legs could take her. His house was inconveniently far away, past Athena's place deep in the woods. But she was making good time.

The setting sun glazed the trees with a deep orange shimmering through rustling leaves. Corre had to squint to where she was going as she entered the forest and followed the uneven trail. Jagged rocks and snapped branches jutting out of clods of mud made for great tripping hazards, and it didn't help that her shoes were already slick with silk.

She dodged and jumped over every obstacle, refusing to stop. Even when her lungs burned, she kept going. It wasn't until a figure appeared in the distance that she slowed to a halt.

Her abrupt stop was a little *too* abrupt and sent her falling to the ground onto a rough patch of thorny brush. She looked up at the figure in the distance, narrowing her eyes to get a better look at the approaching god.

Her eyes widened when she saw who it was. *Phineas.*

His face was warped in pain as he raced toward her. Sweat leaked from his temples like a cracked fountain, sliding down his tightened jaw.

"Corre!" His eyes were wild, frenzied, and bloodshot.

"Phineas!" she gasped, wiping the mud off her shins and grabbing his arms when he finally made it to her. "What happened to you?" She scanned his face and body until realizing the only sign of distress came from his face. He had clearly been injured. But how? There were no marks or external signs of damage, other than his eyes.

"It was him," he said, gripping her biceps "Hades."

"What?" The word came out in a strained whisper. Like all the air had been sucked out of her lungs in a single moment.

"Yes. Now, go! He's coming for you next."

"What? Why? How did he find you?"

"I-I think it was a mistake—" he started, but something held him back. Corre shook her head. "What are you talking about?"

He looked up at her, pain still oozing from his bloodshot eyes. "I went to train with Athena, but when I got there, he tossed her to the ground. At first, he didn't see me, but when he did...I guess he decided to get information out of me." His face tightened. "About you."

An unsettling weight pushed deep into her stomach. "Did you tell him anything?"

"Of course not! You know I would never do that to you. But...he used a power from his mind or something. It was horrible. And he saw things. I don't know what, but he knows where you are now. You have to get out of here before he finds you."

Corre tried to say something, but Phineas grabbed her by the wrist and led her in the other direction. "You have to hide. Go farther into the woods. I'll stay here to make sure Berenice is safe."

The cool night air bit at Corre's skin. Her mind was numb, her forehead cold and fuzzy. Her body was limp as Phineas led her deeper into the forest, but she needed to get it together. She had to let him go. The thought of her mother getting caught in the crossfire made her stomach ache.

"Phin," she said hurriedly. "Go into my room through my window. It's open." When he didn't move, she spoke louder. "Go now! *Please.*" Blood pounded in her ears.

At first, he didn't move. Then he nodded and said, "Be safe, Corre."

"Don't worry about me. Just get to my mother and make sure Hades goes nowhere near her." If he responded, she didn't hear it. The pounding in her ears was overwhelming now. The look in Phineas's eyes was more than enough to send her racing into the woods. But the thought of her mother made her wish she could go back home.

She needed to trust Phineas, though, so she didn't look back. Pumping her arms and legs in a new direction, she sprinted as fast as she could into the middle of the wood. A place that would hopefully offer her refuge until Theron gave up and returned to the Underworld.

Theron

"Where is she?" Theron cried to the new arrival at Athena's cottage. He'd been working his way through the god's senses and thoughts.

"I don't know who you're talking about," the god lied, but his mind was weak. Theron could see her. The vision of the goddess was clearer this time, but he still couldn't make out her face or where she might be. He pushed harder into Athena's pupil's mind. Who was this girl, and where could he find her? So far, all he could make out was the back of her head. The glimmer of a gown beneath rosy hair. He pushed harder.

The god at his feet howled in pain, and something pulled at Theron's chest. A sick feeling pooled through his gut. He ignored it. He needed this. There was something about this girl. She was important. Significant. Someone his master needed to know about. So far, he'd encountered Athena and this pupil of hers, but *this* goddess...the one surrounded by a field of flowers...she had to be Persephone. A goddess of light and life. She was everything he was not. Although he didn't relish the idea of meeting someone so sickeningly antagonistic to him, he had to pursue her for his master.

Theron intensified his concentration, his temples throbbing. Finally, he saw who the god was trying to protect. A place materialized in the young

Hades' mind. A cottage surrounded by a sea of flowers. A plain, gray-stoned home with a cone-like rooftop. The goddess was there, sliding from an exit on the side of the house and falling gently into the grass.

He needed more information. Where was this place? His powers searched the other god's senses, deciphering the thoughts made by these strange vibrations. He couldn't dive directly into someone else's thoughts without first sensing what they were made of, and then they'd materialize in his mind. It was a skill that took years of grueling training—training that was proving to be worth the pain.

Once he figured out that person's vibrations—deciphered what they were made of and understood their mind's movements—he could peer more clearly into their minds. And he had successfully unlocked what was in Athena's pupil who'd come at just the right time.

The vision shifted, and he saw a front door. Trees on every side. Endless entrances to woods. This house was in a large clearing in what appeared to be the center of a forest, like the eye of a lively storm. But as the door of the cottage opened and the flowers faded away, he saw something else.

A bright flash of light, then pitch-black. Like a tangible night had been draped over the sun. An unsettling coldness filled his body, and there was a scream. It wasn't from this god, and it wasn't from anyone in this vision. It was somewhere else. Just like it had been at the village.

He winced.

The loss of focus wrenched him from the young man's thoughts and senses, and he was back. In a separate wood—from what he could gather—from where he needed to be. But he would soon find her, this flower girl.

"You're a monster!" Athena's pupil cried, his round, dark eyes brimmed with fury. Theron studied him carefully. The god was weak but not limp. His muscles were toned enough to indicate he trained, but he had the unblemished skin and uncalloused hands of someone who never knew real pain. The epitome of Olympian luxury.

Theron straightened and wiped the sweat from his face. "Consider this your lucky day. Leave now, and I won't hurt you further."

The panting god studied him as his shoulders rose and fell like an ebbing wave. As soon as sense knocked into him, he shot up and ran off. Theron watched him flee in a different direction from the one he'd come from. The young Hades smirked. If the image of a cottage hadn't been clear, he could have simply followed the god. And why shouldn't he? It only seemed smart. Time-efficient.

He needed to be strategic.

His servants couldn't be around him. They would get him caught more easily. They'd only slow him down anyway. He turned to them. "Return to Tartarus. I'll take it from here."

"But, sire—"

"Go!" Theron yelled, and the demons scattered.

As their humped frames fell into the distance, Theron returned his attention to the escaping god. His boots scraped against the cobblestones that led to Athena's house—the goddess now a fainted heap at the end of the path. He weaved through the mass of trees, keeping his mind firm on Athena's pupil—the signals emanating from his thoughts. He could sense his presence and let it direct him down the winding wood.

As he continued to focus, and as flashes from the young man's mind returned to his own, something tightened in his bones. An odd, unpleasant sensation.

He growled and kept his focus. She *had* to be Persephone. She was too young to be Demeter, from what he could tell. But he needed to see her—to peer into her mind and feel out her powers—to know for certain.

Suddenly, the god's presence vanished. Theron twisted to spot any sign of him, but there was nothing. Twigs and muck cracked and squelched beneath his thick, black boots as he crept toward one end of the forest. There was something there—someone. First, it was a feeling, and then a twin cracking of sticks caught his attention. He froze. Peering around a stalky tree, he heard rustling.

He crept closer, avoiding any possible detection. A beast stalking its prey. He grabbed hold of the thick tree trunk blocking his view and swung around, launching himself at the source of the noise. His shoulders fell when all that was there was a thin fawn hobbling away.

Sighing, and swiping a large hand through his thick, inky black hair, Theron closed his eyes, searching for that male god. A vision materialized. The young god turned toward a clearing. His eyes shot open, and the feeling thickened. Before the sensation dissipated, he made a beeline to his right and weaved through the mass of trees until he reached the end of the forest's gaping mouth. And then the feeling stopped, something else taking its place.

That's when he saw her.

Not in person, but in a clear vision in his mind. In a clearing by that cottage. A waif of a goddess next to Athena's male pupil. He could only see her outline, but he now knew where to go.

Theron's lips curled into a wicked smile.

"I have you, Persephone."

Jumping off a boulder, the young Hades hastened through the trees. Their paths would meet naturally. He just needed to feel out for her.

He kept his mind open but guarded, so he could feel her but she couldn't feel him. Not that she could have his skill, but he couldn't be too careful.

Dodging shrubs, rocks, and more hobbling animals, Theron raced through the maze of the forest, narrowly avoiding smacking into trees at every turn, his cape snagging onto ragged bark, and pushing himself off others. He was getting closer. Her life force was fixed in his mind now, coursing through his veins. It wouldn't be long. Excitement fizzed through him. Her power was strong. Appealing. Delicious. There was something ... *different* about her, and he would find out what it was.

His boots splashed in a thick puddle of mud, squishing as they un-suctioned from the ground, and then he saw it—an enormous boulder next to a tree as tall as a double-story structure. It was wide enough to conceal the body of a slender, young goddess, who'd clearly just been running. Hiding.

His heart raced, but his pace slowed. The last thing he wanted was to have come all this way only for her to hear him and escape before he caught her. He crept closer, slow and calculated, until he made it to the large rock, his gloved fingers pressed against its smooth slope. With one more step, he caught a glimpse of her. The rosy, golden knot tied on the back of her head and the shape of her arm.

A smug, self-satisfied smile broke across his long face. There she was—just one jump away. He had her.

As he made that one last leap, she turned enough for him to glimpse the side of her face, and his foot slipped. He couldn't catch himself, even with his powers. Usually, his mind was quicker than that. He never so much as tripped. His mind was too fast, too refined. The powers that flowed so effortlessly through him always kept him from hitting the ground. But something about her made his mind fill with static.

There was a vulnerability on her face as she turned to survey the area. A smattering of freckles covered the delicate bridge of her nose. He couldn't see her entire face, but he saw enough. Maybe too much. Did all goddesses look like that?

No. Of course not. He'd seen many today, and none of them had come close.

He repressed a grunt and got to his feet, hoping she hadn't heard him, but as he regained his footing, he heard her voice, shaky and loud, calling out from behind the tree. "Who's there?" Her voice was melodic. Bold. He saw beyond the façade.

Theron took a deep breath and pushed himself over the lip in the ground, planting his feet on the grass level with the top of the boulder. The goddess was still partially hidden behind a tree's thick trunk. "You sound so brave," he teased, slowly moving toward her. He could see the sharp outline of her shoulder and the flutter of a shimmering gown. It glinted in the rising moonlight streaming through the trees, like an ethereal blanket of stars.

She turned to face him. And he stopped.

"I'm not afraid of you," she said, her voice low and steady.

Theron wanted to say something back. Banter. Threaten her. Anything. But his throat went dry. The stream of silver from the stars illuminated every beautiful feature on the goddess's face. The freckles dusting her nose and cheekbones. The fullness of her lips. The soft curves of her body, covered only by that light piece of glittering cloth. The longer he looked at her, the more his skin burned in a way he'd never felt before.

When she lifted one of her thin eyebrows, he frantically gathered his thoughts. He couldn't let her have the upper hand. She needed to know that no one was more powerful than the God of the Underworld.

He mustered a smirk. "Is that so?" He laughed softly. "You really aren't afraid of me?" He stepped closer. The quickness of her breath was evident through the shallow movements of her chest.

She stepped away when he got too close, but as she staggered back, a gust of wind rippled through her dress. She caught the cloth but fell back against the tree, not before a branch clawed its way down one side of the skirt.

Theron glanced down at the slit in her gown, and that warm spark in his veins relit at the smooth, sun-kissed glow of her exposed skin. As the burning filled his body, he wondered what kind of power this was. Did the goddess Persephone have powers that could shake him like this? Make him burn? Make his heart race?

His eyes widened when he noticed the very thing he'd expected from the beginning. The thing that reassured him that he was still in control: her legs were shaking. His lips once again curled into a wicked smile. She was in the palm of his hand.

He took the steps necessary to close the gap between them. With her back against the tree, she had nowhere to run. A smarter goddess would have run—tried to, anyway—but she stood her ground, glaring up at him, never once looking away. There was something strong about her—a strength he hadn't seen in anyone since stepping out of Tartarus and into this pathetic land of the living.

She might be brave, but she was incredibly stupid.

His massive frame towered over her, the shadow of his body swallowing her up as he peered down into her eyes. They held a foolishly harsh glare, which stayed fixed beneath her knitted brows. The strikingly vibrant green that swirled in the earthy brown-gold of her eyes only contributed to the enigmatic glow about her. But still, she was a fool.

"Why do you not flee before me?"

"L-like I said," She cleared her throat. "I'm not afraid of you."

He narrowed his eyes. "I think you know that I see through you. That I won't feed on such a lie." His voice had fallen into almost a whisper as the space closed between them, her body almost touching his, and again, that fire tore through him.

"I don't care what you think. I'm not afraid of you, and I would appreciate you leaving Mt. Olympus immediately."

His smile dropped. "What?"

She squared her shoulders and pushed herself away from the tree. Looking straight up into his eyes, she said, "I want you to leave." There was no more tremor in her voice. Her body wasn't shaking. His eyes fell to her leg to be sure, but she swiftly covered it up. "You've overstayed your welcome here."

Fury shot up his chest. "How dare you." He stepped toward her again, but she backed away, her eyes fixed on his, completely unwavering. "Do you know who you're talking to?"

"Yes. Theron, God of the Underworld. I know *all* about you."

"What could *you* possibly know about *me*?"

"I know that you want everyone to be frightened, but for all we know, you could be completely powerless. A regular—albeit *chosen*—god like everyone else. Someone who wants to feel important by acting big and tough."

The fury she'd spiked in him earlier burst into a ferocious storm. He opened his mind and took hold of hers, his power grasping onto her so he could back her up against the tree. "Does this feel like powerlessness to you?" he growled, but she kept her glare steady on his. The frown carved upon his face deepened. "*Well?*"

He made a point not to hurt her. He didn't want her to think he was a raging animal with no control over himself or his powers. That he was some primitive, barbaric, unrefined beast. He knew a certain lackey in Tartarus who always liked to spread those lies, like a pale spider weaving its slimy web. Appearance mattered. So did control.

He needed the gods and goddesses on Mt. Olympus to know that he had the power to do anything he wanted but that he was also an expert in controlling it and wielding it at his every whim and command.

But he'd be lying to himself if he denied the fact that he was also desperately trying to push his power deeper into this goddess so she could feel his unfathomable strength and raw, unmatched power. To feel that he was greater than any other god on or under Olympus. That he was someone to be both feared and respected.

But her mind was a fortress, and no matter how hard he tried, he couldn't make out what she was feeling. How could someone like her block that part off from him? *It must be because I'm holding back*, he thought, so he pushed a little harder into her mind. A slight shock of excitement sizzled through him at the idea of exploring her thoughts. The start of an image flashed before his mind for a spark of a moment before they turned to black, and he was blocked off again. Like he'd run into a thick, icy wall.

His eyes darted to hers. "What are you doing?" Lines formed on her forehead. He let out a low growl and tried harder, pushing as much as he could without making her feel any pain.

That thick wall started to crack.

When he saw that field of flowers pop into his head, he knew he was back in, but it only lasted another instant. This time, she ripped herself away from his mental grasp and was able to back out of his shadow. "I said, *leave!*"

His jaw slowly dropped. Her eyes were ablaze—two unmatchable, fiery stones—and her stance was strong. She'd defied him, both in mind and body.

"Who are you, *really*? Surely, you're not Persephone. You're no Goddess of Life and Nature. You're surely one of war. Of combat or wisdom, or some other source of strength."

Her eyebrows knitted together again. "How did you know that I'm Persephone?" Success soared in his chest.

"I know all about you, too, you know." He lowered his face to be closer to hers. "I've seen you in the thoughts of your friends." Her lips parted slightly. He momentarily faltered. Quickly recovering, he continued, "And now I know you even more. I've felt your strength. I know your mind."

"You know *nothing*," she hissed. The words escaped her mouth in rushes of breath against his throat. Her eyes shot daggers into his. Something in his stomach flipped, and that now-familiar burning intensified.

It was hard for him to breathe, but he made himself stay composed. "We'll see about that." They stared at each other, both refusing to be the first to look away. It wasn't until Theron noticed the darkening sky that he initiated the break.

Thanatos's angry, deformed face crossed his mind, along with the familiar pain of the deity's claws striking his flesh. Fear curdled in Theron's stomach. He had to go.

But . . .

He studied the goddess's face. She watched him carefully, panting and glistening with a thin layer of sweat. Stray hairs had come loose from the knot fastened at the base of her skull, now framing her face in ice-pink tresses. Her stance didn't waver. No matter how much he looked at her. No matter what he did or said, she didn't falter. All fear was gone from her being.

It made no sense. This was no ordinary goddess.

He needed to know her name. Her true identity. Not just the title she bore.

For Thanatos.

"Who are you?" he pressed. She glowered at him. He took a slow, silent step forward, eyes fixed on her, daring her to answer. After another dangerous minute away from Tartarus, he said, "If you tell me your name, I'll leave immediately and return to the Underworld."

She frowned. "Why?"

"Because you're strong. So..." He lifted his hand and trailed the back of his fingers down her neck. "Brave."

Her eyelids fluttered, but then she jerked away. "Do you promise you'll leave?" Color rose to her cheeks.

His mouth twitched into a smile "Of course."

Her eyes narrowed. "Correlia," she said, folding her arms. "My name is Correlia."

Correlia.

"Sire!"

Theron whipped around to see one of his demons bounding toward him.

"Sire! We're late! Thanatos has called for us!"

Fear simmered in Theron's chest. "Let's go. *Now*." He did his best to contain the terror rising in his throat. The demon nodded, but it didn't move. It was waiting for him.

Another feeling Theron didn't recognize flitted through his chest. It happened when he'd thought of leaving and how he'd likely not return. He turned enough to catch a glimpse of the glistening goddess, that feeling intensifying.

"Sire!"

He snapped his eyes forward. "Y-yes, let's go," he said and started his journey back to the Underworld. He wanted to take one last look at the fearless goddess behind him, but he knew his demon might catch something in his eyes that wouldn't bode well for him. Something Thanatos would surely find out about.

A weakness.

So he kept moving. Kept looking ahead. No matter how much he wanted to see that look of fire in her eyes, just one more time.

CHAPTER EIGHT

Corre

C orre couldn't believe what had just happened. She could still feel his breath hot against her skin and the touch of his hand sliding down the slope of her neck. A blazing sizzle skated up her back. Heat rose to her cheeks.

Theron, the God of the Underworld, was *not* what she'd expected.

For the first few minutes after his abrupt departure, she couldn't move. Her feet rooted themselves into the earth as she struggled to process it all. He was no monster disfigured from years of torment in the realm of death and decay. He was ... *captivating*. Attractive.

Her mind lingered on the pitch-blackness of his hair and how it fell in waves almost to his shoulders—his incredibly *broad* shoulders. He wasn't withered and ghoulish. He was well over six feet tall, and strong, with taut muscles that flexed when he moved. She thought of the way he'd inched toward her, his dark eyes fixed on hers. Of the deep richness of his voice.

The alluring air about him that had made her torn between wanting him to go and begging him to stay.

Of course she didn't want him to stay. He was evil. Monstrous. The lowest of the low. He'd dug his way into her friend's mind and sought her out. Hunted her. He'd entered her mind, pushing her against the tree with careful precision. Maybe with a slight tenderness, like he was holding back. It didn't hurt. It was almost *intimate*. His body was so close to hers.

A feeling like ice prickled her nerves, slipping through her veins. With a sharp inhale, she pushed the thoughts of him away. Before she could entertain the confusion in her mind, she flipped around and started home She ignored the exciting sensations swirling through her body at the thought of him. The heat burning her flesh.

He's a monster, she chastised herself. *He wanted nothing more than to get information out of me, like he did to Phineas. That's all.*

Still, she couldn't rid her thoughts of him—couldn't peel him from her mind and abandon the feelings spiking up her body and snaking down her back.

Instead, she focused on the anger in his eyes and the harshness of his speech. On his disregard for anyone other than himself.

But why had he let her go? He had every opportunity to question her—to interrogate her the way he'd tormented Phineas. He could have tortured her for answers, but he'd only asked for her name. And then he let her go. Why? Was it wrong that she'd given it to him?

By the time Corre made it to the clearing where her cottage sat tucked away from the world, the sky's warm purple deepened, rising above the earth in twilight. There was a stillness in the air that only accompanied this time of night, when the moon rose so boldly in the sky. A silence, as if she was the only soul in existence, wandering the earth in the space between life and death. As if there was a time set aside for the worlds of the living and the dead to commune, in those very brief moments before the dawn of a new day began.

Maybe Theron had taken with him the world of the dead as he wandered Mt. Olympus. Maybe he breathed in this air the same as Correlia, in these quiet moments of stillness.

Or maybe it was nothing. Just a passing hour before the world finally woke.

Corre's hand found the doorknob and slowly, quietly, she turned it. With one step, she crept into the entryway. A bright light illuminated the home before she could get her other foot in the door. When the fuzzes from the sudden contrast fled her eyes, she was left gaping at her mother's angry expression.

"H-hi—"

"Correlia! How could you be so foolish?!"

"Mother, I—"

"No!" She grabbed her daughter by the wrist. "You are *not* to leave this house for the next twenty-four hours. I can't believe you broke my trust and did something so dense, so irresponsible, and—" The door to Corre's room creaked open to reveal a very sheepish Phineas. Her head fell back. She closed her eyes, letting out a groan. Berenice rubbed the space between her eyebrows. "I can't believe you two thought you could trick me."

"We weren't trying to trick you. We were trying to protect you," Corre said, her head bobbing back up, but her mother just shot her a furious look.

"By putting yourself at risk?"

"He would have hurt you on his way to me!"

"Is that so?" Her mother scoffed, shaking her head and looking between the two young gods in frustration.

"Yes!"

"And why would he have spared me—or Phineas—if he came to find you here only to find us instead?" Berenice waited for her daughter to speak, but Corre looked away.

Her mother had a point. One Corre hadn't thought of, and one that thankfully hadn't occurred.

"I guess that could have happened, too," she whispered, looking back at Berenice and adding, "But it didn't! He saw me and tried to get something out of me, but nothing happened, and I was fine—"

"*What?*" Her mother's eyes widened even more, her thick eyebrows springing to her hairline. "You *saw* him? He *spoke* to you? He—" Fear filled her eyes as she held onto her daughter's elbows. "What happened?"

Corre gave her a reassuring smile and threaded her hands in her mother's. "I'm okay. He was angry and arrogant, and I'm sure he only showed me an ounce of his strength, but I'm all right. He tried to peer into my mind or something but was unsuccessful. Then he left with one of his servants."

"What?" Phineas gaped. "That doesn't make any sense. I couldn't combat him at all, and he practically tortured me. Did you do something to hold him back?"

"No. I-I don't know. Maybe I did, but I really don't know. I don't fully understand his powers. I don't know how he's able to feel around our minds like that or how he can move someone without his hands."

Phineas's expression twisted. "I don't get it," he said. "Why didn't he attack you?"

"I don't know, Phineas. Should he have?" Corre snapped. This was getting ridiculous. Her mind was still whirring from the encounter. The last thing she needed was an interrogation.

He rolled his eyes. "Of course not. It just doesn't add up. How could you possibly resist his powers at all?" He shook his head. "It just doesn't make sense."

Corre wanted to give them an answer, but she had none. She had no clue what had happened. Theron seemed to have the ability to control people's movements and to peer inside their minds, which is probably how he'd been able to make her heart race the way it had. He possessed some kind of power that drew him to her and made him magnetizing.

He was pure evil. She was sure of it. She just didn't understand him. His motives *or* his powers.

The room fell silent. Phineas didn't seem to know what to say anymore, and her mother was lost in thought, concentrating on something Corre didn't want to explore at the moment.

"Hey, it's all okay! Right?" the young goddess said, trying to lighten the mood. "Hades is back in the Underworld, and we're all fine." She flashed her signature dimpled smile, but the tension in the room remained, the air thick and rotten like spoiled milk.

"Well," her mother said, her eyes still far away. "I suppose all we can do is wait."

Corre frowned. "Wait for what?"

"To discover what he gained by coming here." She sighed. "And to find out what he'll do next."

Theron

Theron's heart wouldn't stop pounding. He couldn't think. He could barely make it through the intricate maze of corridors in his labyrinth. *I'm just worried about Thanatos* he told himself, but Thanatos wasn't the one who appeared in his mind when the throbbing of blood pounded in his ears. The more he let the image of that girl linger in his mind, the worse the pounding became, and the harder it was to breathe. To focus. He couldn't even hear what his servant was saying until it yelled his name in his ear.

"Master Theron!" The young Hades turned to the wiry demon in front of him. Its hollow skull barely reached Theron's waist before it bowed, apologizing. "Master Thanatos wants you straight away. He said not to return to your chambers. He wants you now."

A new pain cut through Theron's mind, but this one wasn't accompanied by that curious burning. It was a memory. A painful recollection that dug through his side like the turn of a blade. The agony that erupted from his body at Thanatos's blow was not something he wanted to relive, but he knew that might be what he was about to walk into.

He couldn't get himself to speak, so he nodded at the creature and moved around it, taking a sharp right to the passage leading to the throne room. As he walked down the ominous corridor, dodging drips of some indeterminate liquid, a figure came toward him, exiting the large doors to Thanatos's grand chamber. Theron could recognize that weasel of a man anywhere.

Nikias.

The gangly man with hair as yellow as wheat, but as slicked back as mud on an old boot, was Thanatos's appointed general. He was here to be trained for battle—to lead one of the fleets of the Underworld not yet under Theron's rule. Nikias had been trained to help with the affairs of Tartarus, and he despised the soon-to-be leader of this world. Neither Theron nor Nikias had ever gotten along, and they couldn't be more of the other's opposite. Nikias liked things organized, rigid, and, in Theron's opinion, unbearably boring. And to the bony general, Theron was unruly, bad-tempered, and not fit for leadership.

Needless to say, the two had never gotten along and didn't pretend to like each other.

When the pale general smirked at Theron as he passed him in the hall, it made him both irritated and uneasy. The smug look on Nikias' face was not a good sign, having just left Thanatos's chamber. Theron picked up his pace. The anticipation and speculation were getting far worse than the pain he was sure would come from the punishment itself.

He reached the chamber doors without another second to lose and threw them open with one heavy push. The muscles in his body were so used to work that the task was effortless, even though the doors were lined with thick, platinum spikes to ward off intruders. The slight pain was nothing to Theron, but the squeezing of his stomach as he faced his master was a different matter entirely.

"Ah, if it isn't my pupil." Thanatos's toad-like voice rattled through the dark cathedral.

Theron tried his best to look strong. Confident. He needed an air about him that would swat unwanted assumptions away when his master prodded his mind and senses. He knelt before Thanatos, bowed his head, and tried to focus his mind on nothing but the present moment. He couldn't show any indication of fear or weakness, or his master would detect it and attack. The powerful leader spoke. "You were gone much longer than I'd hoped, boy." The words echoed through the room. Theron tried even harder to keep his anxiety at bay.

"I had to track down Persephone," he replied, head still bowed. "And she was worth inspecting. She's a goddess much more powerful than she appears. Perhaps stronger than she even knows. I had to learn more about her. I needed to report about her to you."

His master was silent. Theron didn't let his mind or feelings wander. A feat he hadn't accomplished to this extent until this very moment.

Thanatos tapped one sharp nail against the arm of his throne. "So you found her?" The heaviness in Theron's chest lifted. "What did you discover?"

The young god's head flipped up to meet his master. "She's a goddess of nature. Of life. But she's strong and possesses unusual power. She's young, about twenty years of age, very unlikely to have learned the skill of the senses by a tutor." He got to his feet but kept his gaze on the black eyes of his superior.

"Is that all you learned?" his master croaked.

"I didn't have time to learn anything else—"

"Are you not taking the blame again, boy?" Thanatos bellowed, his voice amplified by the size and near-emptiness of the spacious room. "Nasty habit of yours. It almost sounded like you were blaming *me*."

Theron bit his tongue, fighting back the fear rising in the back of his throat.

I'm stronger than this. I'm strong.

"No, of course not. I took too long finding her. It's my fault." Then something pricked up in his mind. Her name. He'd learned her name. "And—" He opened his mouth, but something compelled him to stop. He couldn't fully grasp why, but for some reason, handing her name over to Thanatos felt wrong.

He'd never cared about doing anything wrong before. *Ever.* His whole purpose in life was to do wrong. Why was it so hard to give his master her name?

"What is it?" Thanatos snarled.

"She's the goddess Persephone. She's strong, and she trains with Athena. That's all I know," he said, tucking her real name somewhere in the back of his mind where his master couldn't find it. He was strong enough to protect it, so he kept his mind firm—air-tight—so his master wouldn't press for more.

The large god leaned his bulbous head against the back of his throne. "That isn't much, but it's something," he mused. He tapped his finger against the throne a few more times, each tick longer than the last.

"How odd that you couldn't learn more. Your demon spotted you with her for quite some time."

Theron swallowed hard and avoided his master's heavy gaze. "She's able to control her senses and thoughts more than the others. It was an unexpected occurrence but provided valuable information." He sounded robotic, rattling off such a technical report. It was something Nikias would do. The thought made him sick.

Thanatos cackled. "No wonder you took so long. What a curious discovery." The deity's chapped mouth curved into a ghoulish smile. "We will have to learn more about this Persephone, indeed."

Without warning, one of Theron's defenses fell. Foolishly, he let himself get excited at the thought of learning more. Of possibly seeing her again.

His master saw right through him.

"Why do you feel this way, *Markus*?" he growled.

Theron flinched. Thanatos only ever called him by his former name—the name his birth parents had given him—when Theron was failing him. Things were going to slide sideways fast if he didn't think of something quick.

"Feel what way, master?" he asked, immediately knowing it was the wrong reply.

Thanatos's eyes narrowed. "Why do you want to see this girl again?"

His body tensed, his hands curling into fists so tight his nails carved into his palms through his gloves. He had to stay in control.

He looked into his master's eyes with complete composure and said, "She's someone worth keeping an eye on. Someone who might cause us trouble." Thanatos scrutinized his pupil's stare carefully, so Theron continued quickly. "We need to learn more about her. She's my adversary in every way. I only desire to learn of her weaknesses and strengths so I can take her down when the time comes."

Thanatos's head fell back, but his eyes were still narrowed. "How do you even know what to look for?"

Theron sucked in a shaky breath. "I only know what needs to be done for my reign. I can't have a goddess up there growing the world we need desolate. You said so yourself before I left. And now I know how unexpectedly strong she is. Having someone so powerful and such my opposite is clearly not going to do me any good. I only wish to keep her under my control. That's all."

The room was so quiet even the demons standing attention at Thanatos's sides seemed nervous for the large deity to speak. It took more effort than usual for Theron to keep his heart beating at a normal pace.

Finally, the ashen deity sighed. "Very well." Theron's shoulders relaxed, a weight rising from his shoulders. "But you have no need to go up there any time soon. You'll stay down here and complete your training." The excitement that had sprung to life in Theron's chest immediately deflated. "You can focus on the girl when you're ready to focus on your reign."

Theron bowed his head, avoiding his master's eyes. He felt Thanatos's body bend forward to gaze at him more closely. "Is that all right with you?" he baited.

"Of course."

"Good. Now, go. You're dismissed."

Theron turned around and left in long strides across the room. Once safely in the corridor, he let his defenses fall, finally able to breathe. But there was a tightness that ricocheted up his ribcage and into his chest when he thought of that goddess. Of the swirls of emerald, gold, and earthy browns in her impassioned eyes. Of the way her lips had parted when his body was close to hers. Of the way the tremor left her voice after one small conversation. Of the smooth skin of her neck and the curve of her legs, partially exposed from the slit in her gown.

His blood burned, even worse than before, and when he made it to his quarters, he let himself fall into bed. He replayed their conversation over and over in his mind. He savored every word that had spilled from her pouted lips. His mind hovered over every part of her body. And before long, it was clear that his blood was burning for *her*.

He ached for her.

He had to see her again.

He couldn't wait until his training was complete. Surely, Thanatos had sensed the urgency in his desire to see her, and that's why he wouldn't let him go. But he had to. His training could take months, maybe even another year or two if Thanatos dragged out the process. He couldn't wait that long.

He had to find a way to go again soon.

When the decision was finalized in his mind, he let out a long breath and kept his mind steeped in thoughts of her. He closed his eyes. "Correlia," he said softly, as if the word was something forbidden. In a way, he supposed it was. He'd hidden it from Thanatos—a move he'd never been brave enough to do.

His master had always seen through every one of his lies, weaknesses, and hidden thoughts and secrets. Thanatos would put every vulnerability and secret out on display and lash out at him until Theron was afraid to feel anything other than anger again or to have any thoughts that were just for him.

But somehow, he was able to keep this one.

She was his secret.

And he craved to learn more.

Chapter Nine

Corre

Being confined to her room was the worst way she could have spent the twenty-four hours following her encounter with Theron, but Corre didn't have a choice. She didn't want to cross her mother again. She was already worried she'd lost her trust. The least she could do was listen to her and follow through with the juvenile punishment, even if she *was* an adult who had genuinely tried to do the right thing.

I guess it is an apt punishment for her level of fury, Corre thought. *I mean, what could be worse than being forced to think about that wretched encounter?* Theron's face appeared in her mind, and she remembered how it felt for him to pour his shadow over her—to feel the warmth of his body so close to hers.

She wasn't disgusted or afraid. She was *excited*.

She groaned and twisted in her bed, plunging herself beneath her pillow. "This is so dumb. What's wrong with me?"

She flopped her arms out in a T-shape, her face buried into the mattress. She should be ashamed of these feelings. The God of Death had burrowed into her mind, had practically tortured Athena and Phineas, and she was *excited* about him? What did that say about her?

She rolled over and stared at the wooden boards staggered across her ceiling. *Am I a bad person?* She had no answer for that but chalked it up to the adrenaline of the situation. She was terrified when she first saw him. When he'd walked closer and closer to her. When he peered into her eyes. Those brown, brooding eyes that contained every shadow of the Underworld. He'd cast them over her through his enchantingly dark stare.

"That's it," she said flatly, inspecting the grooves in the wood above her. "It was the rush of nerves." She let out a heavy sigh. Her theory was a good one, and it was the one she was going with. She wasn't completely convinced, but she'd worry about that another time. She didn't want to dig too deeply into her psyche. Not right now. Plus, she'd never see him again anyway, so what did it matter?

Her thoughts dissipated when a knock sounded at the door.

"Come in."

The door creaked open. "Are you doing okay?"

Corre rolled her head to face her mother. "Meeting the God of the Underworld and then being forced to relive it for an entire day is a new form of torture, I think."

The older goddess let out a sigh and closed the door behind her. Phineas had immediately skittered home after the confrontation, leaving Corre and her mother alone in the cottage with a thick air of contention that followed the young Persephone into her room.

The slight goddess took a seat next to Corre on the bed, creating a small wave that bobbed her daughter's head against the sheets. Berenice brushed the frizzed knot that was coming undone on the back of Corre's head. Her hand stilled on her daughter's cheek. "I'm sorry, but you don't understand.

The power of Hades is unmatchable. He's capable of things you couldn't even comprehend."

"How do you know I can't comprehend it? Maybe I'm more capable than you give me credit for."

Her mother's smile softened, and she knew what she was thinking. She was thinking Corre was being naïve. She *always* thought she was being naïve. But what if she wasn't? What if she was the only one who could see this situation clearly? See through Theron? That he wasn't this big bad elusive god that could kill someone with the flick of his hand.

"I don't know what to tell you that will make you believe me, but I was there. I saw him myself. I can hold my own. I'm alive, aren't I?"

Berenice patted the back of Corre's hand. "Yes, but we don't know *why* he let you live. I'm sure he had his reasons. And they likely weren't noble ones."

Corre gathered her knees to her chest and rested her chin against her kneecaps. "I never said he was noble," she said. "He's vile. I just . . . I don't think he's as scary as everyone makes him out to be."

The hand holding Corre's squeezed tighter. "Corre. You cannot underestimate him. The fact that you think he isn't frightening proves how cunning he is."

She sighed. Maybe her mother was right. He certainly had an entrancing ability that made her feel too comfortable with him. Even if she didn't want him around, she wasn't scared of him after a few quick words and exchanged glances. *I guess that is scary,* she thought.

"Then what do I do?"

"You stay away from him. At all costs. He's dangerous." Her mother paused and leaned back, her eyes falling far away, as they had the last time the two spoke.

The silence grew long. Corre fidgeted until she couldn't take it anymore. "What is it?"

"You haven't seen destruction the way I have," Berenice whispered. "What gods can do. What demons and Titans are capable of." She winced, but her eyes were still somewhere else. Somewhere they didn't want to be. Like she was staring at something she desperately wanted to look away from but was forced to watch.

Corre shook her head. "What are you talking about?"

Berenice's eyes fastened to her daughter's. "You . . . don't remember any of it?"

"Any of what?" Corre studied her mother's wide eyes, but Berenice didn't answer.

The silence grew until it nearly choked Corre again. "Mother, can you please stop being cryptic and tell me what's going on? You're scaring me."

The older goddess rubbed the bridge of her nose, the lines on her forehead now engraved in place. "It's probably better that you don't remember."

"No! Please tell me. It's important I know everything that can help me against Theron."

"Absolutely not. If that's what you want the information for, I definitely won't tell you."

"Come on! It's not like I'm going to go out looking for trouble. I just think I should know. Just in case."

Berenice sighed. "I'm sorry, Corre, but there are some things that are better left unsaid."

The young goddess's shoulders dropped. She sighed and let herself fall against the intricate metalwork of her bed's headboard, the tunnel-like designs digging uncomfortably into her back. Berenice put her hands on her knees and slid off the bed, but before she left, she took one last look at her daughter. "One day, I'm sure you'll remember it for yourself."

With that, she closed the door, and Corre was even more lost than before.

Theron

Theron couldn't focus. He moved through the chamber with agility and precision, but it was all through muscle memory. He couldn't get his mind to latch onto his training. The creatures looming over him were hungry. Thanatos prepared them to fight by not feeding them for weeks. *It's the best way to make you become the Hades you need to be,* he always said.

A ghastly noise like shattering glass pierced the dungeon. With it came a stench so putrid it made Theron's eyes burn. There were six of them—dragon-like creatures of fire and shadow, all snapping, snarling, and chomping at the bit to get their rows of blood-soaked teeth sunk deep into Theron's skin.

The long sword at his side was made with a blade of hematite and an ancient mineral found only in Tartarus, with a hilt made of steel. It was long enough that it took the massive god both hands to carry, and the heavy minerals it was forged from made it purposely difficult to wield. It was crucial that he handled it with absolute precision, not only because it was sharpened daily, but because of the power it contained. The Sword of the Underworld was a treasure he'd worked to obtain for years. With it came the power of the God of Death.

It was exactly what he needed to make up for his lack of concentration today. He needed every thought to be centered on his movements with the relic. The ancient mineral at the core of the blade was said to have come from the teeth of the hydra, its venom lining the razor-sharp edges and instantly poisoning those struck by it. There was no room for mistake.

He swung the sword by its gold-encrusted hilt, then quickly pointed it at the closest of the creatures and lunged with all his might. Carefully, he calculated each attack. His movements were swift as he dodged the first creature's snaps, the others following close behind. It only took one calculated swing to swipe the head clear off the first beast, but as soon as the gaping skull rolled across the rocky dungeon floor, oozing black goo sprayed from the creature's exposed neck. The headless body writhed frantically.

Theron took a step back, positioning the sword high in his hands. The bodies of the identical creatures writhed with the bleeding, headless one. It was eerie watching them shake in unison like that—bent and popping and unnatural—but he studied them each carefully. He didn't buckle from the pressure or nerves of what might happen if his next move was the wrong one. He stayed strong and cautious, and as soon as the first of the remaining beasts snapped at him, he ripped through the air and killed it. Unblinking, he listened to his senses and picked off each one after it, fileting scaly flesh and creating a pile of steaming heads in the middle of the dungeon floor.

Once he was sure they were all dead, he took a breath and went over his techniques, playing out every moment of the fight in his head. The task had taken him longer than he'd hoped, but at least it was over now. He knew there would be more beasts, more training, but right now, he could rest. Tired and achy, he moved to his room, his sword vibrating and contracting until it fit securely at his waist.

His quarters were cold and didn't smell of monster flesh—a welcome change as Theron stalked inside. He peeled off his shirt in a daze. His movements were purely from muscle memory. *Clean. Wash. Scrub. Rinse. Dry. Dress.* There was no use rushing his nightly routine after his last fight of the day. He'd just have to wake up and do it all again tomorrow.

He fell onto his bed with a relieved sigh and looked up at his hourglass. He'd finished early tonight. "Oh good," he breathed, stretching out and closing his eyes. Sleep started creeping over him, dulling his senses and relaxing his aching muscles, until the face of that goddess surfaced in his mind. Her freckles like a cluster of stars, dusting her delicate features. Those fiery eyes piercing the darkness.

That familiar burning rushed through his blood, and he couldn't take it. He needed to see her again. He thought of his master, of his routine and each corridor of his labyrinth. Thoughts brewed in frenzied waves as he formulated a plan, figuring out the exact strategies to go about this.

If he could ensure Thanatos wouldn't summon him for the day—at least for a few hours—he could leave Tartarus through a less conspicuous entrance. No one would know he slipped out, and he could go see her.

That's it. It was settled. He was going for it.

He just needed to cover all his bases first.

Corre

It was a new day. Corre could finally breathe in the fresh air of the pastel garden outside the cottage. She crouched to inspect a new hyacinth her mother must have stress-grown. Her hand slid to the grass. *I don't feel like creating anything today.* The emotion was strong, but she was hollow.

Her thoughts were too messy—too clogged with curiosity from the fear in her mother's shaky voice. Theron was dangerous. There was no doubt about it. He'd used his cunning abilities to enrapture her. Even now, it was hard for her to avoid the thought of his eyes on her leg and his body nearly touching hers.

Her fingers absently found the smooth petals of another new flower. Berenice did that often—stress-worked. When her mind was brimming with anxiety, she poured it into the powers she was granted when given her title of Demeter. She was the only goddess, to Corre's knowledge, who was *given* an ability, rather than being born with it—she wasn't born to be Demeter, like Corre was Persephone.

After Corre's parents disappeared, the gods had to improvise. She was never told what happened exactly, but she knew Berenice was chosen to take her in and was given the title of Demeter to help her. Every second wave of Great Ones had to have a mentor who ensured they would properly fulfill their callings and be ready to take on their titles when the time came. But Demeter was the title of her mother, not a mentor. Though her biological mother had vanished, along with her title, to Corre, Berenice was both.

What the young goddess didn't understand was why Berenice had more of her gift than Corre did. Whenever *she* was distressed or confused, she was useless. Even on her best days, she couldn't create half as breathtaking a plant as her adopted mother could make on her bad days.

Corre sprawled out on the grass, letting the soft blanket of green warm her body, breathing in the sweet scent of the lilies outlining her frame. The divine concoction of scents usually lifted her spirits at least some, but not today. *This is hopeless.* Her eyes focused on the clouds churning above her head. *What am I even doing?*

"I knew I'd find you here."

Corre's stomach dropped. *That voice.* She sprung up, her rosy hair falling loosely between her shoulder blades. Standing there in front of her, right outside her home, was Theron. Her eyes darted to the cottage.

"Don't worry," he said, his deep voice pooling through her ears. "I'm not here for anyone but you."

She didn't move, but her eyes followed him as he approached, dressed all in black, a cape billowing behind him and brushing against his ankles. He moved in careful strides. There was a hint of a smirk on his face, a mischievous smile that made her stomach flip.

She tore her eyes from him to look around, but she didn't know what she was looking for. Nothing could help her now, and she didn't want to get anyone else involved. By the time she looked back at him, he was standing above her, his shadow casting over her like a lethal umbrella.

She sucked in a deep, shaky breath and rose to her feet. "What do you want?" Her eyes fixed on his. She didn't want to miss anything—a flinch or sudden flicker in his face. Anything that could indicate his next move.

He chuckled, and when that smirk turned into a gentler smile, she had to look away. Her skin burned. Why was the God of Death so good-looking? That, in and of itself, was a travesty. It should have been against some rule. That Hades' gaze couldn't make a goddess so weak in the knees.

"Isn't it obvious?" he said, and the rich darkness of his voice melted her insides. Her gaze gravitated back to his. She wanted to quip back with a witty reply, but she couldn't speak. Any comeback was stuck behind a large lump lodged in the back of her throat. "I wanted to see you." The words crashed into her like a thrashing wave.

"Why?" She forgot to breathe as he crept closer.

He tugged on each finger of his black glove until it slid off his large hand. "You intrigue me, Correlia." She stepped back, ignoring the sound of her name on his lips.

"Well . . ." she began, but words were a concept so far from her now. He didn't look at her as he pulled off his other glove, but then his dark eyes snapped to hers, and her body froze in place. "Well, *you* don't intrigue *me*," she managed to hiss.

"That's okay. I just needed to see you." His voice rumbled against her chest. Heat coursed through her, and she desperately tried to ignore how hard it was to breathe. His fingers caught hold of a loose strand of her hair, and it was hard to do anything, let alone think.

"Why?" She tried hard to catch her breath. It felt like she'd just run through the entire woods and back again. "What could you possibly gain from seeing me?"

His smile dropped, but his eyes stayed on the hair twirling between his fingertips. "There's something about you I can't get out of my head. Something I desire." The words came out like a purr.

Her knees wobbled. "What?"

"Something is off about you, Correlia, and I need to find out what it is." His voice was liquid silk in her ears, deep and smooth. He was so close she could feel his breath on her lips. Another moment ticked by where they didn't say a thing. The corner of his mouth tipped up, and he let his hand fall along her jawline, his touch white-hot as his fingers swept across her skin.

"Something's off about you, too," she whispered, breathless, "but I already know what it is."

"Oh?" His hand fell to her bare shoulder, and her mind temporarily fizzed to a stop. "And what's that?"

She shook off his hand and stepped away. "You're *sick*," she hissed, "And you can't be trusted. You're not even really a god. You're a *monster*." The muscles in his jaw clenched, his eyes turning into sweltering torches. She expected him to snap back, but instead, he evened his breaths and looked away.

She didn't get it. Why did he care about staying so composed in front of her? He was a bloodthirsty madman. One of those evil gods banished from Mt. Olympus, denounced and deemed to do the dirty work no true god would ever do. A god of decay and darkness. What game was he playing with her?

"I've heard the stories," she continued. "Of how many you've killed. How you show no mercy. How you have no one by your side but your lackeys and demons and your twisted mentor, whose only purpose is to make you a monster."

Darkness flashed in his eyes. "*Stories*," he scoffed. "You've heard *stories*. You really are as naïve as you look." The word pinched something in Corre's skull.

"I am *not* naïve."

He laughed and stepped forward, lowering his face. "I see I've struck a nerve."

"*No*, I just don't like being underestimated. That's all." She crossed her arms, but her legs trembled. Not because she was scared. She wasn't sure what it was from, but she knew the proximity of his body to hers and the flutter of his cape against her skin wasn't helping.

"You're mistaken," he said, his voice low. Each word spilled out like melting syrup. "I don't underestimate you. I think you underestimate me."

"What could I have said to make you think that? I told you I know how ruthless you are."

"Exactly."

She blinked. "What?"

"You think I'm some sort of beast." His head shook slowly, the inky waves of his hair swaying above his shoulders. "But I'm not." The richness of his voice was enticing. Seductive. He trailed his fingers down the slope of her neck, letting them venture to her collarbone. She gasped involuntarily, and goosebumps flashed across her skin.

"You *are*," she said, quickly stepping away. She prayed to the Titans that he hadn't heard her gasp. "And I still don't understand what you're saying."

A smile tugged on his lips. "Has anyone ever told you that your eyelids flutter when you're flustered?"

Her skin flushed. "I am *not* flustered."

His head tilted back with a short, carefree laugh. "You're so cute. So easily riled up."

"Excuse me?" She wished she'd said something wittier, but she'd never been in a situation like this before. Her skin was hot, her mind frazzled.

He stroked her collarbone with two of his fingers. "I said you're cute." The bass of his voice, and the touch of his skin, sent a flurry of confusing messages through her body.

"Th-that's not what I was saying."

He leaned forward, his hand sliding to the nape of her neck. Warmth pooled through her, heating every inch of her skin as he tipped his face down and tugged at the back of her neck, gently, just enough for her to look up. "Then what are you saying, Correlia of Olympus?"

His other hand fell down the side of her dress, resting on her hip, and a rush of heat turned her blood to fire. "I . . ." Her voice failed her. Her mind wandered.

And she made the mistake of getting trapped in his stare.

His dusky eyes peered coyly into hers, but they were warm, steeped in that same seductive nature so entangled in his voice. She couldn't help but notice the fullness of his lips, and the sheer blackness of his hair. Like the feathers of a crow, but darker. A moonless, starless sky.

Her body mindlessly searched for the touch of his hand until she felt it curl along the small of her back. "Do you truly think I'm a beast?"

"Of course." The words came out quiet, weak. She fought every urge that screamed for him to hold her tighter.

He leaned in closer. "Is that so?" Her mind emptied, and just before she could take another ragged breath, he pulled away. "Someone's calling for you." The seduction in his voice dissipated, and his closeness vanished. His hands slipped away and returned to his side. It took more effort than she'd care to admit to tear her eyes from him and look at what he was referring to.

"Corre!" A distant voice cried. She scanned the area but saw no one. *How did he hear that?* "Corre!" Finally, Phineas came into view. Her stomach lurched.

"Oh no—" She swiveled around, but the fear that her friend might see her unwanted guest was backed by nothing. Theron was gone. The God of Death had vanished as quickly as he'd come. There were only the trees and the vastness of the colorful field that formed a gate around her guarded life.

"Corre!"

She stared at where Theron had been standing mere seconds before—at the emptiness of that space—even when Phineas grabbed her shoulder. "Hey, I got done early. Want to come by Athena's and spar?"

Her eyes didn't waver from the trees.

"Corre?"

"Mm?" Finally, she looked, but her mind wasn't present. It raced with thoughts of Theron and mixed emotions she couldn't make sense of. Thoughts she couldn't pull together.

"Do you want to train with me?" He said more clearly, and finally, she nodded.

"Sure. That would be great." The words were hollow, but she followed her friend, forcing herself to stare straight ahead and not wonder what in Zeus' name was going on.

CHAPTER TEN

Corre

*F*ocus, *Correlia.*

The goddess watched her friend's every movement as he circled her. She leapt forward and threw another punch, but Phineas blocked it and took the balance out from beneath her left leg, striking her to the ground. The pain stung, but the humiliation was worse.

"Are you okay?" Phineas's confusion at her incompetence was unbearable.

She rubbed the back of her head and took her friend's hand. "Yeah, I'm fine. Just a little distracted. Let's go again." He nodded, but she could tell he was skeptical. She didn't want to think about the concerns spinning through her mind, let alone discuss them with Phineas. Or anyone, for that matter. She just wanted to fight. Get it all out of her system. Move her body until she was too exhausted to think about anything else.

No matter how hard she tried to focus, Theron's face appeared in her mind. His voice rumbled in her chest, and the ghost of his fingers danced across her skin, pressed inside her memory like a fallen leaf in the pages of a book. She couldn't think or focus or hear the world outside of her head. Those confusing moments with him had fastened themselves in her mind, and she couldn't unlock herself from them.

"Does Demeter know you're here?" Athena asked. The crimson-haired goddess approached with a disapproving look.

Corre grimaced. "She knows I'm working on my training today." Athena raised a brow, and Corre's shoulders fell. "I know what you're thinking, but you know how much *this* training means to me, too. Plus, I'm helping Phineas. So please, don't tell her."

The older goddess narrowed her eyes, then sighed. "All right. But work on the training she expects you to as well. You know how much it means to her that you're ready for your coronation. It's only a month away."

"I know."

She pursed her lips, looking between the two young gods before turning to another pupil. A silver-haired goddess with eyes like a fox. "Hold the arrow lower. No, not like that. Here—" Corre's eyes followed Athena's movements until she was out of earshot.

She turned to Phineas. "It's also not my mother's job to keep us safe from threats, and with Theron lurking about, someone has to know how to fight. We live too far away from anyone else out there in the glen."

Phineas frowned. "Corre, you're talking about your mother here."

"That's why I'm saying it. I know she'd sacrifice herself for me. I *know* it. She always takes the fall for me, and I can't let her do it anymore. Especially not a fall that could cause so much damage—one that could hurt her. Or worse. She doesn't mind my training here anyway. She said so herself. I need to protect her."

For a moment, he didn't look at her, but then he grinned. "Want to go again?"

A matching smile spread across her flushed face "Of course. Let's do this." She didn't let her mind wander this time. There was too much at stake. She focused on the patterns Athena had shown them, gliding along the forest floor with her friend in a warrior's dance, dust rising from the dirt at their feet. As usual, Corre dodged Phineas's every punch. Sweat coated her skin, and the rush of it all made her body soar.

Phineas utilized a few new moves Corre hadn't anticipated, but she managed to dodge them, landing a few punches of her own. As one last throw headed her way, the thought of Theron pierced her mind. His lips. His breath. His hand on the small of her back. She faltered, and Phineas knocked her clean onto the forest floor.

She slid across the dirt until her body hit the base of a tree. Luckily it wasn't hard or fast, but her ego was definitely bruised, and she hated whose fault it was.

"Are you okay?" Phineas offered his hands and pulled her up.

"Yeah, I'm fine. I just got distracted." Her spine throbbed; it had curled itself against that tree in the least pleasant way possible. She was afraid to inspect it when she got home.

"Corre." Phineas kept her hands in his until she looked up at him. "Corre, I know you. Something's off. You usually run circles around me. What's going on?"

"I'm fine!" she snapped, and her heart fell at his wounded expression. "I'm sorry. I just . . . I have a lot on my mind these days."

"Like what?" His voice was soft. She shifted uncomfortably at his worried stare. "You know you can tell me anything."

She wished that were true, but she couldn't tell him *this*. She didn't even want to admit it to herself—that she couldn't shake Hades from her mind. That she might even be drawn to Theron of Tartarus for reasons unknown to her. "I'm just having trouble with my destined path." The words weren't *un*true, and the longer she thought about it, the more she realized how true the sentiment was. The anxieties that had suffocated her before Theron had distracted her came rushing back. "I don't want my life to be growing things. I want to fight. I want to be useful in some way."

Phineas took her by the shoulders. "Hey. Look at me. Your destiny *is* useful. You make the world a beautiful place. You make Mt. Olympus heavenly and provide life for the mortals. You are destined to bring breath and light to the world."

She smiled weakly. "I don't know. I just . . . It doesn't feel right."

This was the real issue plaguing her, she decided. Theron was a distraction. That was why she'd been so intrigued by him. Inside, all she'd wanted was to be distracted from the cold reality she had to face every day—that she was deemed the Goddess of Life and Nature, but she wanted to be somebody else.

Making plants wasn't something she wanted to do. It wasn't even something she was good at. It was something she'd been told she *had* to do. But it didn't feel right. It didn't feel like her. It never had.

So, no. This wasn't about Theron. This was about her.

"Corre," Phineas said, and she looked up again. "You've already improved so much in your craft. You know that, right?" He lowered his face, a broad smile stretching so wide it had to make her smile, too. She nodded. His face lit up even more. "See? You know it's true. You can do anything you set your mind to. You know that. I know that. I'm sure your mother does, too."

"I guess you could be right."

"I *am* right. Don't think what you're destined to do isn't useful. It's something we need. Something beautiful. Something like . . ." Whatever Phineas wanted to say next fell dead on his lips.

"Something like what?" she pressed, but he chuckled awkwardly and scratched the back of his head.

"Nothing. Just," —his arm dropped to his side— "be yourself. You're a wonderful person."

She smiled. "Thank you, Phineas. Should we go again?"

"Definitely!" he said with a laugh, and the two of them took their positions.

Phineas is a great friend, Corre thought as she dodged a punch she knew was too weak to be his best attempt. *But he doesn't get it.*

As the two of them sparred, Corre did her best to hide the aching in her chest. Her friend didn't understand, but how could she tell him the truth? That who she was supposed to be wasn't who she really was. A notion no other god or goddess on Mt. Olympus seemed to understand. And that was the loneliest feeling in the world.

CHAPTER ELEVEN

Theron

*T*he goddess's voice was soft and melodic. The rhythm thrummed in the young boy's chest. Warm sunlight bathed his dark hair, and he laughed as the woman took him by the hand and spun him around. She was smaller than he was, but she was larger in life than any other god or goddess he'd ever seen. Her presence was special, warm like the sunlight pooling around them.

He couldn't make out any words—just the rhythm of her voice. When the deep voice of a god joined her melody, the boy turned and saw the face of a god he recognized from somewhere. But just like with the goddess, he couldn't hear the words or make them out from his lips. The joy that filled him was enough. He didn't need the words.

Theron's eyes opened. The ceiling was a mass of cold darkness—everything that place was not. His eyes burned with a sudden influx of tears, and he turned around as they slithered down his cheek, warm and uninvited. Why did he have to wake up today? For once he wished he'd stayed asleep.

Tossing and turning in his spacious bed, he couldn't take it anymore. Any of it. Had Thanatos known that immersing himself in the world above would be its own challenge? That Theron would realize he needed to choose the world he belonged to—the world of the night—now that he knew what was up there?

He whipped off the blanket and stalked to the washing room. Removing the thin stone carved at the mouth of the fountain, he pushed away the thoughts that bothered him the most. But they kept coming back, with one question burning like hot coals in the forefront of his mind: were those his parents?

He splashed the water on his face until it was hard to breathe, letting the cool slickness wipe away any sweat that had accumulated during the night. *Nonsense*, he decided. *My parents didn't love me. Thanatos told me I wasn't meant to be loved. I have a duty that must be fulfilled.* He blocked the spout once more and dried his face. *It's just the way it is.*

He tossed the towel on the ground and tried anchoring himself to reality. When he peered up into the pristinely polished mirror, he saw the solemn look of a trained killer, and he was reminded again what his place was in the story of the gods. His head dropped. He couldn't stand looking at himself—at the dark circles sagging beneath his eyes or the ruffled, unkempt hair that dangled from his head.

If he couldn't stomach to look at himself, how could anyone else? His hands clutched the sturdy onyx bowl mounted beneath the fountain's spout. *I'm a monster. That's all there is to it.*

That warm sunlight vision was just a dream. Memories like that didn't exist for someone like him.

Corre

'Do you truly think I'm a beast?'

Lying on her bedsheets, Corre remembered every detail of the meeting she shared with Theron those few short days ago. Her mind lingered on the way his fingers fell down the slope of her neck in calculated strokes, and on that spark in his eyes, the seductive warmness of his voice.

"Corre?" Her mother knocked on the other side of the door.

Her heart jumped in her throat. "Come in." The words tripped on each other as she covered her flushed skin with her bedsheets. The door creaked open to reveal her small mother, wound up in an elegant shawl and carrying an oversized travel bag. At Corre's confused expression, the older goddess sighed. "You forgot, didn't you?"

"Forgot what?"

"That I'm leaving today."

"Leaving? Oh!" She *had* forgotten. Berenice was leaving on an important task to grow an entire forest for the humans. Her last big task before Corre would take her place—one that Corre was initially supposed to go on with her. They thought she'd be ready by now. Berenice loved her daughter enough to lie and claim that Corre was perfecting her skills before her coronation next month, though she did promise that Corre would complete the next task on her own.

"Yes '*Oh*,'" Berenice laughed. "I don't know how long I'll be gone. Probably a little under a month. I'll be back by your birthday, though, so don't worry. Don't forget that at least." She winked, but Corre sunk further into her sheets at the thought.

She wished she could forget.

Her birthday was the big one. Twenty. When she was supposed to be ready to take on her role as Persephone. Phineas was lucky. He'd turned twenty last month but was ready enough to take on his role as the warrior god of Olympus. He'd be gathering his army soon and getting ready for whatever lay ahead. He was being cautious at this point, but he was ready. Corre thought he was dragging his feet, but Athena was fine letting him wait to take on his title. His parents were okay with it, too. Zeus, too, apparently. But the world would wither and rot without Corre taking up hers.

Berenice enjoyed her role as Demeter and would never give it up. Corre was fortunate in that way. But she still knew her mother couldn't do it alone, yet here she was, a heavy bag slung upon her slight shoulder, ready to take on an enormous job because Corre wasn't ready to help.

"Thank you," she said with a sad smile. "I'm sorry I can't go."

Her mother waved her hand. "Oh, it's all right. I'm up for the challenge. An entire forest. Whew! I hope I can do it." Her mother laughed again, which only made the guilt twist in Corre's guilt. She knew what it meant when her mother nervously laughed this much. She was hiding what she felt. Masking for Corre's sake, as usual.

This was *her* job. Not her mother's. But just like always, her mother swooped in so that Corre didn't have to push. Or fail.

"I can go with you, you know."

"No, no. Stay here. I want you to practice, anyway." She gave her daughter a kiss on the cheek. "Make something beautiful to show me on your birthday. I'll be back then. I love you."

"Love you, too." Her mother gave her one last smile before shutting the door behind her. Corre let out a long breath and sunk into her bed. *I need to get up and walk or my muscles will get worse.* Too much time in bed over the last couple of days had left her cramped. Sore. She needed to move or she'd be even more useless in her duties while her mother was away.

She allowed enough time for Berenice to disappear into the woods before she emerged from their cottage, thinking back on the day Zeus had summoned her. He'd wanted to ensure that Corre could take up her mantle in one year's time. She remembered being frustrated, wondering why it was so important to him that she was ready. Weren't there more important goddesses to be concerned about?

'The fabrics of fate can get quite chaotic if one doesn't fulfill her destiny,' he'd told her.

She'd nodded. *'Yes, sir.'*

Now it'd been a year, and she felt no closer to becoming Persephone than she had back then. If anything, she felt even worse about it. She wasn't ready, and all eyes would be on her as she was taken before Zeus on her coronation day.

She let herself flop onto the ground. *Mother won't take me if I'm not ready,* she assured herself, but she couldn't help feeling guilty at the embarrassment Berenice would face over it.

'The fabrics of fate can get quite chaotic if one doesn't fulfill her destiny.'

She stared up at the sky. "Surely, it's happened before," she muttered. "And here we all are. Still standing and breathing. The world hasn't collapsed."

She watched the slow dance of clouds moving through the salt-water sky. *Has it happened before?* she wondered. *I bet it has. They're just afraid.* Everyone was always afraid. It was the general reaction to everything on Olympus if things didn't go exactly as planned.

Her chest tightened, her breathing becoming quick and frenzied. She had to keep her body moving. No more thinking.

She took deep breaths and tried focusing on the physical sensations around her. The warm air against her skin. The soft soil and grass that cushioned her bare feet. She looked at that little patch of grass she had to spend almost every waking moment within. The one littered with her half-decent creation and wilted trials. Was that going to be her life? Was that her fate for eternity? To visit endless patches of grass once she conquered the ability to decorate each one?

Her mother had the power, too, and she was so good at it. Was Corre really needed? Would anyone miss her if she was gone?

She couldn't stand it. "I hate that stupid patch of grass." She squeezed her eyes shut, forcing down the urge to run back inside the cottage and sink into her bed. A thick fog wrapped around her, muddling the thoughts ripping through her brain, causing her limbs to turn into heavy bags of sand. A heavy, invisible blanket rolled down her body, weighing on her—crushing her—inside and out.

She was numb. Lost. Alone.

And tonight would serve as a reminder of everything she wasn't ready for. It was Apollo and Artemis's coronation day. The golden children of Olympus—a brother and sister team so committed to each other they refused to hold separate coronations. Their joint birthday wasn't for another half-year, but Artemis had been ready for weeks, and as soon as her brother was equally ready, they pleaded before Zeus for an early ceremony. For whatever reason.

Likely to passive-aggressively gloat behind a shield of success. They were like that.

Corre would have to remember not to roll her eyes while she attended the ceremony. The twins were not the easiest company. She shivered, remembering when she'd met them. Apollo's complete disinterest and Artemis's scrunched face and sticky-sweet smile after Corre had fumbled over an introduction. "Don't want a repeat of that," she grumbled, but then she thought of the worst part. At the ceremony, everyone would ask her when her coronation would be. She'd have to be tactful, put up a wall. Put on a mask. Tears burned in her eyes. "Forget it. I can't do this."

"Can't do what?" A voice like silk rippled through the air.

Corre sucked in a nervous breath. Biting her tongue, she opened her eyes. His hair was brushed back as slickly as his voice, and the cape rippling behind him caused his massive frame to take up even more space—shadowing more of that wretched grass. "You again." She didn't say it as icily as she thought she would.

Theron's lips curled into a wicked smile. "Correlia." Corre hated the way his voice melted in her ears. Worse was the way her body warmed as he slowly made his way to her. Juxtaposed beneath the sunny sky, this unnervingly handsome god with skin pale like a cloud-soaked moon and hair blacker than the night sky, Theron was a walking poison—a personified curse. As far as she knew, there was no elixir for this dark spell he cast upon her whenever they met. Stalking closer, that same black cape snapped in the wind behind him.

"What? You're tracking me now?" She tried to sound indifferent, but it was harder the closer he got.

"What can't you do?" The words purred out of his mouth. Corre had to look away.

"Ignoring the question?" She folded her arms but still couldn't get herself to look directly back at him.

His presence loomed closer, and she had no choice but to return his gaze. "I'm just curious." His dark eyes peered down into hers, "What task could be so difficult that Correlia of Olympus is unable to complete it?"

"Why should I tell you anything? I don't even know why you're here." She managed more of a bite in her voice this time, but it only made that wicked smile spread wider across his face.

"I'm here for a reason, just like before."

"That reason being?"

"Maybe a little of the same, maybe a little more."

"What's that supposed to mean?" she scoffed.

His eyes narrowed and then unnarrowed, like he was impressed or intrigued at her questioning. "It's a secret."

"Then I guess my task is a secret, too."

"I'll tell you what." His breath on her skin made her momentarily falter, but she stayed strong, arms crossed and eyes glowering into his. "You tell me, and I may tell you."

She let out an exasperated laugh and dropped her arms to her side. "I don't care why you're here, so why would I make such a stupid bargain?" It was bold of her to lie, but he seemed to accept it.

"Because I can help you with whatever it is."

"I don't need help. It's just a stupid party." She suppressed a breath and clamped her mouth shut.

His smile widened again at her slip-up. "A party?"

She sighed. "Yes, a party. Are you happy to know that my 'task' is attending a stupid party?"

He laughed, a low, pleasant caress against her eardrums. "A little. I can see the reason you wouldn't want to go. Crowds of people are insufferable."

"How would you know? Are there ceremonies down in the Underworld, too?" She meant it as a joke, but when his smile dropped, she wondered if there were ceremonies and what they were like. "Should I take that as a 'yes'?"

He turned away from her, slowly pacing the field of flowers. His eyes lingered on each one. Crouching down to hold a lavender lily in his hand, he said, "Not the kind someone from Olympus would want to attend."

His fingers stroked the petals gently—a jarring scene from the large, gloomy figure before her. Birds flew overhead, but his eyes stayed on the plant at his feet. He must not be used to colors like these. When his eyes found a blossom with a soft pink hue, he crept toward it, and Corre's heart jumped.

"Wow," he breathed. "This is magnificent."

"Oh, that? It's nothing." But Corre very well knew it wasn't nothing. It was *her* flower. Amongst all the creations that circled the cottage created by her mother, he singled out hers and found it magnificent.

"Did you create this?"

She shifted her weight awkwardly. "Yes, but I'm still working on it."

He took one last look at it before straightening himself. He turned to face her, and her jaw subtly dropped at the sudden change in his expression. His features were soft—his eyes were off somewhere else, his thoughts roaming with the wind.

Her heart sped. *Theron is here.* Here. *At my house. What do I do?* She took another moment to compose herself before clearing her throat. "I have to get ready. You really need to leave." She managed to get the words out boldly, but she was still worried he'd see right through her.

His eyes found hers again, and his face tightened to its usual scowl. A twinge of regret surfaced in her chest, a confusing feeling that made her want to retreat into her house even more quickly. "Goodbye," she said and turned to her house.

"Wait."

She stopped but didn't flip back around.

"What's this party going to be like?"

What? She couldn't help turning around to examine him. His features had softened again. The ever-changing expressions on his face made her even more confused. And intrigued. "Loud," she said. "Crowded. The two gods being given their titles today are insufferable, so a lot of pretending will be involved, I assume."

She jumped when he snorted. "Now *that* is something I understand completely."

"You do?" She caught herself before further revealing any interest. Why should she care what he does or doesn't understand? He wasn't even supposed to be up here.

"Unfortunately." He wiped the dirt off his hands. He wasn't wearing his gloves today, and something about seeing his hands made her breath quicken.

Thoughts she didn't want to entertain knocked on the doors of her mind. Shaking them off, she found herself saying something stupid. "How?" She winced. *What is wrong with me?*

"You may not believe it, but Tartarus isn't swarming with gods. I only really have to deal with one—other than my master—but he's insufferable enough for a thousand others. If I was forced to go to a party honoring him, I'd pull my hair out."

Corre laughed. Again, that voice in her head screamed at her. She was being stupid and reckless. He was cunning. A flatterer. But she thought of the tales. Everyone said he was a monster. That he was malicious and evil and unlike any other.

No one said he was like this. She looked back up at him and saw him examining the world around them, his eyes returning to the plants and a bird perched on the windowsill a few paces behind her. "But," he continued, "I think you could still have a good time. You gods up here are pampered. I'm sure you'll get plenty to eat and drink." Corre wanted to refute and tell him how wrong he was—how insufferable *he* was for saying such a thing—but his voice was seeped in a sort of sadness. Like he was envious of the pampered lives of those he mocked.

What was the Underworld like? Surely his life wasn't as miserable as the tales told. They were vicious depictions of demons wailing and Hades sucking the souls out of humans. She was once told he was rejected even by his family. That he was *that* bad. But that was the part that always bothered her. How could any god be destined to be evil? And if he was, if the stories were true, wouldn't that mean he was raised in that torment?

Were the stories of who he truly was or who he was supposed to become? Just like with Corre and the stories of Persephone and who she ought to be.

"Have you...ever wanted to live on Olympus?" she asked, deciding to permanently shut that voice of reason out of her mind, at least for today.

He didn't look at her. His eyes stayed locked on that pink plant. Her first creation. She hadn't even given it a proper name yet. "Sometimes." He said it quietly. Maybe he hadn't meant for her to hear it.

She wanted to ask what Tartarus was like but decided against it. Instead, she asked something else. Something far less responsible. "Would you like to try? Just for today?"

His eyes snapped up and he stared at her like she was crazy. "What?"

"The party. The coronation...it might be good for you to see. How insufferable it is, I mean. Maybe then you won't wish you lived here." She laughed awkwardly, but fear bundled in her stomach. *This is a bad idea.* "You know what, forget it—"

"All right."

She stared at him in shock.

"But that doesn't mean I want to live here," he quickly added. "I know how gods treat each other on Olympus. It's a different kind of suffering." The words weighed heavy on Corre's shoulders, but she didn't understand them. "It doesn't matter. I can't go. I'll be recognized."

Before she could think better of it, she nodded toward her house. "Follow me. We'll see if it can work."

CHAPTER TWELVE

Corre

Corre didn't let herself process the gravity of inviting Hades into her home—and of what her mother would say if she found out—as she threw clothes out of one of the old trunks gathering dust in the back of Berenice's closet. *Why am I doing this?*

She ignored the thought and pulled out a large cloak with a hood. It was an old one of Phineas's he'd given her one day, after he was gifted a new one by his parents. *"You said you were cold remember?"* he'd said. She had to rack her brain at the time, but she finally did remember she'd recently told him she got cold when training in the garden in the evenings.

She never wore it, and hopefully Phineas wouldn't recognize it if he attended the coronation. *Luckily he hates these things as much as I do.* Corre wasn't sure if she would have even gone if she hadn't heard the pain in Theron's voice. A haunted look usually accompanied his conniving stare, but when he looked at her in shock after her invitation, it was like he'd turned into someone else—someone with childlike delight behind the pain in his eyes. The melancholy feeling that squeezed her stomach at the sight was what got in the way of her better judgment.

"This should do it." She held up the cloak.

"That's a little short," he said, inspecting the ragged material. 'A little' was an understatement. Theron was a good six inches taller than Phineas.

"I didn't say it was perfect. I said it would do." She threw it at him. "Try it on."

He rolled his eyes. "Why do I have to put this on anyway? It's not like my face won't be recognized."

"Your face isn't what people recognize. It's how you move and what you wear." She paused. "And your hair."

"My hair?" He glanced in the long, floor-length mirror in Berenice's bedroom.

"Yes. I haven't seen anyone else with hair like that." When pink crept up her cheeks, she quickly closed the trunk and said, "Get dressed. We may have to figure something out for your clothes beneath the cloak, but that should be good enough until we get there. Or maybe just pin it shut. And I'll help you with your hair." She didn't look at him before closing the door. "Hurry, though! If we're late, it will only draw attention to us."

Wait. "Actually, people will be suspicious of me being with someone they don't recognize. So...just...follow me a few paces behind..." She rambled a little more before he called out through the thick oak door.

"I can't hear a word you're saying!"

She growled. "You really are insufferable," she shouted back. He either didn't hear her or didn't want to respond. The only sound Corre was met with was the shuffling of clothes behind the door before it creaked open.

"I don't know why I had to change in there. It's only a cloak." He came out looking exactly the same but with the cloak fastened around his neck.

"You were supposed to take your shirt off."

"I was?"

She groaned. "Yes!"

"Okay, okay!" He groaned back, making a point for her to hear it, and unpinned the cloak, lifting his shirt over his head. All she saw was a flash of muscle before she averted her eyes. Heat shot up her face.

"You should have gone back in!"

Metal clinked as he pinned the cloak again. When the sound stopped, she turned around. The light brown fabric shrouded his bare skin and went just below his knees. Good enough for a disguise. The fact that it was old and worn helped. Hopefully he wouldn't stand out as much.

"Good enough," she said.

"What about my hair?"

Right. She focused on the inky waves that traveled down the nape of his neck. Even at the bustling markets of Olympus, or when she met Zeus, she'd never seen someone with hair like his. Everyone else's was precisely combed and clipped in a way deemed most suitable. His was thick and untamed, the black waves accentuating the dark brown of his eyes.

She tried not to think about it. This had to be purely platonic. It was a favor. The heat growing beneath her skin had to have nothing to do with it. "Let's go to the washing room. I'll try a few things."

She opened the door next to Berenice's room. It led into a small, cabinet-sized washing room with a fountain for baths and hand washing, as well as a flat surface in the floor with a hole cut in the middle of polished slabs of wood. "Is this really your washing room?" he asked incredulously.

"I don't have to help you," she reminded him, turning the spigot until fresh, cool water ran between her fingers. "I didn't even want you here in the first place."

"You're the one who invited me."

She twisted the spigot to allow for more water flow. "I could tell you wanted to go."

She was surprised when he didn't contest her. "It beats what I would do in Tartarus."

"Which is?" The water was a good temperature, but Corre needed to wait until the debris cleared out so she could wet his hair without having to clear out any dirt.

"That's confidential information."

"Whatever you say," she muttered. The debris had finally waned, so she stood up and pointed to the small fountain. "Kneel."

His eyebrows shot up. "Excuse me?"

"You have to kneel and wet your hair."

He narrowed his eyes, seemingly calculating a comeback, but wordlessly he did as he was told and knelt in front of the small fountain and dunked his head beneath its mouth.

His shoulders were so broad they almost filled the entirety of the room. It reminded Corre of a time she'd seen a fox cub try following a squirrel into the knot of a tree. Only its nose managed to poke through the small opening. At least Theron could fit well enough in the washing room to wet his hair.

The room felt even smaller as he lifted his thick arms to run his fingers through his soaking hair. Her next breath snagged in her throat. She snapped her head away and stared at the tiles on the wall, but she could still feel his elbow brush against her slight bicep. After about a minute, he whipped up his head, spraying water all over her. "Now what?" he said.

Her mouth gaped open, her eyes just as wide. "Are you serious? You got water all over me."

"So? I have water all over *me*." His casual tone was maddening. Corre decided this would be her good deed for the foreseeable future.

"You know that's different." She shook water out of her hair and grabbed a cloth to wipe down her arms. "You have terrible social skills."

"Sorry, Your Greatness, I didn't have the opportunity to learn etiquette while I was being trained to rule the Underworld."

"Is that supposed to impress me?" she quipped. "Whatever. Just come here." She guided him to a chair in the kitchen. He stalked behind her, his footsteps accompanied by the faint drips of water plunking against the wooden floorboards. "May I?" she asked, though it was more of a jeer than a request. He plopped in the seat in front of her, and the chair's poor legs squeaked in agony. *I sure hope that doesn't break. What would I tell Mother?*

"May you what?"

"Do your hair," she said. She was losing patience. Luckily, he nodded, though there was a reluctance in his eyes that threw her off.

"Okay. I'm going to brush it back and pin it. Wear the cloak as much as you can while we're out, but there may be times when taking it off is inevitable. Like when it gets dark."

"That won't be a problem. I won't stay longer than an hour."

"The coronation starts in about an hour," Corre said, her hands hovering above his head. She bit her bottom lip. How could she run her fingers through his hair when she was rendered immobile from the brush of his hand against her skin?

"I guess we'll have to be on time then," he said, but she didn't retort. Her fingers grazed the slick waves of black draping down his face, but the contact made something buzz in her veins that didn't sit well with her. It felt . . . forbidden.

Her hands fell. "You can do this part yourself," she said, trying to sound stern.

"What? Why?"

"I'm not your slave!"

He rolled his eyes. "Fine, just tell me what to do."

She led him back into the bathroom and showed him how to stroke his hands through his hair in a way that would make it easy for her to pin it back. There was a mirror above the basin next to the fountain. Corre had forgotten all about it—the surface was so old and murky it was practically useless. There was even a big crack split across the middle. But that was the one Theron used as he stroked his fingers through his hair.

As if in a trance, she couldn't look away. His dark eyes shone starkly against the smudged glass, somehow parting the clouds of dust and grime. She took pins from her room and placed them carefully on the back of his head. Her fingers began trembling again the moment they touched him. She ignored the spark in her chest as she combed her fingers through his hair. Neither one of them spoke a word.

Carefully, she slid each thin, metal bar in a neat row across the crown of his head. Then in a slanted line down the sides of his hair, leading down to the back of his neck—a hidden staircase in a field of black.

When she was done, he looked back into the glass, and his eyes widened. She looked between him and his murky reflection, ignoring the pounding in her chest. "What?"

He continued staring. "My face."

She cocked an eyebrow. "What about it?"

"It's so long. And pale."

She laughed. "It is." She resisted the urge to tell him what other words came to mind when she looked at his face—especially now that she could see it better. "Do you like what I did with your hair?" His eyes didn't leave his reflection. When he still didn't respond, she said, "You should look in the bigger mirror. That one's useless." The words didn't reach him for a few seconds; when they finally did, he silently left the room and walked over to the floor-length mirror he'd inspected the cloak in.

"Whoa." He turned to his side and leaned forward to inspect himself. Then, to Corre's great astonishment, he smiled—not a smirk or wicked grin. He smiled, and he looked like any other god ready to attend a gathering on Olympus. The strangest part was how normal he looked. Second only to how much it made her cheeks warm.

"I should get ready now, too, and you should go somewhere else until the coronation starts." She tried not to look at him idly running his fingers across the rim of a fruit bowl next to a precarious stack of books.

"Why?" He turned to look at her, and her heart skipped a beat. Even without the dark waves framing his face, he was strikingly handsome. It made it easier to see his eyes and all the power behind them.

"Because we're not supposed to go together, and I don't want you in my house."

He gave her a flat look. "Yes, princess." Their normal rap returned, which offered Corre some relief. A guarded, arms-length relationship was wiser and more comfortable. And much more preferable to the alternative.

She watched him leave, but it took her the greater part of the hour to stop thinking about him and get ready for the coronation, hoping to the Titans nothing would go awry.

CHAPTER THIRTEEN

Theron

It didn't take many strides away from Correlia's cottage before Theron realized he had no bloody clue where to go. He stalked the area around her house, far enough away that she wouldn't see him once she emerged. He stayed hidden in the trees, realizing he didn't care for the birds chirping but could get used to the sweet smell of sap sticking to the bark beneath his fingertips.

He leaned against the tree with a sigh. *What's taking her so long?* He tried adjusting his position, but the moment he shifted, the cloak pushed awkwardly against his throat. He turned to find the brown fabric snagged in the peeling bark of the tree. "Perfect," he grumbled, tugging at the cloth with a tiny ounce of strength he'd thought was gentle enough. But when an unsettling rip tore through the air, he winced and raised the now-tattered cloth to eye level.

A door creaked open, and a nervous chill shot through Theron as he whipped the torn cloak behind him like a child hiding a stolen sweet.

At first, he saw no one, and then a glimmering figure dressed all in silver appeared like a flicker of light. His breath stilled. Her rose-gold hair was pinned in intricate knots on the back of her head, save for two soft tresses framing her freckled face in casual elegance. She looked more than a mere goddess. She was the moon on a dark, dreary night.

The trance she placed him under made him momentarily forget to follow her, until her figure was nearly out of sight. He quickly weaved through the trees, keeping his eyes on her the entire way. It was easy not to think and wonder as he focused merely on her image, but the journey to the coronation was long. He, unfortunately, had the time to wonder. To think.

Why would she invite someone like me?

Unease settled through him, sweat forming in his palms. He stopped. *Maybe this is a trick. Maybe she's leading me into a trap.*

His heart pounded, and the thoughts continued piling into his mind, swarming messily and aggressively on top of each other. "Of course it's a trap. Why wouldn't it be?"

A lump formed in his throat. He'd be stupid to follow her there.

But . . . on the off-chance this wasn't a trap—that she actually *did* want to invite him—wouldn't he want to take the risk?

His eyes found her shimmering form again.

Without a second thought, he took another step.

Corre

What am I doing? This is a mistake.

A knot formed in the pit of her stomach. She focused on her feet as they led her to the coronation. Guilt swirled in her gut. *What if something happens because I invited him?*

Her heart raced. So much could go wrong. She truly was as reckless as her mother accused her of being. When something rustled behind her, she jumped and glanced over her shoulder. No one was there. She scanned the area for any trace of the God of the Underworld, but there was no one. *Maybe he decided against it.* Her shoulders dropped in disappointment, but she quickly corrected herself. *It's for the best.*

She thought of his face. The mystery behind his gaze and how he never hurt her—how he came up from the Underworld simply to speak with her.

Her heart quickened in her chest. She pushed the thoughts aside. *Don't be stupid, Corre. It could be part of a long, elaborate plan.* But for what? What could he gain from hurting her? She wasn't Zeus or Hera or even Artemis. Her duties were benign compared to the others. What reason would he have to hurt her?

The stories of Hades always made him out to be a vicious killer with no humanity, but the way he looked at himself in the mirror was so innocent. So guileless. When he wasn't dressed to intimidate, he looked like everyone else. Corre was never one to blindly believe stories, but that's what got her into this mess. Maybe everyone was right. Maybe she *was* naive.

She chewed on her lower lip, hoping she was wrong about that but right about inviting him. He deserved an invitation like all the others, didn't he?

Despite her justifications, thoughts of destruction and endless worst-case scenarios tormented her the whole way there.

She was stupid for doing this.

No, she wasn't.

Of course she was.

No, he has done nothing to show the stories about him are true. Hasn't Mother always taught me to judge people on their actions?

Every time she thought it was wrong and that something bad would happen, she remembered how normal he looked when he saw himself in that mirror. The unguarded sadness in his eyes before she invited him in. *I guess I'll just have to see what happens*, she thought, but guilt tightened the knot in her gut. *Maybe having him meet me there was the right call after all. I can keep an eye on him.*

When she neared the slope leading up to the Square, she could see the top half of Zeus's castle, and for some reason, it put her at ease. Could she really believe stories that originated from such luxury? Everyone said Zeus was a great god. Charismatic and caring. But she'd only met him once, and just like the stories about Hades, she wasn't sure what to believe. Not anymore.

From what she understood, Zeus was largely the one who explained who Theron was to the others on Olympus—how terrible Hades was and how he should be avoided—but it was hard for Corre to believe everything was so cut and dry. That the leader in this mansion touching the sky was to be revered, while the unknown, young god living in Tartarus should be feared.

She wondered if she was judging Zeus too harshly. After all, it was the Titans who'd given him the luxuries he now lived in. Maybe he didn't have a say in his castle or the affairs of the gods. Maybe she wanted someone else to blame other than herself, just in case her invitation was the worst mistake anyone had ever made.

The hard truth was that there was too much she didn't know, and it was making her head hurt. There was nothing she could do now, though, so she might as well move forward and keep an eye on Theron. It shouldn't be hard to find him once he arrived. He was the tallest Great One she'd ever seen. She just hoped no one else would notice his stature and look too closely at his face.

The lively chatter of Olympus was the first indication that the coronation had already begun. Corre heard laughs and the jubilant singing of whatever gods were invited. At first, she was relieved, as there appeared to be more gods than the Great Ones in attendance, but upon closer inspection, she wasn't sure if that was the case. There were countless unknown faces, but each was adorned with jewels, their bodies dressed in fine silks and fabrics that the non-appointed gods could never afford. Maybe they were the second-tier Great Ones. What were they called? Were they considered 'common gods'? Corre hated the hierarchy, but she wanted to understand how it all worked and who everyone was.

"Welcome!" A golden-haired goddess in bright purple robes greeted Corre as she made her way through an arch of silvery vines ornamented with gemstones of every color. The archway looked magical with its garnets and emeralds, sapphires and onyx. An awe-inspiring, iron rainbow.

"Hello," Corre replied feebly. The girl smiled hazily, and though her eyes were staring right into Corre's, they looked far away and covered in glass. She was clearly intoxicated.

"Help yourself to the feast and drinks at the base of Zeus's castle. The rest of the festivities are set up all along the square and up the mountain at various booths." She rattled on about the different activities and features at each one. By the end, her words slurred, and she giggled.

"I'm sure I'll find my way," Corre said with an awkward laugh. "Thank you."

"Of course! Oh, welcome!" The girl said to the next visitor.

"Hello," a deep voice purred. Corre's stomach dropped. She waited an agonizingly long moment before surreptitiously looking over her shoulder. "Correlia."

She shot him a glare. "How did you get here so fast?"

He smiled beneath the hood of the borrowed cloak. "Years of training."

She glanced around to see if anyone had noticed something off about the tall god, but luckily most of them were too drunk to care. Her shoulders relaxed.

"Well . . ." She looked around again. *What am I supposed to do now? Spend time with him? I didn't think this through.* She wrung her hands.

"Why don't we get a drink?" He gestured to the long table with the same jewel-crested adornments as the silvery entryway.

"Okay, but you can go on your own to the booths, you know. You don't have to follow me around."

"Don't you want my company?" The seductive drawl in his voice made her stomach knot again, only this time it was for a different reason.

"Not particularly."

He laughed. "May I remind you that *you* invited *me* here?"

"No, you may not."

He flashed her a wicked smile and held out his hand. "Come on. There's no harm in a drink."

I'm not so sure. "Fine. But then you can examine an Olympus party on your own and head back to Tartarus." She pushed past him, ignoring his hand and not waiting for a reply. She needed a drink just as much as anyone here. Probably more.

The music grew louder as she walked deeper into the festivities toward where the drinks were being offered. Gods on lyres and drunk groups singing off-key bumbled around the large turquoise fountain in the middle of the Square. The noise intensified the more Corre thought about Theron following close behind. She couldn't hear the blood pounding in her ears.

Everything was too loud, going too fast. She moved quicker, picking up her pace until she made it to the golden table adorned with chalices. "Wow," she breathed, though she couldn't hear herself over the noise. The table stretched across half of the Square, every inch of its surface covered in jeweled goblets with different elixirs sitting inside. Some liquids were a dark burgundy, others ice pink, some brown, mauve, violet, opal—some were too far away to see.

"What are these?" she asked the plump, ember-haired goddess filling a cluster of goblets across from her. When the goddess didn't look up, Corre repeated herself louder.

"These?" The redhead finally said. "The finest elixirs my dear. Whatever you could ever want is in these cups." She gave Corre a wink, but the answer was too ominous for her liking. Did some make you *too* uninhibited? Would she drink the wrong one and do something stupid? *Even more stupid than inviting Hades to a party on Olympus?* She grimaced. Yes, she'd already done something outrageously stupid today, but she didn't feel like adding to it.

"Which ones are safe?" she shouted above the noise, pointing at the goblets.

"Oh, all of them, dear!" The goddess continued pouring, then turned around to fill a pitcher with more curious liquid from one of many diamond-encrusted vats.

Corre groaned. How was she supposed to enjoy herself here if she didn't know what was safe?

"That's a good one!" The goddess said to someone next to Corre. She looked to her left and saw Theron chugging one of the liquids in one go.

Her eyes widened. "What are you doing? You don't even know what's in that one!"

When the goblet left his lips, he cast her an impish smile. "What are you worried about, Correlia? Afraid I might make a fool of myself here? Or worse?" She couldn't tell if he was joking or not, but she didn't like it. She crossed her arms and tried to come up with something to say. Before she could, he laughed. "It's Olympian fig tree wine," he said, placing the empty goblet on the table. The goddess with the pitcher poured more purple liquid into it.

"How do you know?" Corre asked as she watched Theron throw another one back.

"I've had it plenty of times to know. See?" He tilted the cup to her so she could peer inside. She leaned forward and sniffed it. The earthy mixture of berries and something bitter set her at ease.

"Oh. It is."

"I don't know what the others are, but I don't feel like being more daring than I already am by being here." When Corre looked up at him, surprised, he raised an eyebrow. "What? Did you think you were the only one at risk by my being here today? I'm pretty sure you have nothing to worry about personally. If I get caught, nothing will happen to you." The last word went sour on his lips, and his expression shifted.

Is he worried about getting caught? She looked around at the goblets and then back at his. "May I?" she asked quickly, wrapping her hand around the chalice. His dark brown eyes stared at her in surprise. Her fingers brushed along his. He nodded, and she ignored the way his gaze made her skin sizzle, and the way it felt to have her fingers linked with his as they both held the cup. She wrapped her other hand around it too and closed her eyes, sipping the drink and letting the earthy liquid fill her being, warming her body.

When her eyes opened, she saw him still staring, and she released her grip on the goblet. "I don't feel any different," she said, looking away and hoping he didn't notice the heat reddening her cheeks.

"It's a mild wine. It's why I took it. Olympian fig-tree wine is essentially juice."

"How do you know so much about it?"

He hitched a shoulder and took another swig. "I guess my master was okay letting me have something this mild. I've had it since I was a boy."

"Really? Hm. It must be mild then."

He laughed. "I don't think my master was looking out for me. I think he just didn't want me to lose my focus. He *is* in charge of my training, after all."

She nodded, but she couldn't help feeling sorry for him. There was something about his master he was trying to mask. "So you were raised by him?"

"Yes," he said, but the word was clipped. He let the round goddess refill his goblet. "But enough about that. Let's go somewhere quieter. I think my head may explode."

A smile dimpled her cheeks. "I agree." She pointed up the trail of booths. "Let's go over there. They usually have amazing desserts. It's how I manage to get through these things."

"By all means, lead the way."

Corre let the smile stay on her face, ignoring the warning flames of anxiety she was taught to heed as she led Theron up the mountain. The higher they got, the less ear-shattering the air became, and when they made it to a booth littered with decadent palm-sized pies, her eyes brightened with delight. Everything else melted away.

"Here, try this one," she said, plucking a small lemon tart with a dollop of meringue on top. He took it without a word, but the hint of a smile on his face made her heart skip a beat. She quickly turned away and grabbed her own.

"Mm, this is good," he said, his mouth full of lemon meringue.

"I told you." Her teeth sunk into the gooey pastry. She could die of happiness in this little pie. "I forgot how amazing these were." She grabbed another as soon as the last bite was in her mouth. And then another. She could care less about any judgments from Theron. This was the only good thing about these parties.

When she heard the tall god snicker, she glowered at him. "What?" *I don't care what you think*, she wanted to hiss, but he didn't have malice in his eyes. With one finger, he swiped something off her face.

"You have something sticky all over your cheek."

Her face burned. "Don't be a jerk," she said, grumpily waltzing back down the hill, trying not to show how embarrassed she was or how hastily she was trying to make it to the fountain of water in the center of the Square.

"I'm not trying to be a jerk," his voice came from behind. "I think it's cute." The burning in her face intensified.

"Don't mock me."

"I'm not."

It was hard to find a place she could comfortably sit at the fountain. It was a vast, circular monument in the middle of the Square, and usually it was treated with respect. But on coronation days, there were no rules on etiquette. Corre squeezed her way between two wildly laughing gods and splashed water on her face. *What a jerk.* The cool water was a breath of relief to her hot skin. She let her soggy palms rest against her face until she was ready to rejoin her guest.

She groaned at the thought. *I want to eat my pie in peace. I don't care about how messy it gets. I don't need someone ridiculing me.* She sat on the marble fountain and looked back up the hill. The booth with the pies was bustling with guests. From here, it looked so small, but it was much more than a booth. It was a makeshift shop consisting of a long counter and as many pies as one could eat. In the back were two goddesses and another god preparing more goods for the partygoers.

It was the first time Corre realized that the gods and goddesses providing the drinks, treats, and favors at the coronation didn't get to enjoy them like everyone else. They worked tirelessly so those deemed as being 'higher class' or 'chosen' or 'Great' didn't have to go without for a single second. There must have been a lot of pressure on them. These gods that were often thought of as being lesser. "Common gods"—ones without grand prophecies. What made people like Corre and Apollo and Artemis, and anyone else enjoying the coronation party, more worthy than these hard-working gods?

Nothing. There was nothing. Just a scrap of paper designed by the Titans and enforced by the Great Ones. Corre leaned back, her hands curling around the marble rim of the fountain. The sprinkles of water spitting from one of its many heads was cool against the back of her neck. It was then that she realized she hadn't heard an aggravatingly alluring voice for a while now, and panic splintered in her chest.

Her eyes darted along the square and up the path toward the dessert booth, but he was nowhere in sight. "Oh no." She jumped to her feet and looked around, but this was the last place you'd want to lose someone. The music was growing louder, the laughter and voices more obnoxious, and there were hundreds, if not thousands, of gods and goddesses piled in the Square and mountain—some busily working and others enjoying the splendor.

Her blood turned cold. What if he was planning something? *I should have known.* She ran to the other side of the Square, her eyes bolting to every god's face. They were all too short. He stuck out in that ragged cloak. He was enormous. She had a hard time believing he could navigate through the crowd as swiftly as she could with those broad shoulders and the hood partially obscuring his face.

"Help!" A small voice cried. Corre's blood curdled. She whipped around to find its source. "Help!"

The blood drained from her face.

A child.

She bolted toward the noise, frustrated that no one else in the Square even noticed. If they did, they didn't care. The tiny voice cried out again. It was clearer now—somewhere in the trees. She pushed through the crowd to get to the woods surrounding the mountain.

Branches scratched at her exposed skin as she pushed them away. She swore she heard the voice coming from this direction, so she kept pushing her way through the leaves. Finally, she heard something. Voices. Other children. And then she saw him.

Corre's mouth opened to scream out—to rebuke Theron. *How could you hurt a child?* But before she could, the scene played out before her.

"We didn't do anything!" Two young boys cried up at the tall god. They looked to be about twelve years old—one had a pinched face and red hair, and the other was blonde and round. At Theron's side was a third boy, one who was much smaller than the others and now clinging to Hades' cloak.

"Are you going to lie to a superior?" Theron's voice boomed. The two boys facing him grabbed each other.

"We're not lying!"

"Yes, they are!" the boy at Theron's side cried.

"No, we're not, you little wimp," the round boy snapped. When the small boy's fist tightened against Theron's cloak, the God of the Underworld stepped closer to the others.

The older boys shook, clinging to each other as the older god drew closer. Bending down, he looked straight into the boys' faces. "Then how did he get that black eye?"

"I-I don't kn-know. He's clumsy," the pinched-faced one stammered.

"Yeah he's stupid," the blonde one agreed.

Corre couldn't see Theron's face from here, but it must have been terrifying, because the blonde boy yelped and staggered back, tripping on a branch and landing on his backside. "Do you think hurting someone smaller makes you tough?" The pinched-faced boy backed up but didn't help his friend. They both gaped at Theron in fear. "Do you think it makes you a god? Do you think it makes you powerful?" The pudgy boy clasped at his friend's hand, but the pinched-faced boy shook it away. "It *doesn't*,"

Theron boomed. "It shows that you're weak. Because if you weren't, then you would find an opponent with equal strength."

"We're not weak!" the redhead squeaked, and again, Theron's face must have been terrifying, because the boy clamped his mouth shut and the other whimpered.

"Then prove it," Theron growled.

"We can't," Pinched-face whimpered.

"I know you can't. Because you're weak. You're picking on someone who doesn't have a chance. Why don't you be real gods and train until you can fight someone your own size?"

The round boy grabbed his friend's shirt, and this time Pinched-face didn't shake him away. They were frozen in fear as they stared up at the god. "Didn't you hear me?" Theron barked. "Get out of here!"

The boys let out a series of final yelps and booked it out of the trees, passing Theron, the smaller boy, and Corre on their way out. She hid behind the tree so Theron wouldn't spot her. What was he trying to do here? She didn't understand. After another moment, she peered out from behind the leaves.

"You need to toughen up," he told the little boy, to which the dark-haired boy nodded.

"Okay."

"You don't want to live in fear because of goons like them."

"Okay."

"Now get."

The boy gave one simple nod and dashed away, passing Corre on the same way out as the others. Her eyebrows puckered. *What just happened?*

Theron lifted his hood and raked his hands through his hair, though the pins made the task less fluid than usual. "What the hell goes on up here?" he muttered to himself.

"Wow, I didn't know you were such a hero."

He whipped around, eyes growing wide. "What are you doing here?"

"Making sure my guest wasn't wreaking havoc," she said, walking out from her hiding place. "I had no idea he would be doing such a good deed."

He scowled. "I wasn't. I just don't like seeing cowardice."

"Uh-huh." She flashed him a teasing look, which made him visibly more aggravated.

"It isn't my fault Olympians are trained to be so weak. What do you do up here? Does everyone waste their time partying and being glutenous like them?" He nodded to the Square, and she frowned.

"Today is a party," she said defensively. "I invited you, remember? Against my better judgment."

"*Right.*" He shook his head in disgust. "In Tartarus, we don't waste our time with frivolous things."

"I know. That's why you came, isn't it?"

He didn't say anything—he didn't even look at her—but his stern expression momentarily faltered.

"Come on. Enjoy some frivolousness. I think you've earned it."

He shot her a look. "Don't patronize me."

"How was that patronizing?" she said, but he just made a huffing sound. She rolled her eyes. "*Anyway*, it wasn't. Don't you think you should enjoy the party since you're already here? When's the next time you'll get a chance like this?"

"Fine," he grumbled, but his expression didn't change. "I guess those pies *were* delicious."

She couldn't help but smile, despite how much he made her want to pull out her hair. "Wait until you try the cakes."

Corre was still smiling as she led the grumpy Underworld god around the Square and the base of Mt. Olympus, but when she glanced up at him, she saw that Theron wasn't sharing in the merriment. His body was rigid, and his face was carved in a permanent frown. Even when Corre held up one of the strawberry cakes that got her through these blasted coronations, he took it quietly and ate it without so much as a half-smile. "You're right. This *is* good," he said blandly.

"You could have fooled me." She tried to say it light-heartedly, but the words came out tense. His expression didn't change. "Is something wrong?"

He wiped his hand on the ragged cloak. "No, why?"

"Ever since we left the forest, you've seemed off. Did something happen?"

"Other than what you saw, no. And nothing is wrong." He looked around and pointed to another booth. "What's that over there?"

"Oh, that's a fortune counter." She smiled brightly, hoping it would rub off on him.

"Fortune counter?" His eyes followed the giddy group of teenaged goddesses exiting the veiled counter, the shimmering black cloth billowing out with the wind.

"You can find hints of your future there. Do you want to check it ou—"

"No." The word was clipped. Corre's mouth opened to say something, but he turned and started down the mountain path. "Let's get something stronger than the fig-tree wine. I need something to get through this."

Her hands tightened into fists. The nerve he had . . . "Be my guest, but I want to get out of here in one piece."

"Is something wrong with drinking?" he grunted, still walking hastily to the long table of colorful goblets.

"I thought you were the one with the problem. Didn't you say it threw off your clarity or something?" The god ignored her and stopped when he made it to a golden goblet with a black liquid simmering inside. Corre watched in horror as he slid the drink down his throat. "Do you know what that is?" By the tightness that soured his face, she assumed he didn't.

The frustration he caused her immediately sizzled to smoke, replaced by a wicked glee.

"Why are you smiling?" he muttered, attempting to hide how much he wanted to clasp his throat and beg for water.

She suppressed a giggle. "Oh, nothing. I'm simply looking forward to seeing what happens next."

"Is this water?" Theron asked the serving goddess at the counter. When she nodded, he emptied a goblet with clear liquid in one gulp, then turned to Corre. "What, pray tell, will happen next?"

This time, she couldn't hold in the laughter. "You're going to be uninhibited in the best way. That black liquid is a special potion brought out only on occasions like this so you can really let loose. In fact, I'd be surprised if you can hold back anything. Even your darkest secrets." She leaned forward and gave him the most mischievous smile she could muster. The horrified expression bulging out of his brown eyes made it easier.

"You're not telling the truth," he said, but through the horror in his voice, it was evident he believed her.

"I am." She stepped closer, until they were only a goblet-width apart. Staring straight up at him this closely, she could smell the black licorice of the special potion, and the faint aroma of strawberry from the cake. "Tell me, Theron, why did you come up to see me today?" She was surprised at her own boldness, but she wanted to know. Why did he keep appearing and showing her nothing but sarcasm and disdain? "What is your plan?"

His eyes softened, and his lips parted. Heat flashed across her skin. "I don't have one," he said. The words warmed her skin even more.

"Why do you have to talk like that?"

"Like what?"

"So—"

"ATTENTION! Gods of Olympus! The ceremony shall now begin!"

Saved by the sound of a trumpet and a bustling crowd, Corre tore her eyes from his. "We better get going," she said, hiding the blush creeping up her cheeks. "We don't want to look suspicious back here. You can't afford to get caught." Her body trembled as his fingers brushed against her cheekbone, tucking a strand of her hair behind her ear. "What are you doing?"

"You're right. I can't afford to get caught." He held his hand out for her to take, but she hadn't drunk that black liquid. He couldn't make a fool of her so easily. Without a word, she left with the crowd, letting her thoughts get drowned out in the noise of the drunk, boisterous gods piling in front of a stage built at the base of the castle a few paces away.

Her heart pounded, and when Theron found his place beside her, she paid him no mind. She had to ignore him, to keep her composure. But it was hard not to think about his fingers brushing against her skin.

CHAPTER FOURTEEN

Corre

"We are so glad you made it out today," a god Corre didn't recognize addressed the crowd. He was a stalky male of medium build with tight black curly hair. He wore pearl-white robes that shimmered in a kaleidoscope of pastel colors when he moved, like the inside of a seashell. "As you know, we will be crowning Apollo and Artemis with their rightful titles and welcome them to our grand jury here on Olympus.

Artemis smiled in the most over-the-top manner Corre had ever seen, showing all of her teeth and waving to the crowd. She was always one for attention and theatrics. Her bright, blonde curls bobbed as she joined her brother at the front of the stage. Corre rolled her eyes. "Kill me now." A couple of gods in front of her turned around, shooting her a disapproving glance before returning their gazes to the stage. Corre's face turned hot. *Oops. I didn't mean to say that out loud.*

Theron snorted next to her, and she glowered at him. "You find that funny?" she whispered, and he shook his head. His hand was covering his lips, but she could tell he was smiling from the crinkles in the corners of his eyes. As the announcer continued, Theron's snort turned into a string of chuckles, and suddenly, Corre was laughing, too. "Stop it. People are going to stare at us."

"No, they won't. They're too busy looking at little miss and mister priss up there." She bit her tongue and tried not to laugh. Why are things always funnier when you're not supposed to laugh? The rest of the ceremony went the same way. Theron whispering sarcastic remarks, and Corre trying not to burst out laughing.

"I would like to thank every single one of you for coming out here tonight. I know it took us a little longer than we would have liked, but—" Artemis fanned her face as if holding back tears—"we made it. Thank you." The crowd roared with applause and whistles, and Artemis wiped the corners of her eyes and waved, mouthing 'thank you' over and over.

Corre bristled. It had only been a week since Artemis and Apollo turned twenty. The twins stood up on stage—Apollo silent and Artemis waving to adoring admirers—and acted like they were late. Did everyone else think they had been late receiving their titles? If they did, what would they think of her? And Phineas?

At least everyone likely knows Phineas is ready. I'm nowhere close to my coronation, and my birthday is in a month.

Someone nudged her shoulder, but she assumed it was an accident as everyone started piling out of the Square. When it came again, she looked to her right. "Are you okay?" Theron looked down at her with a frown, and she wondered if he would have asked her if he hadn't taken that potion.

"I'm okay. I just need to go home. You should, too. Everyone's potions and wines will be wearing off soon. They may start questioning what the enormous god in the tattered robe's identity is."

She swallowed the lump growing like a rising ball of dough in her throat and headed out the silvery entrance, trying her best to leave Artemis's stupid speech and idiotic admirers behind her. *How could anyone fall for that fake charm?*

Her hands balled up in fists, but about halfway home, the anger swelling in her turned into pain, and tears stung her eyes. When she could finally see her house, she let the tears fall.

"Are you sure you're okay?"

She let out a sharp gasp and whipped around. In the middle of the empty field, only a few paces from her cottage, was Theron, his face illuminated by the rising moon. He'd pulled back his hood at some point and unpinned his hair. "Have you been following me this whole time?"

"Yes?" He said it like she was supposed to have known.

She couldn't fight the tears she'd already allowed to stream down her face, but she couldn't handle him teasing her about them right now, much less talk about what was troubling her. Especially if that black potion was still in his system. "You should go back to Tartarus." She didn't want to look at him. She didn't want to look at anyone. She just wanted to curl up in bed and pretend she didn't exist.

The air in the field was vastly different from the stuffy air of the Square. The atmosphere was clean and quiet, and the rustling of leaves in the surrounding trees eased some of the tension in Corre's chest. At least out here she was alone, and as soon as Theron left, she could cry without anyone watching and then try again tomorrow.

"Here." She looked up and saw the hairpins in his palm. They looked like splinters in his giant hand.

"Thanks," she said quickly, swiping the pins without meeting his gaze. When he didn't reply, and a few more seconds ticked by, she turned around and kept walking. She had to get there before more tears slid down her face. No one could see her like this, especially not him.

"Thank you," he said. She stopped. The words were soft and looped around her, tugging her to him like a lasso. "I didn't think I'd ever be able to experience something like that."

She turned and saw him looking off into the forest. She couldn't be sure from the darkness of the night, but she thought there was something sad in his expression. Strands of his hair fluttered away from his long face, feathered from the wind. Somehow it was even blacker than the sky.

"Theron, I—" She began but was cut off by a thunderous voice splintering through the air. It was coming from the woods, whispering through the fingers of branches and rapidly soaring through the field. Theron's eyes widened. He stumbled as he turned toward the voice, almost falling into Corre. A pucker formed between her thin eyebrows as she processed the fear on his face.

Fear. In *Hades*.

"What are you doing?" the voice growled, followed by a long, unsettling buzzing.

A coldness settled in the air, making Corre's skin crawl. She staggered to the side, expecting to see the source of the demonic voice, but no one was there. She could feel a presence but saw no indication of one.

"I-I needed to come back and investigate what I—"

"You dare lie to me, boy?"

"No! I'm telling the truth! I—"

"Get back here at once!"

The stale air pricked Corre's skin, clawing its way to her bones.

It all disappeared as quickly as it came. The voice. The chill. The low hum like crackling static. The two stood frozen in place, Corre's heart unexpectedly racing as she waited for Theron's next move.

"I . . ." she started, but her voice failed her, almost like the words had been stolen from her tongue. From what had been left by that odd, unsettling presence.

She half-expected Theron to turn around and carry on with his act of coy intimidation, but the only movement he made was a slight flinch before moving forward. She stared at the back of his head, the flowing inky black curls.

"Wait!" she called out, and she couldn't believe the word had come from her. He stopped. Her heart continued racing. "What . . . what was that? Are . . ." She wanted to ask him if he was okay, but why should she care? He was a beguiling murderer. This was probably all linked to some master plan. Maybe he was making her care for him so he could betray her somehow.

He tilted his head to look at her, and her heart stopped. His eyes were still wide—*wild*—with fear. His mouth was a tight line, and his light skin was even paler than usual, as if he'd lost any ounce of color his body had possessed.

"I have to go," he said, but the words weren't strong or calculated like they usually were. They were quiet. Vulnerable.

Terrified.

"But I thought you came here for a reason. Did your mentor not send you?" Worry flooded her voice. Something inside her head screamed *What are you doing? That's Hades!*

His gaze fell. "I don't know why I came."

"What?" she whispered, but before she could question him further, he was gone. The air was colder and suddenly suffocating. But there was no one. Only her.

As she stared into the empty space Theron once stood, all she could do was stand there, trying to understand what had just happened and why that voice sounded so eerily familiar.

Chapter Fifteen

Corre

T he chill that encompassed the field after Theron's departure lingered on Corre's skin. The wind rustled her bed of flowers, but the light of relief was gone. The air was warm, but she still felt cold. Her dress draped across her legs as she fell to the ground, her hands tightly wedged in the crooks of her arms.

Despite the chirping birds and fruity aromas traveling through the air from the trees of the nearby wood, something was very wrong. It crawled beneath her skin and squiggled through the blood in her veins.

What's going on?

She knew lying like this would only make the odd sensation intensify, trapping herself in the spiral of thoughts continuously going back to that voice, but she couldn't move. Something was constricting her. Something unseen but completely real.

Before long, the moon rose to the middle of the sky and the temperature finally met what Corre was feeling on the inside. Her head throbbed.

That voice.

'You dare lie to me, boy?'

'Get back here at once!'

She shivered, but that menacing, unseen presence wasn't what was haunting her the most. It was the fear so deeply embedded in Theron's eyes, the horror etched in every line of his face. That voice meant something to him. It terrified him. *Him.* The God of the Underworld.

The thing that bothered her most—the question that wouldn't leave her mind—was why Theron hadn't hurt her and why he kept coming back to see her.

'I don't know why I came.'

Corre let her face fall into her hands. *What's going on? What do I do?*

Anxiety gripped every inch of her skin. It throbbed in her ears and pulsed in her veins. It took a few tries before Corre finally heard Phineas calling her name. "CORRE!" She looked up.

Sweat lining the ridge of his eyebrows, Phineas peered down at her, frowning. His shirt was dirty and worn. *Great.* The last thing she wanted to do right now was pretend everything was fine.

She sat up. "Hey, Phineas. Just got back from training I see." She forced a smile, trying hard to hide the unevenness in her voice. She didn't need him asking questions, especially ones she didn't know the answers to herself. Something that she realized was becoming increasingly more common these days. "Hey, why didn't you go to the coronation tonight? I didn't see you there."

He sat down in front of her and crossed his legs, ignoring her question. "I'm worried about you."

"Why?"

He sighed. "Ever since you ran into Hades, it seems like something's off about you."

"What do you mean?"

"Like right now, for example. When I got here, you were lying here, in the middle of a field, in a sleeveless dress when the sun has fully set."

She shrugged. "I like contemplation."

"I know you better than that."

"Honestly, Phineas," she said. His frown deepened. He *did* know her better than that.

He lowered his voice. "What happened? Did he hurt you?"

"What? No, he didn't. I'm fine, really."

"He's dangerous, you know?"

Corre rolled her eyes. "Yes, I know. I've heard."

"Then why aren't you more scared? I mean, *are* you scared? I can't tell what you've been thinking these last few days."

Corre tried to ignore his concerned expression, but it was hard to. What could she say? That—for whatever reason—she wasn't frightened of Hades? That maybe there was someone more lethal than Theron of Tartarus? Someone worse than death.

It was best for Phineas not to know.

"Of course I'm scared," she said. "But he didn't hurt me, and I'm okay. You don't have to worry about me." She gave him a soft, reassuring smile, which finally broke the tension.

"I'll never stop worrying about you," he said, placing a hand on her knee. "We've got each other's backs, remember?"

Corre's face brightened, remembering the pact they'd made as kids. They were both newly re-homed orphans in new lives in unfamiliar places. The world around them had been moving so fast, and everything was scary. They were so little. So terrified. But they'd found each other. And after weeks of adventuring the many nooks and crannies of the hills and mountains of Olympus, Corre had given Phineas her pinkie and said, *"Let's make a pact, okay?"*

"A pact?" Phineas said, wiping the dirt from his hands onto his shirt.

"Yeah!" she said, sticking her pinkie closer to him. "We'll always have each other's backs. No matter what. Promise?"

He gave her a wide grin, one of his teeth having recently left a gap in his smile. "Promise," he said. He laced his pinkie in hers, and they both giggled the way only kids know how to.

The adult Phineas lifted his pinkie for her to take. "Do you still promise?"

"Of course," she said, linking her pinkie with his. "I promise."

"Good. Me too. So no keeping secrets, okay?"

Corre's smile fell. She took her hand back. "Well, I mean, we can't tell each other *everything*."

"I didn't mean everything. Just things that could get us hurt, you know?"

Corre looked down at her hands. She couldn't lie to Phineas, but she couldn't tell him the truth, either. She had to keep this one thing from him. It was for his own good. For his safety.

This is how she could keep her end of the deal. This was her having his back.

"Corre?"

She looked up and nodded. "Yeah, I get it. I know what you mean."

"Good," he said, but his eyes narrowed again.

Before he could say anything else, she got to her feet and offered him her hand. "Were you training with Athena?"

"Yeah, and you weren't there." He grabbed hold of her hand and hoisted himself up.

"I was at the coronation with everyone else on Olympus."

"You hate those things. We both do. Hence why I wasn't there." He lifted an incredulous brow. "What made you go this time?"

Panic rose in her chest. "I-I decided it would be a nice change of pace. Mother's not here and I wanted to get out of the glen for a bit."

"You could have come to Athena's and trained with me."

"I don't need to," she said, gesturing to the flowers. "This is my battle-field." Her heart fell just saying it. "My personal war."

"This doesn't have to be your only thing, Corre. You can fight, too."

"I understand that, but it's not what I'm supposed to do right now. I'm supposed to focus on this. You're supposed to focus on that. You don't need me—"

"Of course I need you!" he blurted, then quickly added, "As a friend. I need you beside me."

Corre focused on the woods surrounding the field. Tall trees, varying in height and width, checkered the woods circling the clearing where her cottage sat. A palace of vibrant green. Every creation her mother made was so grand. How could she ever live up to it? And why was it so much easier for Berenice than it was for her?

"Corre?"

Her eyes settled back on his wary expression. "Yeah?"

He smiled, but it didn't quite reach his eyes. "You seem tired, and it's getting late. Maybe we should call it for today. But this isn't over." He gave her a teasing look, and she couldn't help but laugh.

"I get it, I get it. Thanks, Phin. You're a good friend."

His smile flickered slightly when she said it, which she found odd, but he was still smiling as he left. "I'll see you soon. Don't give up on our training, all right?"

"I won't. Don't worry." She waved and watched him leave. Her expression was just about to settle back into how she really felt when he flipped back around down the path.

"Remember our promise, okay?"

She forced another smile. "Okay." He beamed at this and turned back toward the woods, picking up his pace as he fell out of sight.

By the time Corre made it inside, she was exhausted. And racked with guilt.

Theron

Theron resisted the urge to spit out the blood spilling into his mouth from the fresh cut sliced across his face. It stung worse than usual today.

"How dare you defy me, boy?!" Thanatos roared.

Theron kept his head down, but he couldn't stop his legs from shaking. *Please, don't notice. Please, don't notice.*

Thanatos growled. "Have you learned *nothing*?"

The young Hades stood up, evening his breaths and forcing himself to look straight at his master. "I know what I'm doing. That's why I went up there. That—"

"Don't even try to lie to me!" Thanatos yelled, his coarse voice echoing across the chamber. "I feel your intentions. Your desires. You wanted to see the girl."

"Yes, because she's important!"

"How would *you* know? You're just a pathetic boy who still shakes in his boots when reprimanded."

Theron kept himself steady as best he could, but his fingernails were already cutting into his palms. Any kind of pain to distract from the emotional guillotine was more than welcome.

"If you want pain, you know where to go," he said, waving his hand in the direction of the corridor and lounging against the back of his throne.

"No," Theron said. The word sounded so much louder coming from his mouth than he'd expected. He wished it'd stayed trapped behind his lips.

"*What?*" His master sounded like he was regurgitating a small animal.

It was too late to back down now. "I'm going to be the ruler of the Underworld soon," Theron said, swallowing the acidic substance bubbling up his throat. "I should have been given the throne five years ago. I have every right to follow my hunches, and I *know* this is an important hunch to follow."

"You know absolutely *nothing*!" Thanatos swung a long arm against the thin, gold-crested lantern standing next to his throne. The top hit the ground with a *tink*, and three guards hurriedly patted out the flames before the room caught on fire.

"But isn't this what you've always wanted? Isn't this what you've been training me for? To be a leader? To face my fears?" Theron strained to keep his voice strong, despite the violent tremors in his legs.

"Look at yourself, *child*. You are nothing more than that. A child. Cowering in fear, pretending to stand up to Father."

"I—" Theron started, but tears welled in his eyes. He looked away and swallowed the shaky words before Thanatos laughed him out of the room.

"Go," his master bellowed. "Before I think of a worse punishment than the one I have in mind."

Theron's chest clenched, and his fists re-formed at his sides.

He lost.

"And . . . what punishment is that?"

Thanatos smirked. "I think you know."

At first, Theron looked at him blankly, but then his blood turned cold. "No. I haven't been there since I was a child." A shriek split through Theron's head. It made him jerk, but he suppressed the urge to grab his skull.

Thanatos's expression didn't change. "Go, *now*. Before you make me angry."

Hands seized Theron's biceps from behind. The guards turned the young Hades around and forcefully guided him to the door. "I know the way!" he growled, shaking them off. The demons grunted and moved back to Thanatos's side.

He felt the eyes of his master follow him as he walked to the cavernous labyrinth. He only hoped that Thanatos didn't sense how fast his heart was racing or how much he wanted to cry.

Like a child, he thought.

I'm still like a child.

Chapter Sixteen

Theron

He bolted for his chambers as quickly as he could. The tears were coming, whether he liked it or not. He needed to get somewhere safe. Fast. He wasn't ready to go to that *room*. Not yet.

Fortunately, the corridors were empty. It was to be expected at this time of night. The demons, soldiers, and guards who normally bustled through the labyrinth were likely either asleep or working, guarding more crucial areas, as this part of the labyrinth was reserved for him. Things were always so chaotic in Tartarus. In Hades. This Underworld named after him. It didn't bother him that most gods and creatures referred to it as "Tartarus" instead of its official name it shared with his title.

If this is my world, why do I still have to answer to him? The anger was strong in his body, but the fear was greater, which answered his question. He wouldn't be allowed to take over until he could stop being so afraid. So pathetic. Thanatos made it clear that he had a long way to go. And now he had to go back to *that* place. How much time did he have to compose himself until then? How much time could he buy before Thanatos found out he wasn't there?

He couldn't make it to his room before collapsing into tears. He tucked himself into a nook. The cold stone wall was like ice against his back. He bit down on his fist and bundled himself into a ball. He was desperate for the tears to stop, but they were falling in droves down his bloodied face, forming a growing puddle around his feet.

"Pfft. Are you crying?"

Theron's body tensed. He shot a glare up at Nikias. The waspy blonde wore a smug grin on his pinched face. Theron tried to surreptitiously wipe his face as he got to his feet, but he didn't know how to respond. He'd obviously been crying, and Nikias told Thanatos everything. He would love to give him this information.

"I'm focused on training."

Nikias laughed. "Please." His arms were tucked behind his back in his usual prim and completely aggravating stance. He gave Theron one last pretentious look before turning on his heel to leave. "You're pathetic. You know that? And you're supposed to be the god here someday." He let out a sharp, disdainful laugh. "When you're here, sniveling like a child."

The cries Theron had heard echoing through his mind over the last two days came racing back, and suddenly, he felt all the little prods and pulls that awaited him in that room. Because he still acted like a child.

Theron

Twelve years prior

"Get in there, *boy*!" the man hissed, tossing the young teen into the room.

"No! Please!" The pain of his master's claws against Theron's fresh wounds stung like bolts of lightning—what he thought one of Zeus's bolts might feel like. But the deity didn't budge. Fear ripped through Theron's chest. "Please," he whimpered, but the large god only growled and threw him to the floor and locked him in the room.

The moment the door creaked to a close, Theron's heart stopped. His stomach plummeted to his feet. The clammy air was sticky against his skin, made more palpable by the sheer darkness of the room. He couldn't see a thing. Being tossed into the room was like being thrown into a shadow. He curled into a ball in the corner of the room. He felt the cold, stone floor beneath his bare fingers and toes to ensure nothing was lurking behind him before firmly nestling his scrawny spine into the corner closest to the door.

It probably didn't help to be tucked into the corner like that, but it gave him a small sense of safety whenever he was in this room of nightmares. He told himself it could protect him, but whatever protection it offered wasn't enough.

It didn't take long before those things slithered over his bare ankles. Before the voices began to wail. And everything else began. The faceless monsters he only knew by unwanted touch and unrivaled pain.

Expecting something never makes it easier.

When the first slimy claw latched onto his bony ankle, the boy couldn't help but scream. He tried shaking it off, but more unwelcome creatures swarmed his body, these ones smaller but more ravenous as they tore at his skin with broken teeth.

The first shriek was like a harpoon propelling into one ear and bursting through the other. He clapped his hands over his ears to protect them from the sound, but then he couldn't swat anything away. Fear spiked through his chest. Claws ripped at flesh.

He was helpless to the bites and scratches of the creatures but, every once in a while, a fire would ignite and extinguish right before his eyes, long enough that he would catch glimpses of what these hellish creatures looked like, and it made his blood turn cold. Their hollow eye sockets and pointed grins burned into Theron's mind, so even when they weren't sucking his blood, they were gnawing at his psyche.

The noises grew louder, the pain more acute, and the peculiar rotting smell rising around him was more pungent with every passing second. The worst part was knowing it had been his fault that his master had thrown him in here. Thanatos never let him forget it. He said it was for his own good. That he needed to do better—be who he was destined to be—and that this was all part of the process.

But it was hard to care when the pain was so all-consuming that Theron had to remind himself that he was still alive. Despite how little he wanted to be.

Theron

Present Day

Theron's head throbbed the whole way there. Snapshots of women screaming and children crying ruptured through his mind. He winced as he remembered the claws tearing at his flesh. That room. It had been such a large part of his life when he arrived here. How had he forgotten about it?

He still remembered how to get there, and when he saw it, his stomach sank just like it had when he was a boy. He was older now—stronger—and knew there were worse punishments he could be given. So, when he came upon the black door with that gnarled handle, he opened and closed it without so much as a tremor in his hand, shutting himself in and waiting for the creatures to attack.

He had over a decade of training and was more powerful than anyone on Olympus. The creatures couldn't touch him now. He had no need to fear.

Theron swallowed the lump in his throat and willed his body to stop shivering. "You're no child. Get it together." He sucked air into his lungs and readied himself for whatever would come. He wouldn't let fear in the way he had when he was a boy. He'd battled demons a thousand times more lethal than those confined to this room.

At least, he thought he had. The truth was that no matter how much he tried to remember, all his mind could find were the sounds and feelings that pumped through his preteen body back then. He remembered being covered with scratches and having night terrors. But the latter never stopped.

So, surely, whatever was in here was capable of great things.

He took another breath. *No. I was just a boy. I wasn't a warrior yet. Not a true god like I am now.*

So, he waited.

And waited.

And waited.

But nothing came.

It was only him. He couldn't see, feel, hear, or sense anything else. He had been plunged into pure darkness. Nothing was coming.

He turned to find the handle, but it was gone. Panic hit him like a heavy wave. Suddenly, he wasn't the big bad Theron anymore. He was the thirteen-year-old boy sent off to be groomed into the all-powerful Hades. A title he had yet to live up to.

Now, it seemed like he was back at square one.

He fell to the floor and instinctively slid back to that corner, his heart pounding in his chest. He couldn't see—or even sense—a thing.

Nothing is coming, he reassured himself, but slowly, his limbs grew weary, his body going limp. "What's . . . happening?" The words were strained, and it was hard to breathe. It felt like a rock was pressing hard against his chest.

Something was taking over him, sucking his life out and rendering him motionless. Helpless.

And tired.

The more he gasped for air, the harder the effort became. His throat tightened, and all the thoughts in his mind blurred together. Tears silently escaped his eyes, but he couldn't wipe them away.

The man struck him again. This time, Theron couldn't get up. His body had hit the tiled floor at an awkward angle, kinking one of the nerves and sending a bolt of pain ripping up his torso. Tears streamed down his face. What had he done to deserve being hurt like this? His mother and father had never hurt him like this.

"You worthless boy!" Thanatos snarled. "Do you think crying makes you any more of a man?"

But the tears didn't stop, of course. Has anyone ever stopped crying when screamed at?

Theron did his best to suck in the tears. He even bit his tongue until it bled. But it was too late. "Put him back," Thanatos ordered the guard behind Theron.

The young boy's face twisted in horror. "No! Please! I won't cry anymore! I promise!"

His sallow master scoffed. "Maybe next time, you won't miss your strike during your practices or cry when you meet your punishment." He nodded to the guard. "Take him away."

"No! Please!" Theron cried, tears dripping to the floor as the guard dragged his bruised body back to the room.

Theron jerked awake, cool with sweat but still unable to see. The memory was gone in a flash, but the scar it left remained. He was still in the room. Years upon years later. And for what?

Correlia's face materialized in his mind, but he pushed it away. It was all her fault. She'd made him lose focus. He'd gone backward in his training. He couldn't let himself be so selfish and sloppy.

He could never see her again, and that was that.

Slowly, Theron got up. First, by bended knee, placing his hand on his thigh and pushing himself to his feet. He grasped at the wall until he felt something that relaxed his shoulders. The doorknob was back. He could go back to his chambers.

The dim light of the labyrinth was like a bright sunrise compared to the void he'd been encased in. He slammed the door behind him and flinched at the loud noise and subsequent echoes that ricocheted down the corridor.

He heard a cry, and it jolted something in him. A flash of Thanatos's face from back then forced itself into his mind. *'Did that dungeon scare you, boy?'* He heard the past words of his master as he hastily bolted toward his room. *'N-no,'* Theron had said. He remembered it as if it had just happened.

Theron tried shaking the memory out of his head and focused on the door of his chambers, which had just come into view.

'Liar!'

He threw himself into the room and limped toward the fountain in the attached washing area. Blood pulsed in his ears, and the muscles inside his chest turned like a key cranking in a lock.

'No, I wasn't scared today! I was brave!'

The deity struck the boy and grabbed him by his shirt. 'Look at me!'

Theron threw water on his face and tore off his armor and undershirt. He splashed water all over his body and scrubbed his arms as hard as he could. He didn't stop until he could no longer see the memories of his master terrorizing him and slashing at his limbs.

'You make me sick!'

The words stung Theron like a hot iron. He kept scrubbing, but nothing was getting better. The feelings were still there. He ripped off the rest of his clothes and threw himself in the small pool next to the fountain. He sat, curled up, trying to visualize the room around him. *That was a long time ago*, he told himself. *It's okay. I didn't get hurt. I have no reason to limp or wash blood off my arms.*

But it felt like it had happened only moments ago. The pain was tangible.

He wanted it to stop.

Why wouldn't it stop?

He stayed there as the hot water scalded his skin, and as the old pain made way for the new, Theron let himself scream. A loud, crescendoing roar. He didn't care who heard. It would probably scare them anyway.

People feared him now. The guards and the demons—they *feared* him. He wasn't that little boy anymore.

He wasn't.

Chapter Seventeen

Theron

Theron wrapped the cloth around his wounded hand. The task was made difficult by his trembling, which hadn't ceased since leaving that room. Even after scalding his skin in the washing room for who knew how long, he couldn't stop shaking. It wasn't until he dried himself off that he found he'd been gashed pretty good by something in that room. He couldn't help but wonder if it was all in his head. If, somehow, the creatures in that room weren't real, and he'd inflicted himself unknowingly while trying to escape.

No. That's not likely. He'd seen the creatures before. Long ago. And while the room was terrifying, he would have known if the pain had been self-inflicted. Besides, all that mattered was that it happened—that these wounds and fears were real, and that he somehow hadn't grown since childhood in the way he'd hoped. He was no closer to the throne than he'd been half a decade ago when he'd conquered his initial fears of the room. 'Learned to hide his fears' was more accurate, but Thanatos had granted his graduation of that room all the same back then. And Theron never had to return until today.

Why now?

"I must have royally screwed up," he muttered as he finished bandaging his hand. He fell onto his bed and thought of Correlia and the way she looked when he first laid eyes on her. On that shimmering dress and that spark in her eyes. How could he have gone through so much pain and punishment and still ache to see her?

He was beginning to think she tormented him more than anything Thanatos could throw at him. And he liked it. He liked her fire and the way she poisoned his thoughts and made him yearn for her. The way she'd turned him into an addict after just one glance.

Being unable to go up to the surface and touch her was agonizing, but he had to resist if he wanted to pass his training. He needed to resist that hunger she gave him.

And that room . . .

Theron shivered and curled himself under his sheets.

That room was terrifying enough to keep him in line until he could run this place his way. Then he could do and take whatever he wanted.

Just hang in there, he told himself. *That day will come soon.*

But when Correlia rematerialized in his thoughts, his body tensed.

Not soon enough.

Corre

When Corre opened her eyes the next morning, her first thought was of Theron. His raven hair framing his long, solemn face. His enticing smirk and even more enticing, somehow soothingly, dark eyes.

His eyes. She thought back on the fear etched across his face. *Why would someone like him be so afraid?* She wondered what secrets lay hidden in his world and what they might look like.

She had so many questions. Had he chosen to be the God of the Underworld, or had he just embraced it? He sure was good at it. Every soul on Mt. Olympus was petrified by the mere thought of him.

"He must be truly despicable," she muttered, staring at the boards on her ceiling and wishing she believed it. She couldn't envision the bad god he was said to be. She could only envision what she saw—a young god just like her enjoying a party like everyone else. And of him helping a child when no one else did. She rolled onto her stomach and continued thinking, but none of her conclusions amounted to anything convincing. She had a hard time believing anyone was supposed to be evil. *But there was always supposed to be a Hades, right?*

She groaned and rolled onto her back again, planting a pillow over her face. There was still so much she didn't understand.

The clock ticked by, and she knew it would get slower the longer she was left alone with her thoughts. Her mother was out creating a new forest on one of Earth's largest continents. She'd be gone for weeks. What was Corre supposed to do in the meantime? Realistically, she wouldn't spend the whole time working.

And then it hit her.

Shooting up in bed, she looked out her bedside window. It was still bright out, and it would be for a while.

She had an idea.

An incredibly stupid, wonderful idea.

She sprung up from her bed and grabbed her darkest cloak—one that at least blended into the soft brown dirt and trees in the forest around her house.

A reckless, terrible, idiotic idea.

She grabbed a small woven basket from the wicker box her mother left next to the pantry and filled it with fruit, vegetables, cheese, and two small slices of bread. Every passing second grew longer, each heartbeat quicker.

Something creaked, and Corre jumped, letting out an involuntary squeal. It was just a common field mouse snacking on the crumbs Corre had forgotten to sweep up the night before. *I have to get it together.* She tucked the basket under her cloak and fled the cottage.

As she slammed the door behind her, she couldn't stop thinking about how reckless this was. Still, she couldn't help but smile and welcome the thrill that fizzed through her as she ran into the forest and headed toward the River Styx.

A truly stupid idea.

Chapter Eighteen

Theron

The beasts were getting more vicious. This one nearly gutted him today. Thanatos wasn't going easy on him anymore. Theron didn't know if it was a punishment for going behind his master's back, or if it meant his training was finally coming to an end—that the throne was so close to his grasp he could almost feel it between his fingers.

The pain subdued any excitement or hope as he wrapped his bleeding side. He hated doing this. He had no clue how to bandage wounds properly, but Thanatos always made him do it himself. The only time he'd ever gotten help was before his powers had fully come in when he was just a boy, and his master had been mildly afraid Theron would become crippled from infection. Then he'd have to deal with a withered apprentice with no hope of glory. The Titans wouldn't look kindly on a mentor who had failed at his one job.

Theron didn't understand how being a god worked. Could he be killed and kept captive in his own kingdom? Then Thanatos would always be his master. For eternity.

He shuddered.

As he stuck the other end of the bandage across his abdomen, he studied the gauze wrapped around his ribcage. *That should do it for now.* His stomach sank. It was time for him to go back into the dungeon. He had more training to do today. It wasn't even mid-day.

Corre

Corre's heart pounded as she raced through the part of the woods she was never allowed to wander. It was forbidden for gods and goddesses to come out here unless they had specific duties and dealings with the Underworld. But Corre had heard enough whispers and rumors from those who had approached the River Styx with their own bargains to know that it wasn't fatal to enter Tartarus's throng.

Her heart leapt when she saw the maw at the edge of the wood, leading her one step closer to the Underworld. Before she could rejoice, something invisible hit her chest. The air was shallow in her lungs, and her mind momentarily faltered. It took her a minute to realize it was just an effect of being so close to it—the entrance to Tartarus.

Out of the lush green earth stood a gray, grooved cavern, opening up like a gaping mouth, half submerged in the earth and the other half a hood for the gloomy river that flowed into its gullet. There was a thin border of soil surrounding the cave-like entrance, where a crude rowboat was docked. A hooded ferryman Corre knew to be Charon stood at the bow of the boat, with the black waves ebbing beneath. He was waiting for someone.

This was her chance.

Don't think. Just do it.

She mustered up the courage and ran to the lanky creature at the edge of the river. As soon as Charon saw the goddess, he let out a groan and opened his skeleton-like hand. Hope rippled through her. She lifted her hand to put into his, assuming he wanted to help her into the boat. He quickly retracted his hand, shaking his head. She peered up into his hood, but his face wasn't visible. The only thing she could see was what looked like the jaw and teeth of a corpse. The rest of his face was obscured in shadow.

"Payment?" His voice creaked like loose floorboards.

Corre blinked. "Payment?"

"Yes. To travel the river."

"I-I don't have pa—"

Charon swung a scythe from his robes and thumped it against the stones beneath Corre's feet. The sound made a crackling boom. "No payment, no entry."

"But—" Corre searched her mind for possible pleas to beg him to allow her passage, but she was interrupted by a voice. A female voice. The words it spoke weren't clear, but something was definitely there.

Corre searched the landscape but saw no one, until a pair of new voices resonated through the trees. Two male voices. It didn't take long for the owners of these two voices to come into view, and Corre recognized one as Hermes.

"Oh no." She looked around, panicked, hoping to find a quick place to hide. All the trees around Tartarus's entrance were thin and withered—not great options to conceal herself behind.

"Psst. Over here."

Corre turned, once again scanning the trees. She *knew* she heard it that time. That female voice.

"Here!" the voice said, a little louder. A hand waved from behind one of the trees, then out stepped a young, teenaged goddess with silvery hair that fell to her feet. "Come here!" She was as pale as a flickering star, with hair so light she looked like a silvery beam from the moon.

Corre looked around for Hermes. She didn't have a choice—it was either get help from this girl or be completely lost. So, she bolted for the tree, which was slightly behind the entrance to the River Styx. When she got to the girl, the young goddess grabbed Corre's hand and pulled her deeper into the forest.

"What are you doing?!" Corre whispered, panic flopping in her gut.

"Trying to help you!"

Corre let her feet carry her behind the silver-haired goddess as they ran deeper into the forest. She'd never gone this far and didn't expect the snow that started to fall. Wasn't she in charge of that sort of thing, or was weather in another god's jurisdiction? Regardless, it didn't make sense why the wind was suddenly icy and the trees in the near distance were leafless—*that* she knew *was* in her jurisdiction.

Finally, the girl let go of Corre's hand and dipped behind a boulder. When she emerged, there was a long, black cloak draped over one of her shoulders. "Here, take this. It's thick and warm, and it isn't as noticeable as that burgundy one you're wearing now."

Corre took the bundled cloth, immediately reveling in the smooth outer layer and woolen interior. "I don't understand. Who are you?"

The girl smiled and, up close, Corre could see the dazzling pale purple of her eyes. It wasn't until now that Corre realized just how young the goddess was. She looked to be about twelve or thirteen years old. And there was something ethereal about her. Something mystical.

"I'm Tyche," she said. "You're Correlia."

"How did you—"

"Please. Everyone knows who you are."

Her stomach dipped. "Great. No pressure."

Tyche laughed, a melodic chirp. "Don't think of it like that. Now, come on. Give me that cloak you're wearing." She waved her hand greedily, but Corre held on tighter to what she was wearing.

"This is my mother's."

Tyche arched a razor-thin brow. "I'm not going to steal it, but you're trying to get into Tartarus, right?"

She nodded slowly. "Yes . . . but—"

"But nothing. You'll be easily detectable in what you're wearing now, and mine is so much thicker. You're obviously not used to the cold." Corre still couldn't get her mind wrapped around this. Who was this girl?

She had no reason to argue. This goddess seemed to know her way around Tartarus, and she had no other choice. She shimmied off her cloak. "You know how to get in? How?"

Tyche flashed Corre a wicked grin. "Let's just say I get bored a lot." She shrugged one shoulder as she helped Corre into the thicker cloak. "Zeus lets me do pretty much anything I want, and this is the most interesting part of Mt. Olympus."

The cloak was as warm as a goose-down blanket and incredibly comfortable. Corre wanted to ask what precisely it was made of but decided on a different, more important question. "I don't have any money. Charon won't bring me across—"

"Oh, please. Only dead gods and humans go to Tartarus that way. Are *you* dead?"

Corre bit her tongue and resisted the urge to show her rising irritation. "No," she said, nearly growling.

Tyche snickered. "I thought not. Now. There are a couple of back ways to get into the Underworld. One is a lot easier, but you cannot stray from the path I'm going to lay out for you. Okay?"

Corre studied the girl's face. "Why are you helping me?"

Tyche crossed her arms. "Like I said, I get bored a lot. And," she flashed that wicked smile again, "judging from the fact that you're out here, I can tell you're feistier than you ought to be. I like that."

"Than I ought to be?"

Her arms flopped to her side. "You know what I mean! Feistier than they want you to be! Zeus and the others! There needs to be more goddesses like us." She gave Corre an approving nod.

"That's as good a reason as any, I guess," Corre said, suppressing a smile. This Tyche was more interesting than most, and she liked their mutual understanding of escaping the mundane. "Okay. How do I get in?"

Tyche grinned. "Yes! I've never sneaked someone into Tartarus before! This will be fun!"

Corre's eyes widened. "What do you mean you've never—"

"Oh, come on. It will be fun! I've done it myself loads of times! Okay, follow me." She grabbed Corre's hand and led her down a narrow path between rows of withered trees. "There's going to be a new forest up here. It looks completely different than this one, and it's next to a beautiful field of flowers. There will be a lot of people there, but don't talk to any of them until you get safely through to the forest that lies beyond the field."

"What—" Corre started, but Tyche kept going.

"See the horizon up there? That line of trees? That's where you'll need to go. There's a fork in the road with three paths. Don't take any of them. Instead, go sideways through the forest."

"Sideways?"

"Yeah, like, cut through the forest horizontally. The paths will be going vertically." Tyche gestured up and down with both hands and then cut through her invisible map with one hand.

"What will happen if I accidentally go the wrong way?"

Tyche grimaced. "Yeah . . . Don't do that. You'll be stuck in Tartarus forever, I think. Unless someone pays some price to get you out."

Corre gaped at the young goddess. "No way. I can't do this." She turned around and started back home. "This was a big mistake."

"No! It's really simple. I promise. I can even take you."

"No thanks."

"The cloak will help you sneak through, and all you have to do is not take those three paths. And don't speak to any of the souls you pass until you cut through the forest. It's really simple. Plus, I don't think you'll actually be stuck in Tartarus forever. I don't think Zeus or the Titans would allow that."

Corre narrowed her eyes. "Are you sure?"

Tyche grimaced. "*Pretty* sure."

"That's not reassuring," Corre said with an agitated sigh and started back to her house. *This was a mistake.*

"No! Wait!" Tyche swung her body in front of Corre. "I really don't think you'll get stuck in there forever. It was mostly a stupid joke."

Corre's eyes were still narrowed as she studied the girl's expression. "Why do you want me to sneak in so badly anyway?"

Tyche swung her head back and groaned. "Because this is so interesting. I want to know what you do next." She straightened and leapt forward, taking Corre by the hands. "You're my hero right now. You're telling everyone, 'Screw you! I make my own destiny!' Am I right?"

Corre pulled her hands free. "No. I just . . . wanted to see someone." She couldn't believe the words had actually come from her mouth, but the truth was out in the open now.

The silver-haired goddess nodded but, this time, that mischievous grin wasn't sprawled across her face, and there was nothing sly in her eyes. There was something sad. Her smile was soft. "You're going to see M—um, Theron, right?"

Corre's hand tightened on the fabric of the borrowed cloak. "Yes."

Tyche looked to her feet and didn't say anything for a while, until she finally looked back up at Corre, with that soft gaze. "That's a better reason than being bored." She kicked a small rock by her feet, then looked at the Goddess of Nature again. "Follow the path I described, and you'll be all right." Neither of them moved while Corre considered it. *Surely she has to be right—no one would be allowed to be stuck in there. And the directions seem easy enough.*

Before Corre finished mulling it over, Tyche turned to leave.

"Wait! Where are you going?"

"I'm going back to my place. You can leave my cloak by the boulder I had it behind earlier if you choose not to go in. I'm pretty much the only one who sticks around here."

Corre hesitated again, weighing what she should do, and then trying her best to push down any doubts or worried feelings of logic. "But I don't know if I can make it through Tartarus alone."

Tyche smiled. "Of course you can. Just follow the path. Don't go to the palace. If you go for the wood, I'm sure someone there will be able to help you. Just don't talk to any demons or people who wear the Underworld crest. Or damned souls, of course. Okay?"

The girl was so earnest, her words so bold, that Corre couldn't help but believe them. Something in her knew that Tyche was telling the truth and that she wasn't setting her up for failure. Maybe it was something in her violet eyes, or the way Corre saw herself in the young goddess. Whatever it was, there was an unspoken agreement between the two of them, though Corre wasn't sure what it was exactly.

For whatever reason, she knew she could trust her. "Thank you."

Tyche laughed softly. "No, thank *you*," she said, then swiveled around and disappeared into the chilly wood, evaporating like smoke. Corre wanted to ask why she had thanked her, along with a host of other things, but the sun was rising higher in the sky, and she wanted to pass through Tartarus while the instructions were still fresh in her mind.

She knew where to go now. That was a start.

After an hour or two of wandering, Corre worried she'd made a huge mistake. She might have been able to focus if it weren't for the unsettling cacophony of moans, groans, and cries everywhere. She'd go mad if she had to spend one more minute in this terrifying wasteland. She already couldn't hear herself think. She kept trudging forward, though. It was her only option—she was just as much lost going into Tartarus as she would be leaving it.

Finally, she passed the field of souls where the screams were the loudest. Doing her best to avoid eye contact with any creature or soul that brushed against her and shrieked at her was harder than she thought it would be. And agonizing. It was like every soul was reaching out to claw her face—to force her to look at them. She could feel their eyes burning into her, but she resisted the urge to look. She didn't want to be stuck here for eternity because she'd disobeyed a simple instruction. Just in case that really was a possibility.

Why was she risking such a possible fate to see the God of the Underworld anyway? She shook the thought away. There was no point questioning her choice now. She was already here. She needed to focus and keep going.

The voices soon faded, and Corre could, at last, safely look around. Everything was so desolate here. The trees were withered and bony like the fingers of a corpse beneath a blood-red, hazy sky, and the field was dry and lifeless. It crunched beneath her feet as she hiked to the horizon of trees.

She breathed a sigh of relief when she saw it. That fork in the road. Three paths leading into a forest, with no clear direction. There wasn't so much as a crude, wooden sign indicating what lay ahead.

"Okay. I need to cut through it," Corre said, scanning the forest. Up close, it was a thick landscape of black and gray, the trees a dead, artificial creation of muted colors and shadows of reality. There was no clear beginning or end to any of it, except for the roads leading straight into it. The ones she wasn't supposed to take.

"Which way am I supposed to cut through?" she whispered. The longer she looked, the more nauseous she felt. She took a step forward but was too afraid to go farther. "This was so stupid. I have no idea where to go."

You have to move, she told herself. *You can't go back now. Just choose—left or right. You can't go through.*

Slowly, she took a step forward and then pivoted to her right. *This is the way Tyche had gestured, right?* She moved in her chosen direction, swallowing the fear creeping up her throat, suffocating her every few seconds. She tried not to focus on that part. One foot in front of the other. That was what she had to focus on, even when the cold chill of those shadow-like trees gobbled her up. But then she heard a noise, like a twig snapping. She was allowed to look at whatever was there now, right? She'd passed the field.

A low growl buzzed in her ears. Another twig snapped. Her blood turned cold.

Just before she turned around, a calloused hand grabbed hold of her arm, and a man's voice cried, "Look out!"

Corre tripped and skidded against twigs and rocks as she fell against the forest floor. The growl rumbled directly above her. Her body froze, but she couldn't stop the gasp that escaped her lungs at the wolf-like creature. Its fur was gray and matted with red-black blood, and its yellow eyes stared right into hers as it bared its thick, pale teeth.

It all happened in a flash.

First, she saw its jaws unhinging, and then she saw a flash of dark. And then a man pounced on the massive creature with something in his right hand. The two forms fumbled around until the man stuck a blade through the creature's mouth, and it vanished like a puff of dust. She stared, wide-eyed, at the gray-haired man as he placed his knife back into his belt and walked closer to her. She couldn't move. "What just happened?" she gasped. "What was that thing?"

"Just a hellhound. They're everywhere around here." The man said the words so nonchalantly that Corre couldn't believe it. She searched his bland clothes for the Underworld crest but found it nowhere. "You're not from around here," he said, his fuzzy brows furrowing. "Why are you here?"

She couldn't speak, but she didn't have a good explanation anyway. Why *was* she here?

The man sighed and offered her his hand. "It doesn't matter. Let's get you out before you get yourself killed."

Corre let him help her up, but as she made it to her feet, she said, "I'm not leaving. I came here to see Theron, and I'm not leaving until I do." She kept her voice steady and firm, recreating the staunch bravery she'd exhibited when facing Theron himself. But just like then, her shaking legs gave her away.

The man looked her up and down. "And why is that?" Corre didn't know how to answer that. While she was trying to figure it out, the man narrowed his eyes and said, "You think about that while we head out."

"No!" she cried, immediately wincing.

The man stared at her. "We're not leaving Tartarus. We're just going to my place. It's right down here. You look hungry. And tired. You could use a rest if you're so determined to make it there."

Corre cast her eyes to the ground but nodded and followed the mysterious figure through the forest. She couldn't tell if she was being stupid or strategic by following this stranger. She was awfully trusting today. Maybe 'reckless' was a better word. But he had just saved her life. That was worth something, wasn't it?

Chapter Nineteen

Corre

"Did Tyche put you up to this?" the man said as he handed Corre a cup of hot tea. She took it happily and bundled herself next to the crackling fire. Her feet were killing her, and her body ached more now than it had this morning. She was definitely reckless. None of this had been thought through and she was paying for it, but there was no looking back now.

"No," she replied, taking a sip of the tea. It was scorching hot and burnt her tongue the moment it made contact. She lowered it and let the cup warm her hands instead. "I mean, she did help me. Gave me directions and everything. But I came here on my own." The man had a permanent scowl on his face, and Corre couldn't tell if he was a weathered old man who had lived a terrible life and was unimpressed with naïve, young goddesses trespassing into his forest and making him save their lives, or if he just had that grouchy look all old mortal men seemed to adopt at some point.

But that was what was odd. He wasn't a god. Gods aged to a certain point, but they never *looked* old. This was a human. What was he doing walking around and living in Tartarus?

"Hmph," the man said gruffly, poking the fire with a long stick.

"I hope you don't mind me asking, but who are you?"

The man gave a half-smile and sat on a log on the opposite side of the fire. He'd implied he lived here, but . . . *here*? How did a man—a *mortal* man—of his age live in such a dingy cave in the middle of the Underworld?

"Who I am isn't important." He sifted through a rucksack by his feet, took out an apple, and threw it to her. "Eat up. You don't know when you'll eat again."

"But I brought my own food," she said, revealing the small basket from beneath her cloak.

"I know, but that won't last you long. Especially if you want to get past Cerberus."

"Cerberus?"

"You don't mean to tell me you planned on going this way to Hades and didn't even know about Cerberus?" He grunted and sipped from his steaming cup. "Damn that kid. I don't know if she forgot or was just being her usual self."

"Tyche was trying to help," she said, holding onto the only hope she had. "She must have just forgotten."

"Regardless, you need food to get past Cerberus. He's the three-headed hound that sits at the edge of Hades' labyrinth. You'll have to get in good with that thing and feed him something that isn't you if you want to get by."

Corre's face fell. "Wonderful." At this point, she wasn't shocked anymore. She'd be facing certain death throughout the rest of her journey. She was sure of it. What did it matter which types of threats they were? All she hoped now was that she'd make it out again one day.

This was such a stupid idea. I can't believe I did this.

"Ah, don't be too hard on yourself," the man said, stoking the flames with a long stick. Corre looked up.

"How did—"

"It's written across your face. You're regretting this little escapade. I don't blame you. It was really idiotic."

She scowled, but she knew he was right, and he was helping her more than she deserved. She blew off her tea and took another sip, then bit off a piece of the apple, which was surprisingly delicious.

"Despite how foolish your actions have been, I admire your courage. Not just anyone would traipse into Tartarus." The old man chuckled. Why did you do it, anyway? You said you wanted to go to Theron. Why?"

The fire crackled at Corre's knees. She soaked in its comforting warmth and woody smell. "Yes, I came to see Theron. The truth is, I was worried about him."

His hand stilled, the stick he was holding surrendering to the flames. "You were worried about him?"

"Yes, and I know what you're thinking. You think I'm crazy and delusional to worry about the God of the Underworld. The fearsome, powerful Hades." Corre tapped her finger on her mug and collected her thoughts. "But there was something in his expression when I saw him last. He looked ... scared. I couldn't help but wonder what his life was like."

"So you risked your own to find out?"

Corre bristled, keeping her eyes focused on the steaming tea in her hands. "I didn't realize how stupidly dangerous it would be until I got here."

"Because you thought Tartarus would be a blissful field of roses?"

"You know what? Never mind. You wouldn't understand. You're just some filthy, crazy person, living in this place you're judging me for entering."

The man laughed. "I'm not judging you. I'm impressed."

Her eyes shot up, finding the old man in wonder. "What?"

His gray-blue eyes crinkled at the sides, where they were adorned with wrinkles. "It takes someone with a lot of strength and character to risk so much for someone else. Especially, someone as unworthy of affection as Theron."

Corre's gaze dropped to the fire between them. "But that's the thing. I don't know who he is or what he's worthy of." Her soft voice hardened as she added, "I know he's the despicable God of Death, so I'm sure he isn't worth this effort I've accidentally thrown myself into. But . . ." Her voice quieted again. "Still. I want to learn more about him. There's something I don't know. Something no one knows. I know it." As soon as her mind welcomed the thought of him, Corre couldn't stop thinking of the way he'd looked at her when they'd last met, or of the words he'd spoken to her—of how he'd wanted to see her.

When she registered the silence that had fallen between her and the old man, she wondered how much of her notions were naivety and how much was curiosity. And maybe something else.

"I don't know what it is you're looking to find out, but I know a couple things about Theron myself if you're interested."

"Really?" Her face lit up.

The old man smiled and nodded. "Yes. Though, I don't know how much of a help it will be to you."

"Well, what do you know?"

The man's demeanor shifted into one of unease. "Since you seem to see past the monster in him—or at least are open to the idea—I'll let you in on a secret: he's been treated like an animal for over a decade." He shook his head. "His master loves inflicting pain on him. Makes him feel powerful, I think. Especially since he knows his days left on the throne are numbered. Theron should have taken the throne when he turned 20 five years ago, but Thanatos is having a hard time letting go."

"Is that allowed?" Corre asked, but the man's initial statement still hung in the air like something sour. *He's been treated like an animal for over a decade.*

"I've been trying to figure that out myself," the man said. "It's one of the reasons I'm down here. Gathering information and all that."

"But why do you care?"

The man stared at the shimmering flames. "Thanatos is a monster. He should have never been given the throne, even as a placeholder, but Zeus agreed to the Titans' demands without a second thought. He didn't care. No one has ever cared about Theron. That's why I find you so interesting ... What did you say your name was?"

"I didn't," she said, "but it's Correlia."

"Well, Correlia, I hope you find what you're looking for when you meet him."

"Wait, that's it? That's all you have to say about him?"

"I don't know what else to tell you. The only thing I know is that Theron should have taken the throne long ago and that Thanatos is abusing his power. And I believe you're right. I don't think Theron is a monster, and it's about time someone cared enough to look."

The words settled in Corre's mind. If what this guy said was true, then maybe this mission of hers wasn't just a stupid, reckless decision after all. Maybe there really was more to Theron than met the eye. And maybe she could be the one to find out what that was.

"I'm glad," she said, a smile dimpling her cheeks. "I'm glad to know my journey here won't be in vain."

"I didn't say that. It's incredibly dangerous for you to go. Theron's still extremely lethal and unpredictable, not to mention Thanatos and all the demons. I can't, in good conscience, send you out there."

"Then it's a good thing you aren't sending me out there, isn't it?" she said smugly as she collected her things.

"It's your funeral, kid."

She scowled. "You're sending me a lot of mixed messages, you know? Do you or do you not want someone to find the light in Hades?"

"I don't want you to risk your life trying to find it. It may not even be there anymore."

Corre kept her gaze steadily on his for a moment, before replying, "I'm going to find out. And then I'm going home. Now, which way do I go to get there?"

"Are you kidding me? Did you not hear what I—"

"You know I'm going whether you like it or not. So, just tell me: which way to Cerberus?"

The man grunted before throwing one thumb over his shoulder. "Go out the back way and follow the smoke. Cerberus is past the back entrance of the Asphodel Field. Give him the food and follow the labyrinth into Hades' quarters."

Corre smiled. "Thank you, sir." With a jump in her step, she swiveled around and started to leave.

"Wait, wait, wait!"

She cast a glance over her shoulder. "What?"

The man got to his feet and gave Corre one more apple. "Keep this for yourself. Don't give Cerberus too much of your food. You're going to need as much as you can keep, and when you get to the labyrinth, make sure you don't go to the palace. That's Thanatos's domain." He sighed. "For now, anyway."

"Thanatos. Right." *The current ruler here.* The crackle of his voice filled her mind once more, and she wondered how much power he held and what he could do with it to make Hades fear him so.

The grouchy old man grumbled a "yes" and evaded her gaze. After the silence between them grew, she cleared her throat. "Thank you. Wish me luck."

Then she left, and the man didn't say another word.

The Asphodel Field was a murky, hazy warzone. The moans chilled her blood and sent gooseflesh skating across her skin. It wasn't as bad as what she'd endured earlier, but it was close. While these souls weren't trying to claw their way into her mind and turn her eyes to them like the others, they were still. Living corpses of gods and humans alike. Though they weren't actual corpses, of course, they were like scattered bones in a graveyard—some standing, some sitting, but all looking at nothing.

It was eerie.

She breathed a deep sigh of relief when she finally entered the smoke-misted labyrinth, but it soon proved to be its own challenge. The deeper she crept through its many tunnels, the darker it became. Eventually, she couldn't see at all, only making it step after step by hearing the clap of each footstep as it echoed across the cavern. Whenever she was unsure of where the next turn led—or *what* it led to—she slapped her hand against the slick wall and steadied herself as much as the damp rock allowed.

A dim light appeared and Corre was finally able to breathe. Until she remembered what lay ahead. She crept even more slowly as she made it down a set of uneven rock slabs that served as stairs into the mouth of another cave inside the winding gut of the Underworld. The roof of the cavern's mouth leaked a putrid liquid onto her head in clammy plops. They were impossible to avoid in the near blackness, so she did her best to ignore the wet sensation sliding down her neck. It was easier when she heard it.

The sound of a grumble too loud to be from anything the size of a god. No. This was the growl of a beast.

Cerberus.

Corre's heart raced as she crept the last few steps into the creature's lair, and then it stopped completely. Her eyes widened at the enormous canine, curled up in slumber. Its fur was as black as Theron's long, inky hair—maybe even darker. It was like staring into a shadow with three heads reassembling that of a pup's, only each skull was easily a foot taller than Corre and ten times as wide.

Its long exhales puffed against her face as she inched closer, carefully placing one foot in front of the other as she ignored the unsettling scent of meat on the canine's breath. Its growling rumbled the cavern's floor with each exhale, sending prickling needles up Corre's spine.

Until it stopped.

The blood drained from her face as the beast opened one eye. And then another. And then the other four. Its massive body rose without taking any eye off of her. Its heads craned to stay close, examining the goddess at its thick, enormous paws.

The beast bared its teeth, and Corre swiftly reached into her pack to take out bread, fruit, and cheese. She panicked as grapes and a small bun rolled out of her trembling hands, especially as the creature's growling intensified into an ear-splitting bark. Its jaws unhinged just before she grabbed hold of the assortment of food and hurled as much as she could at one of its heads. To her immense relief, the food landed on the purple tongue of the middle head.

The head bounced in surprise, floppy ears flapping, and then its tongue furled around the food and pulled it into its throat. The head's eyes closed in delight, and it licked its black lips. The adjacent heads stared in envy before turning to Corre in anticipation. She swiftly took most of the remaining food and tossed it at the other two heads. The first one barked—that middle, awaiting head—so Corre did the only thing she could think of. She leapt forward and scratched its belly.

Cerberus paused. And Corre's heart froze again.

Thumping shook the cavern, and she took cover with her hands above her head. She squeezed her eyes shut, ready to face her death, until she heard the soft whimpers once the thumping stopped. She looked up at the happy creature—that middle head happily staring down at her with a tongue hanging out of its mouth. She looked back down at its night-dark belly and reached out and scratched it again. This time, when the thumping started, she didn't close her eyes.

Laughter escaped her lips when she realized what it was. She scratched it more, lending another hand to its delight. The thumping intensified—the loud glee of a happy dog's wagging tail.

Theron

Black liquid soaked into the stone as the creature's head flopped to the floor, Theron's sword clattering alongside it. He did it. He'd killed it. The beast that had nearly ripped him to shreds earlier that day. He'd destroyed it in record time.

Dropping to his knees, Theron let his body fall onto the stone-scattered ground. He didn't care how coarse the dungeon floor was; he let the chilly stones cool his hot, sweat-soaked skin. He was exhausted and in a great deal of pain. His torso was wet with blood, and he knew he needed it re-bandaged, but he didn't have the stomach to stare at the gaping wound right now. He wanted to rest. To recover. To eat.

To eat.

His stomach cramped. He couldn't remember when he'd eaten last, but it had been long enough. Thanatos had taken away his meal privileges. It was for his own good. He needed to be taught a lesson for what he'd done. He was used to this type of punishment, but never before had he been tasked with killing an extraordinary foe on an empty stomach, dizzy from exhaustion.

Was it worth it? he wanted to ask himself when he got to his feet, and she was the first thing that surfaced in his mind. How was it that she was still the only thing he could think of when he was this tired and ravenous and in so much pain?

Theron picked up his sword and limped to the dungeon doors. He needed to shower. To re-bandage himself and then look for any scraps of food he could sneak without Thanatos suspecting anything. He knew he shouldn't go against his master, but his vision was blurring. He needed to eat.

He stumbled down the passages of the labyrinth, trying his best not to crumple onto the floor. That was the last thing he wanted Nikias to see. He'd never hear the end of it. Especially from Thanatos.

"Theron?" A voice pooled through his ears. He froze.

Was that . . . ? No. I'm hearing things.

He kept moving, willing his body to keep going long enough to fall into his room unnoticed. But then he heard it again.

"Theron?"

He whipped around and stumbled back, falling into the wall behind him. He blinked over and over, wiping the sweat from his eyes and focusing his blurred vision. No matter how many times he focused, the freckled goddess in a long, dark cloak didn't disappear. It was her.

"Correlia?" he mumbled, but his vision was still blurry.

"Are you okay?" she asked, but it was muffled like he'd been submerged in water. "You're hurt!"

A ringing sounded in his ears, and he felt his legs give out. He heard her gasp when his body fell to the floor, but when his head didn't hit the hard stone, he looked up and saw that she'd partially caught his fall.

It was really her. He wasn't imagining things. "Correlia," he said again, and suddenly the fear of Nikias catching them was far worse than the physical pain shooting from his side and gnawing at his empty stomach. He quickly stumbled to his feet, Correlia steadying him the whole time. "Quick—come with me," he said, slurring his words as he grabbed her hand.

"Where are we—"

"Shh! Don't speak!" he managed to say, fighting through the pain as he spoke. "We're going to my chambers. No one can know you're here."

Despite himself and everything plaguing him—the pain, the hunger, the fear, and the fatigue—Theron smiled.

CHAPTER TWENTY

Theron

"What are you doing here?" he asked as they tumbled into his room.

Correlia tried steadying him, but she wouldn't be able to hold his weight if he started to fall. He reluctantly unhooked her arm from his so he could fall onto the bed. "Are you okay?" she asked again, but he couldn't answer. The pain in his side was throbbing, and his suspicions were confirmed when he heard her gasp. "Your side is bleeding!"

"I know," he muttered. His body decided to betray him once more, letting out an enormous growling sound.

"You're in really bad shape," she said, that tone of shock still planted in her voice.

"Thanks." He winced. His stomach was starting to churn. He needed to eat. Or throw up. Or pass out. He didn't know what he needed, but she was right. He *was* in really bad shape.

"Let me help you." Before he could object, she was gently laying him on his back, propping his head up on a pillow.

He blinked a couple of times until his eyes cooperated enough to allow him to see her. To drink her in. Seeing her pursed lips as she looked down at him with concern was a better balm than anything he could have found for himself. He should have protested to her helping him, but he didn't want to. He didn't know how long this would last, and he wasn't in a state where his thoughts were rational.

"Okay," he said, "But I don't know how you can."

Thin lines crinkled on her forehead, and she brushed the hair from his face. With every touch of her fingertips, his heart beat faster. Something inside his chest lifted. He was about to let his eyes close when she took her hand away and said, "Your skin is hot . . . I'll get you a cloth." She got up from the bed and looked around.

"In there," he said weakly, nodding to the washing room. She padded through the doors, and as he heard her clink around in there, he was grateful he wasn't a slob.

He heard a brief splash before she reappeared. "Here." She placed a damp, rolled-up cloth on his forehead. "Is this all right?" He nodded, and she patted it down his face, then placed it back on his forehead. "Now, about those bandages. They really need to be changed, but I can tell you're weak."

His stomach growled again, and he felt the color rise to his cheeks. *How embarrassing*, he thought, but she didn't seem to mind. "Here," she said, bending down and fishing something out of a basket by the door. She unpinned her cloak and threw it on top of it. Her shoulders were bare, and she was wearing that same shimmery gown she'd had on when they'd first met, or something very similar, with warm stockings underneath.

She stopped for a second so she could pull them off, and Theron couldn't stop himself from watching the way the stockings slid off her calves and the dress shifted on her curves. He quickly looked away when she turned back around. "Eat this," she said, handing him a slice of bread and an apple. "You need it far more than I do."

"No, I couldn't take your food—"

"Nonsense," she said firmly. "Eat it. I'll find something to bandage you up."

He took the food from her and waited until she turned back around to stuff it in his face. He'd never tasted anything so good. "The bandages are in the drawer by the wardrobe," he said between bites. "As are the glasses." He needed a drink stronger than water, but he would take anything right now.

She filled a glass in the washing room and gave it to him before heading back for the bandages.

"Take off your shirt," she said, and the color rushed back to his face.

"What?"

Excitement must have flashed in his eyes because she gave him an unimpressed look and said, "Not like that. I need you shirtless so I can change your bandage."

"R-right," he said, lifting himself on the bed. He let out an involuntary grunt, which made Correlia spring closer.

"Be careful!" she said. "Here, I'll help. Do you mind?" She tugged at the hem of his shirt, and he emphatically shook his head. She smiled. "Good. Lift your arms, and I'll pull this off on the count of three." She looked him in the eyes, and his heart snagged in his chest. "Okay?" He nodded. "Okay. One, two, three!" When she lifted his shirt, she paused, her eyes trailing down his chest and then down to his side.

He slid the shirt the rest of the way off his arm and threw it to the floor, but he couldn't stop looking at her and the way the color was now creeping along her cheekbones.

"O-oh, this is bad." She got up and tucked her hair behind her ears. "The wound. The wound is bad. I-I need to get more cloths," she said quickly, avoiding his eyes as she turned back to the washing room.

"Why are you so flustered?" he teased, his energy starting to come back now that he had some food in his stomach.

"I am *not* flustered," she protested, wetting another cloth. "Your wound is just really bad. I wasn't expecting it."

He grinned. "Whatever you say."

She dunked a cloth in the fountain and shot him a look through the doorway. "Do you want help or not?"

"Yes . . ." he mumbled.

She wrung out the towel, but as soon as she sat on the bed, her frown deepened. "This is terrible," she said, examining the wound. He winced when she touched the cloth to it.

"Be careful," he grunted.

"I am. Just . . . Hold still." She gently pressed on the wound, trying her best to soak up the blood. He was used to pain, which may have been why he barely felt it as he watched her—someone who obviously was *not* used to pain or bloody gashes. Her frown was heavy, but her eyes were focused. Something about her genuine interest in helping him and her deep concentration was endearing. He could watch her like this all day.

But he was glad when she took the cloth away and grabbed the bandages. "I must admit that I'm not exactly a nurse, and I don't have healing powers, so you'll want someone else to look at this after I'm done. Sit up." Theron did as he was told, and she leaned closer, wrapping the roll of gauze around his back and waist, unraveling it over him, over and over again.

She was so close he could feel her breath graze his skin as she moved. It was still hard for him to believe. He'd tried so hard to get her out of his mind, yet here she was, her hair smelling of flowers and sunlight, and her full lips pursed in concentration as her body brushed against his. As she cared for him.

Why was she caring for him?

When she finished wrapping his wound, she sat back and smiled. "There," she said, looking up at him. Her smile dropped to a frown again. "What?"

"Why are you helping me?"

"What do you mean? You were in rough shape. Anyone would have—"

"*No.* No. No one does this. No one . . . cares. Or helps. At least, not here."

"They should."

"Well, they don't!"

"I'm sorry, but are you mad that I helped you?"

Theron's stomach jerked. "What? No! I'm . . . I'm grateful. Really, I am."

"Then why are you talking to me like that?"

"Like what?"

"Angrily!"

"I'm not angry!"

Correlia scowled. "Fine. Just . . . take it easy, okay?" She looked away, and the pout on her face made him smile.

"You're cute when you do that."

She jerked up. "What?"

He smiled to himself. "Am I flustering you?" He chuckled, but his teasing was cut short by an intense pain erupting from his side.

"Are you all right?"

"I'm fine," he said, but it came out in an incoherent grumble. He could act unaffected all he wanted, but even with all his training and previous injuries, he couldn't pretend that this didn't hurt. "Ah!" He winced and placed his hand on his stomach; the gash extended from his navel to the side of his ribcage.

"Nonsense," she said and crawled over to where he sat on the bed.

He tried not to scan her body as she approached.

"I can't imagine what this feels like." The light touch of her fingertips trailing across his bandages forced his attention back to her.

"It's not sunshine and roses," he spat. "You have no idea."

She glared at him. "I just said I couldn't imagine. Are you intent on getting me not to like you?" When he didn't say anything, she added, "Is this how you always treat people who try to help you?" Theron didn't have to reply. Her face changed immediately after she asked the question. "Oh. Right. You said no one helps you . . ." He nodded slowly. "But why?"

He didn't know how to answer that through anything but another question. "Why would anyone help me?"

"Surely you have someone here who cares . . ." Her voice trailed off, and now she was the one wincing. "Sorry. I didn't mean to imply—"

"No. You're right. No one cares. Why would they?"

"What do you mean? You're a person—a god. You deserve to be cared for."

He laughed bitterly. "I'm not a person. A god." She frowned, and he hated that he had to explain it to her. "I'm a monster."

"No," she whispered, but there was no conviction behind it. *Olympian flattery.* He knew she knew better than to argue with that simple fact. She knew his reputation. He remembered their previous meetings.

"Don't give me that look. I'm *supposed* to be a monster. It doesn't bother me."

Correlia's gaze fell, and silence filled the room.

Finally, she checked his wound again. "What hurt you so badly?"

"A beast. I fight for my training. I'm going to be the ruler here soon. I can't let a small set of scratches affect me."

"These are a lot more than scratches."

He took his glass of water and gulped the rest of it down. "Yeah, well, it is what it is." He placed his fists on either side of him, attempting to hoist himself up.

"What are you doing?" she asked, reaching out to help him.

"I need more water."

"I can get that for you."

He narrowed his eyes *Something isn't right. Why is she helping me?* "No. I've got it." He held his breath and attempted to slide off the bed. It hurt like a bugger, but he couldn't let it show. Straightening his back, he strode to the bathroom. He was stronger than she knew, and she was up to something. He couldn't show weakness. That was one of the first rules Thanatos had taught him. Show no weakness. Show no mercy.

He moved a piece of stone blocking the opening of the smaller fountain he used to wash his hands and drink from. As he filled his cup, he heard her gasp.

"Theron, what's on your back?"

He covered the fountain's head again. "What are you talking about?" He threw back another full glass of water.

"Your back. It's torn up with scars."

He looked at her through the reflection in the mirror. Her eyes were wide with horror.

Oh. That.

"It's nothing."

"*Nothing?*"

He filled his glass one more time and then walked past her. "Yes, nothing." But before he could get any farther, she caught hold of his forearm, and their eyes locked. Her mouth was in a tight line, her eyebrows tilted downward over her concerned eyes.

"What?" he asked, completely lost.

"Theron, you shouldn't have to be subjected to so much abuse. Is this .
. . is this because of your master?"

His blood boiled. "What are you trying to say?" He shook her hand from
his forearm.

Her somber expression turned to one of fury. "I'm trying to say you're
not being treated well here. That your master is putting you through too
much."

"You don't know what you're talking about," he hissed. "My master is
the reason I am who I am today. This pain has made me stronger."

Something shifted in her gaze, then quietly, she said, "Are some of those
scars from him? Personally?"

"Of course," he said, still lost. "It's all a part of my training."

A hand rose to her mouth, which only confused him further. Was she
really horrified? *No. This is part of her ploy. No one would be surprised by
that. It's just how things are done.*

"This is how gods are made," he said. "But I'm sure you know that.
Don't play dumb with me."

"I'm not playing dumb! No one should treat you like that. It's barbaric."

"This doesn't concern you," he growled and strode back to his bed. "Just
go back to that field of flowers and live your sunny little life, and I'll live
mine." He avoided her gaze for as long as he could, but the silence was
suffocating, and he could feel her eyes on him as she returned to his side.

The mattress moved slightly as she sat down next to him. "Theron?"

Reluctantly, he turned, and the heartbeats pounding in his chest tripped
over each other. The sparkling sunflower pattern of brown, green, and gold
in her eyes shone like a kaleidoscope of stained glass. There was tenderness
in them. A softness that warmed his body, even more so as she placed her
hand on his face.

"What?" he whispered back. He shouldn't love the way her fingers felt
against his skin, or the way she looked at him like she cared, but he couldn't

help it. Just like he couldn't help that, for whatever reason, tears were forming in his eyes.

"I don't know what your master says to you or what you think, but you're not a monster. No one should treat you like one."

Flashes of fire tore through his mind. A fragment of a memory he longed to forget. One that confused him and wasn't complete but was something that confirmed what he knew to be true—that he *was* a monster.

"I am," he whispered, emotion welling in his throat. He swallowed the lump but couldn't look away from her.

Her full lips were weighed down in a frown, the freckles across the bridge of her nose splattered like a litter of stars. She was perfect. With a perfect life. How could she know what he did and didn't deserve? What he was or wasn't. If she really was here sincerely and had no plot up her sleeve, then she was just naïve. Completely, hopelessly naïve.

"No," she said, stroking his face with the back of her hand. "No one is born a monster. No one is *supposed* to be a monster." When he turned his head, she turned it back, so he looked into her eyes. "No one should be treated like one, either."

"You're wrong." He closed his eyes and let out a shaky exhale. "It doesn't matter." His heart pounded in heavy thuds. He knew her hand would soon leave his face and that she would be gone, and none of this would be real anymore. She would go back to her place on Mt. Olympus, sheltered and protected from the likes of him and everything else.

He would keep being a monster. Keep training to take his throne in the world of the dead, while she brought light and life to the world. And that would be that. It was the way things were supposed to be.

When her fingers inevitably left his face, she let out a sigh, but she didn't contest what he said.

"Now what?" he said, turning to her again. She was staring off, and all he could see was her perfect profile. Her delicate nose, her pink lips, the curves of her chest. "You shouldn't be here."

"I know," she said, still staring off.

"Then why did you come?" Things had been so crazy since she got here that Theron hadn't stopped to ask her the obvious. "You're a bewildering goddess."

"Why is that?" She gave him a smile, one that showed the dimples in her cheeks, and it was hard for him to put two words together.

"Um, well, you're here. It's dangerous to get here. How did you manage, and why did you risk it?"

"It's a long story." She was drawing circles on the bed with her finger. "But on that note, I can't go back today, so I'll need to stay here tonight."

Theron's eyebrows shot up. "Excuse me?"

"You didn't expect me to come all this way and leave after feeding you and cleaning your wounds, did you?"

"N-no, but you haven't even told me why you came."

Her lips scrunched to one side. "I . . . wanted to see you again . . . I guess."

Something in his chest skipped, and he couldn't hide the shock elongating his face. "You did?" He immediately regretted the unguarded tone in his voice. He cleared his throat and tried not to look excited.

"Yes, but now I'm not so sure I should have come all this way just for you to chew me out and get mad at me for helping you." She glared at him, and his heart sank.

"Oh. I'm sorry. I'm not too good with . . . people. But I *am* grateful for your help." His face tightened.

What's gotten into me?

She smiled. "It's okay." She turned to face him and crossed her legs. "I know you're not a people person." She winked, and the blood rushed to his face.

"You don't know the half of it."

She laughed and fell onto her back. "Ooh, this bed is cozy."

"Yeah, well don't get too comfortable. You need to leave immediately."

She rolled over and perched out her bottom lip. "I'm exhausted. You wouldn't make me go back across the Asphodel Field and the woods *tonight*, would you?"

It was futile to keep his gaze from her lips. Then her eyes. Then her leg, which had become exposed through the slit of her skirt when she'd rolled over.

His whole body burned.

"I guess not," he grumbled.

"Thank you!" she squealed, scooting next to him and resting her back against the pillows.

"What are you doing?" he said, shifting his body away from hers.

"You said I could stay here."

"I didn't say you could sleep in my bed!"

A sharp inhale shot through his lungs. Her face was inches from his. Her lips were so close that he could feel the warmth of her breath on his neck. She gave him another dimpled smile and burrowed into his sheets. Sparks sizzled across his skin.

"You don't have to sleep with me," she said. "You could sleep on the floor. I'll only be here this one night. Then I'll be gone, and you can have your bed back all to yourself."

That isn't a very hard sell. He tried not to look too eager for her to stay, but he detested the thought of her leaving. Of this room being empty again. His bed only for him.

He turned back around. "Fine, but stay as far to that side of the bed as possible."

He grabbed one of his pillows and tried scooting as far to the left as he could. But then he felt her body against his back, her arm around his waist.

"Thank you."

He swallowed and tried to think of training. Of the beast that gashed his side. Of demons. Anything. Anything but the way her leg felt behind his. Or the way her hand slid away from his bare skin as she rolled back to her side of the bed.

He tried not to think about how she looked lying next to him, or how he wanted to reach out and touch her. To kiss her. To make her his. To grab her and suck out her soul from her teeth. To steal her senses and entwine her in him.

There was something about her that made him want to go mad. But he couldn't do anything about it. He had to lie here next to her, aching for her with no relief.

"Good night," she said cheerily.

"Good night," he grumbled, waving his hand to turn off the light. He never went to bed this early, but she was driving him crazy. He needed to sleep.

As the light flickered off, Theron had never been so grateful for darkness in his life. He didn't know what he would do if she noticed how red his face was. Among other things.

And if he turned around and looked into her eyes, there was no way he could stop himself from kissing her.

All he could do was squeeze his eyes shut and hope to fall asleep.

Why had she insisted on sleeping in his bed?

There was no way he was sleeping well tonight.

CHAPTER
TWENTY-ONE

Corre

I t wasn't that late, but Corre didn't mind going to bed. In fact, she welcomed it with open arms. She was exhausted. The ordeal of traveling down and through the Underworld, running into Hades, and nursing him to health had been a lot more tiring than she'd bargained for. Go figure.

Granted, she hadn't known she would be doing the whole 'nursing him to health' part. But that wasn't what had been tiring. She'd actually kind of liked that part, which was odd because she usually got sick at the sight of too much blood. She'd gotten woozy once after she and Phineas had sparred too close to a bed of rocks and he'd scraped up his shins.

But helping Theron was different. There had been more blood in one place than Corre had ever seen, but she didn't mind helping him clean it up and get it bandaged and squared away. It was strange that no one had ever done that for him before. Maybe that was part of why she liked helping him. He liked it, too. She could tell. That helped. And she'd be lying if she said she hadn't enjoyed seeing him without his shirt on. Something she was acutely aware of as he slept in the bed next to her. She desperately wanted to ask him if he was asleep, but what then?

She needed to rest.

Suppressing a groan, she wiggled into a more comfortable position, but the thought of the next day's travels weighed heavily on her mind. *Tomorrow's going to be another long journey. Why did I even come here?*

She looked around the dark room. Theron's place was surprisingly nice. It was dark and kind of dull—not a touch of anything homey in sight—but it was cozy. She'd half-expected him to live in a dingy grotto like the adjacent halls, but this looked more like a room taken from a palace. A bit plainer, maybe, but it had a grandness to it. Almost every surface was carved from dark marble or onyx, the sheets as soft as the field around her house, and the pillows felt how Corre imagined clouds would feel beneath her head. It was like she was dreaming.

Kind of.

Her heart wouldn't stop racing. *What if I wake up and I'm snoring or drooling or something?* She begged herself not to think about it. *Just go to sleep. Tomorrow will probably be rough.*

⁖⁖⁖ ⁖⁖⁖

When Corre's eyes fluttered open the next morning, she was surprisingly well-rested. And warm. It took her a second to realize why. When she saw Theron's arm wrapped around her, she jolted upright.

"What are you doing?!" she cried.

He mumbled something before opening his eyes and processing where he was and what was going on. His eyes shot wide open. He was a blur as he threw himself backward on the bed, almost falling off the other edge.

"I-I don't know!" he replied.

Corre covered her mouth, but a giggle still escaped.

He narrowed his eyes. "You think this is funny?"

"You were holding me! Your legs were—"

"Stop! Don't say it!" he yelled, covering his head with his pillow.

She snickered at his childish antics. It was endearing. "You're the one who was doing it!"

"I was asleep! I didn't know what I was doing!"

She dropped her hand to reveal a teasing smile. "You're blushing."

"No, I'm not."

"Yes, you are." She laughed and crawled closer to him. "You liked it, didn't you?"

His face turned crimson. "That's ridiculous! Why would I want to hold you? I'm not—"

As he fumbled to find the words to say, Corre threw her head back in a fit of laughter. "You're so cute," she said and immediately clamped her mouth shut.

Did I say that out loud?

Now he was the one wearing a playful grin. "What was that?"

"Nothing," she said quickly, but she felt the heat rising on her face. It didn't help that he was still shirtless and now crawling toward her.

"You said I'm cute."

"N-no . . ." She couldn't finish her sentence. He was so close to her. Too close. His face was only inches from hers now. She could smell the alluring scent of his skin. A rich, earthy scent with a hint of something masculine that only flustered her further. The air escaped her lungs.

The base of his voice rumbled in her ears as he said, "Yes, you did." His voice was low, and his eyes flickered to her lips.

Her heart sped. "I was joking," she whispered, but she knew it lacked conviction.

He gently stroked her face with the back of his hand, and it took her way more self-control than she'd care to admit to force herself from closing her eyes and leaning into his touch. But she managed to keep her eyes on his, even though his stare followed his fingers as they fell down her cheekbones and tucked her hair behind her ear.

What's happening? She wasn't sure if she was more confused by the way he was looking at her or by the way her body was suddenly so warm, her stomach queasy.

She swallowed and slapped his hand away. "I didn't say you could touch me."

He retracted his hand with a frown. "I'm sorry." The genuine remorse in his voice filled her with guilt. His gaze fell as he backed away.

Was that too harsh?

"It's okay," she said, shifting awkwardly on the bed. They avoided each other's stare until Corre took a deep breath and said, "I have to get ready. I have a long journey ahead of me today," and slid off the bed.

"Wait!" She turned. His jaw tightened, but he didn't say anything, and when she decided to turn back around, he quickly added, "You don't have to go. Not yet, anyway . . . if you don't want to."

"What?" The room was quiet, darkness still surrounding them from the lack of windows. It was only the candles that illuminated his face as she studied it.

"I just mean . . . You came all this way. Surely, you had a reason for coming here. And I assume you wouldn't want to turn around and make that same journey so soon. I—" he paused and looked away. "I just mean . . . you can stay. If you want. At least another day."

The light from the candles grew, as if some sort of magic stoked it as the minutes ticked on. He'd been so adamant about her leaving, and she'd made it clear last night that she didn't know why she was here and that she'd be leaving today. Why would he want her to stay?

She tried to remember why she'd come and whether staying an extra day was the right thing to do. Of course, she *wanted* to do it, even though she wasn't sure why.

She wanted to stay.

One more day couldn't hurt.

"Okay," she said, and his eyes snapped up to hers. "I'll stay." She lifted a finger. "One more day. Just to figure out what this Underworld place is all about." She plopped back on the bed. "I need to get to the bottom of why you went to Mt. Olympus. It wasn't a *complete* lie, and the excuse masked the full truth well enough.

She wasn't ready to admit why she'd made the jump to come here—that maybe she had worried about him. A notion that only intensified when she'd seen the state he'd been in last night. Staying another night was the right call, she decided. *There's obviously more to the story than Theron being the big bad God of the Dead. There is something bigger at play here.*

She thought back on the old man who'd given her food. How he'd said Theron wasn't a monster, and that it was about time someone looked into that. As she stared down at Theron now, trying her best to act intimidating, her stomach tightened. Was it okay for her to admit to herself that she was worried about him? That she was wondering why and how someone he trusted so much could inflict such pain and abuse on him?

How could anyone—especially a mentor or father figure—be so callous to their pupil?

She thought about her mother. About how caring Berenice had been when she was placed in her care. Was Thanatos Theron's Berenice? Because if he was, Theron had been through more anguish than Corre could comprehend.

Yes. Staying one more day was the right thing to do. Even though she wondered what one more day could actually do in the grand scheme of things. Her thoughts were interrupted by Theron laughing. "Is that why you're here?" he said and, for a second, she'd forgotten what she'd told him. "Do you really think I'll tell you why I went up there?"

Right. She let out a half-laugh. *Mt. Olympus.*

He flipped the blanket off his legs and moved far too close to him again. A habit of his that tormented her in a way she didn't understand.

Corre evaded his gaze, but he tilted her chin so she had no choice but to look up at him. Theron's eyes fell to her lips again. Just for a second. Then he looked back into her eyes. "I'm not going to tell you anything, so if that's the reason you're here, maybe you should just go back."

"I don't need to prove myself to you. I . . . um . . ." Her lackluster lie started to crumble. "I don't need to explain myself. I'm, um, I'm tired from yesterday's journey, but I get it if you want me to leave. I'll just bathe and pack up my things—"

"No!" he shouted. He raked a hand through his hair. "Sorry." His face twisted in frustration. "Get ready if you wish. But stay here. In this room. I have to go train, and I can't have you wandering the labyrinth, or both our heads will be on a chopping block."

She nodded. "I understand."

His body relaxed. "Okay. Stay here. I'll come back at midday and bring you some food. We can decide what to do then. If you want to leave, I'll find a way to escort you back, but if you decide to stay, you need to figure out how to spend the rest of your day in here." He cast her a stern look. "Because you *cannot* leave this room. Under *any* circumstances. Okay?"

"Okay," she said, suddenly wishing she'd at least brought something to paint with, or maybe train with, to pass the time. Maybe weights—or soil and seeds—whatever would have fit in that small basket.

"Get going," he said, pointing to the washing room. "I have to go right away."

"Don't you need to use it first?"

He fidgeted and let out a grumble. "I guess, but I'm already behind. Just—" His mouth hung open for a second before he clamped it shut and strode into the washing room, slamming the door behind him. He was only in there about five minutes before he walked back out and started peeling off his clothes.

"What are you doing!?" Corre squealed, quickly turning to face the wall. "I have to get ready!"

"You don't have to do it in front of me!"

He laughed. "I know, but I like to see your face turn pink."

"You're cruel, you know that?"

He shut the wardrobe door. "So I've been told."

A chair creaked, so Corre thought it safe to look. He was putting his boots on. She turned back around and crossed her arms, leaning against the wall. "Have fun training," she spat.

"Oh, yeah. It will be a blast." He grabbed something behind his door. It was long and pointed with an onyx body and gold, swirled embellishments. When he hooked it to his belt, she realized it was a sword.

He grabbed the doorknob with his freshly gloved hands, then paused. "Don't make a sound in here," he said, without turning to face her. "There are ears everywhere."

Before she could utter a response, the door closed, and he was gone.

Theron

She had some nerve prancing into Tartarus and demanding he tell her about his mission on Mt. Olympus. Theron grumbled as he made it to his training dungeon. He was almost to the door when it flung open and Nikias emerged.

The blonde general sneered. "Aren't you a little late this morning?"

"Why were you in there? That's *my* training chamber."

"You weren't in there, and I needed to train." He smirked. "Just in case."

"In case of *what*?"

Nikias snickered to himself and walked away, his arms firmly planted at his sides. His pretentiousness, smugness, and love of order and all things boring made Theron hate him with a passion, but he didn't feel like getting into a verbal spar with him today, so he just rolled his eyes and entered the dungeon.

Enveloped in darkness, the only sounds Theron could hear were the echoes of his boots scraping against the uneven, rocky floor beneath. As his eyes adjusted to the dim light, his gaze shifted to the other side of the room. *Something isn't right. Where is the*—"Ah!" A piercing stroke lashed him on the shoulder. The pain was white-hot, causing him to stagger back, his hand thrusting against the stinging wound. Blood trickled through his fingers.

He whipped around and was met with the belly of a beast greater than any he'd seen as of late. His eyes scrolled up its long, silvery neck as he gaped at the five-headed serpent snarling down at him. The entirety of its body was covered in thick, metallic scales like pointed bars of gold as sharp as the blade at Theron's side. Its mouth peeled back to reveal five rows of dripping, black teeth.

Thanatos was determined to break him.

The beast wailed an unearthly screech and pounced at him. Theron's hand groped at his side, unsheathing his sword, but his mind was cluttered. He needed a clear head to fight something like this, but all he could think about was her. About the way her eyelashes batted in that sultry way when their eyes locked. The way her breathing changed when he crawled to her.

The way she smelled so sweet and intoxicating. The way her body felt against his in that brief moment of accidental contact earlier that morning. It had only lasted a fraction of a second, but it was enough to enrapture him with thoughts of her when he least wanted to think at all.

Theron focused his stare on that five-headed beast—on its beady, black eyes and dragonic form—in total concentration. He had to stop thinking about her, but no matter how hard he tried, all he could see and feel was her. The softness of her skin. The curves of her body. He swung the sword at the beast and tried to stop his mind from turning, his skin from blazing. Tried to erase all the memories from the last twelve hours for this one match. But a task that hefty would take a lot more training—the kind he had no experience in.

For now, he had to fight this thing and try his best not to think about anything but the weight of the sword in his hands and the movements of the creature stalking his every move. And hope to Zeus that the distraction of knowing Correlia was currently lying in his bed would eventually go away.

CHAPTER
TWENTY-TWO

Phineas

T hings had gone from mild distress to near hysteria since Hades' appearance. It was hard for Phineas to even go to the marketplace for food. Gods and goddesses were scattered everywhere, some whispering, some shouting, but all with strained faces.

He looked at the fruits in the crate before him. The vendor was usually pleasant—a black-haired goddess who always greeted him cheerily when he strode through with Corre. But today, her expression was dark, and her sapphire eyes were somewhere else.

"Are these the same as last time?" he asked, though he knew full well that they were—she sold the same fruits every week. She nodded but said nothing. Her expression was past him. He looked back at the fruit. It was dark red and oblong, with one small leaf fluttering on the twig at its head. It looked more like candy than fruit. Corre loved them. She always grabbed an armful and bit into them as if she'd never eaten something so tangy and delicious in her life.

He smiled at the thought of her laughing with her mouth full, shoving him playfully on their weekly journey home from the grocers at the market square, baskets filled to the brim with their spoils. His smile vanished at the thought of her absence. She was always here on Saturdays. They met at this exact time, too, when the sun was in that perfect spot in the sky and they could find the freshest food for lunch.

But she was nowhere to be seen. Even on the off times they didn't plan on meeting ahead of time, they'd run into each other. It was always constant. Something had to be wrong.

"You're just being paranoid," he muttered to himself and fumbled with the fruits. She's probably focused on training. Her mother's been on her about that.

"I am *not* paranoid," a voice said.

He looked up, locking eyes with the blue-eyed vendor. "I didn't say you were—"

"I am realistic," she said, annunciating every syllable.

Phineas looked back down, picking up another piece of fruit. "I—"

"He's going to come again, isn't he?" This time, her voice was shaky.

"I don't know," he said quietly. "I can't imagine he'd stay away after coming up here."

The woman nodded at a lightning pace. "Exactly. He's planning something, and we're all in danger."

"That's not necessarily true," Phineas lied, knowing mass hysteria could be even deadlier than a god from Tartarus.

She scoffed. "Well. Think what you want, but I'm going to prepare." Her eyes bolted to his. "You better, too. More than any of us. You're Ares, for pity's sake. Act like it." The words stung, and before he could stand up for himself, she added, "One drachma for the fruit. And I think it's best if you leave."

He tossed her a coin and nodded, still stung by her words. He knew it was true, though. It was time to buckle down.

No more games.

Instead of heading home, Phineas took a sharp turn to Athena's. He weaved through the woods, the vendor's words heavy in his mind. He was supposed to be the greatest warrior on Olympus. If something happened—if Hades did anything—it would be up to him to take action.

"Time to live up to the legacy," he told himself, despite the uneasiness filling his chest. Athena's place was straight ahead. As the cottage came into view, he worried that the older goddess may not be home. She wasn't expecting him today. He usually took grocery days off to spend with Correlia.

But the door opened, and the scarlet-haired goddess spotted him and stopped. "Phineas. I wasn't—"

"I need to train." The words echoed through the wood. A gust of wind blew between them, and Athena's long hair rippled at her sides.

"Okay," she said. "Let's get to it."

Corre

Corre watched as her feet swiped back and forth on the bed. She groaned and flopped her arms out into a T. "This is so boring." She shifted to her side and sucked in a breath. When Theron's recognizable scent wafted through her nose, a spark sizzled through her body.

She closed her eyes and breathed in again. In her mind, she saw him lying there as he slept, his black hair spilling onto his pillow, his body moving in steady breaths. He turned around, still fast asleep, and grabbed hold of her, his body enveloping hers, and together they slept, molded into one shape.

If she'd woken up to his embrace deeper into the night, would she have turned around, sleepy-eyed and uninhibited, and touched him back? Feeling the arc of each sculpted muscle beneath her fingertips? What if he'd grabbed hold of her willingly? For all she knew, he had. He could have easily swept her into his grasp, his face nuzzling into the crook of her neck as he breathed in the tulip scent of her hair.

If he'd done so willingly, and she'd known . . .

Air snagged in her throat. She thought of him wrapping his arm around her waist in the darkness of the night. Of her turning around and facing him, dizzy in a state of half-sleep. Him swiping his hand up her back and across her stomach. His fingers trailing across her skin. His hands—

The door swung open, and she inhaled a breath so fierce it made her cough. "Why are you so flushed?" Theron asked as the door closed. He was gripping the top of a lumpy sack, eyeing her with a cocked head.

"I-I'm not. I mean I'm hot." She laughed. "I'm used to fresh air."

"Really? I find it cold in here. And damp. It's a lot chillier than where you live, that's for sure."

"What's in there?" she said quickly, pointing to the cloth in his hand.

He threw it to her. "Food. Take whatever you want. I need to go."

"What? Already? You just got here—" She stopped the moment she heard the eagerness in her voice, then leveled it. "You have to eat. You're all sweaty, and—Theron! Your arm!"

He looked at the wound—a bloody claw mark slashed down his shoulder, skidding to a stop right above his chest. "Oh, that?"

"Yes, that!"

"It's nothing," he said, genuinely confused at her alarm. "Really. It happens all the time."

It happens all the time?

Corre's insides knotted. How could someone be so used to a life of pain? So desensitized to violence?

"What did it to you?"

"Another beast. One I've never seen before." He sat next to her on the bed and flashed her a smile. "But I got him. He's a pile of flesh and ash now." Corre looked at the food but, thinking of that lovely image, lost her appetite. Theron got off the bed, swung off his cloak, and hung it over a rack by the door. "I must go. I'll be back in a few hours."

"Can I come?"

"What? Of course not." He pointed at her clothes. "That's hardly armor. And you can't fight."

Her eyebrow twitched. "Of course I can."

"Sure, princess," he said with a chuckle.

The blood boiled in her veins. She slid to her feet, her fists balled at her sides. "How dare you call me that!"

"I'm not wrong. Besides, you can't be seen by anyone, remember?"

"I won't! I'll be careful."

"What are you even going on about? Just stay here."

"No! I'm going with you! I know how to fight! I want to train—"

"No!" he shouted, then left the room before she could protest again.

"RAH! He's so irritating!" She sat back on the bed with her arms crossed, the anger still pulsing through her. She looked at the food now spilling onto the bed. There were two rolls, three apples, and a branch with about a dozen grapes on it. Her stomach growled, but she thought of Theron's arrogant attitude, the state of his shoulder, and her desire to do anything but waste her day in this mind-numbing room.

Quickly, she plucked a handful of grapes off the branch, popped them into her mouth, and raced to the door. She placed an ear next to the crack beside the doorknob. Nothing. No one was out there. She grabbed Theron's cloak and threw it over her shoulders, quickly opened the door, shut it, and followed the hallway until she heard Theron's even stride.

At least, she thought it was his. She peered around the corner. Sure enough, she saw the towering Hades striding down one of the hallways in the black maze. She tiptoed to the other side and waited until his footsteps were far enough away that she could tail him without him suspecting anything.

She followed the echo of his footsteps until she heard the heavy dungeon door creaking open. When it slammed shut, the noise echoing across the entire labyrinth, she turned the corner and ran to it. She waited as long as she could before throwing herself in and ducking behind the nearest pile of rubble. When she poked her head out, she stifled a gasp.

This was no room. Some sort of sorcery must have played into the creation of such a chamber. Or maybe a Titan had built it. There was no way this place was hidden below the ground in any natural way. Its ceiling was so high Corre couldn't make out where it was. There was nothing concrete above her head. No dirt or tile or earth. It seemed to go on endlessly, eventually turning into a shrouded mass of shadow above the rocky cliffs and towering stone walls that stood scattered across the spacious dungeon.

It was incredible. Unnerving, but incredible.

Corre quietly crawled on her hands and knees to another spot she could hide behind—a wall of ruddy stones, each jagged and misshapen—until she saw where Theron stood. His body moved in careful motions, his sword slicing through the air in graceful strides. It was like a dance. He was strong. Confident. And she liked the way his muscles tensed beneath his thin black shirt. He'd taken off his heavy cowl, belt, and any other form of armor he usually wore beneath the cloak she was now gripping against her chest.

He looked free, but his motions were calculated. His arms were still strong, despite being injured, and his legs were solid and planted firmly on the ground by his long black boots. She loved the way he moved. It was captivating.

His foot skidded back as he wielded the long sword, his upper body moving forward with the momentum. Of all the times Corre had witnessed fighting—mostly from watching Athena and training with Phineas—she'd never seen something so elite. So precise.

The beast he was facing came into view. It was the most horrifying thing she'd ever seen. With four—no, five—snake-like heads the length of three maple trees stacked from root to tip and black eyes that squared in on Theron, Corre didn't know how he wasn't more afraid. Despite its thin necks, its body was robust—thick, like a meaty elephant with four stocky legs. Every inch of its skin was covered in sharp, glass-like scales that allowed it to blend into its surroundings, making it even more lethal.

One of its beaked mouths let out a cry that shook the ground, causing her to fall onto her tailbone. Her dominant hand scraped against the rough dirt. That was when she realized how realistic the floor looked to the world above. It was like a piece of Mt. Olympus had been taken from outside her house and placed in this chamber. She sifted through the coarse, sandy material with her fingers, then reached out and felt the smoothness of the stone beside where she'd been hiding. It was probably odd to be studying dirt and rocks at a time like this—she understood that, but she couldn't help it. Maybe it was the Persephone in her.

A scream sliced through the room, but it wasn't from the beast this time. Corre jumped out to see Theron on his knees, holding his wounded side. It was split back open and leaking blood onto the floor. His head hung, chin resting against his broad chest, but she couldn't see his expression through his falling waves of hair.

The creature wailed, one of its heads bending back, winding up for its next attack. Corre sucked in a breath and looked to Theron. He was still bent over, swaying dizzily.

"Theron! Look out!"

His head shot up. He looked at her for a split second before swiveling around and spotting the serpent-like head snapping toward him.

There was a loud pinging sound, like metal blades scraping against each other, and a furious spark. A light flashed across the room. Its blinding strength temporarily fuzzed Corre's vision, and in those brief moments of uncertainty, she couldn't fight off the panic. She rubbed her eyes furiously until she spotted Theron again. His back was against the dirt, his sword stretched out in front of him, its blade impaling the roof of the serpent's mouth, bursting out the top of its head.

It must have been the only head in control because soon the other heads shriveled and coiled up, and the pierced head crumbled into dust. The beast's lifeless body crashed to the ground, puffing a large cloud of dirt to life. The dirt swept through the dungeon in an enormous, earthy wave. When the haze dissipated, Corre spotted Theron clutching his side and hobbling to his feet. "Are you okay?"

"You shouldn't be here," he said, his voice strained. He tried putting weight on one of his legs, but then toppled to the ground and grunted in pain.

"Let me help you." She grabbed hold of his arm, half-expecting him to jerk away, but he didn't resist. He let her steady him, and he took hold of his sword's hilt with his free hand as he inched up into a standing position.

He started to fall against her and lose his footing, but she managed to keep him upright. "Whoa, hang in there," she said, steadying him as best she could.

"You shouldn't be here," he grumbled again.

"How about a 'thank you'?" She glowered at him while she helped him find a place to sit. "I've saved you twice now."

"I was fine," he said, sliding onto a flat rock.

"Right." She rolled her eyes. With the dust now settled and the beast not so much as twitching, Corre let herself breathe and scan the room more closely. "How was this chamber created?" she asked, looking again at the impossibly high ceiling and the overwhelming size of the dungeon.

"Magic, what else?" he replied as if it was the most normal thing in the world.

"Magic?" She lifted a brow. "Seriously? How am I supposed to believe that?"

He winced as he repositioned himself on the rock and pressed his arm against his injured side. "Believe what you want, but that's the reality of it. Besides, how is magic really that different than the powers you use to create life on Olympus?"

She looked back up at the ceiling, or at least where the ceiling should have been, instead of a sea of shadow. "You use magic," she said, more of a statement and more to herself. "Trust me, it's different. I use what flows in me through skills I've acquired through training. I can't whip up illusions."

"What you described *is* magic. Just because you can make illusions with it doesn't make it a different source of power. I have to train to do what I do, too."

Something flickered and swirled in the abyss above her. Her eyes followed the odd movements as she pondered his statement. She'd always been told that magic was evil. That it wasn't true skill—that it was taken from the energy of others and created through falsities. Surely that was what was at play here. This dungeon couldn't really exist like this. "Magic isn't real. My powers are."

Theron snorted. "Whatever you say." She frowned and shot him another glare, but she couldn't bare argue with him. He looked terrible. His eyes were barely open, and the color was rapidly draining from his face.

Without another word, his eyes closed, and his body slumped. He almost slid off the rock before she jumped up to catch him. "We need to get you patched up again. Right away—"

"No. I need to train."

She grabbed hold of his arms. "You really are something," she snapped. "How do you expect to live through another fight like this?"

He didn't retort, but he also didn't move. His face lost more color by the second. It was only a matter of time before he hit the ground and passed out.

"Come on. Let's get you back to your room."

It took them a painful amount of time to make it to the door, and as they did, it swung open. Corre couldn't so much as blink before Theron pushed her behind a pile of debris and masked her from whoever was at the door. She almost hit the wall but was more shocked and confused than anything else.

Theron stood upright, bracing himself, but his legs were trembling. He couldn't mask the pain completely.

"Sir, you are expected for a meal with Thanatos," a scratchy male voice said.

"Oh. Right."

"Forgive me, but had you forgotten? I could tell the master—"

"No! No. I just . . . I may be a few minutes late. I was training again. I took on another match and—"

"You'd forgotten. I understand. I will tell—"

"No!" Theron snapped. The other being fell silent. Theron leveled his voice. "I didn't forget. I simply lost track of time."

Another moment of silence passed. "Very well," the voice said. "I will tell the master that you will be there shortly."

Corre hadn't seen what the god looked like, or even if it was a god. There were a lot of demons crawling around Tartarus; she never knew what to expect. But when the being finally left, Theron let himself hunch back over and turn to her, his face strained.

"You forgot, didn't you?" she said with an impish smile, but he wasn't looking at her. He was bent over and heaving uneven breaths. "We should get going right away," she said, correcting her behavior. "If you want that side of yours stitched up before you eat with your master."

"Stitched up?"

"It's going to keep bleeding if it's only bandaged. We need to stitch it. Your opponent today knew where to hit you. You were bleeding all over the place." The image of his blood spilling to the floor and between his fingers made Corre's blood drain from her face. She shook the thought away. "Come on, we—"

"No. Someone will see you. I'll go first, and if the coast is clear, I'll wave to you and you can follow."

"But you're hurt. You're going to fall—"

"Please!" His voice echoed across the dungeon. Her heart nearly stopped. His deep brown eyes stared down at her, pleading.

"Okay," she conceded quietly.

"Let's go. If you want to 'stitch my side' before I dine with Thanatos, we have no time to lose."

Corre rolled her eyes. "Yes, Your Majesty," she said, but she couldn't hold back a smile as she followed him out of the room.

CHAPTER TWENTY-THREE

Theron

T hey were almost to his quarters when that insolent guard reappeared. Theron sprawled his hand out behind him so Correlia knew to not take another step. "What is it, Therius?"

"Sir, Thanatos wants to see you right away."

"I know, but—"

"Right now," the creature urged. "He wants to see you *now*."

Theron's jaw clenched. "How dare you speak to me like that? I'm your master."

Therius bowed, but Theron's eyes flashed with fury. Most of the demons and creatures crawling through Tartarus were afraid of him, but General Nikias and some of his soldiers didn't seem to think he was anything more than a glorified general.

"Forgive me, sir," the soldier said stalely, standing upright. "But Master Thanatos wants to see you immediately."

Theron's fists tightened, but his body was only rigid for half a second before the pain of his split side struck through him. He bent forward slightly but bit into his tongue to avoid making a sound. Even after the taste of iron pooled through his mouth, he didn't budge.

"Psst. Theron!"

He shot up in panic at the sound of Correlia's voice, but when he noticed Therius had left, he relaxed slightly. He'd been so focused on keeping himself together that he hadn't seen the creature flee.

"Psst! Theron!"

"Stay in my quarters, Correlia," he replied icily. He moved forward, preparing himself to look and feel strong before Thanatos. To reveal no weakness.

His thoughts needed to be stuck on nothing. Reveal nothing. He needed to get as far from Correlia as possible, in every way, until he left the throne room. He just needed to get through the conversation with his master, take whatever he needed to be given—no matter how unpleasant that might be—and then hurry back before losing too much blood.

To his surprise, Correlia didn't follow him as he fumbled down the hall. Each corridor grew harder to tread, the walls around him blurring as a high-pitched noise pierced his eardrums. Finally, he made it. He wiped the sweat off his forehead before entering the throne room.

"Ah, there he is," Thanatos said as Theron entered the chamber, his voice drawn out like the sound of a door slowly unhinging. "And you're *injured*." The last word was drenched in disgust.

Theron didn't let it phase him. "I'm sorry for missing our meeting. I tried to pick up another match—"

"'Tried' is right, by the looks of it." Thanatos scoffed and looked away.

Theron paused briefly, then said, "I beat it, master. I believe it was worth the effort."

The giant deity laughed. "I don't find making it out barely alive a feat. Do you truly think you could rule Tartarus in such a way?"

Theron bowed his head, eyes fixed on the floor.

Thanatos continued, "I suppose it is noteworthy that you chose to take on another battle. So, I will let you go with a warning today. But do *not* disappoint me again. You will dine with me in one hour. Get yourself cleaned up. I can wait to converse with you until then."

The young god's spirit soared. He looked up at his master, trying his best to hold back a smile. "Thank you, sir," he said calmly, then turned around and strode to his room.

I can't believe it. I actually did something right.

He was on cloud nine all the way to his quarters, almost forgetting to stop at the infirmary for supplies to patch up his wounds. He was so consumed with what had just transpired that it took him a second to register that Correlia was talking to him. He looked over his shoulder and saw her there, concern etched across her face.

He opened the door. "I thought I told you to stay in my quarters until I came back." He allowed himself to finally let go of his tough façade once he walked through the threshold of his room. His body bent forward, his hand clasping his bleeding side, as he limped to the bed.

"I wanted to know if you'd be okay."

"And you thought you could protect me if, what? If someone were to attack me on my way there?"

Correlia sat at the foot of the bed, but she was still frowning. "No. I was afraid of what Thanatos might do to you."

He shot her a glare. "Thanatos is my master. My teacher. He raised me."

"So? I've seen the scars on your back."

Something rippled through him. Not anger, but something like it. "It's for my own good." Correlia stared at him but said nothing. "Besides. You saw him today. He didn't hurt me even though I disobeyed him." His face softened, his mouth curving into a smile.

"How did you disobey him?" Correlia quipped. Theron's smile faded. "You simply forgot an engagement because he's working you so hard. Because he's in your head so—"

"You don't know what you're talking about!" His voice came out louder than he'd intended. He could still hear its echo as Correlia's mouth clamped shut. But he was shaking, and annoyed. Or sad. Something.

She took a breath before quietly breaking the awkward silence. "Does he always treat you like that?"

Theron's head jerked back. "Like what?"

"He puts you down and treats you like rubbish."

"He does what he must to shape me."

"And he must do it through putting you down? Through making you feel guilty for doing the things he asks you to do?"

"He didn't—" Theron stopped and lowered his voice. "He didn't ask me to do anything."

"He doesn't ask you to fight until you're tattered to shreds every day? He doesn't ask you to train until you nearly bleed to death?"

"I'm a god. I can't die so easily. And I'm the God of Death—"
"So?!"

He shook his head. "Why do you care how my master treats me?"

They stared at each other, their gazes locked, until Correlia finally looked down at her hands. "We need to get your side stitched up." Her voice was quieter. She reached for the supplies in his hand and didn't look at his face. "Take your shirt off. We don't have much time before you must present yourself in front of him again."

Theron's brows furrowed. "What's . . ." *What's wrong?* He couldn't say it. Maybe he didn't want to know the answer. He slid off his shirt, despite how much it hurt to feel the cloth peel from his gaping side, and watched Correlia's face as she investigated the wound. The subtle lines on her forehead wrinkled, the space between her eyebrows puckering.

"I'll get some wet cloths. Do you have anything for the pain?"

"Like what?"

She shrugged. "I don't know. Some medicinal herbs I can dab the wound with before I stitch you up?"

He let out a half-laugh, then winced. Laughing was not an option right now. He rested his head against the headboard, closing his eyes and hoping his vision wasn't blurry when he opened them again. "No. I don't use anything for pain. This is how I can become Hades. Surely, you've gathered that's a big part of my training by now." He waited to hear her quip back, but all he heard was the distant running of the spout and the absence of her breath.

He opened his eyes when he felt her dab the cloth on the gash. He tried not to let out a groan, instead studying the wound himself. It was like the creature had infected half his body. His left side was covered in so much blood it looked black, except for the occasional curls of flesh that were bunched between each claw mark.

"Then this might sting a bit," Correlia said, taking the needle and carefully prodding it into the swollen skin.

He silenced a cry as she weaved the needle through the tender outline of the wound, doing her best to seal up his mangled torso. Neither one of them said a thing as she patched one side of his wound until he finally couldn't take it anymore. "My master does what's best for me."

She kept sewing.

"He wants me to be strong."

Correlia's hand stilled. "I don't think he wants you to be anything."

"What? What are you saying?"

Finally, she looked up at him. "Just that. I think he puts you down to make himself feel superior. I think he gets off on hurting you." She looked back down and continued to sew.

Theron's jaw clenched. "How would you know how a god of the Underworld is made? All you have to do is grow flowers and live in your little naïve bubble up on Mt. Olympus. Safe from everyone and everything. Safe from reality."

Her eyes snapped up. "I know more about pain than you think." There was a slight rattle in her voice. It made him uneasy—angered him, even. Not at her. At *something*. It was accompanied by a slight twinge of guilt, too.

"Forgive me," he said, his gaze falling to her delicate features as she sewed. Watching her mend him—care for him, for whatever reason—made the pain so much less intense. It made him feel warm, despite the icy patches of his exposed skin.

"What are you hiding?" he asked before realizing it might have been a bad idea to ask. But he had to know.

"What do you mean?"

"You're caring for me. *Me*. Why?"

She let out a long sigh. "Does everyone need an ulterior motive to do something nice for someone else?"

"Yes," he said bluntly.

"Well, I don't." She tugged on the string as it made its last ascent from his skin. "And maybe you should learn that, too." She tied the thread and broke it free from the needle. Her gold-green eyes looked up into his. "Maybe you need to learn that not everyone is a monster. That there are actually people capable of compassion." She stood up and took the bloodied cloth and needle to the fountain.

"Thanatos could have hurt me today," he called out. She blocked the spout, cutting the water off and creating a brief silence between them. "I did something wrong. I'd forgotten an obligation. But he spared me." He followed her gait from the washing room. "That shows the compassion he has for me."

"You need to put on a new shirt," she said, looking through his things to find one. "You have to leave soon." She opened a trunk made of tightly knit black straw that stood next to his wardrobe.

"*Correlia.*"

She closed the lid and looked at him.

"You don't know me. You think you understand my life, but you don't. You can't. You're from a completely different world. So don't judge me. And don't judge my master for something you don't understand."

The silence was suffocating as he awaited her reply, but she said nothing as she got up and walked back to the bed, tossing him a shirt. He expected her to have that fiery look in her eyes. For them to fight. But as she sat next to him on the bed, there was only a sadness in the way she looked at him. "I know that I don't understand your world or what you've been through," she said, "but there's something I understand that you don't: you don't deserve to be treated the way he treats you, and you're stronger than you think."

He scoffed and looked away. "I know I'm strong—"

"Not like that. *Inside.* He can't break you, and he probably sees that. So don't let him." She gave him one last look before standing up again. "Now, tell me where the rest of your clean clothes are. You need to change completely before you go to dinner. You reek."

He glowered at her, but there was nothing real behind it. He didn't know what to say to her. He didn't understand her. He thought about Thanatos. About his punishments. About the rigorous training he'd put him through. He wanted to believe her that he was strong enough not to break. Maybe then he could finally take up the mantle and be Hades once and for all.

But she knew nothing about this. About him or anything of his life here.

"I'll get it myself," he said, but she vehemently shook her head.

"No, you need to save your energy for when you're gone."

"I'm fine."

"No, you're not—"

"Who do you think you are?" he spat, and at the sight of her wounded expression, wished he could be the one hurt instead. "I'm sorry," he said quickly. "You just don't understand."

"Stop saying I don't understand! You can't tell me this life has made you happy."

"This life isn't supposed to make me happy."

She gaped at him, her eyes wide. "Don't you want to be?"

"I— Of course, but . . . Being crowned Hades will make me happy."

She placed a hand on his face. The warmth of her palm against his cheek opened a part of him he didn't know existed. "You *are* Hades. Whether or not you're on the throne doesn't change that. You're allowed to be happy. You're allowed to dislike your master and admit to yourself that you're worth more than what he says you are."

Tears stung his eyes, but he blinked them away and turned away. He took her hand from his face, though he hated the cold nothingness that replaced it. "No. This is how it's meant to be for me. My master knows what's best, and I enjoy my life because I know I'll become the god I'm supposed to be one day, and it will be because of him." He looked back at her, his eyes no longer threatening him with tears.

Her eyes narrowed, that sadness still inside them. "You can't tell me there's never been a time in your life that you wanted something else. That you wished he treated you differently."

The words cut through him and resurfaced a memory he'd thought was lost. From when he was a boy. Just a year after he'd come here.

After one of the evenings in that room . . .

"No. This is my life. I'm perfectly fine with it."

She cupped his face again and looked tenderly into his eyes. He studied her back, unsure of what she was thinking or doing. A look of pain flashed in her sunflower eyes. "I'm so sorry that all you've known in your life is pain."

Something in him flipped. Snagged. Tore through him like claws.

He looked away, shoving down the feelings twisting in his chest. He shifted in the bed and got to his feet. "I have to go. My master is waiting for me."

He half-expected her to say something else as he slipped into the clean shirt and fished for a cowl in his wardrobe adjacent to the front door. When he pinned his cape across his chest, he left without saying anything else. Trying as hard as he could not to think.

CHAPTER TWENTY-FOUR

Corre

When Corre was six years old, she couldn't speak. There wasn't much she remembered about that time, but she did remember how patient her mother had been. She remembered that, despite how scared she was to be with this unknown goddess in this strange, tiny house, Berenice always tried, and she always wore a gentle smile. Corre never felt that she must hurry up and speak or do exactly the right thing. And that was probably what got her to finally speak one day—when she finally let herself utter something other than that song.

When she looked back on it now, she couldn't remember the details of it—only snippets and how Berenice made her feel. That was enough to tell her one part of the story, but it haunted her that she couldn't remember what her life had been like before that point. Before her voice had been snatched from her and everything became confusing and strange. She couldn't remember why she'd sung that haunting melody or ceased speaking. She didn't even know if she'd spoken at all before she was six. For all she knew, she'd been born without speech.

But Berenice said she'd sing. She'd sing that melancholy tune, even when she wouldn't utter an un-cadenced word. For weeks—months—she sang that song. Until one day, she finally spoke, and the song vanished from her memory.

It was eerie. When Corre thought about it too long, it scratched at the parts of her brain she didn't like to think about. At the memories she didn't understand. The pain she didn't know how to locate and do away with.

But that song . . .

It hadn't vanished. Because all of a sudden, she started singing it again. Even now, after stitching up Hades and wondering what was happening to him in that dining hall, that song was playing inside her head, as if it'd been locked away in a lost music box deep in the cracks of her mind, stuck shut until she was old enough to pry it open and listen to it again.

She desperately wished she could close it. Seal it back up. She didn't like it. With its unnerving ebbs and flows, ups and downs, and sideways notes. It didn't sit well with her. It wasn't right.

It was easier for her to push it aside and get up to wander about the labyrinth, even though she knew how dangerous it was. How incredibly reckless it was. It was better than being alone, to sit there and listen to that song playing over and over until Theron returned, when she could listen to his soothingly deep voice instead. Until then, she had to do something else. Something reckless. So that song would stop playing in her head.

Theron

"Why are you so afraid?" He scoffed.

"I'm not afraid," the boy said, lifting his head.

His master sat back on his throne. "Prove it." He pointed a crooked finger toward the corridor.

Theron's body trembled until he couldn't stop the shaking. It overpowered him. Still, he walked, following the path of that crooked finger until he had no choice but to open the door.

"You haven't touched your food," Thanatos said.

Theron sat upright. "I'm sorry. I'm just..." *I can't say 'tired'. I can't say 'worn out'.* "I was thinking. I will eat it now. My apologies."

"Ts. Stop apologizing, boy. It makes you look weak."

"Yes, sir." Theron picked at the dark meat soaked in red and thick, gooey black on his plate. This meat was rare, and he almost didn't want to know what beast it had come from, but it was probably the thing he'd slain earlier. He looked down at the blood as he slowly chewed.

"Eat it," Thanatos commanded.

"I don't like meat!" the boy cried. A hot clap flashed across his cheek, and blood trickled into his mouth. He hated when his master hit him. Even more than he hated meat. "Yes, sir," he said, trying to control the tremor in his voice.

Theron took a swig of his wine and tried not to think, but Correlia's voice echoed in his mind. *'You can't tell me there's never been a time in your life that you wanted something else.'*

"Is something wrong with the food?" Thanatos said, anger gurgling in his throat.

"No, sir." Theron took another bite. "It really is delicious."

"Hmph." The giant, pale creature took a swig from his massive goblet and turned to speak to his general. "Did you receive any news?"

"I'm afraid my soldiers have found nothing yet, sir."

Theron looked up. "What are you talking about?"

Nikias sneered. "What is wrong with you lately? You're—"

"Elsewhere," Thanatos drawled, narrowing his eyes.

"I'm preoccupied with my training. That's all."

Thanatos's eyes stayed narrowed. "We were talking about the girl."

Theron's heart stopped. "The . . .girl?"

"Nikias's soldiers haven't found her anywhere."

Theron's stomach turned to lead. He downed his wine. "Where have you looked?"

Stay calm. Keep your mind steady.

"Everywhere," Nikias said with a huff. "We've looked in and around her house and all over Olympus. We can't find her anywhere."

"Oh." *Stay. Calm.* "Why are you searching for her?" *Keep your mind steady.*

Thanatos scoffed. "This was your idea." Theron looked up, his heart racing. "You said she was someone to look out for. I had thought as much, but it was confirmed when you found her. We need her."

"Need her for what?"

"Interrogation, what else?" Nikias said, poking at the last bite of his meat. He popped it into his mouth and looked at Theron like he was stupid. He'd always been like that.

"You're Hades?" the young teen had said with a scoff when both boys had been taken to their chambers that first night in Tartarus. He'd looked him up and down. *"Not much of a god if you ask me."*

They'd never gotten along, but Theron couldn't stand Nikias, either. That insipid, tight-laced, stick up his—

"And you'll be heading it," Thanatos said, pointing a gnarled finger at Theron.

His stomach dropped to his knees. "Me?"

"Yes. *You*. You do want to be Hades, don't you?"

He forced down a piece of meat. *This could be good*, he reasoned. If he had to interrogate her, he could be in control. Keep her safe. "What are we trying to get out of her?"

"Everything," his master said, then looked back at Nikias. "As Theron previously mentioned, she's stronger than she should be. There's something about her that doesn't sit right with me. Find her and bring her to me. Don't stop until you do. Or you might as well not come back at all."

Theron's stomach twisted.

The bloodthirsty spark in Nikias's eyes flickered. "Of course, master. I won't disappoint you."

Suddenly things were much, much worse.

Corre

Corre's footsteps echoed as she padded down the corridor. She wasn't sure how long she'd been walking and turning right, then left, then another left, and so on, but it'd been too long. Especially for her to think she was in any sort of control of her situation. Finally, after another loop around nothing but more passageways and dirt floors crawling with mice and insects she'd never seen before, she let herself admit it.

She was lost.

She couldn't believe she'd gotten herself lost in Tartarus. Of all the idiotic—

"Come this way," a voice whistled through the air. It was so faint that Corre second-guessed if she'd truly heard it. But then it spoke again. "Come, girl. Come."

She turned around but still saw nothing. A light breeze brushed against her ankles, lightly pushing her in the direction of the voice. She flipped back around and stifled a gasp at the white image of an old woman floating in front of her.

"Come," it said again before turning around and slipping through the wall.

Corre knew better than to follow a mirage in the heart of Tartarus but, at this point, she was desperate. She was completely lost. Besides, she could just follow it part of the way and then fight her way out of whatever situation she got herself into, right? Right.

It was her only option.

Before she let herself think too hard about it, she took a step forward and followed it into the dark.

Theron

There were hundreds of possible things Thanatos could do to and with Correlia, and every single one that came to mind made his insides twist. The worst part was that he knew she wouldn't know what to say or not to say to his master if he decided to be a part of the interrogation.

He was convinced she really was as naïve as she'd seemed upon their first meeting. Unaware of how the world worked or what to be afraid of.

As he swung the door open to his chambers, he tried to get it all out of his head, but one look at the empty room made his stomach sink. "Correlia?" Panic ricocheted through his gut. "*Correlia?*"

His stomach squeezed tighter.

He thought of Thanatos. Of Nikias and that devilish gleam in his eyes—so desperate to please Thanatos and become his favorite. He'd do anything to please their master. He'd always been furious that he wasn't deemed the god-to-be, and Theron knew that the general was trying to prove he was a more worthy fit. That maybe he could usurp the throne or replace him before Theron even finished his training.

"Correlia, this isn't funny. Where are you?"

Silence.

The room spun around him as he staggered to the door, slamming it shut as he ran out into the labyrinth. He sped down each corridor, frantically searching every nook and hiding place. Fear racked his body.

Where are *you?*

Corre

The air continued pulling her closer to the voice. A mesmerizing warmth saturated her senses as she followed the path the mysterious spirit-like goddess had taken. But the wisp of a woman was nowhere in sight. Corre decided to at least follow the labyrinth in the opposite direction of the one that led to Thanatos's chambers—the one attached to that castle. It seemed to be the best bet if she didn't want to get caught. It would at least buy her some time to think and figure out how to make it back to Theron's quarters.

If she wanted to understand more about Hades and how the Underworld worked, and everything else that went on down here, she needed to memorize her surroundings, so she could make her way back if necessary. This journey wasn't stupid. It was strategic. It would probably serve useful one day.

She thought back on Thanatos and when she'd peeked in on Theron bowing before his master. How small he had looked in comparison. In that moment, Theron wasn't the big, bad Hades everyone cowered from. He looked like a boy, afraid of getting scolded by a cold, erratic parent.

Who was Thanatos to taunt him anyway? To sit on his throne?

It was strange that the throne room was said to be part of the castle when it had looked detached on the outside. Still, she knew to avoid that area at all costs, so she crept along the paths she was pretty sure she hadn't taken before, carefully keeping an ear out for any straggling demons or lost souls, or whatever else was down here. As well as that odd, melodic whisper.

She was glad the tunnels were hollow. If anyone stepped a foot—or claw—into a path anywhere near her, she'd hear the echoes long before they found her. Hopefully no one would hear her, either, as she crept along, turn after turn.

After taking too many rights, she met a dead end with nowhere to go but through a grooved entrance of some kind, carved into the wall. She peered over her shoulder at the deep, shadowy labyrinth. There was nowhere else to go but through the gaping hole in the middle of the onyx wall. It looked like the mouth of a beast, whose acid had burnt through the stone and melted the area around it.

Her heart raced. She almost didn't go for it until she heard that voice again, this time on the other side of that opening. Slowly, she crept through the gaping maw. The air grew thick and even damper than the rest of Hades' labyrinth. The ceiling leaked something foul onto Corre's shoulder. She shimmied it off and rushed faster through the cavern.

Darkness shrouded her surroundings, growing thicker with each step, until she spotted a glowing light, green and shimmering like fairies dancing against the cobalt walls. The closer she crept, the more obvious the source of the iridescent light became. It was the glimmer of a pool—a peridot expression gleaming from a thick body of flowing water, starting about eight or ten feet from where the opening expanded into a much larger cave. The length of the river was unknown as it tunneled through the far side of the open cavern, turning sharply behind the back wall of the grotto.

There was something magnetizing about it—the river like liquid jewels or molten candy. She wanted to reach out and touch it. Feel it flow through her fingers.

She heard that voice again—a mesmerizing call from the glowing water.

Corre crouched next to the mouth of the river, peering in as puffs of steam rose from the surface. Green mist poured through the cavern, creating a thick fog between Corre and the water.

She crawled closer. The pull to peer deeper inside was inexplicable. She needed to do it. It physically pained her not to. She waited for the fog to pass long enough to see what lay beyond the strikingly green surface.

A dark shape formed deep beneath the surface. It grew larger and more concrete with each passing second. It swam closer, and that pull to peer inside engulfed Corre's senses. She reached out to touch it when her name broke through the room like shattering glass.

"Correlia, stop!"

She whipped around to face the voice, but in that same breath, something clutched her wrist and yanked her into the river. The hypnotic appearance of the absinthe water was deceiving. As soon as Corre's skin touched the liquid, it burned like she was being scalded with boiling oil.

She opened her mouth to let out a scream, but her head was completely submerged. The water stung her throat on its way down.

Only one calf was out of the water now, and as that last piece of her started slipping in, a hand grabbed hold of her ankle and started pulling her out. It was like being caught in a current of fire as her body was propelled backward in the water. And even though it was likely only half a second before she was back on dry ground, it felt like she'd burned for eternity. She gasped for breath when her head made it above the surface, but tiny claw-like hands grabbed hold of her wrists again and started pulling her back in.

Her skin bubbled in blistering pain. She wished she could cry to release some of the agony, but her throat was too dry. Whatever the little creatures were, they were no match for the strength of the god who pulled her out. It only took one extra tug for Corre to be unlatched from those tiny claws for good and back onto the ground by the river, far from its alluring surface.

She skittered away from the water, her body shaking violently. Her limbs ached, her head throbbed, and she couldn't stop herself from pulling at the skin on her face. Dry whimpers escaped her burning throat. Despair encompassed her. What was happening? What was that? Her eyes lost focus as she curled within herself.

"It's all right," Theron cooed. His hand brushed against the back of her head and down her damp hair. She looked up at him, still shaking and breathing in little gasps. Her skin was no longer burning, but she felt awful. The liquid in that mystical river seeped deep beneath her skin. She swore she could feel little singes and zaps every few seconds on various parts of her body.

She desperately wanted it to stop.

It was hard to breathe. It was hard to speak. And she couldn't help the tears that spilled down her face.

"It's okay," he assured her again, gathering her into his arms. He scooped her up, one hand beneath her bent knees and the other firmly holding her torso against his chest. Even when her body was raised from the floor and she felt him moving her along through the corridors, she couldn't speak or stop the shivering. And she couldn't stop remembering the feeling of those claws sinking into her boiling skin.

Her eyes were closed when he placed her in his bed, his arms wrapped tightly around her, but even wrapped up in him and a shield of blankets, she couldn't stop the violent shaking or the sobs now pouring out of her. She couldn't even make out the comforting words he whispered in her ears. All she could hear were cries. Wailing. Screaming. And they weren't hers.

She curled her body in tighter, burying her hands in her ears, and squeezed her eyes shut.

Please. Stop.

Her mind whirred. It felt like tiny twigs were splintering throughout her body, each nerve fraying and snapping apart. The sounds intensified—louder, faster, more chaotic—until a warmth spread along her back, and a hand cupped her cheek.

Finally, her eyes peeled open, revealing Theron looking down at her, and it took her a second to realize he was shushing her softly. He grabbed her shaking palm and pressed it to his chest. "Focus on the beating. Count each one. Keep your mind focused."

She nodded unsteadily, her neck aching, and fixed her eyes on her hand splayed on the black cloth of his tunic. She tried to even her breaths as she felt each thump of his heart. It worked for a second, but then the screams broke through again. Her hand started to slip, but he caught it and held it against his chest, this time keeping it secured there.

"I can't," she breathed, barely able to hear her own voice.

"Yes, you can. Focus on my eyes."

She looked up at his concerned stare, at the chocolate color of his eyes, but the voices were too loud. She tried to mouth something but couldn't find the words to speak.

His frown deepened, and he looked around the room. "Find five things and describe them to me—their color, how they feel—and if that doesn't help, keep naming things until it does."

She floundered until she found her voice. "Th-There's a black wardrobe. I-it's made of some kind of stone."

"Good. What else?"

"Um, a chest. A chair. A—" Pain split through the side of her head. She reached to grab it, and her vision blurred. Panic flooded her until his skin brushed against hers and he gently moved her fingers back to his chest.

"And beyond the door?"

She stared up at him, exhaling slowly and feeling his heart thump against her hand. She looked to the door straight back from the foot of the bed. "Towels," she said. "A fountain."

He used his other hand to gently stroke the side of her face before placing his forehead on hers. "Breathe," he said, and she did. She hadn't realized she'd stopped. She let her eyes close as she listened to his breath. "Everything is okay." His voice rolled through her ears, warming her shivering body.

Calm slowly washed through her, and when her trembling finally ceased, the voices and wails gone, all she could feel were the tears stinging her eyes. "What was that?" she whispered.

"The souls of the damned. You went down the wrong corridor." He sighed. "Why did you leave the room?" His voice wasn't accusatory. It was soft.

He had the same look in his eyes that she'd often seen in her mother's—distressed concern. She scooted herself up in the bed and rested against the headboard. "I don't know. I just needed to get out of here. If that makes sense."

"Well, yeah. The Underworld isn't a place for someone like you."

She didn't have the energy to toss him a scowl. "No. Not Tartarus. I just . . . I needed to get out of this room. Out of my head."

There was a pause before he gave a brief nod and placed his back against the headboard next to her. His fingers fidgeted with his gloves. "I understand that impulse." His eyes were focused on his gloves as he took them off, but Corre had a feeling he just didn't know where else to look, until he finally turned to look at her. "What do you need to get out of your head for? Your life is so easy."

Her eyebrows shot up. "*Easy?*" She laughed in disbelief. "Are you serious?"

"Explain it to me, since I clearly don't know."

She sighed. "I'm sorry, but you can't assume things about me, okay? I know my life isn't as hard as yours, but I've still got things I don't want to deal with."

"I guess I shouldn't have said that," he said, as if processing the rules of social etiquette. She glanced up at him and studied his frowning profile. Maybe she shouldn't be so adamant about her life not being easy. Because, truthfully, it did seem that way, at least when she thought about his. About the torture he went through daily. The lack of love in his life.

"No," she finally said, "You should have. You're right. I have nothing to complain about."

"That's not what I said—"

"It's true, though. My life isn't hard."

"I . . ." He looked down at his hands again. "I don't know what your life is like, but I know it can't be as easy as I think if you're struggling so much. If you wanted to run to the Underworld."

His eyes flickered back to hers, and something about the softness inside them made her stomach flip. She had to look away. "It's not really something that's hard right now. I'm having a hard time with something that happened a long time ago. Something I don't understand."

"What is it?"

She thought about the song and the way it felt engrained in her bones. A haunting siren song, pulling at her lungs and clawing at her mind. "A song."

"A song?"

She nodded. "I remember a song. It feels both good and bad when I think about it. I'd forgotten it existed until recently, and now I can't get it out of my head. And I hate it. I don't know why, but I hate it." Her hands curled in her lap.

"I have something like that, too."

Corre looked up. "You do?"

Theron's expression twisted, his gaze cast to the wall. "But I know what it was. It was a day I can't forget. No matter how much I've tried to rip it from my mind."

"What happened?"

"It doesn't matter. Plus, it was for my good. It helped shape me."

She could tell by the shadowed look cast across his face that he didn't believe his words. "Did Thanatos tell you that?"

He shot her a look. "Tell me what?"

She gathered her words carefully. "You . . . I don't think you should believe everything he tells you. He spouts nonsense to—"

He rolled his eyes. "Are you really still on that?"

"Yes! Because someone needs to tell you!"

"Tell me *what*?"

"That you deserve better than this!"

He stared at her in frustration, the muscles in his jaw clenching and unclenching.

Corre lowered her voice. "You deserve an easier life. One without so much pain. So many scars." She lifted her hand to his neck, where the tip of one of his past wounds poked out of his shirt.

He shrugged her hand away. "You don't understand."

She glowered. "The only thing I don't understand is why you don't want to believe me. Why you don't want a better life."

"Of course I want a better life!" he shouted, and when he met her gaze again, she could see tears forming in his eyes. He swallowed hard, his jaw setting and tightening again.

"Then do something to make it happen," she said gently, but he shook his head and refused to look at her. She thought that might be the end of the conversation, but then he spoke again.

"How do you propose I do that?" he muttered.

She tried thinking of a reasonable answer, but there wasn't one. She couldn't think of any solution, which she realized might have been why he felt so trapped. "What are you going to do?"

"I don't know," he said through clenched teeth. "All I can do is keep trying to take the throne. That's all. Then, when I'm finally crowned the ruler here, I'll be able to do whatever I want. I'll be free."

Something in his voice still lacked conviction. She wished she knew why, but the truth of the matter was that she really didn't know much about Theron—just that he'd been abused for so long and that there was a gentleness in him that no one else had ever cared enough to see. He deserved better than to be torn to shreds every day, hoping that one day he would get a title and a throne that he'd always been told he'd receive.

"You don't believe me," he said.

"What? No?"

He chuckled. "Very convincing." He smiled at her, but there was pain in his eyes. "It's okay. I don't know if I believe it either."

"Do you really want it?" she blurted. "The throne."

He thought for a moment. "I don't know. I don't know what I want."

Those words were the most honest ones he'd spoken tonight. The way he'd said them reminded her of that last time they'd met near her house. When he'd said he wasn't sure why he'd come to see her.

The uncertainty in his eyes, the confusion and conflict, reminded her of something else, too.

"I know how you feel," she said.

He lifted an eyebrow. "You do?"

She nodded, but her gaze fell. How could she express this? She'd never said it out loud. Not even to Phineas.

"I don't want to be a Great One," she said. "I don't think I've ever wanted to be. I just want to be Correlia. I don't want to be forced to plant fields and flowers and trees. I want to live my life. I want to practice fighting and have fun. I can work—I don't want to not work and be lazy or something. I just . . . I don't want to be . . . Persephone, Goddess of Life and Nature."

Saying the words out loud didn't feel like she'd expected. It didn't feel wrong. It was *relieving*. An enormous weight lifted from her shoulders the moment the words left her lips. And when she breathed out in relief, she looked up at Theron and studied his expression, wondering what was going on in that enigmatic mind of his.

"I don't want to be Hades." He said it quietly, like it was a scandalous secret, and perhaps it was.

She couldn't hide her stunned expression. "You don't?"

"No. I never have. I hate it. All of this. I absolutely hate it, but I have no choice." His jaw tightened again. "It's just the way it is. We're given what we're supposed to be given. We can't change our fates."

"Do you think that's true?" she asked, but she knew it was a long shot to even wonder if he knew the answer. She'd been sheltered most of her life, but even so, this didn't seem like the type of question given out at coronations or during training sessions. It was likely one of those answers locked away where only the Titans could find it.

"I don't know. It doesn't seem like it. I don't see how any of us can get out of it. We're doomed to whatever the Titans declared."

"There has to be a way we can change our destinies. Maybe we can figure something out. Maybe—"

"Don't be naïve."

"I'm just trying to help." She glared at him.

His face fell into his hands. "I'm sorry. Let's drop it. There's nothing we can do about it. There's no point dwelling on it."

"There has to be something," she said, but now she was the one who lacked conviction. She needed hope, and by the looks of his draped frame, Theron did, too.

"I've tried everything," he said, his voice shaky. He looked into her eyes and repeated, "*Everything*." The word came out ragged, and a tear fell down his face. As soon as it dropped, he sniffed and wiped his cheek, looking away. "You must be hungry," he said abruptly. "I'll get you something—"

Corre reached forward and wrapped her arms around him. "I'm so sorry," she whispered. "I wish I could take your pain away." After a quiet moment, she leaned back, starting to let go, but he wrapped his arms around her and squeezed her against him even tighter, burying his face in her neck.

Surprise rushed through her, but so did something else. Something like the feeling of butterflies landing on her skin on a warm day. She embraced him more fully, then lifted one of her hands to trail her fingers through his wavy hair, gathering it softly when she reached the ends. "I wish we could choose our fates."

Gently, his arms loosened, and he pulled back slightly. She did the same, and they locked eyes. As Corre sucked in a breath, Theron took her face in his hands and brought her lips to his. The softness of his kiss melted every bad feeling in her body and released them from her pores. Her brain was dizzy, and her legs were weak.

Her whole body was weak.

She let it fall against him, kissing him back, her arms resting on his shoulders, wrapped around his neck. He pressed into her, and she fell in a foggy wave onto the bed. He planted one more kiss on her mouth before releasing her.

When her eyes opened, she couldn't believe what had just happened. She sat up and touched a hand to her face. It was warm. *Really* warm. She looked to Theron, but he was already off the bed and flinging on his cloak.

"I have to train," he said, but his face was red.

"Okay," she said as he opened the door.

When he turned to look at her, her stomach fluttered, and she smiled.

The red dusting his cheeks darkened. "I'll see you soon," he said, then gently closed the door.

Long after he was gone, she still couldn't stop smiling.

CHAPTER TWENTY-FIVE

Theron

Theron sat in the cavernous battle chamber, his back resting against the cold stone wall. He welcomed the chilly air of the dungeon, despite there being no monster to fight.

Why did I tell her I had to train?

His face fell into his hands.

Why did I kiss her?

But he knew the answer.

He desperately wanted to.

He couldn't stop thinking about the fullness of her lips and how they felt on his. The way she tasted. The way she made his body ache, or how she made him go crazy inside.

He let out a calculated breath and rested against the wall.

"Correlia . . ."

The warm thoughts of her turned cold when he remembered the fear on her face. The way she'd shaken uncontrollably in his arms after he'd pulled her from the river. The panic he'd felt when she was sucked beneath the surface.

He thought he'd lost her.

The moment he saw those claws latch onto her.

Those claws.

"Isn't there any way?" Theron cried to the withered soul.

He tried shaking the memory away, but it was burned in his mind.

"I'm afraid not. Just be happy you were chosen to be one of the greats." The soul slunk away, dipping back into the bottomless pool.

He thought he'd erased that memory—pushed it into the deepest recesses of his mind.

He crouched down. He wanted to sink, too. Far, far away. Into complete nothingness.

No matter how much he wished it, he could never forget that day.

"This can't be it," he screamed at the creature. He couldn't believe there was no way out of this. That death couldn't come to its god. The creature popped her head back out of the neon river and nodded, a sinister smile stretched across her hollow cheeks. "I'm sorry, child, but it's the truth."

"It can't be."

The creature started back into the pool when Theron grabbed her arm and whipped it up, his arm burning from the acidic water. He saw something in the soul's face that made him despise this life even more. This mangled, eye-less creature was somehow staring at him with pity. With those empty sockets facing his reddened eyes.

Finally, milky eyes appeared in the sockets as she honed in on the wounds lashed across his face and the cuts on his arms. "I'm sorry, boy, but you're stuck here. Gods can't die so easily. Especially you."

"But—"

"Just be grateful you're one of the greats," the creature said again, and then she vanished into the Kokytus River.

Theron was left alone again.

It had only been a year since he was sent here, and already he wanted to die.

"What if I don't want to be one of the greats?" he whimpered, collapsing onto the freezing ground. He curled his body into a tight knot, tensing it until he felt nothing. Nothing and everything. His body was no longer in pain, but the emotions thrashing inside him were growing. They were too intense. He couldn't take it.

He dug his fingernails into his skin.

He needed the pain to go away.

He needed relief.

Because he didn't want to be here at all.

Theron shook his head and got to his feet. *Enough of that.* He left the dungeon and searched for one of his minions. *The past only drags you down.* When one of the familiar creatures was in view, he called after it. "You! Put a monster in the chamber. I need to train."

"Yes, sire," it said and fled down the corridor.

Theron stood there, frozen in place as he remembered the withered soul. That creature in the river who had swum with all the others. The female demon who wanted every soul to be sucked into the neon river's depths but his. He tried not to think of it. There was no use dwelling on the past.

But then he remembered that second creature. The one that had slithered from the cavern that day. The one that had come from the other side of the river.

"I can take you somewhere," it said. "Somewhere you can forget." It was a vulture with a blue, pointed beak, thick bones, and a corpse-like pallor. Its eyes were the same milky white as the Kokytus creature's disappearing ones.

"Somewhere I can forget?"

It nodded. "Another river. The one by the cave of Hypnos."

Theron frowned. "Hypnos?"

"You have never heard of the great Hypnos?"

He shook his head, but he was still numb inside. He didn't care what this creature thought of him or what lay ahead, or anything at all.

"He is the Great Deity of Slumber. I can take you to his river. There, you can forget everything."

The offer was tempting. The chance to lose the memories behind every scar could relieve part of his suffering, but even so, it wouldn't do any good. If he forgot everything, he'd have to continue on anyway, only without the memory of his training. The pain would be even worse, the punishments more severe. The time in that room would multiply.

It would only cause more pain.

"No," he finally said to the creature. "Forgetting will make me weak."

He got to his feet and ran as fast as he could to his room before he could change his mind. He ran until his lungs stung. If he was late to his next post, Thanatos would have his head, and then it would get sewn back on his body and he'd have to keep going, in even more pain than before.

'I need to grow up,' he thought. 'I need to become Hades. When I take the throne, no one can hurt me anymore.'

"I'll be feared by everyone," he whispered to himself with a grin. "Even Nikias."

He made the final turn to his room, but the sight of the blonde-headed boy made him freeze. Next to him were three other teens. Demons, but teenaged ones. Just like them. They all shared identical sneers.

"Well, well, well. Look who wasn't at his post," the boy said.

Theron's stomach soured.

Nikias stepped forward, his mouth curled into an impish smile. "Wait until I tell Master."

"Only weaklings need to cower behind others," he growled.

The demons around the boy cackled. Nikias stepped closer. The foes were the same height, both just as skinny, too, but there was something especially sinister about the blonde. Something he kept hidden behind his obnoxious composure.

He pushed the dark-haired boy into the wall. The shock of the blow made Theron trip and bash his head hard against the ground. Nikias and the others laughed. Theron's blood boiled. He got up and screamed, lunging at the other boy, pummeling him in the face. He knocked the blonde over and sat on him, punching his face over and over until blood spilled from Nikias's nose.

"I'm telling Master!" Nikias squealed, his voice breaking. He pushed against Theron's chest, but the god wouldn't back down.

Theron punched him harder and harder, not letting himself think about the punishment until after the two demons fled and came back with one of Thanatos's henchmen. The adult pulled Theron off his peer and tossed him against the wall.

"Come, boy," the henchman growled. "We're going to Thanatos." He snatched the dark-haired boy by the arm and led him to the throne room. The last thing Theron saw before he was taken to his master was Nikias's grin as he wiped the blood off his smackable face.

"Have fun in your playpen," the blonde said with a laugh.

Theron scowled and gave him a vulgar hand gesture before the henchman whirled him back around. The rest of the way to the throne room was agonizing, and as soon as he was brought before Thanatos, his master walked forward and struck him across the face.

"You will never be the great Hades if you let words affect you enough to attack your men," he shouted. He took the boy by the shirt and tossed him back toward the hallway. "You know your way."

Theron nodded and fought back tears as he walked to the room. The henchman stayed close behind so the boy wouldn't be found anywhere other than that palace of nightmares.

His hand shook as he opened the door, but he stayed strong. He thought about Nikias, and he thought about his plan.

'I'll be Hades one day. And then you'll be sorry. Everyone will be.'

"Sire?"

Theron jumped at the voice of his servant, his heart still pounding from the surfaced memory. "Yes? What is it?"

Its hunched frame bowed when it met his eyes. "The beast will be here shortly. Your sword will be fetched from your room."

"All right," he said, but as the demon turned, Theron's eyes widened. *Correlia.*

"No! Wait! I'll fetch it myself!"

"But, sire—"

"I said I'll fetch it myself!"

The creature bowed. "As you wish."

He raked a hand through his hair and pushed past the demon to make it back to his chambers. His heart raced even faster as he thought of Correlia. About her delicate body, and the fire in her eyes. Of the way she tasted when he kissed her.

His face reddened, and he wondered how he was going to face her when he opened the door. But when he did, he found her standing in a fighting stance in the middle of his room.

He lunged forward and prepared to fight whatever was there. She burst into laughter. "What are you doing?"

He frantically scanned the room, but no one else was there. "I thought you were in trouble."

She laughed again. "No, I'm just practicing."

His eyebrows lifted. "Practicing fighting?"

"Yes, what else? I told you I don't just grow flowers."

"I didn't think you—" He spotted his sword and remembered he needed to hurry. "Well, you can have fun practicing in here to your heart's content. Just don't make any noise."

He picked up his sword and started to leave when she said, "Wait! Can I come with you?"

His eyes widened. "No!"

"Come on! I'm stronger than I look."

"*No.*"

She scowled. "I'm coming whether you like it or not."

He paused. "Fine. Just . . . be careful." The tips of his ears warmed. "I don't want you to get hurt."

She flashed him a grin. "You care about me," she teased.

His face instantly went white-hot. "No, I don't! I just don't want—" He stopped and closed his eyes. He pondered before saying it, but he didn't let himself think too hard about it before he blurted it out. "Fine. I do care about you. Happy?" When he opened his eyes, she wasn't smiling anymore, and panic flooded through him. "I-I mean—"

"No," she said, shaking her head slowly and walking toward him.

"No?"

"I mean . . . I don't want you to take it back." She was close to him now, looking straight up at him with those mystical eyes and long, curled eyelashes. "I care about you, too," she whispered, pink rising along her cheekbones. "But I want to train with you. So let me. I'll be careful."

Her lips formed a small pout, and he couldn't resist leaning down and kissing her again. A short but needful kiss. Her eyes were wide when he pulled away.

"Put this on and be quiet as you follow me," he said quickly, taking off his cloak and draping it over her shoulders.

A shade of pink swept across the freckles on her nose as she nodded, but she didn't say another word.

He smiled. "I didn't know I could make you so flustered."

She shot him a glare. "Let's just go," but as she walked past him into the labyrinth, he could see the corner of her mouth turn up into a smile.

Corre

Corre watched him strike down yet another monster, but this one was small compared to the last one. It was a mix between a lion and some kind of horned, shape-shifting feline. It didn't take him long before the creature was dead on the floor. Maybe it was because he was putting more effort into it. He wielded his sword with even more precision than she'd seen earlier that day, but he'd ultimately killed it with some unseen power.

She couldn't help but feel like the added effort was for her benefit, which made that same butterfly sensation extend to her chest.

When he turned around, she clapped. "Bravo!"

"Ts," he said as he kicked the sword to the side of the wall. "It was nothing."

"It did look like nothing for you. It was effortless. You're very good." She smiled up at him, but he turned away, shifting uncomfortably. She frowned. "What?"

"What?" he said, almost defensively.

She searched the trace of discomfort in his eyes, deciphering his reaction. "Are you not used to compliments?"

He looked down and kicked a rock. She took his silence as a 'no' and reached up to kiss him on the cheek.

He looked at her with surprise, and she winked. "We'll work on that."

His gaze returned to the ground. "You liked the fight?"

"I did." She smiled. "It put up quite a fight, but . . . How do you do that?"

"Do what?"

"That power." She lifted her hands and made the face he'd used to take down the beast.

He threw his head back in laughter.

"What?" she said, her smile widening.

"Your face. Do I really look like that?"

"You do!" She made the face again, and he laughed.

"I do not." He bit down a smile, and she giggled.

"Show me," she said, nudging him playfully.

"My face?"

"No!" She laughed. "How you do that!"

"My power?"

"Yes!"

He inched closer and looked into her eyes. "You have to focus. *Really* focus, and then get into the other person's thoughts. Feel out their senses until you can envision what's in their mind." He lifted his hand to show her, but he was still smiling.

"I can't tell if you're being serious or not."

"I *am* being serious, but it's a lot harder than it looks, and it would take more than me telling you how it works to teach you how to do it."

She gasped in delight. "You'll teach me how to do it?"

Regret flashed across his face. "What?"

"If you teach me, I'll teach you how *I* fight."

He bit his bottom lip, tucking in a smile. "Is that so?"

"Hey, you don't know my moves."

He laughed. "And what moves are those?"

She took a step back, stood in her regular fighting stance with her arms propped up, and then kicked in the air, twirling swiftly, and then ending it facing him in the other direction. He clapped with an exaggerated impressed look on his face.

She straightened. "Ha ha," She rolled her eyes, smiling. "You don't have to act impressed."

"I *am* impressed!"

"Whatever!" she said with a laugh, heat rising up her cheeks again. "If mine is so lame, then why don't you show me how you would do it?"

"I never said it was lame," he said, walking behind her, "but I would do it like this." He pressed his body against her back and slid his hands down her arms, repositioning them to be higher and at a slightly different angle. "There. Now, move your legs a bit."

She shifted forward, but it was hard to focus with her heart pounding at the way his body felt against hers. "Like this?"

"Yeah, there you go."

She whipped around with her new stance. "How do I look?"

He smiled. "Beautiful."

Something tugged in her chest, and her stomach fluttered. He took a slow step forward.

"Are you sure?"

"You're perfect," he said softly, and his body pressed softly against hers.

Her lips parted, and she moved her hands up his arms. She tried to think of something to say but couldn't find her voice. She watched her fingertips trail along the perfectly sculpted muscles on his arms before looking back up. When her eyes locked back on his, he grabbed her face and kissed her.

The moment she tasted his lips, her body sparked to life. Her mind hazed as the blood rushed through her veins in fiery waves. She pushed into him, kissing him deeply.

This kiss was different than the last. It was urgent and beautifully intense. She was addicted to every movement of his lips and brush of his tongue. When she pushed herself into him even more, he staggered back, his back pressing into a wall. Her heart thumped wildly against his. He grabbed her wrists and whipped her around, pinning her to the wall. Excitement surged through her. His hands rushed up her sides and grasped the back of her neck. The fire in her veins continued its delicious rage as she melted into his touch.

She was delighted by this newfound discovery. This pandora's box of sensations. She'd never known such feelings existed. It was like lightning rushing through her body, sparking through her blood and warming every muscle and nerve.

His hands made their way to the small of her back, and he pulled her up into his arms. With her body lifted against his, she let her legs wrap around his waist. Her face was higher than his now, and she kissed him even deeper as her hair fell around him. He released his lips from hers and kissed her cheek, trailing down her neck. She forgot to breathe when he kissed beneath her ear and down to her collarbone. When his lips made it just above her chest, he licked up to her mouth, and she thought her soul had left her body completely.

She slid back to the ground and grabbed him hungrily, kissing him with everything in her. He sunk his kiss deeper into her, sucking on her bottom lip and trailing his tongue across hers. She never wanted this to end. She never wanted to be released from this spell.

She wanted him to ignite this fire in her blood forever.

"We should go back to my room," he said, kissing her slowly one more time.

"Okay," she said breathlessly. "But you'll need to take me there."

He smiled and kissed her again. "As you wish."

CHAPTER TWENTY-SIX

Theron

Theron laid her on the bed, his lips refusing to leave hers as he fell on top of her. His blood pulsed through his body in blazing surges as he kissed her in feverish urgency, feeling her body move beneath his. The passion in her was electric—a wild force, unleashed and feral. It made that burning sensation rising within him burn further with unbridled intensity.

Her hands gripped his back, gathering his shirt in her fingers as he nipped at her neck. He'd never felt like this before. It was like all the pain he'd ever experienced had melted away. Like everything was suddenly okay because of this fire between them. This untamed, affectionate feeling. This ravenous need. It was lightning shooting through his body, making him yearn to become one with her, unsatisfied with any space left between them.

He kissed down her neck, lightly trailing his teeth against her skin. His hands moved up her legs and started grazing her inner thighs when she pulled back. Suppressing a sad grumble, he looked up at her.

"I-I don't think I'm ready to go further," she said.

He swallowed, nodding as he kept the river of fire surging through his body at bay. "Okay." He smiled, leaning down and pressing his lips against hers one last time before falling next to her. He closed his eyes and steadied his breath, easing the feelings still raging inside him.

She turned on her side and smiled, scrunching her nose in the most adorable way as she brushed the side of his face with the back of her hand. He forced himself to ignore the way her legs were exposed and the way her chest was half-poured out of her dress and kept his gaze fixed on her eyes.

"Sorry," she said.

He smiled back and placed his hand gently on her cheek. "Don't be. It's okay. Whatever you're ready for is more than enough." He kept a reassuring smile plastered on his face.

The last thing he'd ever want was to make her uncomfortable. As he looked at her now, flushed and smiling, something gleaming in her eyes, he suddenly wished he could gift her the world and everything in it. Everything good and worth having.

He would move Mt. Olympus for her. Give everything he had just to see her this happy forever.

"Thank you," she whispered, scooting closer to him and resting her head on his pillow.

He wrapped his arm around her and held her against his chest. Closing his eyes, he took in her warmth, her heart beating in rhythmic thumps with his. "I should be the one thanking you."

She looked up at him. "For what?"

"For making me feel like I could actually be cared for."

The gleam in her eyes faded, and a spike of worry splintered through his chest until she said, "You're worthy of being cared for." Her frown softened into a smile. "I'm very fond of you."

He smiled, swallowing the emotion lumped in his throat. "I'm very fond of you, too. And I've never been fond of anyone." He leaned down and kissed her, then closed his eyes and placed his forehead on hers. "You're the embodiment of happiness, Correlia. I wish I could keep you forever."

She didn't say anything for a moment, then finally whispered, "I wish you could, too."

Tears threatened to fall down his face, so he kissed her again. And kissed her. And kissed her. Until she leaned back and whispered, "It isn't fair."

"What isn't?"

"That we were born to be enemies."

Her eyes welled with tears as they searched his. The pain in her sunflower eyes cranked something deep within his chest. He wished he could take away the pain, but all he could offer her was this embrace and the words that sat at the tip of his tongue. With one large palm, he cupped the side of her face and leaned in close. His nose brushed against hers as he whispered her name. "Correlia," he breathed, "you could never be my enemy."

She blinked away the dewy tears with a half-sob, half-laugh, but he still spotted something sad in her eyes before she nestled into his chest. He stroked her hair, twirling it between his fingers as it fell between her shoulder blades. He loved the unique color of it. Like the sun setting in a blushing sky. From afar, her hair looked like golden light poured from the stars, but the closer she got, the more he could see the beautiful rose tint that made it a light, golden pink. She was truly the embodiment of life at its brightest and most beautiful.

"I don't know how much longer we can stay like this," she whispered, emotion brimming in her voice.

"Let's not think about it," he said, but he couldn't *not* think about it. His heart cracked every time he thought of never seeing her again and never being able to hold her like this or feel her lips on his. "Tell me something. Anything."

"Okay," she said with a sniff. She hummed thoughtfully. "I don't remember my life before I was six."

His hand stopped on her back. "Oh?"

She nodded against his chest. "I think something very bad happened to me, but I don't know what."

He slowly started stroking her hair again, running his fingers down her back. "I don't remember mine either."

She leaned back. "Really?"

"Yeah . . . I mean, I remember enough. I was thirteen when I came."

She frowned. "That's somehow worse."

"Than what?"

She combed her fingers through his hair. "Than losing your memory as a child. You would have remembered your life before this one. And that would make that pain so much worse." Her eyes flickered to his. "Did it?"

"I don't know. I don't remember much of my life before coming here. I remember my parents, and I thought they cared about me, especially my mother, but they let me get sent here, and I think they were glad."

"Glad? Why?"

His stomach twisted as he remembered the look his mother gave him right before they were told he was Hades. "I think she was afraid of me."

Correlia's fingers gently scratched his head as they trailed through his hair. "I'm sorry," she whispered, the sincerity in her voice so genuine, so kind.

"It's okay," he lied.

"No. It's not. It's okay to say that it's not."

It is okay, he wanted to say, but the truth was that a day didn't go by when he didn't think about his mother. When he didn't wonder what had gone through her mind as he'd been grabbed and dragged to the Underworld by a drove of demons—creatures that were so terrifying that the mere sight of them had ripped at his insides as they'd sunk their claws into his skinny arms.

Tears slid down his cheeks in warm streaks. "I don't know how they could let that happen." He looked at Correlia, his breath shuddering. "I don't know how they could let me go. Their screaming, terrified son." He shook his head as more tears slithered down his face. "I don't believe they loved me. I can't imagine how they could have. I don't know much about love, but I don't think you could do that to someone if you loved them."

Correlia wrapped her arms around him, and he grabbed onto her, crying into her as silently as he could. Thanatos would have given him the worst punishment imaginable if he knew he was letting himself cry, let alone to her. Such a beautiful, powerful goddess who might actually care about him. Somehow. For some reason.

"How can you care about someone like me?" he whispered.

She reached up and kissed him, cradling his face in her hands. "It's easy. You're stronger and kinder than you realize."

He scoffed. "Don't tell anyone, or I'll be a dead man. Well—worse. A forever tortured god."

She stroked along his jawline. "Don't worry. Your secret's safe with me."

He stared at her, still completely baffled. Surely, she was lying. "No one could care about a monster like me."

"You're not a monster. And I do care about you. No matter what you tell yourself, or what Thanatos or anyone else tells you. I care about you, and you're worthy of being cared for." She leaned in closer, burying her gaze into his. "Okay?"

He smiled, more effortlessly than he knew he could, and swallowed the welling emotion gathering in his throat. "Okay."

"Okay. Good," she said, her smile widening, dimpling her cheeks.

He thought for a minute, then said, "So you don't remember any of your childhood? Before you were six?"

"No. Not even bits or pieces. I think my parents died, but I don't know how or why. They may have abandoned me. I'm not sure. I was raised by

Demeter. Her real name is Berenice. She's the only mother I've ever known, and she's always loved me. I'm grateful for that. Really, I am, but . . . it's just . . . I don't know. I wish I knew what happened to my other parents. You know?"

"I understand."

"I'm sorry. I must sound spoiled."

"No. Not at all. You have every right to be upset and confused. Sometimes, not knowing is worse than knowing the truth, regardless of how bad it is."

She sighed. "Yeah, but you've had it so much worse."

"That doesn't matter. It doesn't matter what anyone else has gone through. Don't discount the hardships of your life because they've been different than mine."

She smiled softly, the white of her eyes reddening. "Thank you, Theron. That means a lot to me."

The way she looked at him made something in him churn. He wished he could take every ounce of pain away from her. Someone so good should never have to suffer. After a moment, he looked down and said, "Markus."

"What?"

"My real name. It's Markus."

When he looked back at her, his heart fluttered. Her smile was soft, her freckles like stars beneath her green-gold eyes.

"Markus. I like it. It suits you."

Hearing his name on her lips warmed something inside him. He didn't know what to say. No one had called him by his real name in a long time.

"Why did you change it?" she asked. "Especially if you'd be named Hades anyway."

"I didn't. Thanatos did. He didn't want me tied to my past, but he wasn't ready to call me Hades until I earned it. So, he gave me a warrior's name. That's what he said, anyway."

"Well, I'll call you Markus. If that's okay with you."

He couldn't help but smile, his chest still warm. "Yes, it's okay with me."

It's more than okay, he wanted to say. *It's everything to me.*

"Good," she said before letting out a yawn and stretching out her free arm. "I'm exhausted. Let's go to bed."

"Okay." He kissed her one more time. First on the mouth, then on the tip of her nose and her forehead. "Good night, Correlia."

"Good night, Markus."

Markus.

He didn't think he'd ever get sick of her calling him that, even though he was supposed to have forgotten it long ago. If Thanatos knew he'd told anyone—let alone her—he'd get the beating of a lifetime. But he didn't care. It was worth it just to hear it in her voice, coming from the soft lips that sent ripples of light through his veins.

He watched as her eyes fluttered closed and the breaths on her chest evened and slowed. He nestled closer to her and rested his chin on the top of her head, pressing his lips gently against her hair as she fell deeply into sleep.

He loved holding her, but it also made him realize how much he was starting to care for her. It was terrifying. What if something happened to her? She was so vulnerable in a place like this, where monsters and evil creatures lurked, ready to sink their claws and teeth into someone so pure and full of sunshine. He couldn't stand the thought of anything happening to her.

As he held her in his arms, it was impossible to ignore the intense need he felt to protect her. To shield her from everything he'd ever been subjected to. He had to protect her from beings like Snoke and Nikias at all costs, and he would do anything it took to protect her.

He tried not to think about what his life would be like when she went back to Mt. Olympus. When all of this faded into a cruelly beautiful dream.

He tried to think only of what he could do to keep her with him when he became Hades for good. When this place was his, and he called the shots and made the rules.

Things could be different then. He let himself believe that. That he could be happy one day. In love, even. Just like everyone else.

Even if it was a lie, he let himself believe it. Whatever let him keep this glorious feeling alive—this feeling that numbed his broken, bruised bones and filled him with warmth and sunlight instead. Just so he could cherish it as long as he possibly could. Because he knew it wouldn't last forever. It couldn't. It wasn't in the stars for someone like him.

CHAPTER
TWENTY-SEVEN

Phineas

P hineas hit the target with the iron arrow, threw the bow to the ground, and ran to the armed warrior head-on. His opponent was more skilled than the others, but he'd improved enough in his technique that it only took him one stride and the right footwork to take out the curly-haired god before he could dodge any subsequent attacks and make it to the other side of the trees, marking the end of the course.

The curly-haired god was around the same age as Phineas and was one of the best opponents he'd ever faced. He had the broad shoulders and wide build of a warrior but lacked the proper training to match how far the young Ares had come over the last few months. On top of that, the training course had become even more rigorous, which served Phineas well. He was getting better. He was focused and finally overcoming some of the obstacles he'd never been able to.

It helped that Corre wasn't there. It was hard for him to think whenever she was around.

"Good work, Terraceus," Phineas said, offering a hand to the fallen soldier and lifting him out of the dirt.

"Thanks," the god mumbled, avoiding Phineas's gaze. Terraceus had been one of Athena's top pupils, and, for a while, Phineas was pretty sure they'd all thought he'd never surpass him. He was bound to at some point, though. He *was* Ares. It was his duty. His birthright.

When Terraceus walked by him, Phineas clapped a hand on his shoulder. "Hey, can you hold on?"

The other god stopped but still didn't meet Phineas's gaze. "What is it?"

The young Ares let his shoulder go and walked over to face him. "You're the best warrior I've ever seen." Terraceus huffed and started to leave again when Phineas quickly added, "I'm going to recruit soon. I need to get my army together."

The curly-haired warrior stopped, then slowly swiveled on his heel to study Phineas with narrowed eyes. "What's gotten into you?"

"What do you mean?"

"You're different."

"I was going to say the same thing," a melodic voice interjected.

Phineas turned to see Athena, whose ruby lips were turned into a half-smile. "I watched you carefully today, and with that clear shot," she nodded toward the fallen bow, "you could give Apollo a run for his money."

"Just focused on the craft," Phineas said, but he couldn't hide the satisfaction on his face. Athena wasn't one to throw around compliments.

"Of war?"

Phineas gave one nod. "Of war."

She eyed him steadily. "Why the sudden focus?"

"Exactly what I was wondering," Terraceus said. His pinched face still watched Phineas warily.

He flinched. Maybe it wasn't the best idea to bring Terraceus on as one of his soldiers.

No, I need to. He's the best.

"I just—"

"You're worried," Athena said. It wasn't a question, and Phineas knew there was no lying to his mentor, so he gave her another quick nod.

"There's been a lot of talk—"

"Of Hades," she said. Again, not a question.

"Yes. Of Hades."

"His men have been everywhere," she said with a sigh.

Phineas nodded again, but his fists clenched at the thought of him. *Theron.* Just thinking about him made his blood boil. It wasn't even what he'd done to him that day that had made him so angry. It was what he'd done to Corre.

He'd done *something* to her. Phineas was sure of it. The way her eyes looked after she'd run into him was more than enough indication that something was off, and she'd been off ever since. Like her mind had been altered. He'd taken her focus away and beguiled her somehow. And she hadn't even been scared. It was almost as if she'd found him *intriguing.* There was no telling the kind of wicked power the monster held. Corre might not be strong enough to resist that curiosity of hers or her notorious recklessness. It had gotten them in trouble more than once in their lives.

"Phineas, let's go to Lerna. I heard you can see the new baby dragons there," she'd said when they were about ten years old. He'd vehemently shook his head.

"No, Corre, we'll get caught, and that old Belen will get after us again." The giant, boar-like man hated children more than his pets' excrements, and he especially hated children who messed with his things, riling up his creatures and forcing him to chase after them and move faster than a tortoise.

"So?" she said, one of her teeth missing as she grinned mischievously. He was convinced she enjoyed getting into trouble.

"So? So we could get our butts whooped again!" he said, but she just laughed and said they were twice as fast as the old brute and could outrun him.

"We didn't outrun him last time," Phineas said flatly.

She'd groaned and continued pleading her case until he finally relented. And, lo and behold, they'd gotten caught, and Phineas's heart had practically ground its way into powder at how fast and hard it pounded in his chest to the other edge of the woods.

After they'd finally caught their breath and Corre had sprawled herself out onto the thick grass, moving her palms through the dirt like she was swimming on the forest floor, she'd said, *"See? I told you we could outrun 'im."*

Although Phineas had been furious at the ordeal she'd put him through, he smiled. She was the bravest girl he'd ever met. The bravest kid period. And he'd been in awe.

"All right, I'll do it."

Phineas stared at the platinum-curled god in shock. "What?"

"I'll do it. I'll be in your army. But I have to be second-in-command."

Phineas's heart leapt. "Yes, of course." A smile stretched across his face, but Terraceus's expression only darkened.

"If what you and everyone else have said is true, a war is coming, and I want to be prepared." He looked at Phineas in a way that made the young Ares swallow hard.

A war was coming. And he needed to lead.

"Okay," Phineas said weakly, but Athena clapped him on the back.

"You'll do great," she said, and he tried his best not to show what he was really feeling.

"Yeah," he whispered, still very much uncertain, but he knew he needed to trust her. He had to live up to his title. He squared his shoulders and looked up. "Okay," he said again, firmer this time. "Terraceus." The god looked at him, and Phineas gestured to the woods behind him. "Let's go again."

Corre

Corre woke up the next morning, giddy to see Theron still sleeping in the bed next to her. No. *Markus.*

She trailed her fingers along his jawline, moving her hand up to brush one of his dark curls out of his face. She stroked his hair and marveled at the blackness of it. It looked like a liquid night sky without any stars. Like a potion made from the universe.

When he made a pained moan, her stomach dropped. His face was strained, and his body jerked slightly. His teeth clenched as he began writhing, sweating. She shook him gently. "Markus. Wake up." He didn't budge. "Wake up," she pleaded. "You're having a nightmare."

His body jerked again.

"Markus!"

He gasped, his torso lunging forward. Sweat had stuck his hair to the back of his neck, and his chest was heaving.

"Markus," she said again, but his name came out in a gasp. He looked at her in shock, his eyes still reeling from some unseen thing in his dreams. "What's wrong?" He wiped a hand down his face, taking calculated breaths.

Corre scooted closer and rested her head on his shoulder. When he was okay with that, she placed an arm loosely around his shirtless torso. She closed her eyes and held him like that until his heart stopped racing and his breathing returned to normal.

"It was just a nightmare," he said at last, the bass of his voice humming in her ear. He looked down at her, his frown deepening. "What?"

"I'm worried. You were in so much distress."

He took another deep breath. "Yeah. I was."

"Do you always have nightmares?"

He paused. "Yes."

"Like that?" He nodded. She hesitated before asking, "What are they about?" He shifted his body awkwardly, and she rested her back on the headboard. "It's okay. You don't have to tell me."

"No. It's all right. It's just . . . a memory-night from when I was young. The day I came here. It was horrendous." He gave her a forced smile. "Seems like my mind is bent on torturing me. I can't even rest while I'm asleep."

Corre's head fell to his shoulder again. "Sounds terrible."

"It is."

"You were thirteen, right?"

"Yes, and it was only the beginning of a life of nightmares."

"It doesn't have to be like that. Your life doesn't have to be full of nightmares."

He snorted. "Right."

"I'm serious. You can change your life."

He laughed tightly. "You think my situation is better than it is."

"No, I don't, which is why I want to help you change it."

"How could we possibly do that?"

"I don't know." Her mind reeled. There had to be something.

"Well . . . I guess I could change things . . ."

A smile broke across her face. "Really?"

"Maybe. When I take the throne."

"Markus! Yes! Of course. We should focus on that!" She grabbed his hand, but his body was still rigid, and his eyes were no happier than they'd been when he'd woken up. Her shoulders fell. "Why don't you seem happy? Or hopeful?"

His eyes shifted to hers, but his body stayed stuck in place. "Correlia . . ." His voice trailed off and, for a long time, he didn't speak. He looked like he wanted to, so she waited. Finally, he said, "Do you know why we were appointed our roles on Mt. Olympus?"

She frowned. "Yes, I think so."

"So you know who made the Decree."

The Decree. She learned of it in school and was taught by her mother. She knew the story backward and forward. It was the only thing that held any answers. "The Mighty Decree."

"The Mighty Decree," he spat like the words were poison on his tongue.

The Mighty Decree was created by the Titans and a certain set of Great Deities at the beginning of everything. When the world was created and Mt. Olympus was formed, the twelve mighty Titans created the first round of gods and goddesses. The Original Chosen. These included Zeus, Hera, Athena, Hermes, Demeter, and many others. They hadn't been given any titles at the time of their creation, and thus, there'd been no order. The world was in chaos. Confusion and disarray.

Seeing the mayhem, the Titans and the greatest, most powerful deities formed what was now referred to as the Mighty Decree. This set the laws and regulations of Mt. Olympus that would then spread to the remaining world. It was in this decree that each god and goddess had been given his or her respective title and responsibilities. There needed to be order, so each Titan made a plan to make it so.

There needed to be a god or goddess for absolutely everything. And when the Original Chosen had children—and there were still many other roles that needed to be filled—more titles were appointed. Most children were taken to the Moirai—beings who could see the prophecies of each child as an infant—and then the Titans bestowed upon them their titles and gave their parents their responsibilities to fill, and any other information they needed to know.

Which was why it was odd that Markus had been so old when he was taken to the Underworld, and that his parents weren't his guardians. Had he also been appointed as a baby? Had he always known his fate?

Not every child was given a title, so it was very possible that he'd been an 'unblessed god' before being burdened with the title of Hades. Corre never liked that term. Unblessed gods and goddesses had 'lesser' abilities and no grand purposes for the mortals of Earth. To Corre, each god and goddess had a unique purpose, but the Titans didn't see it that way. Therefore, the Great Ones on Olympus often didn't see it that way, which caused a lot of contention, and undue and undeserved respect on the worthy and disrespect on the innocent.

"The Mighty Decree is just a piece of paper," she said.

"A powerful piece of indestructible paper." He cast her a wry smile.

"I'm serious."

"So am I." His smile fell. "There's nothing we can do."

"Then why bring it up?"

"Because I will be Hades one day. But," his voice quieted, his body tensing, "you know I have no choice but to wait. The Titans give us our titles—with Zeus's help—and we have to deal with it and do what we're told."

"Exactly. The Might Decree says you're Hades, and, Markus, you're twenty-five. You should have been given the throne by now."

Pain flickered in his eyes. "I *will* take the throne one day. I'm simply not ready yet."

"*Thanatos* says you're not ready, but does he get to decide that?"

"What?"

"It isn't his call, is it? The Titans appointed which god would rule the Underworld. You were chosen as part of the Mighty Decree." She squeezed his hand. "If it's not up to him, you can find a way to it. To take what's rightfully yours."

The shadow of a smile passed on his lips but vanished almost instantly. "There's no way for me to know. Thanatos is the only Great Deity here, and he says I'm not ready. So that's that, I guess."

"That can't be it," she said, running a hand gently through his hair. "You're the strongest god I've ever seen. Something isn't right."

Markus stared off but didn't speak. She didn't expect him to, but she'd hoped he would. She hoped he might have some idea of how he could finally take his place as ruler of the Underworld.

She wasn't sure if she should say it, but she needed him to know.

She looked right at him and said, "Someone told me that Thanatos was a placeholder and that his days are numbered on the throne. Is that true?"

He blinked. "What? Who told you that?"

"I don't know his name. I found him here, actually. He was a scruffy-looking mortal."

"A mortal? In Tartarus?" She nodded. He pondered it, still frowning. "That doesn't make any sense. Are you sure he was mortal?"

"I guess I can't be completely sure, but he looked like one."

He leaned back, raking his hand through his hair. "So, this person—this mortal—said Thanatos's days are numbered?"

"Yes. That he's a placeholder."

"Well, I know that. He's not Hades. I am."

"Exactly. There must be something we can do so you can take the throne. Because Markus," she scooted closer and took his hands in hers. "I don't think he'll ever give it to you willingly."

He shook his head and got to his feet. "He's been training me. He's made me who I am. He'll do it. I'm just not ready."

Corre's stomach dropped. She was losing him. "Markus, no. Are you listening?"

"Yes, I am." The words came out clipped. His eyes were still lost in thought. One feeling between them was mutual: nothing was making any sense. Finally, he sighed, and any edginess in his voice faded away. "Maybe you're right."

The knot in her stomach loosened. "So will you help me?" The hope in her chest soared, but when he turned and looked at her, he didn't have to say a thing. She knew what he was thinking.

And just like that, all the hope she'd held in her body crashed to the ground.

"I'm sorry," he muttered. "I just don't think I can."

"You *can*," she said, rising to her feet. She held his face in her hands and looked deep into his eyes. "I promise you, you can."

He didn't shake her off. He didn't resist. He didn't do anything but look at her with tears forming in his eyes. When his lip started to quiver, he gathered her in his arms and held her against his chest. As he silently cried, she held him.

There was no use making him feel more torn than he already did right now. Or to make him admit the abuse he was finally starting to see. He didn't need to decide anything right now.

It was okay for him to just *be*.

"It's okay," she whispered, brushing her hand along his back. "It'll be okay. I promise."

She held him until he was ready to start his training for the day. After he silently got ready, she kissed him on the cheek and wished him good luck. He smiled and thanked her, then quietly left the room.

And although the pain in her heart was getting worse, she knew that he needed rest for the time being. Mental rest.

They could talk about this another day.

She just hoped it wouldn't be too late.

Corre spent the following hours paralyzed in thought. She couldn't stop thinking about Markus and how little time she had left here. She thought about her mother, of Phineas, and her looming 20th birthday. Her chest tightened.

She welcomed the sound of Markus's voice when he came back mid-day, just as her stomach started to growl. "I brought bread and cheese," he said, eyes bright with no hint of the conversation they'd had earlier.

She let out a deep sigh of relief and took the food from his bruised hands, but the relief soon turned to horror when she saw his purple, tattered hands. "Your knuckles! What did you fight today? Did you not have your sword?"

He took a hunk of cheese and sat next to her. "I had my sword. I just didn't have the chance to use it." He tossed the food in his mouth.

"Because?"

"Because it was a chimera," he said with a groan, lying back on the bed.

A pang of terror scurried up her back. "A chimera? Markus, I—"

He sat up and kissed her, and the zing of his lips blurred her thoughts and left her dizzy.

"I love when you call me that." When she opened her eyes, he was smiling so fully she couldn't think of anything else.

Her nose crinkled as she smiled and kissed him on the cheek. "I like *calling* you that."

He leaned forward and kissed her on the cheek, and then her lips, her neck, and down to her collarbone. When a breath snagged in her throat, she closed her eyes and let herself fall onto the bed. He moved to hover over her and kissed her deeply. She flung her arms around him right before her stomach let out an agonizingly long growl.

His lips let go of hers, and he burst into peals of laughter.

Her cheeks warmed. "That's so embarrassing," she said, slapping her hand to her forehead.

"No, you need to eat. Come on. Up!" He took her hands and pulled her up. He handed her a generous piece of bread. "If you hurry, you can come train with me."

Her face lit up. "Really?" He nodded, his lips stretched into another wide smile. She beamed and took the bread, throwing the whole thing into her mouth.

"What are you doing?!" he cried, and she laughed, her cheeks as full as a squirrel's.

"I nee' to 'urry," she said before gulping it down. She regretted swallowing the whole thing when it stuck in a great bump in her throat. While she struggled to work it down, he chuckled. "What?" she asked flatly, finally gulping it down.

"Do you want something to drink?"

"Yes." She glared at his amused expression. "And then we'll train, right?"

His eyes softened, and he stroked the side of her face, letting his fingers fall down her neck. "Of course. Whatever you'd like."

She leaned forward and kissed him, and when he grabbed hold of her, kissing her in that marvelous way that made her head spin, she decided she could wait to train. The dungeon wasn't going anywhere.

CHAPTER TWENTY-EIGHT

Corre

A lthough bringing color and life to the world was her calling, Corre had never been good at it. Combat, on the other hand, had always come easily, which was why her inability to master or even wrap her head around the basics of Markus's techniques was excruciatingly frustrating. His abilities were unlike anything she'd ever seen or heard of, but he made them look effortless. His power was immense and a little intimidating.

She couldn't comprehend what was behind it all. Even with her greatest efforts, she couldn't get the basics down. Her face scrunched as she held her hands out in front of her, trying to form the ball of power he'd told her to concentrate between her palms. "I don't feel anything," she said, her voice strained. The muscles in her temples were starting to throb, but she kept her eyes focused between her hands.

"You need to focus—"

"I *am* focusing!"

He grumbled something under his breath, then cupped her hands in his. The warmth of his touch derailed her focus even more. She tried to get back to it, but it was like her mind had tripped and she was trying to force it to sprint again. He closed her fingers in his hands. "Not like that," he said calmly. She let her muscles relax, her arms dropping limply in front of her, her fingers still entangled with his. Her body ached from the tension.

"I don't get how I'm supposed to do this. You just gather some kind of power in your hands?"

"No, not—" He ran his hand through his hair as he stopped to think. "You have to focus on something you really want, and you can't have any distractions, at least not when you're starting out. You need to be able to focus on something you really want and then channel that feeling into gathering power from the space around you. Then, with that concentrated matter, you can push into your opponent."

"Mentally?"

"No, physically. The mental part is a different technique."

She closed her eyes, her head falling back in defeat. She wanted to scream. This was so confusing. So incredibly frustrating. "I *am* focusing on something I want. I want to gather that blasted power."

"That's not enough," he said, kicking at a rock on the dusty ground. The dirt was soaked with dried blood from the chimera he'd pulverized earlier.

How did he do it? How did he become so strong?

She thought about the scars on his back and of that gaping wound and the state he'd been in when she'd found him here. Maybe she needed to be patient. She'd only been at this for a couple of hours. Not over a decade. She let out a breath and rolled her shoulders back, lifting her arms again, her hands out in front of her like she was holding a ball in front of her chest. "Okay. I'll try harder."

He smiled and gave her a nod. "Good. It's important to focus on something you truly, deeply desire—something much more significant to you than learning these techniques. Let those feelings guide you to a deeper strength. That's the first step. You need to channel passion. But first, you need to find what that is."

She closed her eyes and searched. What was something she wanted so deeply that she could steal from the matter around her? Something from her soul. She thought about growing fields of flowers, but that wasn't good enough. That was a duty she was expected to perform, not one she was passionate about. Not something she desired.

She thought about protecting her mother and about becoming Persephone to make her proud.

Still nothing.

Beating Athena in a training round? No. Plus, that would never happen. And Corre could care less if it ever did.

What do I want?

The air in her chest clenched, her lungs working to pump it evenly. *Maybe I can't do this.* Her mind reeled, but then she thought of Markus. The way he smiled at her so unabashedly. The way he was growing less and less inhibited around her. The way he'd kissed her neck and held her while they slept.

And she thought about leaving him. Of the pain she would soon face when they had to part, knowing she was leaving him here in the hands of an evil puppet master who knew exactly what to say and do to make him feel small.

She fumed at the thought. Her chest ached.

Suddenly, her body was bright and loud and unleashed, and a spark fizzed through her palms. She opened her eyes to see if anything was there, but she saw nothing. Anything she'd felt disappeared.

Her arms flopped back down. "I thought I had something!"

"You did." He grabbed her hand and kissed it. "I sensed it." He trailed a finger across her palm, then looked into her eyes. "Right here."

Her cheeks burned, and a gust of air whirred around them. She looked everywhere but still saw nothing. "What was that?"

He chuckled. "You won't be able to see it. You're gathering power from what's around you, and you'll be able to keep it concentrated enough to use it." He shook his head. "But you won't be able to see it."

Now that he mentioned it, Corre realized she'd never seen power spring from his hands or move around him. It was invisible. "But what am I doing right this time? All I did was think about something I was upset about . . . and cared about. But I do that all the time. In my room, in the fields. Why would the power suddenly show up now?"

"Because you're focused on gathering it," he said, but she crossed her arms, one of her eyebrows rising incredulously. He laughed and said, "*And* because I'm here."

"I knew it wasn't just me," she said with a groan.

"No, it's not like that. You did that all by yourself. I'm just sensitive to the matter around us. I live with the control constantly—always focused and always manipulating it, at least somewhat, even when I don't realize it."

"Pfft. Well. Then it *wasn't* me, like I said."

"No, *you* did that. Trust me, Correlia." His voice was so gentle and pleading that she couldn't resist looking up into his eyes, his dark irises like pools of dark honey or the water from her favorite rich, earth-filled lake.

Everything about him made her ache and pulled her to him in ways she never knew was possible. She was connected to him in a way she couldn't explain and didn't understand. But she loved the feeling of it—the power that rushed through her like fiery rays of light.

"Trust me," he said again, and she nodded, entranced by the darkness of his eyes and the deep richness of his voice. She would follow him to the depths of Tartarus and back again. She would even peer back into that absinthe water mere inches from her flesh if it meant keeping him close and making sure they were bound together.

She'd do it without a second thought because she couldn't stay away. She wanted him in every way.

"Good. Then let's try again," he said. He let go of her hand, and she had to focus on her breathing before her legs felt less like liquid and her body felt more solid again. She needed to train. If she wanted to do something about any of this, she needed to learn how to do these things. Anything she could to make her stronger. So he wouldn't have to do it alone anymore.

Corre lifted her arms and closed her eyes.

She wouldn't let him go through life alone.

She would fight. With him. For him.

And that was what fueled her.

Corre flopped onto the bed, every muscle in her body screaming with fatigue. "How does he do it?" she whispered under her breath and rolled over. She slipped herself into the sheets and tried to rest. Her body was tired, but her mind was alert.

She couldn't stop thinking about Markus. Almost seconds after they'd returned from hours of training, he was summoned to report to Thanatos. What he needed to report, she wasn't sure, and by the expression on his face before he left, she guessed he didn't know either. It gave her an uneasiness she couldn't swat away or shut out long enough to sleep it off.

She grabbed one of the pillows and wrapped it over her head, her face planted firmly against the mattress. *Go to bed*, she urged herself. *You can only help if you rest.*

But sleep didn't come until Markus finally came back, looking even more tired than he had when he'd left.

"What happened?"

He silently slid off his boots, then ripped off his shirt and slid into the bed next to her. "Nothing. Let's just go to sleep."

That uneasy feeling grew and coiled within her gut, but she knew better than to press him on the matter. "Good night, Markus," she said, leaning forward and pressing a kiss on his lips.

"Good night, Correlia," he whispered, then with a wave of his hand, the light in the room faded to black.

Two hours earlier

Markus tried not to let the thought of Correlia linger in his mind as he walked to Thanatos's chambers. It had been a while since he was summoned to the castle. To Thanatos's *actual* chambers. The throne room was one thing, as was the dining hall, but going straight into his chambers in the castle meant something serious. Something too urgent for the old deity to bring himself to the throne for in the detached portion of the labyrinth.

When the dark, stone walls faded into a pristine tunnel of silver, Markus knew he was almost there. He followed it to a marble staircase, his feet no longer causing loud clacks against the stone. They were now muffled by the plush scarlet rug that led into the large, colosseum-sized chamber in the grand palace of Tartarus. His fists tightened. This was *his* palace. Yet here he was, trying not to tremble as he was summoned by his captor.

Captor.

He'd never thought of Thanatos like that before, but he didn't have time to analyze it. He was too distracted by the hideous, unsuspecting god waiting for their master before the onyx throne. He wanted to spit when the blonde turned to smirk at him. Could the muscles on Nikias's face form any other expression? Had he shot out of his mother looking like a pompous ass?

"Thank you for finally joining me," the lanky general said with a ghoulish smile.

Markus glowered. "The pleasure's entirely yours." Nikias's face tightened. He opened his mouth to retort when Thanatos's guards strode through with their spears, leading the mighty deity to his seat in the center of the room—an extravagant, ruby-crested throne. The throne that belonged to Hades.

"Ah. My pupils," Thanatos said, then waved for his soldiers to go and stand attention at the back of the room. To ensure there were no intrusions.

"Master," Nikias said in the most saccharine fashion Markus had ever heard. It took everything in him not to roll his eyes.

"Master," Markus said, a little more than a grumble, kneeling and bowing alongside the blonde.

"General Nikias. What news do you bring from Olympus?"

"We can't find the girl anywhere," he said.

Markus tensed but immediately forced himself to relax and push out any thought or feeling. *Stay blank*, he begged himself. *Stay blank*.

"How is that possible?" Thanatos growled, his long, talon-like fingers scratching against the arm of the throne.

"We have searched every inch of the world above, but we have seen no sign of her."

"Have you interrogated anyone?"

Nikias flinched. "A few, but—"

Thanatos leaned forward with gritted teeth. "You have yet to lead a full interrogation? Do you think a mistake like that would be made by Theron?"

Markus bit down a smile and shot a triumphant glance at his enemy.

Nikias pretended not to notice. "I'm sorry, master. We will question her family and friends."

"Why haven't you done that already?"

"Her home has been empty."

"So, you—" Thanatos started, then stopped. He sat back in his chair, his face falling into an odd expression that made Markus ill at ease. "Her home has been empty? Curious." Markus's stomach soured, his triumphant smile wiped clean off his face. "Do *you* know anything of this?"

Markus looked up and saw his master's eyes on him. He swallowed hard but kept his voice steady. "No, master. Why would I know anything about that?"

The wrinkled creature narrowed his eyes. "I thought you found her most intriguing. You even sneaked to see her behind my back."

Stay blank. Stay calm. Stay focused.

"No, master. I learned my lesson the first time."

Thanatos tapped a gnarled finger, his eyes still narrowed on his apprentice.

A bead of sweat crept down the back of Markus's neck, and he hoped to whatever beings that existed beyond the Titans that his master wouldn't notice.

But Nikias was the one to speak. "*Have* you?"

Markus shot him a look, but he couldn't hide the unguarded shock that rippled through him at the accusation. "What are you implying?"

Nikias smiled, his face as smug as ever. "You haven't been training as much as usual."

"That's a lie!"

"Oh? Then why have you been retiring at supper every night? You usually take on one more beast, or at least train your swordsmanship and form."

Markus's jaw slowly dropped. "Are you keeping tabs on me, general? Because the last time I checked, *I* rank above *you*." Nikias's smile tightened, his eyes staring daggers into Markus's. "Keep your ugly face out of my business."

"And what business is that?" Thanatos croaked.

Markus couldn't stop how fast his heart was racing. His thoughts were slipping. His composure was falling apart. He was losing control. "Nothing of note," he said quickly. "I just don't like the idea of being followed and spied on like some filthy low-level demon." He kept his arms firm at his sides, his nails digging into his palms. He wished he could take a good swing at Nikias right now.

"Understandable," Thanatos said, and Markus relaxed slightly, but then Thanatos added, "But if you have nothing to hide, you wouldn't mind if my servants check on you after supper from time to time? To make sure you're training properly."

The blood drained from his face. "Of course not. I have nothing to hide." His hands were freezing despite being balled up so tightly his knuckles were white.

"Good. Because you need to prepare to take the throne, and you're far from that point right now." Markus swallowed hard but kept his composure. "And my pupil next to you says you're hiding something."

His eyes snapped to Nikias. "Hiding *what* exactly?"

That smug grin was still plastered on the blonde's face as he said, "I'm not sure yet. Maybe I'm wrong, but, as our master said, if you have nothing to hide, you wouldn't mind the occasional check now and then, would you?"

"Of—"

The two were interrupted by Thanatos's gravelly laughter booming through the room. "My boy, you need not worry. You rank higher than the general. He is simply sore because he hasn't done his job." Nikias turned red. "So do it," Thanatos growled at the blonde with a sudden crack in his expression, "Or you might as well never come back to Tartarus again."

Markus looked to his feet, trying his best to conceal the satisfaction on his face.

"Yes, sir," Nikias said shakily.

"Now, the both of you, go. Keep looking for the girl. Her coronation is only a few sun-falls away. We need to find her before then."

"Why?" Markus blurted.

Thanatos narrowed his eyes again. "We can't let someone so dangerous start blooming the world. Or our plans will fall apart. Don't you remember?"

"No. You never told me the depths of your plans, or what you want with her."

"Silence! Find her!" His voice roared through the room.

Nikias bolted upright and bowed. "I won't let you down, master."

"You already have, general," Thanatos drawled, then looked to his star apprentice. "Don't disappoint me, Theron. You know what happens when you disappoint me."

Markus swallowed and nodded slowly, his nails finally piercing the first layer of skin on his palms. A trickle of blood dripped through his fingers. He smeared it discreetly beneath his tightening fist before his master could spot it.

"Go," Thanatos said lazily, waving his hand. "I'm tired."

Markus didn't bow as he left. He had to get out of there fast. He didn't care what Thanatos did to him, but he couldn't let him get his claw-like fingers on Correlia. The thought of Thanatos doing anything to her made him sick. It made him want to scream and wield that all-mighty sword across his master's chest.

"You can't win," a voice hissed behind him.

"You've already lost," Markus said, opening the doors from the palace and weaving back into the labyrinth.

"I know you're hiding something, and I'll find out what." Nikias pushed past the larger, dark-haired god and rushed down the corridor. Markus wondered if he should worry. Logically, he should. Nikias was onto him. But Thanatos didn't take the general seriously. He saw through his brown-nosing. The spindly god was weak.

Still, Markus needed to be less sloppy. He couldn't give Nikias the chance to win. Not this match. There was too much at stake. He needed to go to the dungeon before returning to his chambers. He had to at least look like he was training as much as he was supposed to. He moved as quickly as he could to the dungeon. He didn't want to leave Correlia unattended for too long, especially now that he knew Nikias was snooping around in the shadows.

When he made it to the practice chamber, he tried focusing and training himself mentally, but every time he tried, he'd get thrown off by the thought of Correlia. The way her nose crinkled when something made her laugh. The way her cheeks dimpled when he somehow managed to make her smile. To make her happy.

And then he thought of what she'd said about the throne. It wasn't until she talked to him that he started reconsidering things—realizing things—and he came to the conclusion that something in him might have unconsciously resigned to his fate of forever being Thanatos's underling long ago. Maybe he'd never realized it so he wouldn't be let down one day. Maybe he'd wanted to protect himself from the disappointment that his crown would never come. But the crown had never looked as vital to him as it did now. The way Thanatos's eyes had looked so viciously hungry and Nikias had looked so desperate made Markus know that he had no choice but to take over the throne. It was the only way to keep her safe.

That beautiful, sunshine person who'd woken him up and rescued him from that recurring nightmare. The goddess with skin so soft she felt like feathers beneath his fingertips.

He would do anything for her.

She might never fully grasp how much her kindness meant to him. He wasn't sure how he could describe it to her—how he could tell her that she'd saved a part of him. Most days, he had to live through that nightmare of fire and heartache. The memory that had tormented him since he was a boy. But today, he'd been rescued from it. For the first time in his life, he'd been rescued by someone who cared.

Not even his own mother had rescued him that day, and he wasn't convinced she'd even wanted to. He could never forget the expression of fear and disgust on her face. She'd *wanted* him gone. But now, even the memory of her face was smudged, wiped away like it'd been scrubbed clean.

It was for the best.

After about an hour, Markus gave up. There was no way he could train anymore today. He left the dungeon and headed back to his room, still tense and afraid of what Thanatos's plans for Correlia were, and what Nikias might know.

What would happen if Markus slipped up?

The twisted knots tightening his muscles were combed out a bit when he opened the door and saw Correlia lying there, waiting for him. But then his stomach dropped.

If Thanatos got a hold of her, what would he do?

He couldn't bear the thought.

CHAPTER
TWENTY-NINE

Corre

T he days passed into a week, and then another, and Corre couldn't
bring herself to mention the throne again, despite the clock ticking
before she had to leave. She had to figure out a plan, but she didn't want to
ruin anything. When she was with him, she was light and free. Everything
was somehow okay when his arms were wrapped around her or when they
sparred after his dungeon battles and he taught her how to use her mind
and passions to gather the powers around her. She just wanted to enjoy the
moments she got to see him before it all had to end. Because even if he did
take the throne, what then? She was the goddess who was to bring life and
beauty to the Earth, and he was the god of death and darkness.

She didn't let herself think about it too much, even though she hadn't
gotten to see him much the last week or so. Thanatos had him on a tighter
leash, for some reason. She'd heard one of the demons say something about

it in front of his room when he'd left a few mornings prior, but she couldn't make out what it had said.

Whatever the reason, Markus was being worked half to death. Corre supposed it was relatively usual, but it felt different. Worse. He came back more and more tired every time she saw him. She wasn't sure when he'd come back today, but as she folded his towels into bouquets of flowers, she hoped tonight he'd be done early.

Because today was the day. The one she'd been dreading. Her twentieth birthday.

She didn't tell him because it had slipped her mind until he'd already left that morning, but all she'd been able to do since he'd left was fold the towels into various flower shapes, trying to figure out how she could ever make real ones the way her mother did.

Her mother.

The thought tightened her stomach into a knot. Berenice would be home from that forest mission any day now. Hopefully, it wasn't today. She'd said she'd be back by Corre's birthday. Luckily, the older goddess notoriously lost track of time. But Corre had a feeling that her mother wouldn't do that this time.

She was out of time.

But she'd think about it tomorrow. Tomorrow, she'd plan. She'd let herself have one more day. One more day with Markus. With Hades.

She ran out of towels halfway through the day, so she messed them all up and made more intricate ones as if the talent would somehow transfer to actual plant-making. She was so concentrated on not thinking about anything other than the cloth in her hands that she nearly jumped out of her skin when she heard Markus say, "What are you doing on the floor?" She looked up at him in shock, her heart in her throat. He laughed. "Did I scare you?"

She pursed her lips. "No."

"You're so cute," he said with another laugh, and the tension in her body drifted away.

She tugged on the faux petals. "Thank you." She looked up at him coyly and said, "What a kind thing to say to the birthday girl."

His eyes widened. "It's your birthday?"

She giggled, then sighed. "Yeah, but I wish it wasn't. It's my twentieth."

"Ah," he said, about to sit down when he suddenly straightened. "But still, you deserve a celebration."

She passed him another coy grin. "Oh? And what do you have in mind?"

"Wait here," he said with a smile that made her knees weak.

"O-Okay," she said, but he was already halfway out the door. She sunk against the wall, smiling to herself giddily, eagerly waiting for his return. Already missing him.

Markus

There had to be something here. He sifted through pans and opened pots and cupboards. Nothing. How was there nothing in the kitchen? When he heard someone come in, he started to duck, but it was too late.

"Master Theron?"

He shot up. "Y-yes. Um, I mean, *yes*?" He said the last word more firmly, more authoritatively.

The hunched demon skittered over to him, its hollow eyes gaping in confusion. "Is something amiss? Did you forget a meal?"

"Um . . . Yes! I'm starving. Do you have anything sweet?"

"Sweet?" it said, its scratchy voice rising. Markus had never wanted anything sweet before.

"Yes, I'm quite hungry for something sweet."

The creature turned around and said, "There is nothing ready at the moment, but if you wait a few minutes, I can have a pie finished for you. There's already one being prepared for General Nikias."

Markus suppressed a wicked smile. "That one would be perfect."

Corre

When Markus returned, Corre jumped, her heart fluttering at the sight of him holding a freshly baked pie. Its crust was the perfect shade of brown, plump and steaming. It had a warm, fruity aroma that made her drool. "Mmm! What is that?"

"Pomegranate pie for the birthday girl." His eyes crinkled at the sides, turning her legs into gelatin.

"Sounds delicious."

"I imagine it is. I've never tried it, but it looks amazing."

"What are we waiting for?" she said, practically yelling. Markus lifted his finger to his lips, unable to contain a smile. "Oops. Sorry," she whispered, and he laughed.

"Make a wish," he said. Her heart skipped at the way he looked at her. Giddiness bubbled through her, and she wondered if she'd ever been this happy before. She closed her eyes, knowing the answer.

She hadn't. She'd never been so happy in her entire life.

So she wished for the one thing she wanted more than anything and then opened her eyes. "Okay, I did it."

"Was it a good one?"

She nodded, her dimpled smile stretched so far across her face it made her cheeks sore. It must have been infectious because his smile widened, too.

"Good. Now, let's eat. You get the first bite." He whipped out a knife from his tunic and started slicing. He cut each slice into perfect triangles.

"Wow. I'm impressed."

"With what?" he laughed, dropping a piece into her hands. It was filled thickly with purple seeds and gooey jam. "Sorry. I forgot plates."

"That's okay. We can use my artwork." She took one of the folded towels and shook it until it was flat again.

"Aw, but they were so pretty."

"Not as pretty as your excellent pie-slicing work."

He chuckled. "Right. Okay." His smile was bright, and there was a faint shade of pink creeping along his cheeks.

She eagerly took a piece of the pie, warm and sticky in her fingers, and tossed it into her mouth. The taste was tangy and perfect, each seed melting in her mouth. "Mmmmm." Her eyes closed in pure bliss.

"Whoa," he said with a teasing smile.

She shoved him playfully. "Shush. It's so good."

He took a bite of his piece, his eyebrows rising. "It *is* good."

"See?" She went for the rest of her piece, dropping it all in her mouth without feeling the need to pretend to daintily rip it into proper fragments. "Mmmmm," she said again, eyes rolling to the back of her head. Markus burst out a laugh. "What?" she said with her mouth full.

"You have pomegranate juice all over your face," he said, leaning forward and dabbing it off with a towel.

Suddenly, the taste of the pie was second to the feeling of his fingers touching her skin and the warmth of his breath. She leaned forward and kissed him, tasting the sweetness of the pie in his mouth, before leaning back in a dizzy flush.

He put down the towel and smiled, then leaned forward and licked her cheek.

She squealed. "What are you doing?"

"You have juice all over you!" he said, licking her again.

"You're such a weirdo!" she said, laughing, but he was on top of her, and she was lying on the floor, throwing her arms around him as he leaned in to kiss her.

When the sweetness of his lips returned, she welcomed the flurry of sparks and starlight that beamed through her. She reveled in the way he touched her and the way his mouth left purple kisses down her neck.

She squealed in delight as he picked her up and threw her on the bed, jumping on top of her and kissing her deeply. She let her mind go numb and her senses be taken over by him and the breaths he left on her neck and chest, and the sweet static that crackled through her when his mouth trailed all over her body.

Her skin grew warmer the more he touched her, and it turned white-hot when his hands moved up the skirt of her dress. He moved down to kiss her legs, and her body ached as he moved up her thigh, his tongue finding its way to the soft skin beneath her hipbone. The sensation was overwhelming, and she loved it. She gathered his shirt in her fingers, and he sat up as she ripped it off him.

When he looked back at her, the insatiable desire in his eyes made something ignite in her blood. Everything was urgent and heated, and she couldn't stop herself from grabbing him and sinking her lips back into his. She loved the taste of his tongue and the movements of his body, so tight and hard against her. She wanted every part of him, and she wanted to give him every part of her.

He trailed his hands up her arms and threaded his fingers in hers. She loved the feeling of his body on hers, his knees on either side of her hips. And as his mouth trailed to her chest, she fell into bliss. Her body was completely his. His fingers ran through her hair, grasping it as he kissed her. She wrapped her legs around his waist and let her hands run down his bare back, nails lightly scratching his skin.

As they kissed fervently, passionately, he sat up and pulled her onto his lap, but they never stopped kissing. Her hair fell around him. His hands trailed down her back. He sucked on her tongue. Her bottom lip. Her neck. She breathlessly fell into him.

"You make me feel wonderful," she whispered into his ear, gently biting his earlobe.

He wrapped his arms around her, squeezed her, then fell back with a smile. "I think you make me feel even better," he said, touching his thumb to her lips, and holding onto her chin before letting his hand fall to her exposed thigh.

She bent over and kissed him. "You're a fantastic kisser."

He laughed and kissed her nose. "I can't say I have a lot of experience."

She lifted an eyebrow. "Oh?"

"Funnily enough, you don't get to court many goddesses when you're getting your ass whooped by demons and monsters all the time."

She gave him a tight smile. "I'm sorry."

"It's okay," he said, chuckling, "but I *am* curious about *your* experience."

She rolled her eyes with a smile and lay down next to him. "There's not a lot to talk about. *But* I wasn't the most work-oriented goddess on Mt. Olympus growing up. So, I may have kissed a fella or two."

He trailed the back of his hand down her arm, his eyes drinking in every inch of her skin before flickering back to her gaze. "Don't make me jealous now."

She scrunched her nose and laughed. "I didn't realize I *could* make you jealous. Maybe I should tell you about aaall of my suitors, then."

He shot her a playful glare. "You wouldn't dare."

"Oh, I would."

He lifted himself onto his elbow and kissed her so deeply that all the memories of those past kisses muddled together and fell away.

"Did you make love to them?" he asked, his voice low.

Her face went hot. She shook her head. "No, I've never had sex."

Something in his eyes lit up, and as her gaze trailed down his body, memorizing every muscle and curve, she wondered what it would be like. To become one with him and feel their passion even stronger, more intense.

"But I'd like to," she said. Their eyes locked. She loved the way he looked at her. Like she was the most beautiful creature in the entire world. "With you," she added quietly, heat blaring on her cheeks.

He sucked in an excited breath and leaned forward to kiss her, pulling her back into him. She grabbed hold of his shoulders as she fell back onto the bed. He smiled and looked down at her, the waves of his black hair brushing along the side of her face. And then it all hit her.

This moment wouldn't last forever.

None of this would.

And suddenly, it was all too much.

He pressed a soft kiss against her lips, but before he could continue, her voice filled the small space between them. "Don't forget me," she whispered.

He shook his head, keeping his eyes on hers. "I could never forget you." He lay next to her, took her hand in his, and kissed her knuckles. He placed the other hand gently on her cheek. "Where is this coming from?"

Tears burned in her eyes. She swallowed, but her breath was shuddery as she spoke. "I have to leave soon. My mother will be back any day now if she isn't already. It's been weeks since I came here, but—" A sob cut through her voice. "I may never see you again." She tried to contain it, but she couldn't anymore. As soon as one tear slid down her face, the rest followed, and she burst into sobs. "I'm so sorry," she said. "I ruined the mood."

He hushed her softly and gathered her into his arms. "You could never ruin anything." He held her against him, and she cried into his chest as he stroked the back of her head. "We'll see each other again. I promise."

She sniffed and wiped her face before looking up at him. "You do?"

"I do," he whispered, placing his forehead on hers.

She closed her eyes and let his warmth blanket her body. "How do you know?'

He grabbed her face gently and looked at her with such tenderness in his eyes it made her want to cry even more. She couldn't lose this. "Because I love you," he said. "And I can't bear living a life without you."

Through the tears, a smile broke across her face. Something within her soared. She let out a quiet, joyful laugh through her trembling. "I love you, too."

They looked at each other one moment longer before he kissed her again, slowly this time, and she savored every second of it.

"No matter what happens, I'll find you," he whispered, "and you'll be mine. Always." She nodded, and he lifted her chin toward him. He smiled softly when their eyes met again, and he wiped the tears from her face, then kissed the spots where they'd been. "I'll always take care of you." He kissed her again. "That's a promise, too."

"Okay," she whispered back, and she let him hold her until every sad feeling fell away. The way his arms felt around her, strong and protective, made her feel safe. She wanted to believe him. So she chose to. She would never let her life be without him. "I promise, too. I don't want a life without you in it."

A smile stretched across his face, and he scooped her face into his hands again and kissed her. Her entire life, Corre had never felt so beautifully alive—so wonderfully free—as she did when she was with him. She never wanted the feeling to end. Safely together, tangled in bliss.

She laid her body flat, and when he saw her lying there, he gave her a hungry, playful look and jumped on top of her. He pinned her wrists against the bed, and she could hardly breathe. Excitement buzzed through every nerve, burning every inch of her skin. But as soon as he kissed her, the door swung open.

"I knew it! I knew you were hiding something!"

Corre's stomach dropped. Her eyes darted to the lanky man standing in the doorway. He had the pinched, smug face of a rat and tightly combed-back blonde hair.

"Guards! In here! He has the girl!" he called, and her stomach was sick.

The look on Markus's face said everything she was feeling. He jumped off the bed and to his feet, shielding her from the guards pouring into the room. "Don't you dare touch her!" he shouted, but the demons pushed into him. "Get back!" He lifted his hands and pushed his power against them.

All four of them crashed into the opposite wall.

"Thanatos will—" the god in the doorway began, but Markus pushed another bout of power against him, too, and sent the man flying into the hall.

Markus turned around and grabbed Corre by the hand. "We have to get you out of here!" She jumped out of bed. She could taste the fear on her tongue like a hot iron. They were bolting down the hall when another group of guards flocked toward them. Markus tried pushing through them with his power, but there were too many coming at him in every direction, and they were stronger than the others. Large, gray creatures with no eyes and withered skin, but giant bodies of pure muscle. Each one was armed with sharp weapons and covered in thick plates of armor.

Markus's back pressed against Corre. His arms formed a rounded T to protect her, but more footsteps marched at them from behind. The four guards and the thin blonde man pushed through the mass of bodies.

They were surrounded with no way out.

"There's no use trying, Theron," the pale man spat. "They have the chains. And you know you can't get out of those."

The look on Markus's face told a story of pain Corre would have to ask him about later, but for now, she had to do something. She lifted her hands and tried to remember what he'd taught her in their spare moments of training these last few weeks. She used the desire she felt to keep Markus safe to fuel her power and then pushed it at the guards in front of her. When Markus saw this, he turned around and tried the same with the others.

She managed to bowl five of the muscled demons over. *This might actually work.* Power gathered between her fingers again, but then Markus cried out, and before she could turn around, she was on the floor, chains shackling her wrists. The metal pierced her with an electric energy that vibrated through her bones.

Her body was filled with painful static.

She couldn't move.

"Take them to Thanatos," the blonde god said. Corre turned to Markus and saw him looking so desperately at her that she wanted to cry. Tears were forming in his eyes, and she could tell he felt guilty about this. As if this was somehow his fault. They were pulled to their feet by their chains, the metal digging into her wrist bones. The pain was so sudden and intense that she let out a cry.

"I said don't hurt her!" Markus roared. He writhed and growled, tackling one of the demonic guards holding Corre in place, knocking it to the ground. But it was futile. Another one of the guards took him by the chains and kicked him, then violently struck him in the face with the bottom of its spear.

Corre gasped, but the guards pulled her forward, grabbing her skull and forcing her to stare straight ahead.

Markus, she wanted to whisper, but she knew it would make things worse.

They were headed for the chopping block.

They were headed to his master.

CHAPTER THIRTY

Phineas

Phineas's hands fell to his thighs as he slumped over to catch his breath. Lately, training had gone by in a blur of pain and fatigue. He'd been working hard, but he'd had enough for today. It was Corre's birthday, and after not seeing her for the last few weeks, he could finally see that beautiful smile of hers as he handed her the gift he'd spent a long time creating. It was a locket made of wood. A heart with perfectly sculpted edges that took him about a thousand times to get right. He'd carved it from one of the trees around the forest near her house. They used to play there for hours every day as kids. He knew she'd appreciate the deep sentiment. Those bygone days meant just as much to her as they did to him.

"I'm heading out," he yelled to Athena, throwing a towel over his shoulder and heading to the watering hole.

"Wish Corre a happy birthday for me," she called back, her melodious voice whisking through the trees.

"I will," he said, but he didn't look back. He already feared she knew his plan, at least somewhat. Athena was the most intuitive goddess he'd ever known. If she saw the nervousness in his eyes, she'd probably give him a teasing look that would psyche him out. She could read him like a picture book. It was best to just think of Corre, and of her gift. And not throwing up when he thought about saying what he'd practiced.

He tried not to think about it as he washed himself off and got dressed in new clothes, but the closer he got to the moment he'd see her, then inevitably tell her, the worse he felt. *I don't know if I can go through with this.* He reached for the perfectly wrapped box with the purple ribbon. He'd saved up to buy the best wrapping at the market. It ended up being a good thing she'd been absent from his shopping trips lately.

It was more of a surprise this way.

When he made it home, he let out a relieved breath at the silence he met as he walked through the doors. Not having to worry about talking to his parents about his plans was preferable. His blood was already pumping with nerves. The only sound he could hear in the quietness of his cottage was the pounding in his ears. He needed as little interaction with anyone who may psych him out as possible, and while well-meaning, his parents weren't always the most eloquent or articulate in the encouragement department. He got his lack of verbal grace from them.

Hesitantly, Phineas stepped in front of the mirror to scrutinize himself. He was wearing the nicest clothes he owned: a dark leather tunic with a tan belt and matching pants. He only had his work boots, though, but they'd have to do. He'd just have to clean them off on his way there.

His forehead crinkled as he studied his rigid frame in the mirror. He looked *tense.* It was to be expected, he supposed, but he tried shaking out his limbs as he moved to the door. He breathed in and out as steadily as he could, then squared his shoulders and left.

He weaved mindlessly through the trees, wiping his boots on a dewy patch of grass on his way to Corre's cottage. He thought again of how it was good that his parents hadn't been home because his mother would have needled him until he admitted what he wanted to say to Corre, and then she would have instructed him on how to do it properly because he had planned it all wrong.

On second thought, maybe he should have asked for advice ahead of time.

He was about half a second away from peeling out of there and coming up with a whole new birthday plan when he spotted the smoke billowing from Corre's chimney. She was home. If he turned back now, she might see him, and then things would get really awkward really fast. He had no choice but to keep going.

He cleared his throat. "Corre, I know we've known each other a long time," he rehearsed, "and I think we know each other better than anyone. I know I feel that way about you . . . Argh." He scratched the back of his head. How was he supposed to do this? A lifetime of friendship would be hanging in the balance. If she didn't feel the same way, he could ruin everything.

No. He promised himself he would do this. He needed to tell her how he felt. It'd been long enough already.

Phineas was only a handful of paces from the cottage when he heard the wooden door on the other side of the home swing open in a quick, high-pitched squeak. Then a slam.

"Corre?" he called, but it wasn't the young goddess he saw frazzled and tearing away from the small house, hastily running toward town. "Berenice?" The goddess didn't hear him. There was something rabid in her eyes. "Berenice!" he called louder. The woman stopped. She flipped around, and her wild expression made him freeze.

"Berenice? Is everything okay?"

"Have you seen Correlia?" she cried.

"What? Isn't she—" He pointed to the cottage, but she shook her head in fiercely quick wobbles.

"I don't know where she could be. She was supposed to be home. She—"

"Hold on. It's all right. Don't worry. I'm sure she's just out—"

"No! She promised she would be here! I told her I'd be here! It's her birthday! And if she isn't with you . . ." Her voice trailed off before a hand raised to her mouth and her eyes widened in horror. "You don't think . . ."

Panic surged through him, but he tried not to act on it. "I'm sure it's nothing. She's probably training or swimming or something."

"Has she been training with *you*? Because she's not in the fields."

Something wavered in his gut. "No, I haven't seen her."

"Since when?" she said, her eyes bulging and unblinking as she stumbled toward him and grabbed hold of his forearms. She shook them as she stared up at him. "Since *when*? When did you last see her?"

He racked his brain, but it was so flurried it was hard to think straight. "Um . . . I think . . ." His mouth turned dry when he remembered. "After Hades. Before you left."

Horror struck her face, pasting her eyelids open against her crepe-paper skin. "Phineas," she gasped through a sob, and he knew what she was thinking.

Ice pricked the back of his neck. "Berenice, Theron's demons have been swarming Mt. Olympus this whole week, but . . ." Where was he going with this? He needed to decide if he should comfort the harried goddess or figure out a plan.

She teetered back, terror twisting her face, so he made his decision.

He quickly caught hold of her before she fell to the ground. "We can save her. We just need to go to Zeus."

Her chest was quick, her breaths short and panicked. "We don't have time."

"We have no choice."

She put a hand to her chest as she caught her breath. "Okay. You're right." But the terror still hung in her eyes. Her mind was elsewhere, and without another word, she turned around and headed back on her trail toward the top of Mt. Olympus. Phineas wasn't sure what else to do other than to follow her, but he soon realized how long it could take for them to make it to the top of the mountain and plead their case to Zeus, get ready, and make the trip all the way to Tartarus. What would all of that entail? Would they need Hermes to bring them to the River Styx? Any official process could take ages.

Zeus was probably extremely busy with a variety of matters, too. How long would it take to get in front of him once they were there? But he was the only one who could assert any kind of authority over Hades, if even just a little. Plus, he had the fleets. The power.

Still, there was no telling how long the process would take, and the longer Corre was down there . . .

The fear inside him boiled into rage as he thought about what Theron could be doing to Corre right now.

Phineas was Ares, so *he* could do something about this.

"I'll go down there with my army," he said quickly.

"Army?" He could hear the incredulity in her voice despite her not so much as turning to face him.

"It's kind of an army. I'm still recruiting, but there are enough of us, and we've all been training for years under Athena. It will at least buy us some time before Zeus sends anyone down."

She stopped and looked over her shoulder. The conflict in her eyes was intense. For a goddess half his size, Berenice sure had an intimidating presence. "Are you sure you're ready for something of this caliber?" she asked. "I don't know if you should try something so risky."

He stepped closer and placed his hands on her narrow shoulders. "It's the only choice we have." She opened her mouth to protest "I have to, Berenice. It's Corre." The pleading in his voice and the desperation in his eyes were apparently enough to convince her. There was no stopping him.

"Be careful," she said firmly.

"I will be."

She turned back around and continued. "Zeus will help us. I *know* he will. All you need to do is buy us some time. I'll be quick."

Phineas's heart swelled. "Yes, ma'am." Then he ran for the trees as fast and hard as he could. He needed to go to Athena and find Terraceus and the handful of others they sparred with. He'd somehow have to come up with an army that wouldn't get killed the moment they stormed the Underworld.

We're strong. We'll be fine. Phineas had more motivation now than ever before as he skidded down the path to Athena's training course, yelling, "We have to go! Now!"

The crimson-haired goddess approached him with a worried, puzzled look on her face. Some of her students straggled close behind.

"Corre's in trouble!" he shouted. "Which way to the armory? Where's—"

"Whoa, whoa, whoa. Calm down, Phineas. Tell me what's going on."

It was hard for him to breathe, let alone think, but he did his best to recount the events and explain what they needed to do. More students gathered around, some already putting on heavier training gear and preparing to go into town to fetch more weapons.

"Okay," Athena said calmly, but the worry was written across her face. "Let's get ready. We have a lot to do in a short amount of time. Follow me."

He gave her one quick nod before he and the others followed her into their preparations. As he readied himself, he let the anger sweltering within him fuel his concentration. "You won't live after this, Theron," he growled under his breath, tightening his boots and fetching his bow. "You're dead."

Markus

The throne room doors opened. The thought of seeing Thanatos's look of delight as Correlia was dragged in front of him pained Markus a lot more than the bleeding gash the guard had cracked above the bridge of his nose. But the throne was empty. The whole room was empty.

The guards pushed Markus to his knees, and though he wanted to jump up, grab Correlia's hand, and run, he knew he needed to resist. He had to think first. He needed to be strategic. But when Correlia grunted in pain as she was forced to her knees, he couldn't stop himself. He sprung to his feet and lashed out at the guards holding her chains. As soon as he pushed his powers out on them, most of the entire lot flung to the doorway, some crashing against the frame leading to the labyrinth, their backs snapping against the iron walls. But the guards holding his chains unleashed the soul-sucking energy that sizzled through the restraints, rendering him powerless as he was brought back to his knees, flinching and groaning in pain.

"Markus," Correlia whimpered, and the sadness in her eyes made his soul splinter into a thousand pieces.

He had done this to her. If he had never gone to Olympus that second time, this never would have happened. He lifted himself to his knees, ignoring the pain searing his wrists and fizzing through his muscles, and scooted closer to her. "Correlia," he whispered, desperate and urgent. He held her face in his hands. The chains binding his wrists clinked down his arms. "You'll be okay. I promise you. No one can touch you if you're with me. I'll always take care of you." He lifted his lips to her forehead and kissed it. A tear rolled down her cheek and sunk into his palm. He tilted her face up and looked firmly in her eyes. "I told you that, didn't I? I promised you."

Her eyes shut as more tears fell into his hands. He pulled her into his chest, holding her against him as he fought back his own tears and the shaking in his legs and tremors quaking through his body. He had no idea how he would do it, but he needed to protect her. No matter what it cost him.

Her body was enveloped in his arms as he held her against his chest. Her hands curled against his bare back, and he nestled his face into the crook of her neck. His arms wrapped tightly around her. He couldn't let go.

The throne room doors slammed shut, and then, slowly, another set of doors at the back of the room creaked open. A familiar sinister shuffling echoed through the room. Correlia's breathing quickened, so he held her tighter.

"It'll be okay," he whispered into her ear. "Just stay calm. And remember what I taught you. Focus, when the time comes. Try to guard your mind. Like you did that day you met me."

She pulled back slightly, but her hands were still tight against his back. "I don't know how I did that."

"But it's in you," he whispered. "That's all that matters. You're strong, Correlia. So, so, *so* strong."

She looked up. The whites of her eyes had turned pink, and her cheeks were damp. "But what about you?"

His head jerked back. "Me?" She nodded, her lower lip quivering. "What *about* me?"

"What will he do to you?"

He blinked. Why was she worrying about him at a time like this? Didn't she know she was the vulnerable one here? That she was the one Thanatos was after?

She had no idea what she was up against or of the kind of monster that lurked in these halls. No matter how much she recognized Thanatos's evil, there was no comprehension of it until you felt the cruelty of his hand, his nails, and his mind as they slashed through your skin and psyche and drove you half insane.

"Don't worry about me," he said, but her expression didn't change. Her eyes still searched him in fear. It killed him to not have the ability to take that terror from her—to not be able to assure her wholeheartedly that nothing would happen to them and to have her believe it. "Just remember what I taught you. Focus on what you want, and it will come."

"My, my, what is this I'm witnessing?" Thanatos drawled, but Markus kept his eyes on Correlia.

A bold move he'd never attempted before, but he needed her to see the look in his eyes so she knew he would keep her safe. "It will be okay," he whispered again, but before she could respond, he was thrown to his feet by a powerful force. Thanatos's power sucked the young god into his mammoth grasp. Markus's body rushed to his master's enormous hand, but before the deity's gangly claw could grab hold of him, Markus used his own power to break himself free.

He slid back but remained firmly on his feet. His mind was strong, and the power flooding through him far exceeded his usual abilities. He'd never had this much passion to work with before. This much purpose.

Thanatos's eyes were as black as thick, dried blood as they narrowed in on him, and an unamused expression stiffened his crooked face. "Are you defying your master, *boy*?"

Markus's fists tightened, the power in his veins pulsing through him in unbridled waves. A shield of energy formed behind him, blocking Correlia from the creature on the throne. He did it all without breaking a sweat.

"Yes," he said, his voice strong, his eyes locked on his master's. "I am."

CHAPTER THIRTY-ONE

Berenice

"Correlia's been taken to the Underworld!" Berenice said, and the goddesses around the throne gasped. They chattered amongst themselves as Zeus stroked his silvery beard and peered down at the slight goddess by his feet.

"Are you certain?"

"N-no, but no one knows where she is. Can you look? Please? We don't have much time! Hades could be—"

He lifted a hand. "I will check, but I'm sure there is no cause for alarm." He snapped his fingers, and one of his aides came to the throne. "Check the looking glass for Persephone. Find where she is located."

"Yes, sir, right away," the young god said with a bow, then fled across the room and out into a hall.

Zeus's palace was said to be the most elegant and intricate in the entire world. She'd been to it at least half a dozen times before, but each time was just as breathtaking as the last. Except for today. The beauty of the palace seemed so frivolous at a moment like this. Her world was dark right now. A cold, barren wasteland. She needed to find her daughter. Fast.

"There," Zeus said, but Berenice was still wringing her hands. He sighed. "If she *is* there, Demeter, we will bring her back. There is no need to worry."

"But what if he's captured her?"

"I assure you she will be fine, even if we have to go down there ourselves."

Fear twisted in Berenice's stomach. There was no way even Zeus could assure her that Corre would be fine. If she was indeed in the Underworld, there was no telling what could have happened to her. She could have gotten lost in any of the rivers, eaten by Cerberus, or killed by Hades himself. Or Thanatos.

"Sir, we have word that the goddess Persephone is, indeed, in Tartarus."

Berenice's blood turned cold. "Oh, no," she whimpered. "Correlia, no."

Zeus sighed. "Prepare our forces," he said, gesturing to one of his guards. "I suppose we're going to war."

Corre

Markus's chains shattered at his feet. His shoulders were back, and his eyes were focused as he stood against his colossal master. There was a blind rage in Thanatos's eyes, but there was a greater surge of power breaking through the room, rushing with a force beyond her understanding.

And it was coming from Markus.

Despite the fear sinking deeper in her gut, she had hope. She watched the god she loved move with flawless precision and believed he could do this. She knew how much it meant just to see him try.

It wasn't enough to try now, though. He had to take his master down. Thanatos wouldn't hold back if he felt the need to split Markus apart. And if that happened, she didn't know if she could live the rest of eternity knowing that the one soul who truly understood her had been condemned to a god-death and that it had been because of her.

God-deaths were especially atrocious—one great drawback of being immortal. They weren't something that lasted a moment, as the only option for death in the human world was. God-deaths were eternal sentences, often spent in Tartarus. The god would either be tortured, thrown in solitude, or in great pain for all eternity. That was her understanding, anyway, and since it was up to Thanatos to decide Markus's fate, she couldn't imagine he'd spare him with an easy sentence. It would be an eternity of everlasting torment and torture of the cruelest form.

So Corre chose to believe in him. She couldn't let Markus feel her waver through the space between them. In case he sensed what was in her heart, she was strong. He needed her to believe in him. Because no one else ever had.

When Markus took his first lunge at his master, her stomach lurched. She instinctively moved forward, reaching out to help him, but one of her captors tugged on the electric chains around her wrists. They singed her skin as they clanked against her bones, and she bit her lip so she wouldn't make a sound. Any indication she was in pain might make Markus falter, and that one moment could cost him his life.

You can do this, Markus. You can do this.

In almost the blink of an eye, he leapt forward and pushed the growing energy at his master. The great creature moved his massive hands over his face to block the attack, but the power was too great. It knocked the leader off the throne and left him skidding across the floor. Markus moved faster, throwing another unseen blow. His hands were in a tight position across his chest when he dealt another one. And another. And another.

A few of the guards ran up behind him with their spears. "Markus!" Corre cried, but he'd already sensed them coming. He whipped around and smacked the guards with one sweeping motion that pushed his power in a cutting wave across their chests. The handful of gold-plated demons crashed in a heap on the other side of the room.

When Corre felt the chains attached to her wrists fall, she expected the guards behind her to rush at Markus next, but she didn't see them pass her. Instead, she heard the great doors they'd come from slam as they escaped. She got to her feet and rushed to one of the fallen spears. Out of the corner of her eye, she saw Thanatos rising to his feet. Panic surged through her. Her adrenaline spiked. She pushed the spear over to Markus and called to him.

He turned and grabbed the metallic object, flipped it, turned back to face his master, and then stabbed the weapon through Thanatos's side. Corre's face lit up, and she ran over to Markus, but he held out a hand to her. She stopped as the cuffs around her wrists clattered to the ground. Even while focused on his master, he'd been able to unchain her. She smiled, unable to suppress how much he impressed her. Was it wrong that she was so attracted to him right now?

He repositioned himself and took one more stab at his master, but Thanatos's hand grabbed hold of the staff and snapped it in two. The deity tossed the pieces to the side and sent his own sweeping wave at Markus. Terror swelled in Corre's abdomen.

The apprentice fell to the ground before Thanatos pushed him back farther. Markus struggled to get up but was soon back on his feet and rushing at his master, screaming with his hands raised and his body rigid. Thanatos jumped forward but staggered because of the wound gaping at his side. Black blood trickled out of it. He held one claw against it and stumbled as he leapt toward Markus again.

"You worthless child!" he growled. He took one long leap his apprentice couldn't dodge. His nails slashed across Markus's face, forcing him to the ground. Corre gasped.

"Markus . . ." She kept her eyes focused as she ran to him. He bent forward in pain, holding his face. He groaned through gritted teeth. Blood leaked out from between his fingers, falling in thick droplets onto the floor. "Oh, no," she whispered and wrapped an arm around his back. "Markus, let me see." She tried peeling his hand away, but it was as though it was sealed to his face. The amount of blood dripping to the floor told her he was probably afraid of what would happen if the wound wasn't held together by the force of his hand.

After one more moment of soul-sucking worry, she decided to do something. She got to her feet and stared Thanatos down herself. Her legs wobbled, but she couldn't sit here and do nothing.

She looked at the horrid beast of a god now flopped back onto the throne. His evil eyes were irritated, but his mouth was carved into a smile. This was the evil master who had tortured Markus for over a decade. This was the one who stood in the way of his happiness and freedom and of the life they could have together.

She moved her hands out at her sides, gathering all the energy she could from the space around her. The surge of instant power squeezed her bones as it flooded through her. It felt like stones were pushed against every part of her, and she yelled—a growing yell that boomed louder by the second—but she withstood it, focused on Thanatos, her hands now outstretched and her mind beckoning two of the spears to come to her palms.

The cool, slick metal hit her skin in both palms. She curled her fingers around them and took a step toward Thanatos. She remembered the combat training with Phineas. Of the sparring she had always done at Athena's. Of the techniques Markus had taught her here. And of course, she thought of Markus, and the blood forming a pond around his knees.

With an ear-splitting war cry, she ran to Thanatos, both spears in hand. She jumped at the throne, the end of one just about to hit his eye and plunge through his skull when the giant monster broke into laughter. He swiped a hand in one unstrained motion that left Corre falling to the floor. Her back nearly snapped as she hit the hard ground, and she let out an earth-rattling, involuntary cry—one far less threatening than the last.

"You bastard!" Markus roared, struggling to his feet. She rolled to her side to look at him, but she could only see his slightly bent form and the back of his head as he staggered to Thanatos. He grabbed one of the weapons she'd dropped and limped toward his master.

"Markus, no!" she cried, but he kept going. Despite the pain. Despite everything.

He lifted the weapon, and his master laughed. But Markus's body was tight again, one of his hands outstretched in a hard line, the muscles on his back constricted. His master was focused, too. And laughing. He was an expert caster of deception, but Markus wasn't biting this time.

The two powerful beings stayed locked in a match of power until Thanatos jolted forward and struck Markus across the side that had only recently started to heal. The young Hades let out a cry, and Corre gasped in horror, running to him as he fell in a heap on the floor. Her back throbbed with every step, but she didn't care.

"Markus—" Her voice failed her as tears welled in her eyes. She pulled his upper body onto her lap and gently moved his head so she could see his face. When she brushed the black hair from his eyes, her throat tightened. He was covered in blood, and his eyes were squinted shut. He was shaking. "No," she whispered, tears breaking through and falling into his hair. She put her forehead on his and cried softly. "Please, don't give up, Markus. Please. I can't lose you."

He lifted his hand and gently grabbed her elbow. "I'll be okay," he whispered, and she lifted her face to look at him. His eyes were open. He was smiling through the pain. "I promised I'd keep you safe, remember?" His face fell, and he broke into a fit of coughs. Blood spewed from his mouth, and her stomach constricted even more.

Corre brushed her hand along the side of his face and tried to smile for him. He lifted his hand to cup her cheek. The pain seemed to vanish in his eyes as he looked at her, which made the situation hurt even more. He lifted his face to hers and kissed her. When she felt the familiar sensation of his lips, her mind momentarily fell into numbness. But then he was gone. When she opened her eyes, he was back up, and she was too stunned to know what to do.

Markus grabbed hold of a spear and threw it at his master's chest with precision, but he was too weak. The weapon barely pierced Thanatos's thick, grey tunic before the great god slapped it away and grabbed hold of Markus's arm.

"Let him go!" Corre yelled as she got to her feet.

The deity's eyes shifted to examine the quaking young goddess before him. Her breaths were shallow, her anger rising again. Then, surprisingly, he let Markus go and cackled at her baffled expression. "My dear." His booming voice was rickety, like a claw scraping across cobblestone. "Why do you care what happens to my apprentice?"

Corre's fingers curled into tight fists. "He's more than your apprentice," she said, her voice surprisingly strong. "He's a bigger god than *you*."

"Correlia—" Markus started, but Thanatos cut in.

"My dear, I am one of the Great Deities that came before your kind. Theron is no match for me." He swiveled his yellow eyes to Markus. "And *you*. Did you really think I wouldn't find out about your little secret?" He snarled as he uttered the last word.

Markus's face lowered. "I—"

"Did you think I wouldn't find out about her?"

Markus's head snapped up. "How *did* you?" He scowled at his master, and Corre had to blink a few times to see if Markus was still trying to defy him. A part of her was impressed, desperate to believe things could change for him, but the rest of her went cold.

Markus. Don't.

His master leaned forward. "I. Know. *Everything*!" The roar blasted through Corre's ears. Markus flinched. "And *you*!" Thanatos's soulless eyes shot to Corre. His crooked mouth lifted in a smile. He let out a quick laugh, wheezed, then said, "How did he manage to fool you?"

"He didn't fool me."

He narrowed his eyes. "Ah, he told you then?"

Nausea formed in her gut. "Told me what?"

Thanatos chuckled and nestled deeper in his seat. "Do you think he gave you that cursed gift by mistake?

The nausea thickened. "Gift?" She looked to Markus, but he wasn't looking back. His gaze had fallen to his feet. His eyebrows were drawn together.

"That pie," the deity bellowed.

The blood drained from Corre's face. "What?" Her eyes were still on Markus. "What is he talking about?"

"I don't know," he said, finally looking back at her. "Truly, I don't."

Thanatos laughed. "My, my. You do know how to trick her, don't you?"

"I am *not* tricking her. What—"

"Come on, *boy*. You know the rules of this place. You will be the god here soon."

As if something struck him, Markus's face changed. He took a step back, shaking his head. "No."

"What? What is it?" Corre cried.

Thanatos laughed again. This was clearly amusing him. Corre and Markus were two bugs beneath his magnifying glass.

"My apprentice, as you know, is the mighty Theron of Tartarus." He took his time between each word, but Corre couldn't stop looking at Markus, her body growing colder by the second. He wouldn't return her gaze. "He knows the ins and outs of the Underworld better than anyone. And yet he gave you that pie." He guffawed and turned to Markus. "Does she truly believe that you did that by *accident*? *You?* The feared *Hades*?"

Markus's face twisted in anguish, and Corre couldn't take it anymore. "What? What did he do? What's going on?"

"What my apprentice failed to mention, I'm sure, is that that pie he gave you—the one swiped from the kitchen earlier this evening—was made of pomegranate."

"S-so?" Her skin was cold, her fingers trembling in lackluster fists at her sides.

"*So,* you are bound here now." The wicked creature's mouth curled. "There's no escape for you. You are stuck here. Just like he is."

Her cheeks burned, but her body was still cold. "Markus, is this true?"

Tears brimmed in his eyes. "Correlia, I'd forgotten. I swear—"

"This has been his plan all along, dear," Thanatos said, but Markus snapped back.

"That's not true!"

"How can you believe him?" the deity barked, his eyes on her, "when he *also* lied to you about that day."

A ringing sounded in her ears. "That . . . that day?"

Thanatos chuckled and sat back in his seat. "As I suspected." He let out a dramatic sigh. "He never told you."

"Told me what?" she said, but the words came out shaky. A lump formed in her throat. She looked to Markus. "Told me *what*?" But he was staring at the ground again, as if in a trance, or maybe searching for something.

"That he was the one who ripped you from your parents. Who murdered them before your eyes that day."

The words filled Corre's ears like bags of sand. Her mouth went dry. "What?" she whispered, but that day rushed back to her like a flash of lightning. Like a missing part of her mind had been found, and the memories were sliding back into place.

She saw the fire. She heard the screams. And she saw *her*—the beautiful, blonde-haired woman with eyes like her own. The woman who'd sung to her every night and told her she could be anything.

She saw destruction. Countless cottages set ablaze. Children being torn from their homes. Gods and goddesses of all stations and ages being executed. She remembered shadowy figures draped in billowing cloaks. She remembered swords. And crying. Her mother's cold body hitting the ground, blood spilling from her lips.

The mother she'd forgotten about.

The day before her life with Berenice had begun. Before the only memories Corre had ever known.

But now there were more. There was too much.

Too much.

She swallowed a sob, but the tears broke through, and she turned to Markus. His head was bowed. She couldn't make out his expression. "Were you there that day?"

His body shifted, and his eyes found hers. "I don't know," he said, but the words were liquid. Like there was nothing behind them.

"You're lying," she whispered. "Markus . . . you're lying."

"No! I—"

Thanatos laughed. "Don't let him fool you, girl. He remembers. He's remembered for some time now."

Markus's hands clamped the sides of his head. He let out a loud growl. "What are you talking about?" he yelled, baring his teeth to his master.

"You know, *boy*!"

Something stung Markus's face. He sucked in a breath, but his eyes went to Corre's. Horror filled his gaze. "Correlia, I—"

She staggered back. "No . . ." This was some kind of dream. A horrific nightmare. It had to be. "Markus, what is he talking about?" her voice faltered as more sobs crept up her throat.

He opened his mouth to say something when Thanatos boomed through the room. "He *did* keep it from you, then. All of it." The giant creature laughed. "I figured as much."

Corre's blood turned cold. She felt like vomiting. She kept her eyes on Markus for an explanation, but all he gave her was a look that made her want to cry.

"You took my family from me?" she whimpered, a tear escaping down her face.

"Correlia, I didn't know. Really, not until this very moment—"

"But you *did* do it?"

Sorrow was deep in his eyes, but it was too late. Corre let out a half-sob. In disgust. In disbelief. Disgust in herself that she had trusted the God of the Underworld. Disbelief that her hope of a future with him had been an illusion. A lie.

She sniffed as more tears fell down her cheeks. "What did you do to them?"

"Correlia, I told you about those dreams. Those nightmares of that day. I didn't remember much until now. . . And I-I didn't know what I was doing. Thanatos had just taken me from my parents—"

"Stop making excuses!" she screamed. "What did you do to them?" The words echoed through the room, hanging in the air.

Tears streamed down his face. "I'm so sorry, Correlia. I was a child. I don't remember. I don't remember you or your parents, so I can't tell you either way. But I do remember that day. And that song. I'm so sorry."

Something hardened in her chest. "That song?"

"The one you sometimes sing at night. When you fall asleep." His voice wobbled, and that pain in his face intensified. "I . . . I think it's the one you told me about. I didn't remember it then, but I do now. I remember a goddess singing it to a little girl—"

"Before he executed her," Thanatos finished.

Corre let out a small cry and covered her mouth. *This isn't happening.* Tears streamed down her face. *This can't be happening.*

"No, I didn't!" Markus cried. "I was there that day, but I never executed anybody!"

"You're sure of that?" Thanatos bellowed, but the young god fell silent.

When Corre looked back at Markus, he shook his head again. "I'm so sorry."

She staggered back. She wanted to get out of here. She needed air. Needed escape.

"Correlia, I don't remember. And whatever happened, I didn't know—"

"Stop!" she cried, falling to her knees and covering her ears. She sobbed into the ground, huddled in a tight ball. This was all too much. She didn't know what to believe anymore. "You lied to me."

"No, Correlia, please—" he said through tears.

Her gaze shot up. "I trusted you. And you didn't even tell me you knew about that song! I was there for you!"

"I didn't remember where I'd heard it until now!"

"How can I believe you? When you hadn't told me anything and then trapped me here under the ruse that you wanted to do something nice for me?" She scoffed and looked away. "A pie for my birthday. I was such a fool."

"Correlia," he whispered, but she didn't want to hear it. She couldn't even look at him. Because if she did, she knew she wouldn't be able to stop herself from running over and holding him until the tears stopped falling down his face. But he was the one who'd ripped her life from her. Who'd deceived her.

"I really did want to give you something special." His voice was little more than a whimper as he continued to cry. "Nothing I ever said or did to you was a lie."

She couldn't look at him. She didn't know what to think. And the worst part was that she didn't even want to go home. But she didn't want to be here. Her whole life had been flipped upside down.

Happiness had been within her reach for the first time. Because of him. Because she thought she'd found belonging. Someone who understood. But it had just been an elaborate fabrication all along. A foolish dream.

She didn't know what to do anymore. Where to go. What to think.

A cry splintered through the air. Not one of sorrow—a wail of pain. She looked up and saw an arrow piercing Markus's left shoulder. It only took her half a second to recognize whose arrows they were.

The kind that could strike through anything.

She jumped to her feet. "Markus!"

"Stop!" a familiar voice shouted, and she turned, hoping it wasn't who she thought it was.

Holding one of Apollo's bows was Phineas, standing armored before a cavalry—a group of well-suited warriors, some from Athena's academy, some Corre had never seen before. Then there were Apollo and Athena. Phineas was leading an army as Ares for the first time. And it had to be here.

"Phineas, you don't know what you're doing!" she called to him, moving toward Markus.

"No, Corre, *you* don't know what you're doing. He's beguiled you."

Corre shot Phineas a glare and walked to Markus anyway. Every arrow was pointed toward him, and every warrior with a spear or an ax was standing at the ready. She kept her gaze locked on Phineas. He knew better than to cross her.

When she saw that the arrow in Markus's shoulder was leaking something into his skin, she gasped. "It's poisoned!" She grabbed hold of the golden body. She tried tugging it out, but the young Hades stopped her.

His hand was on hers as he slowly turned to look at her. "Leave while you can," he said. His voice was strained, and the agony on his face made more tears fall down her cheeks. "Please," he whispered.

"Markus, no." The words were barely audible. Another arrow struck his back, and he fell limply to the ground.

She looked at Phineas in horror. "What are you doing?"

"We need to take you back," he said, sliding another arrow in place on the bow.

Her cold blood started to burn. "Don't you *dare* hurt him again, Phineas, or I will *not* come back at all."

Thanatos let out a long, drawn-out cackle. "No need to worry, dear. You cannot leave here anyway."

"She can, and she will," a voice said, but this one filled Corre with relief. She turned to see her mother, walking alongside Zeus.

"Mother—"

"You cannot keep her here, Thanatos," Zeus said, his deep voice rattling the broken chains on the throne room floor. His silvery beard fell halfway down his chest. He was almost as tall as Markus's master and about ten times more robust.

Thanatos's mouth pinched shut. "She has eaten the pomegranate. She cannot leave."

Berenice gasped, but Zeus lifted a hand, gesturing for her to be at ease. "The pomegranate only ties her here. It does not force her to spend every day here, so she will be returning to Olympus today."

"She lives *here* now," Thanatos said firmly, but Zeus shook his head.

"She's leaving here with us. You and I can discuss the details after she is gone, but for now, she is leaving."

Thanatos narrowed his eyes on the god, tapping one sharpened nail against the throne. "If we must," he growled.

Corre looked down at Markus again, but he wasn't moving. His eyes were squeezed shut. "Markus?"

He flinched before peeling his eyes open to look up at her. "Go, Correlia. Just go."

Pain stung every part of her. It wasn't supposed to be like this. "Did you do it?" she whispered, but his eyes closed again. "Markus?" She let out a sob. "What's happened to him!?"

"It's just the poison," Phineas said, and she whipped around. Her friend let the bow fall to his side. "He'll be awake in an hour or two."

She gritted her teeth. She'd never wanted to smack someone harder than she wanted to hit Phineas right now. "How could you do that?" *I still had so many questions.*

"You've been through a lot. Let's get you home."

Corre's fists tightened.

"Don't worry, dear," Thanatos said with a smirk. "You will be back here soon enough."

"Come on, Corre," Phineas said, grabbing her wrist.

She snatched her arm away and glared at him. "Don't touch me, Phineas."

He frowned, wounded, and she wished she could wound him even more. She looked back at Markus, but one of the guards was chaining him again, his limp body soaked with blood and sticky, black poison.

"Take the arrows from his back," Thanatos said lazily to another of his guards.

The demon did as the deity commanded. Markus let out grunts of pain as each arrow was plucked out. Tears stung Corre's eyes. She wanted to leap over to him, but she wasn't even sure who he was anymore. She was stupid for thinking she knew him so intimately after such a short time.

But still, as Phineas and the others escorted her out of the throne room, she couldn't stop looking at Markus and wondering—after she was gone, who would be there to stitch up his wounds?

CHAPTER THIRTY-TWO

Corre

If someone were to ask Corre about her journey from the Underworld that day, she wouldn't be able to tell them. Her mind was gone as her mother led her home. Her body was cold. Everything was numb. Everything except the heavy weight sinking deeper inside her stomach.

Even after her mother tearfully hugged her, kissing her cheeks and telling her to sleep, Corre felt nothing. Yet, somehow, she still ached with pain. She felt both everything and nothing—a simultaneous dance of daggers deep within herself, in a place that couldn't be reached. Her body hurt the moment it hit the sheets, her ribs a fragile cage that creaked in agony when she breathed against her too-soft mattress.

The room was cold, the air stale. Maybe she'd gotten used to the muggy air of Tartarus. It didn't feel right to be here.

It didn't feel right to be without him.

Her hands tightened, coiling as her body curled in on itself. When she wasn't tensed and guarding her body, she felt too vulnerable, too out of control. It was easier to bear everything when she was balled up. As if not keeping herself like this would expose her to more agony.

Despite her best efforts, the pain only grew. It branched from her stomach into her veins, and soon, her insides were burning, but her skin remained ice cold. She didn't know how she was supposed to feel, or what she was supposed to think. Was she supposed to believe Markus was the bad guy? Or was her immense anxiety over him being left alone with that monster fully justified?

His smile surfaced in her mind. The way he looked at her when she did nothing special. Whether it was just a laugh, a playful look, or sometimes nothing at all. He always looked at her with such awe. Like she'd just done something spectacular.

Throughout her time there, his eyes had softened. His jaw had clenched less often. His body had become less tense. He'd let himself go more. Not in the way Thanatos wanted him to, or in the way people would expect. He had let the *pain* go. The expectations. The fear. Even if it had only been in small bursts, in thin slivers of time. When they were together, he let himself be hers and let Markus slip through Theron's mask. If even just for a little while.

It didn't matter how hard she tried to peel the image of him from her head. He was still there. Those dark, brooding eyes that lit up when she smiled. The strength of his frame as he trained. As he'd stood up to Thanatos. As he'd tried to protect her.

Corre watched her hand slowly uncoil. Tiny half-moons had imprinted on her palms from her nails. She stared at her fingers, at the lines on her palm, remembering Markus's touch. Remembering everything she didn't want to remember. The way he'd held her hands when he'd promised to keep her safe.

She thought of the waves of his black hair, the taste of his mouth, and the feel of his body. But worst of all, she remembered the pain slashed across his face just before she'd left. His limp, almost lifeless body being dragged away.

What would they do to him now?

As she lay there, she couldn't help wondering what was going on at that precise moment, despite not really wanting to know. Because whatever it was, Thanatos was behind it, and it was likely beyond her comprehension.

Her eyes squeezed shut, and her body curled tighter. "Markus..." A tear rolled sideways down her face. What would he go through while she was away? How often would Thanatos rip him apart and sew him haphazardly back together, just so he could rip him apart again?

Eventually, her mind found what it wanted to focus on most, which, naturally, was what *she* wanted to focus on least. Those final few moments before the cavalry had arrived. Thanatos's sinister grin as he revealed that Markus had killed her family. The unreadable expression on Markus's face as his master spoke those words. The sorrow in the young Hades' eyes when he finally looked at her.

But what he'd said...

"I don't remember you or your parents... but I do remember that day. And that song. I'm so sorry."

She couldn't take it anymore. She couldn't stop the sobs barreling through the room. The loudest, hardest cries she'd ever produced. Her body shook violently as the tears continued to flow.

"Corre?" her mother's voice came through the wooden door.

She didn't answer. She cried until her body hurt too much to move. Until she was too exhausted to do anything but sleep.

She didn't know how long she'd cried before passing out, but it had been long enough that the night sky had already shifted to dawn. The light blue beams pooled onto her bed as if the sun was begging her to stop relying on the night.

She couldn't stay in the darkness forever.

No matter how much she wanted to.

When she woke up for the day, she was miserable. Her body ached. Her eyes were puffy, and her stomach was cramped. She'd barely eaten anything in Tartarus because of the excitement she'd let herself get swept into. But even now, she wasn't hungry. The thought of food made her sick. When her mother asked what she wanted for breakfast, despite it being late afternoon, Corre mumbled that she didn't want to eat.

She couldn't even move. She was still numb, hollow, lifeless. The only times she didn't feel numb were when the thoughts of Markus resurfaced, and her eyes stung again, and her stomach lurched. The pain was beyond anything she'd ever experienced.

The next day went by like that, too. And then the next.

Finally, on the third day, Berenice let herself into Corre's room and placed her hand on her daughter's arm. "Sweetheart, you have to eat something. You've barely eaten."

"I'm not hungry," she replied. Her voice was hoarse from lack of use. And probably from crying.

Her mother paused, then quietly said, "We never celebrated your birthday."

My birthday.

She thought of Markus and the joy in his eyes when he brought in that damned pie. There was no way he'd known the fate behind it. He couldn't have.

Could he?

Tears filled her eyes, and she hated that she couldn't stop crying. She tried to hide it as best she could, but her shoulders betrayed her.

Berenice rubbed her daughter's arm. "You poor thing. You must have been through so much down there."

Corre blinked away the tears and wiped her face before sitting up. She gathered her knees to her chest and rested against them. "I didn't go through what you think," she said, sniffing and clearing her throat.

"What do you mean?"

She wanted to tell her mother everything, but how could she understand? How could she tell her that she'd fallen in love with the God of the Underworld?

She studied the floral patterns on her quilt. Her feet were little unmoving lumps beneath the sheets. She took in a deep breath and huffed it out, then rolled her head to the side so she could face her mother.

Berenice smiled. "Hi, sweetie. Are you doing okay?"

"Mother . . ."

"Yes?" Berenice's voice was light, and guilt stirred in Corre's stomach.

She must have worried her mother sick these last few days. She opened her mouth, but then her throat went dry.

Her mother frowned. "What is it?"

She took another deep breath, squeezed the last few tears from her eyes, and then asked a question she didn't want to know the answer to. "What happened the night my parents died?"

Berenice's eyes fell, her mouth tightening into a line. "I never told you they died."

"I know. You never told me *anything*." She felt a little bad about the indignation in her voice, but enough was enough. "Don't you think you've sheltered me long enough? I'm twenty, Mother. I can handle it."

There was still a deep sense of worry in Berenice's gaze. "Who told you they died?"

Something twisted in Corre's chest. "So they *did* die." She puffed out an angry laugh and shook her head. "Thanatos was telling the truth."

"Thanatos?"

Corre jolted at the sudden rise in Berenice's voice. "Yeah?"

"You mean the one who took on Hades to train? The current ruler of the Underworld? *That* Thanatos?"

Corre's forehead crinkled. "Yes . . . What about him?"

"What did he say?"

Corre's head jerked back in surprise, and she tried to find the words. "Um . . . Well . . . He said . . ." Her mouth clamped shut. She couldn't say it. Just thinking about the allegation made her sick. And it brought back the memories.

The one of her biological mother hitting the ground.

She let out a sharp, quick cry and buried her face in her hands.

"What's wrong? What is it?"

Her breathing quickened, her chest tightening. "I remember it," she said.

"Remember what?"

"That day." She looked up. "I remember my mother. My other mother. The one who sang me that song. That . . . that melody. I remember her death now."

Berenice's eyes widened. "What?" Her voice was shaky and quiet, and all Corre could do was slowly nod. "How? When did this happen?"

"The day you fetched me from Tartarus. Thanatos told me that . . ." Corre closed her eyes and took a deep breath. As she exhaled, she forced the words out. "That Markus killed them. I mean . . . Theron. Hades. He killed my parents."

"Thanatos told you that?"

"So, it's true?" Her heart nearly stopped, the blood draining down her body.

"No. It's not."

Chills pricked Corre's skin. "I don't understand. Markus didn't kill them?" The words barely made their way out.

Berenice gave her a sad smile. "You know that he's Markus."

Corre gaped at her. "*You* know his real name?"

"Of course," she said. "I was there that day, too. I saw everything."

Markus

When Markus awoke the day after Correlia left, he was in the most excru-
ciating pain of his life. And to make matters worse, the first thing he saw
when he opened his eyes was Nikias standing above him. One of his lackeys
had dumped ice water on his face to shock him back to consciousness. He
didn't know what was worse—the pain, the freezing water, or having to see
that smug face staring down at him.

It was the pain. Definitely the pain.

It was searing through him like a hot knife peeling through the layers
of his flesh. His insides were shocked and jumbled. His blood was like the
acidic water of the Kokytus River.

"Get up, you filthy traitor," Nikias hissed, shoving him before turning to
leave. Markus reached out and grabbed him by the arm before Nikias could
get far. His hand was large enough to almost completely wrap around the
skinny man's bicep. Nikias scowled at him, but Markus could see the fear
in his eyes. The blonde knew he was no match for him, even in this state.
"Let go of me!"

"No," Markus said through gritted teeth. "You took my life from me."
He tightened his grip on Nikias's arm, and the slender man bent forward
in pain. "You will live to regret this."

"I took nothing from you," Nikias growled, struggling to free himself from Markus's grasp. When he managed to snap his arm away, he stumbled back and nearly fell to the floor. "That goddess is nothing."

"Not to me," Markus said, sitting up and sliding to his feet. He took a step toward Nikias, who nervously walked back with every move the bigger god made.

The young Hades stalked toward him faster, ignoring that every step was like walking on broken glass. Fear widened the skinny god's eyes as the Underworld's successor cornered him and grabbed him by the shirt. Markus pushed him against the wall. "Not. To me," he repeated in a low growl. "To me, she is everything." He wished he could kill Nikias. Cave his pretentious skull in. But there was no point, so he threw him to the ground and stepped over him to leave the room.

"Get him!" Nikias cried, and the demons slithered over to Markus and tried holding him down. The young Hades did his best to fight them off. If he wasn't this injured, he could have pulverized them with no effort at all, but the pain welling inside him was getting worse, and it wasn't long before he crumpled to the ground, his vision going white.

It was a struggle to breathe, and he still couldn't see anything when he felt someone pick him up by the back of the shirt. They tore it off him and threw him against the wall of the labyrinth, which was far worse than the one he'd thrown Nikias against back in his room. Every surface of the corridor was rocky. Being smacked against it was like getting scraped with serrated stones, and his body already burned like he'd been doused with fire.

He grunted in pain, then fell to the floor, his head hitting the hard surface. Nikias laughed hysterically, each laugh getting louder as he approached. "Get up, you pathetic excuse for a god." He kicked Markus hard in the stomach. "You'll be happy to know that we can't get a hold of that girl until she's here again."

Panic flared in Markus's chest. "When will that be?" he managed to grumble.

Nikias chuckled. His voice was muffled now, and Markus had to strain to hear the answer. "Three months' time."

The fear erupted into flames. Three months? He only had three months? He'd trained for a decade and couldn't even take Thanatos down. Now he was in a state worse than death. What could he possibly accomplish in three months?

It wasn't enough time.

If he was to protect her, he needed to be a lot stronger.

"Don't get your hopes up. You won't be allowed to see her."

Markus's eyes shot open, and though breathing was a struggle, he said, "What are you talking about?"

"Are you stupid? It means you won't be allowed to touch her!" Nikias's evil smile lengthened. "Don't worry. I'll touch her enough for the both of us."

A new fire lit in Markus's soul. He roared and got to his feet, knocking Nikias over and punching him in the face. "Touch her and you're dead, you pompous bastard!" he yelled, and struck him again. He wound his arm back to land another punch, but Nikias's lackeys grabbed hold of his arms and restrained him.

Just like when they were boys, Nikias was spared from another punch. Only this time, Markus wasn't sure he ever would have stopped.

The demons kicked him to his knees and chains were once again placed on his wrists, locking his arms behind his back. Nikias wiped the blood from his nose and strode over, crouching down to get leveled with Markus's face. "You don't have what it takes to be Hades." He spat on his face, and Markus tried jumping at him but only fell to the ground in a blaring bout of pain.

His torso scratched against the rocky ground, burning his skin as the chains on his wrists sent shocks through his bones. Nikias laughed again, but Markus couldn't keep his eyes open anymore.

Before everything went black, the last thing he heard was the general's muffled voice. "And now you'll never get the throne. You're done."

CHAPTER THIRTY-THREE

Corre

"It was the most terrible night of my life. It was the most horrific thing I'd ever witnessed. To this day, I've never seen so much terror. So much destruction." Berenice's eyes were gone to another time, and goosebumps quickly rose on Corre's skin. "Thanatos and his men had come up from the Underworld. He'd been appointed the leader there until Markus was of age. When the boy was deemed old enough to train, he needed to be fetched." Berenice let out a shaky sigh. "That day was his thirteenth birthday, and Thanatos decided to make it a show."

Corre nervously tugged on a loose string hanging from the corner of her quilt, processing her mother's words. The world around them was still.

"I lived in the village with many of the others at that time. The ones without special titles, you know." She let out a tight laugh. "Back then, it was no better than it is now. We weren't seen as important. It's concerning how much better I was treated after being deemed the new Demeter. But that's beside the point. The point is—if I had been home, I would have missed the sight completely. And I don't think I was supposed to miss it."

She smiled softly and lifted a hand to her daughter's cheek. "Because witnessing what I did that night was one of the reasons Zeus let me be your mother. Probably *the* reason." Corre swallowed hard but stayed silent. "I was walking home from the marketplace that night when I heard screaming. I rushed to the sound. Before I got there, a burst of smoke funneled into the sky, and another wave of screams filled the air. I ran there as fast as I could."

"Weren't you scared?" Corre asked.

"Of course I was."

"So why did you do it? You don't have the skills of a fighter. You could have been tortured or burned alive."

"It was the right thing to do, and the screams were too much. Especially, the screams of a child." Something darkened in her eyes. "I heard *you*." Corre watched her mother, forgetting to breathe every couple of seconds. "I hid. I saw everything. You and your birth mother. I saw it all. I saw him ripping you from her, pulling your tiny arms from hers. You had wrapped them around her so tightly."

Corre's hands turned to ice. She stopped tugging on the string. "Why couldn't I remember any of this until now?"

"It was very traumatic for you. I'm sure you blocked it out as soon as you knew you were safe here."

Corre paused. "You said he ripped me from her. Was that Markus?"

"No," Berenice said with a small smile, but her eyes were still dark. "It was Thanatos."

Thanatos. Of course.

Guilt pinched her chest. Why had she been so quick to believe that demonic beast? Why couldn't she have stood her ground, stuck to her belief that Markus was good the night she'd left Tartarus?

A lump formed in her throat. She had to concentrate hard on the words she wanted to say so she wouldn't cry. "So, Markus didn't do anything?"

"No, he didn't."

Markus wasn't lying. I was right before.

He is good.

"Then why did he remember that day?"

"Because he was there, too. It was his birthday 'celebration,' remember?" Berenice shook her head, sadness deep in her eyes. "But he didn't hurt you or anybody else. He was just a frightened boy back then, trembling behind his new master. He'd just been taken from his own family. He was terrified."

"Why didn't anyone do anything about it? I got placed in *your* care. Why didn't he get a chance like that?"

Berenice rubbed her forehead, grimacing. "Because Markus wasn't born from the same parents as you, and he was the one who was supposed to go with Thanatos. No one had a choice. His parents had to watch him get sent to the Underworld."

"What do you mean 'the same parents as me'? Because my mother was Demeter?"

"Because your father is Zeus."

Corre froze. "What?"

Berenice squeezed Corre's hand and kept her eyes steady on her daughter. "He wanted to give you a good life, despite . . ." she didn't want to finish the sentence, but she didn't have to.

"Despite not wanting to be a part of it," Corre finished. *My father is Zeus. My father is Zeus.* No matter how many times she thought the words, she couldn't get herself to fully believe them. "I thought Zeus was a good guy. Everyone always talks about how personable he is, and he went down to rescue me . . ." *Because I'm his daughter.* "Right." She started pulling on that string again, desperately wishing this moment would end. Wishing she was back in Tartarus, wrapped in Markus's arms.

Her chest ached at the thought of him.

"Zeus always seemed so good," the young goddess added, trying her best to ignore that ache burrowing deeper in her chest. She looked to her mother, hoping she'd assure her that her father *was* good and that he had a good reason for his absence in her life. For hiding that he was her father.

But Berenice only held her daughter's hand and gave her that same sad smile. "Unfortunately, appearances and reputations are deceiving, especially when shaped by public opinion." She patted Corre's hand. "But I'm sure you know that by now."

Her stomach twisted as she thought about Markus and the vile things people had always said about him. The way rumors were steeped so far into their community that Phineas was willing to storm the Underworld and strike a complete stranger with an arrow. All because he—and everyone else—didn't know Hades. Because they *thought* they did. But they didn't. They only knew stories that were never backed by fact. And Markus was never there to defend himself. Nobody was.

To them, he was a monster, and no one bothered to question it.

Corre's mind drifted to the other part of what her mother said, and of what Markus had mentioned about his parents before. "They cared that he was sent there? Markus said he'd been abandoned by them."

"Of course they cared, though I suppose I'm not surprised that he thinks otherwise. He's been down there with Thanatos all this time." She let out a sigh. "But yes, they cared very much. His father was even cast out of Olympus trying to stop it. He'd tried so hard to keep Markus from going, but the Titans had already declared that Markus would be Hades, and there was nothing anyone could do about it."

"What about Zeus? Couldn't he have done something about it?"

"Unfortunately, Zeus didn't care. Hades was destined to be his rival. It was deemed as much, in different words, by the Titans. Zeus was only to follow their orders, though he had his influence. I think he knew that

Thanatos would be a difficult master. I think he secretly hoped that no true Hades would ever take the throne." She looked sadly into Corre's eyes. "I think he liked that Thanatos took Markus. He knew that the creature would be hard on him. He saw the evil in Thanatos."

"That's terrible!" Anger rippled through her. "Why would he enjoy sentencing a young boy to that? And what made Markus such a good candidate?" She scoffed, fury rising in her voice.

"He was a very emotional child, and troublesome. Zeus didn't want anything to do with him, and he wanted Markus's mother. If you ask me, I think he agreed so vehemently with the Titans' choice because he wanted Markus out of the way, and when Markus's father, Thomas, tried fighting back to save the boy, Zeus leapt on the opportunity to cast him out. He even took away his status as a god and made him mortal. Then Zeus took Markus's mother for himself. Against her wishes. Though he's moved on now."

Corre wanted to scream at Zeus. Markus had been the object of detest his entire life, just because he'd struggled with his emotions. How was that fair? And how was Zeus their leader? What kind of leader destroyed lives like that, and for his own gain, no less? And how was someone like that her father?

Markus's father risked immortality for his son, and mine is the source of such pain.

"How despicable," Corre muttered in disbelief.

Berenice nodded. "Yes. He had a child with the goddess, too."

Corre blinked. "He did?"

"Yes. She's grown up to be quite mischievous, but Zeus doesn't really pay attention to her. She's not a threat to him."

"Who is she?"

"Her name is Tyche. She's probably about twelve years old now."

Corre's body froze. Tyche. That platinum-haired goddess who'd helped her into Tartarus. She was her half-sister? And Markus's on his mother's side? "Does Markus know about her?"

"No. Markus was completely cut off from everyone but Thanatos that day. He was forced to watch all the destruction and was taken to Tartarus afterward, and no one heard from him again. Naturally, he became a folk legend on Olympus. He was renamed Theron by his master, and rumors grew over the years. That's how he became a monster-under-the-bed type of being to everyone here."

Berenice looked out the window, her eyes following the happy trots of a bird on the other side of the glass. "You likely won't find sympathy for him on Olympus, but I know what I saw that day. Amongst the destruction was a trembling boy, scrawny and sobbing, and whenever Thanatos caught him showing emotion, he would strike him, which would obviously make the boy cry harder." Corre's chest ached at the thought of a young Markus being treated so horrendously. She clasped the cloth of the quilt and tried not to dwell on it, but her mother continued. "I saw Thanatos grab him by the shoulders and scream at him, telling him he needed to whip him into shape if he ever wanted to be Hades. Markus cried that he didn't want to be Hades, but Thanatos just hit him and told him not to speak back to him." She let out a sad, audible sigh. "And that was that."

"That's so awful. I don't understand why anyone would allow such things to happen. Did Zeus at least know about the destruction Thanatos was causing?"

"Not until it was already over. He came with his army just as Thanatos was about to kill you."

When he was about to kill me?

The thought made her blood run cold. "Why was he killing children?"

"He wasn't. He was only after you."

"What?" All the air left her lungs. Each time she thought nothing else could shock her further, her mother revealed even more.

"Thanatos wanted to make a statement that day, which was the reason for all the burning and theatrics. He also knew you were to be Hades' opposite. He wanted you dead in case you caused trouble for him one day." At the sight of her daughter's anguish, Berenice leaned forward and gave her a compassionate smile. "You were to bring light and life to the world, my dear, and Thanatos wanted to rule through darkness. He wanted only death. He was scared of what you might one day become, and you should be proud of yourself that you've grown even stronger than what he feared."

Corre couldn't respond. Her mouth was dry, and her body was weak. It was like she wasn't in her body at all. Berenice patted her daughter's hand again and gently continued. "After Zeus chased him out, and after you had been carefully taken from your mother ... who had passed before your eyes ... you were placed in my care. I was given the role your mother had—to be Demeter. You needed to be taught. Then, more than ever."

Something twisted in Corre's gut. What would have happened if Berenice hadn't found her that day? She felt even guiltier. "I'm sorry. For not taking my role seriously. I had no idea."

"No, no, it's my fault," Berenice said. "I sheltered you from all of this. After you finally accepted me and trusted me when you were a child, something shifted in you. You were happier, and you slowly stopped re-membering the terrors of that day, including your old life. I didn't want to see you as listless and despondent as you had been. I wanted you to be happy. But you're a grown woman now. I should have told you long ago."

Corre stroked her mother's hair. "It's okay. I know now." She tried to force a smile, but she couldn't stop thinking about Markus. What he'd gone through made her sick. And furious.

"You care about him, don't you?" Berenice said softly.

"I do. He's not what everyone thinks. He's especially not what Phineas thinks."

There was a pause before Berenice said, "You should explain it to Phineas."

Corre snorted. "Right. That would go over well."

"He deserves to know."

The young goddess's eyes snapped up. "Why? Why does *Phineas* deserve to know? *He*'s the one who hurt Markus."

"Not that. He deserves to know how you feel about Markus."

Corre's mouth hung open. "Why?"

Berenice chuckled. "For someone so beautifully astute and understanding of the God of the Underworld, you sure have a hard time seeing what's in front of you in your own life."

Corre frowned. "What are you talking about?"

Berenice looked out the window. "I think Phineas has something to tell you. You should talk to him. Try to explain things. Who knows—maybe he will change his mind about Markus. You never know." Corre suppressed the urge to roll her eyes. The last person she wanted to see right now was Phineas, after what he'd done. Berenice brushed a loose strand of hair behind Corre's ear. "I'm glad you told me how you feel about him."

"I'm glad you believe me," Corre said, realizing she could finally let relief loosen the tension in her body. The most important person in her life validated her feelings and believed her. It took a huge weight off her chest. "I'm glad that you know that he's not what people think."

Berenice smiled sadly. "Child, I've always known he's not what people think." Corre smiled, tears filling her eyes. "But I'm glad to know Thanatos hasn't changed his heart. At least not to the point that he would be too far gone by the time he met my lovely daughter."

"You warned me about seeing him, though. You were afraid of him. You were so worried about me being down there you sent Zeus to fetch me."

Berenice let out a short laugh. "You were in Tartarus, my dear. Thanatos is evil and, as I said, I had no idea what state Theron was in." She smiled. "But I'm glad to know he still has Markus left in him."

Corre nodded, trying to smile, but her heart wasn't in it. She looked back down at her hands, pulling that loose string on her quilt again. "He's not perfect, of course, but he's not what people think."

"Is anybody?" Berenice said, and Corre looked up. "Are any of us what everyone else thinks?" She pondered this but said nothing. It didn't matter what it was like for anybody else. No one else was Hades. He was the most hated god on Olympus. There may never be hope for him.

"Let me make you something to eat," Berenice said, patting her daughter on the knee and getting off the bed. Halfway out the door, she stopped and turned back around. "Oh. I almost forgot. Zeus summoned me to his palace yesterday."

Corre frowned. "Why?"

"He told me the agreement he struck with Thanatos." The room went silent. When her mother realized Corre wouldn't reply, she continued. "He said you will be there half the year." Pain twisted her mother's features.

Half the year?

Would she get to see Markus during that time?

"You will report in three months."

Corre's stomach dropped. "That's so far away," she said, and Berenice gaped at her.

"Correlia." She shook her head in disbelief. "I know you have seen the light in him, but Tartarus is dangerous, and Markus is still a powerful god who has been trained by the worst creature I've ever seen."

"He's not a monster, Mother. Really, he isn't," she pleaded, but she could tell the older goddess was still skeptical. She had to come to terms with the fact that although her mother understood better than most, no one would know Markus the way she did. She just wished her mother could understand a little more. "He won't hurt me. I know it. He sacrificed himself to protect me on more than one occasion."

Berenice let out a long sigh. "Even so, you won't be reporting to him. You'll be reporting to Thanatos." The older goddess's hand curled along the door frame. "I don't know what he plans to do with you—" her voice cut off, and, to Corre's surprise, she broke into tears.

Corre rushed to her mother and threw her into an embrace. "It'll be okay. I promise. I'll train. I've been training in combat for years, and Markus taught me some things, too. I'll be okay."

Berenice wiped her face and looked up at her daughter. She gently placed her hands on the girl's shoulders. "Don't focus on your duties as Persephone, okay? Train with Athena as much as possible. Learn from her." She leaned in closer. "Will you do that for me, please?"

"Of course. I promise."

The older goddess dropped her arms to her sides. "Okay. Now, there's no use focusing on such melancholy things. Let me make you some soup. I baked a fresh loaf of bread this morning. I'll bring it to you."

"Thank you," Corre said, and her mother kissed her on the forehead and closed the door.

When she was alone again, Markus came back to her mind. All his suffering. The pain his parents must have gone through. The pain he'd been enduring for so long.

The darkness had faded in him at a rapid pace.

Maybe he just needed someone to believe in him.

To help him not be afraid.

To love him.

Corre fell onto the bed and curled herself into a ball again. She couldn't take it. She couldn't take the pain and the not knowing. She couldn't take his absence. She couldn't even sleep well anymore because he wasn't there to hold her.

She was desperate for him. The thought of him being stuck there and in so much pain, without her. Being tormented by his master. It was too much.

Three months. I'll see him in three months.

She closed her eyes and waited desperately for the turmoil inside her to stop. She had to believe he'd be okay in the meantime, but then she remembered his apologetic look as she'd accused him of being a liar, and her insides practically crumbled. She curled her body in tighter, tensing it to keep out the pain. To guard her against the guilt and agony. "I'm so sorry, Markus," she whispered.

What did he think of her now?

The way she'd looked at him must have cut him up inside, and then she'd left, and he was alone again. Alone with his abuser and his lackeys. Without knowing she still believed in him. That she still loved him.

She had to keep it together. If she let the guilt build and stay there, she'd go crazy, and she'd be of no use when she returned to Tartarus. She couldn't let herself be consumed by all the horrible thoughts and feelings. She needed to think about him—about how she'd be there to save him soon and how she'd apologize and kiss him, and hopefully, everything would be okay.

In the meantime, she had to train. But she'd get to that tomorrow. She was still too weak right now. Hopefully, she'd be better tomorrow.

Hopefully.

Markus

Markus went through a grueling punishment process the whole week after Correlia was torn from him, but none of it hurt more than losing her, or the memory of her face as she'd stepped away from him with such sorrow and shock. The look of someone who had been betrayed.

"I'm so sorry, Correlia," he whispered to the empty space beside him every night. "I wish I could remember."

Part of his punishment was for Thanatos to strike and scorn him for his disobedience, and he'd scream that Markus was worthless—that he was such scum that he'd even tricked a girl whose parents he'd killed into falling in love with him. But Markus couldn't get himself to believe any of it. Correlia believed in him, and though it had taken him some getting used to, he'd started to believe her. And he didn't fully remember that night.

He couldn't even stomach killing the villagers a couple of weeks ago. He couldn't imagine having killed people when he was a boy, before his training. It just didn't make sense. Maybe he was only hoping it wasn't true because the thought of hurting Correlia in any way made him feel completely gutted.

Day after day, the abuse continued, and he couldn't help but feel he deserved it. He'd put Correlia in harm's way. He even fed her the pomegranate. How could he have been so stupid? How had he forgotten the curse of that fruit—the fruit that was only grown in Tartarus and came with such a price?

And he'd given it to Correlia. Like a complete moron.

Guilt racked his body every night when he no longer had pain and training rendering him too weary to think. He'd doomed her to an eternity of agony because he couldn't stop thinking about her the day they'd met, and because he'd been sloppy. He had no idea how he'd take the throne anymore.

The only reason he hadn't resigned completely was that there was no alternative. He *had* to take the throne. He needed to be able to free her, and only he could do it. But only from his place as Hades, ruler of Tartarus.

He couldn't give up. No matter the odds, he had to keep going. Whenever he thought of her uninhibited laughter and intoxicating smile, the light in her eyes and the softness of her lips, he knew he had to keep her safe. He couldn't let anyone hurt her.

The thought of her kept him going. Every night, he let his mind wander back to her. He'd recall every part of her—every lively, bright, and beautiful detail—and relive the moments they'd shared.

Weeks of agony went by, but the moment he'd fall into bed each night, he thought of her. And for a moment, the pain would subside. And that kept him going.

She was the most brilliantly beautiful person he'd ever known. Her soul radiated perfection. He was used to such disgusting corruption and evil creatures, but she was the complete opposite. She was light incarnate. She was free, like the air on Olympus—the air she breathed when she was safely away from this place.

The selfish part of him lingered on the image of her lying next to him, wishing she was still here. Wishing he could hold her as she slept. Wishing he could feel the familiar warmth of her body. That body that housed his heart and soul. He was starting to wonder if he could even exist without her now that he'd given so much of himself to her. Part of him only existed within her now.

He did know that he didn't *want* to exist without her. That he would gladly give his entire existence to her if it meant keeping her safe and happy. So freely alive. And though she didn't know it, she was already home to most of his soul. The moment she'd first looked at him, part of his soul had left his body and entered hers. The more enamored he became, the more of him went into her, and when they finally kissed, he became hers completely.

The only way he could feel complete now was if she was next to him. He wanted to weave their souls together and become wholly one. He wanted to kiss her until her mind buzzed to a stop. To feel her body beneath him as he took control of her desires. He wanted to make her feel every good sensation in the world. To see her eyes light up the way he imagined they would when they were finally one in body. He wanted her to breathe his name and be his forever.

He ached for her so much it hurt.

Before she waltzed into his life, he'd resigned to just barely hanging on. But knowing her and feeling her, tasting her, and being loved by her had changed him. It awoke desires he didn't know he had. Emotionally and physically. And he wanted to live now. Really, truly live.

It wasn't enough to dream of her, but it was all he could do for now. So every night, he thought of the softness of her skin and the curve of her hips, and the way she lit fire through his bloodstream.

And that's how he got through those next three months.

CHAPTER THIRTY-FOUR

Corre

Markus's arms wrapped around her, his body pressed against her back. His hands slid up her forearms as he helped her get into the right position for the technique. She could feel the massive amounts of power flooding through him like it was wind rushing from his soul to hers. She'd never felt such power from anyone before. It scared her a bit, but in a way that sucked her into him.

Her stomach fluttered as his breath grazed the back of her neck. She found her eyes closing and her body falling into his. He must have realized she wasn't paying attention anymore because her head grew dizzy as she felt his mouth trail up her neck. Her eyes didn't have time to flutter open before his lips found hers and they were kissing in heated waves, each kiss more urgent than the last. A rush of warmth rose to her cheeks, his fingers finding the flushed skin on the nape of her neck.

But then he grew cold. His lips like ice. And when she finally did open her eyes, he was gone. The dungeon was empty. And she was alone. Tears fell down her face, but she couldn't hear the cries leaking from her mouth until her violent shaking roused her from sleep.

Leaving her dreams only made her cry more. The intense shock of remembering where she was and who she was without never ceased to hollow out her stomach. She tried silencing her cries by curling her body up and sobbing into her pillow. She let the muffled sounds mix with the liquid falling from her eyes and into puddles near her nose.

Outside, the birds chirped, and the sun was bright, but Corre couldn't have felt more detached from it all. She was cold and so completely alone. Every morning, she woke up feeling empty and sick. There was a weight in her stomach that made her want to vomit. Sometimes, her dreams were happy, filled with sweet, stolen kisses, with memories of Markus training her or sleeping next to her in his chambers. But other times, they were even worse than the agonizing hours she spent awake each day.

And sometimes they were nightmares. Of Markus's face as she'd left Tartarus, sorrow and agony carved in an expression she couldn't peel from her mind, no matter how hard she tried. Or of Thanatos lashing out at him with a cold strike of his claw-like hand, his apprentice falling into a pool of blood at his feet.

She always woke up with that same sick feeling, but there was nothing she could do about it. That's what killed her most. That helpless guilt. Or guilty helplessness. She wasn't sure which it was. All she knew was that there was nothing she could do to help Markus and that she'd broken his heart before leaving him to break in front of his master—by the hands of his master, who was doing who knew what to him at this very moment.

Corre couldn't let herself think about it. All it did was make her collapse into a lifeless, useless shell. She knew that was the last thing she should let happen in the weeks leading up to her return to the Underworld, so she forced herself to train. Day in and day out.

No distractions. No looking forward or back. Just fighting. Training.

She didn't even talk to Phineas; she hadn't since arriving back on Olympus. But today, as she made the trek through the woods to Athena's, she knew there was no more escaping him. She'd managed to evade him for a month, but there he was now, blocking her way to the training course, arms crossed and eyes set in a heavy stare.

She tried moving past him, but he wouldn't let her. He stepped in front of her every time she tried to go by. She let out an irritated grumble. "Let me by, Phineas."

"No. Not until you talk to me."

She glowered at him. "I have nothing to say to you."

"You've been avoiding me," he said, as if she hadn't spoken. "Why?"

Her jaw dropped, and an exasperated laugh rolled out. "Are you serious?"

"What?"

She shook her head and laughed again. An annoyed, astonished laugh. "I can't believe you don't know."

He scowled. "Why don't you enlighten me?"

"For one thing, you shot Mark—um, I mean, *Theron*—without even knowing anything beforehand. Have you always been like that? Shoot first, ask questions later?"

"You were in danger. What else was I supposed to do?"

"And how did you know I was in any danger? Hm?"

"*Weren't* you? Because it sure didn't look like you were in the middle of a picnic when we got down there."

Corre let out another tight laugh. "You have no idea, do you? You have no idea what you're doing."

This set something aflame in his eyes. "I saved you, Corre! This is the thanks I get? Sure, I don't know how to lead an army yet, but last I checked, you didn't know anything either. About *anything*."

"I know more than you," she spat.

"Yeah? About what?"

"About the Underworld. About the way this whole place works! About Theron. He isn't to be feared. Everything anyone's ever said about him is a lie."

"And you know that for a fact?"

"Yes, I do."

"After, what, a few weeks of knowing him?"

"That's not fair—"

"Oh, and avoiding your lifelong best friend after he risked everything to save your life *is* fair?"

Tears stung Corre's eyes. "You don't understand, Phineas. He's a good man."

"I thought you were smarter than that," he scoffed.

Corre's blood boiled. "*What*?"

He stepped closer, lowering his voice. "I thought you were smarter than to trust an evil god you barely know just because he's easy on the eyes."

It took everything in Corre not to reach out and slap him. "Get out of my way," she growled, pushing past him.

"You know I'm right about him."

She whipped around. "You don't know anything about him, Phineas. You have no idea at all. You just walk around this place, trusting all your friends and everyone who looks remotely innocent. But you don't look into what may or may not be true about someone you know nothing about."

"And you know him? Theron of Tartarus?"

"Yes, I do. I know that people have used him as a scapegoat that they can pin their hatred on for far too long."

"He's the scapegoat for a reason, Corre! He's God of the Underworld!"

"So? You're the God of War! Should I see you as a ruthless killer?"

His mouth formed a hard line, but he didn't say anything.

"Do you see?" she said, exasperated. "Do you see why you can't trust someone based solely on words alone and the title they've been given? A title they may not want? One that was thrust upon them—"

"That's ridiculous. Everyone wants their titles. It's what we were born to do. We wouldn't have been given our titles if it wasn't what we were destined to be."

"What does that have to do with it? What does destiny have to do with what we want?"

Phineas frowned. "What are you saying?"

She sucked in a sharp breath and tried to stay composed. She kept her voice leveled as she looked up at her friend, if she could still call him that. "Some of us don't want the titles we've been given. Just because you like yours doesn't mean I like mine, or that Theron likes his." His face fell, but she continued before he could say anything. "I don't know if our titles are our destinies anyway. Maybe the Titans and Zeus randomly decide everything."

"I don't believe that."

She shrugged. "Well, for all you know, it could be true. All I know is that no one would want to be the God of the Underworld and be taken from their home at thirteen, only to be tormented and hated for eternity. So why don't you think about that? Chew on that a while, and then come back to me and throw allegations at Theron and call me naïve for finally seeing the truth of things."

He let out a half-chuckle, but one of his eyebrows flickered in frustration. "The truth of things?" He tried to avoid her gaze, but she didn't let him off the hook.

She kept her eyes on him with such focus that he had to look straight down at her as she replied. "Yes. The truth. That sometimes looks and reputations are deceiving. That sometimes the people we trust most are the ones we should trust the least." Her scowl burned into him before she pushed past him and headed toward the training course. She paused for a moment, and, without looking back, she quietly added, "And sometimes, people are afraid of the wrong monsters."

"Are you talking about me?" he asked in disbelief.

"No," she said, still facing forward. "Not the last part . . ." She turned her head just enough to briefly make eye contact with him before saying, "But I don't think I can trust you anymore. I think you should re-evaluate who you trust up here. There may be more enemies in your social circle than you realize." She blinked back tears as she took the first steps toward the course. "It's hard to believe what's right in front of us sometimes."

She didn't know if he'd heard the last part, and maybe she didn't want him to. She wasn't sure who it was aimed at. Things were so sideways now. She didn't know what to think anymore.

"Corre—" Phineas started, but she kept going. She had nothing else to say to him.

Everything was jumbled. In a little over a month, her whole world had turned upside down. She couldn't blame Phineas for not being able to process the situation. She could barely process it herself. And if she were to tell her former self—the Correlia she'd been just before meeting Markus—would she have believed it? Would she have believed Markus's innocence? Or would she have been like Phineas and believed she was being naively beguiled?

Maybe past Corre wouldn't want to believe it, but present Corre knew it was true. She realized the gods she knew around her could be anybody. *Anything.* Monsters and killers, or peacemakers and friends.

She picked up her speed, tearing through the woods, hoping the brisk air skimming her skin would shock her out of her mind.

But nothing could tear her from this mess.

Nothing made sense anymore.

Not even the character of gods she was supposed to believe in, like Zeus. He was worshiped by the humans and revered on Mt. Olympus, but he was nothing more than a monster himself. Yet everyone trusted him. Goddesses let themselves fall for him, and the ones clever enough to avoid him still found themselves attached to him somehow. Everyone thought he was a glorious legend. But he was nothing more than a psychopathic sham.

And Markus was a god who was strong, despite possessing a heart and spirit so battered and broken he barely wanted to breathe. With his openly warring emotions, his large stature, his dark hair and deep voice, he was easy to pin as the bad guy.

But . . .

She thought of the way he'd looked at her when she'd tended to his wounds. About the way he'd held her and kissed her. The way he'd cried. The way he'd loved her and wept for her. The way he'd trusted her. The way he'd risked everything for her and attempted to attack his master. His abuser. For her.

Nothing could convince Corre that Markus was the bad guy. She knew he wasn't. In fact, he may have been the least bad god she'd ever met, and when she took a step back from everything, the notion was shocking. How many gods had she wrongly trusted, and how many had she wrongly despised?

This new knowledge of the way the world worked left a bad taste in her mouth. It was disturbing. Unsettling. To know how easy it was to believe the cunning and well-liked gods, like Zeus and countless others. How easy it was to believe the crowd and hate someone who was apparently born to be hated.

It had taken everything she'd gone through to learn the truth of things, and she didn't like it. If all of this was true, then she couldn't trust anybody. And if she couldn't trust anybody, what then?

She stopped running and grabbed the cloth in her back pocket—the one used to bind her fists. To prepare her to fight—to pulverize the trees and wield weapons she wasn't yet accustomed to or experienced in. Markus surfaced in her mind again, as if he'd ever left. She thought about the way his hands had shadowed hers as he'd taught her how to use those powers known only to him and his master.

What was his master doing with that power now?

A bolt of pain ricocheted through her ribcage, and she dropped the cloth. Watching as it unraveled from her fingers and fell to the earth, she took a deep breath and steadied her mind. Markus's voice entered her mind, and it was like he was right there next to her. *"Trust me,"* he said, and the velvet sound of his voice warmed her chest. She could feel his breath against her skin. Smell the warm, masculine scent from his sweat-soaked body after a day of training. The scent that, for whatever reason, made her hungry for him.

"You have to focus," his voice said, and she straightened, her eyes still closed. Her forehead scrunched tight as she tried remembering what he'd taught her. And then she heard it like he was telling her now: *"You have to focus on something you really want. You can't have any distractions."*

How was she supposed to not be distracted when all she could think about was him? About the pain he was going through while she was up here in complete safety, with people who cared about her. No one cared about him. No one but her. He might not even realize she still did. And without that hope . . . what would he . . .?

"No," she snapped at herself and got into the position he'd taught her. "I have to focus."

"On what?"

Her eyes shot open, and she whipped back around. For a small sliver of time between the world of her imaginings and the one she was in now, she half-thought she'd heard Markus behind her. That, somehow, he was here.

But, of course, she was wrong. That fleeting bit of hope had been only that, and she found herself scowling at Phineas. "Why are you following me?"

"I'm not—" he started, his voice almost blaring. He stopped himself from saying anything else, took a deep breath, and tried again. "I'm not. I just . . ." He walked closer, and she could see the concern in his eyes. "I'm worried about you."

"Don't be," she snapped. "I'm fine."

His gaze fell to the ground, and when he didn't retort, guilt twisted in her stomach. The wind whistled softly through the trees, filling the awkward space between them until Phineas finally spoke. "I've never seen you look at someone the way you looked at him." His voice was quiet. His eyes met hers. "When I saw that . . . I didn't know what to make of it . . . and I . . ."

"You shot him," she said curtly, and he flinched.

"I-I did, but you have to believe me, Corre. I did it for your own good."

She shook her head in disbelief. "Why do you think I can't take care of myself? You of all people should know that I can."

His face was strained, and she didn't know what to make of his new-found silence and his odd energy. Why was he acting so weird?

"Don't you trust me?" she asked.

"Of course I do." He sounded agonized, which made her even more confused.

"I feel like there's something you're not telling me, so just spit it out." The frustration coursing through her was only getting worse. She had no time or patience for this right now.

"I love you, Corre," he said, and she jerked back, wide-eyed.

"What?"

"I've loved you for a long time, and I'm worried about you. How could I not be? Just like how . . ." He paused before saying it. "Just like how you were worried about *him*."

Corre wanted to be mad at the way he'd said it, but she couldn't be. She was too shocked, and the sorrow in his eyes was too real. "What are you saying?"

"Don't pretend you don't know. Please. For me."

Her stomach clenched tighter. She didn't know what to say. She stared at him until he finally continued, "I'll always worry about you, and . . . I-I went down there to save you. But when I saw you look at him like that . . . I couldn't control it. I was furious. I was mad that he could beguile you into feeling for him in a way you've never felt for me."

"He didn't beguile me, Phineas," she said, and for whatever reason, her eyes filled with tears.

He nodded. "I know." His gaze fell again. "I know."

The world inside her head whirred, and everything was suddenly too hot, the wind and birds too loud around her.

Tears stung her eyes as one escaped down her face. "Why?" The word came out like a plea.

"Why, what?"

"Why did you have to hurt him? And why do you have to . . ." *Why do you have to feel like this?* she wanted to say, but she knew it wasn't fair.

Phineas surmised what she was getting at regardless. "I can't help how I feel, and you should know that more than anyone. Right?" It sounded like an accusation.

"You're like a brother to me, Phineas."

"Great. That's what every guy wants to hear." He tried to laugh, but her bloodshot eyes seemed to stop him.

"I mean it. I've seen you as a brother. A friend. And now . . ." Nausea curdled in her gut. "Now, nothing will be the same."

"Nothing was ever going to be the same after you went down there with him. After you fell for—"

"For what?" she challenged, and he should have known better than to answer.

"A monster." He said it as if daring her to spar. Like it was just another mock fight. The kind they'd been using to train their whole lives. A time that seemed so distant now.

She wanted to yell at him, but she knew there was no point. "No," she said, shaking her head. "My falling for Hades wasn't why things will never be the same. That switch happened the moment you shot that arrow." Her bleary glare stayed locked on him one more silent moment before she decided to walk back to town. She couldn't train like this.

"I have to get out of here," she said, but as she ran past him, he grabbed her arm. She shot him a look and said, "Please, let me go, Phineas. I can't talk about this anymore."

Tears were in his eyes, too, which made hers spill like rain down her cheeks.

"Please, tell me we can still be friends," he whispered.

She sniffed back tears and turned away, yanking her arm free and wiping her face. "I can't." She didn't look at him. She couldn't.

She ran toward town, without looking back.

To get anywhere but here.

CHAPTER THIRTY-FIVE

Corre

Corre didn't stop running until she made it to the village. Her throat was dry and her legs were wobbly, but she had to get away from Phineas. She'd circle back and train later, but she couldn't face him anymore today.

She was confused, but mostly, she was furious. After what he had done to Markus, how dare he? And after all the condescending remarks and the way he'd thought of her—that she was some fragile, brain-washable girl—did he think she would just fall at his feet? She didn't know if she wanted to scream or cry, because despite how mad she was at him—for everything—he was still her friend. At least, he had been. Her best friend. Nearly her entire life.

She walked through the marketplace in a daze, despondent as she picked up the colorful fruits and tried not to remember all the times she and Phineas had gathered every fruit imaginable, like colorful jewels shoved deep in their pockets. They'd worked hard for the small amounts of money they'd earned as kids, and then they'd splurge here. They'd head for the hills. For the places in the forest known only to them. At least, that's what their young minds had assumed.

And they'd laugh. For hours, they'd laugh and eat those gem-like fruits until their stomachs ached from the combination of the two. The world had been so bright. Maybe it was simply because they were children, and the world is so much brighter to kids. Everything is possible when you're a child. There's a glow about you when you're young, and somewhere along the way, it gets dimmer until you lose it completely. And once you realize it's gone, you may spend your whole life trying to find it, and that's what it means to grow up.

Corre wasn't sure where that glow had gone for her, but she imagined it lived within Markus now. Her little glimmer of the possible and the free had materialized when they'd been together. When he'd looked at her with his dark eyes, so earnest and gentle, when he'd laughed with her, and when he'd covered her with those purple pomegranate kisses on her birthday, it had been like that joyful spark had returned. A more mature version of that impossible glow of happiness only children seemed to possess.

"Are you going to pay for that?"

Corre looked up, momentarily disoriented. "Oh, I'm sorry. I was just looking." She placed the ruby-colored fruit back in the crate on the vendor's stand. The plump woman behind the counter narrowed her eyes and let out a *hmph* under her breath.

It must be frustrating for her to stay under the blazing sun, waiting for customers.

Maybe she should leave.

She sighed and walked past the rest of the vendors on her way back home. She could have lunch and wait things out. Eventually, Phineas would leave or be too deep into his training to scout her out, and then she could go back and train the rest of the day.

But then she heard her name. And Markus's alias. She didn't turn to face whoever was speaking, but she listened. They were attempting to whisper, from the way their voices were warped into a hushed manner of speaking, but the volume was loud, undoing any attempt at subtlety.

"Poor thing," one voice cooed.

"Go ask her," another whispered.

Corre walked up to one of the booths and pretended to inspect the vegetables the booth had to offer. She gave the gruff-looking god a tight smile. "How much is this one?" she asked, but she didn't hear him when he replied. She was too busy listening to the goddesses behind her.

"No way," the first goddess said to the other. "She looks so sad."

"Of course she's sad. He likely tortured her."

"Oh, you're probably right."

A bolt of fury tore through her, and her fist tightened around the fruit. Its juice spilled through her fingers, and the vendor gasped.

"What are you doing? You have to pay for that now!" he said, but Corre kept listening.

"Hades is a vile creature, isn't he?" the other goddess said. "Poor girl."

"We should leave her be."

"Especially if you don't want Hades coming after you, too," a male voice chimed in.

The two women gasped. "You're right," one of them said. "Can you imagine? He's terrifying."

"Mm-hm. We shouldn't get involved. She's probably okay, anyway. She has her mother."

Corre's heart raced. She turned around and threw the mangled fruit at their feet. They both let out a shriek and looked at Corre with wide, gaping eyes. One of them even placed a hand on her chest.

"What are you doing?!" the vendor cried.

It was hard for her to hear or think, but when she compelled herself to breathe, Corre processed what she was doing. She looked away, then swiveled around and handed the vendor two coins. Those people weren't worth it. She needed to focus on going home, and then on training.

"He probably forced himself on her, too," the male voice said, clicking his tongue. "Poor thing." Corre's stomach tightened, along with her fists. "We should stay away, though. To give her space, I mean. She'll be all right."

"Yes, I'm sure she will be. She'll reach out if she needs help, right?"

"Oh, yes," the other woman said. "But I'm sure she won't need any. She's fine."

"Right. I'm sure she's fine."

"And you don't want to get too close," the man said. "He could go after you next."

"Shut up," Corre growled, her knuckles white. The words came out scratchy, like gravel rolling from her throat.

"Excuse me?" the male god said.

"I said, shut up!" she shouted, whipping around and shooting daggers at him with reddening eyes. When tears began swelling and falling down her face, she tried blinking them away. The three stared at her in disbelief. "You have no idea what you're talking about," she said, her voice shaky. "You don't know Markus at all. He's not a monster."

Realizing she'd used his real name, she bit her tongue and turned around. "Just . . . Shut up. You're making fools of yourselves. And you should be ashamed. People in pain don't reach out." She glowered at them one last time. "But I wouldn't want help from the likes of you three anyway. You're far viler than he could ever be."

She made sure to cast them all a nasty look. They looked like a peculiar bunch together, too. One so stout and crinkled she looked like a cream puff, and the other hunched and gangly, leaning over her friend like she was her umbrella. And the man was wearing such a gaudy robe it almost hurt Corre to look directly at him.

As she made her way out, she figured the three would be wise enough not to speak again, but just before they were out of earshot, she heard the man say, "He sure got to her, didn't he?"

"I should say so," one of the goddesses replied. "Poor thing was tormented and manipulated more than she realizes."

They kept talking but Corre ran away as fast as she could. She needed to go home. Then she wouldn't have to hear those wretched people talk anymore, spouting their nonsense and their faux well-wishes that only allowed them to gossip and judge without feeling so guilty. All they had to do was claim to each other they'd help someone in need, but Corre doubted they'd helped a soul in their infinite lifetimes.

Mt. Olympus wasn't the place she'd once thought it was. Every day here since Tartarus only reminded her of that fact and made her want to crawl back down to the Underworld even more.

She trudged home after she couldn't run anymore, but the words of the villagers echoed in her head.

"He likely tortured her."

"Hades is a vile creature, isn't he?"

"He probably forced himself on her, too."

She couldn't help the tears dampening her cheeks. Markus treated Corre so gently. He would never hurt her. That was something that had become clearer and clearer with each passing day. He'd always been honest with her. In every way.

He'd risked everything for her.

He wasn't a monster. He wasn't a torturous demon like they were accusing him of being. His heart was kind. And what mattered more—appearances or truth?

The more Corre thought about her interactions with Markus and the way he'd looked when Thanatos scolded him and lied to them the day she'd been brought back to Olympus, the more she realized how stupid she'd been for believing the evil master. All he'd ever done was lie and twist things, manipulating Markus into thinking he was worthless and that everything wrong with the world was his fault.

As soon as she got home, she flung herself on her bed and squeezed her eyes shut. She buried her face in her hands, unable to scrape those images from her mind.

I shouldn't have left him like that. I should have believed him. Now, he's down there all alone. And Thanatos is probably torturing him in every way possible.

Then Markus's softened face passed through her mind, and she remembered how it felt to see him smile, once he'd finally trusted that she could love him. When the unbridled, unyielding passion between them had become palpable and real, and their souls had been bared in front of the other. They'd both taken that jump. The risk of crashing and burning in a way that could take every shielded, vulnerable place in their hearts and shatter it to pieces.

After what she'd said to him when she left, where were those pieces now?

She sucked in a sharp breath and rolled over. Another tear skated down her cheek.

When she saw him again, would she be able to put those pieces together again? Or had the damage been done forever?

As Corre sunk deeper into the darkness of her mind, she wondered if she'd screwed up everything and if Markus could ever really trust her again.

Or if he even loved her anymore.

She couldn't let herself think like that or she'd go mad.

As more tears trickled onto her bedspread, Corre closed her eyes and thought of him, but that only made her cry harder. Her body shook, coiling as she sobbed.

"I don't know what to do," she whimpered. *Nothing. The answer is nothing.*

I can't do anything.

CHAPTER THIRTY-SIX

Markus

Three months had finally passed, and Markus knew Correlia would be here any day, pulled back down to this place against her will. Because of him.

The guilt was a constant source of pain, on top of the throbbing physical pain that accompanied him every second of the day. When he opened the door to his chambers each night, after a long day of training, the pain was made so much worse. Because, every day, he foolishly hoped she'd be there, sitting on his bed with a smile on her face and a roll of bandages in her hand, ready to wrap him up and take away the pain.

She was a balm to his soul that nothing else could match. He wasn't sure what had healed him more—the cleaned wounds and bandages she'd wrapped him in or the gentleness of her help, the careful way she'd cleaned his cuts and frowned in concern at the state of his pain.

He wasn't used to that. Sympathy. Thanatos only ever expected more cuts and bruises, inflicting many of them upon Markus himself. But Correlia cared. She cared about the cuts. She cared about his pain. She wanted to heal him.

But ever since she left, and he found that Correlia was, of course, not on his bed or folding towels into flowers on his floor, the wound in his soul gaped open all over again. The pain of what he'd done to her rushed back. He remembered what he doomed her to because of his pull to her and the danger she was now placed in. That same danger he had to face, day in and day out. And he probably wouldn't get the chance to see her. To protect her from any of it.

He slammed the door behind him, staggering into his room. Like always, it was cold and empty. He struggled to pick up an old pile of bandages at the foot of his bed. The pain from his latest gash was bordering on unbearable. He hated to touch it, but he had to stop the bleeding.

Markus grabbed hold of the long, winding gauze Correlia had used on him months before and tried ignoring the pang of homesickness that pulled at his insides when he inspected it. It probably wasn't the smartest thing to do—to reuse this bandage over and over again—but using it comforted him. It brought him a tiny pinch of solace as he tended to his injuries. And he couldn't get himself to throw it away and let it go. Maybe he was afraid that once he did, the memories of her would leave with it.

He pushed down the thoughts of her and rinsed the bandages in the fountain. He barely had the strength to stand right now. He couldn't afford the hollow feeling that gutted him when he remembered her absence. So he focused on the water falling onto the old material, but the thoughts of her returned. Her dimpled smile and her sunflower eyes. The warmth of her soul. The comfort of her body. The beauty that radiated from every pore. Every inch of skin and bone.

He blocked off the spout and toweled the gauze down until he could use it to wrap himself. He winced as it pressed against that gash, every swipe of the bandage made the festering wound slashed across his ribs wail. The creature he fought today had poison oozing from its claws, so any contact with the gash on Markus's skin was a recipe for both instant and lasting pain. But it would only get worse—*feel* worse—if he let it stick to his sheets and brush against everything he touched.

The minutes ticked by, and he was unsuccessful in every attempt. He couldn't get the bandage to stay in place, partly because it hurt too much to tighten, and partly because he was losing consciousness. The peeled flesh was too tender, the gash too raw. His left arm was useless, too. He couldn't move it without nearly blacking out.

He finally sucked it up and tightened the bandage around his torso, even after his face drained of blood and his forehead turned cold and slick with sweat. He let his right arm drop after he tied the ends of the bandage together and let out a long sigh. Carefully, he placed himself on the bed, lying completely straight on his back. The room was spinning, and his forehead was still clammy and cold, but all he could do was rest. There was no other respite for him here.

He let out labored breaths and begged his mind to stop racing so he could sleep. If the pain hadn't made the task difficult enough, he also had to lie as flat as the sheets beneath his back to avoid any zings of pain. With another labored breath, he closed his eyes.

Of course, the first image to pop into his mind was Correlia, but he welcomed it. His favorite part of the day was this tiny spot of time between work and rest when he could let all his guards down and just think of her. *She'll be here any day*, he thought, smiling for a fraction of a second until that dreaded follow-up question surfaced in his mind and left him melancholy.

Then what?

Corre

"I can manage this myself, thank you," Corre said curtly, pulling herself onto the back of the glossy black mare. The freshly embroidered crest of Phineas's new army was a stain on the side of its leather saddle.

"I was only trying to help," the red-headed soldier scoffed.

"I can take care of myself," she said, keeping her eyes forward. She hid the struggle of straddling a horse in the dress she'd chosen to wear today. It was one she'd insisted on wearing, despite her mother's skeptical remarks. Corre had no choices of her own to make today. Everyone had scheduled and dictated what was to happen, who was to escort her, and everything else before her descent into the Underworld. Once she was down there, there was no telling what would happen, but it was safe to say she would have no choices of her own to make.

The only choice she could make for herself today, without anyone being able to protest, was what she would wear and how she would present herself. So she chose the most beautiful gown her limited amount of saved money could buy: a long, layered dress of light blue silk that fell like feathered flower petals from her shoulders to her feet, with slits just above her knees. The sleeves fell off her shoulders and flowed down into the careful folds of the iridescent skirt of the dress. She looked like an upside-down rose, blooming with soft, opulent petals and covered in star-lit dew.

The young, red-bearded god huffed again, and a familiar voice joined in his frustration. "She's been like that for months now," Phineas said, coming up behind him and slapping him on the shoulder. "Don't take it personally."

Corre rolled her eyes. "What are you doing here?"

His expression fell, something sad sitting in his dark brown irises. Despite everything, she felt sorry for him, and guilty. About what, she wasn't sure, but it was always accompanied by the fear that their friendship was beyond saving. They hadn't spoken since that day in the forest. She had nothing left to say to him, and perhaps that was where the problem lay.

She fixed her gaze on a tree before her and silenced her thoughts. She couldn't think about this today. Today wasn't about Phineas. It was about Markus. She was finally going down to Tartarus, and she would do everything in her power to see him again. Even if it risked her being punished by Thanatos. She had a way out of that place. Markus didn't. She could endure the pain before coming back to her cottage on Mt. Olympus.

The risk was worth it. She needed Markus to know she didn't blame him for anything. That he wasn't guilty of what Thanatos had accused him of—of what she'd accepted as truth the last time their eyes had locked, and she'd left him. She had to apologize and wipe away the tears that had formed in his eyes that day when she'd told him she couldn't trust him.

The thought made her sick.

What if he didn't want to see her?

She wouldn't blame him if he didn't.

"It will be okay," a light voice reached Corre from below. It was her mother, whose bloodshot eyes were swollen from tears. The sobs kept Corre up half the night. She wondered if the older goddess had slept at all.

She forced a smile and leaned down to kiss her on the forehead. "I know it will be. Don't worry about me. I was thinking about something else. I'm not worried. I'll be okay. I promise." She tried to make her smile convincing, but her mother knew better.

She took her daughter's hands in hers, kissed them, and then patted her on the cheek. "I love you. I'll see you soon."

"I love you, too," Corre said, straightening on the horse and grabbing hold of the reins. "I won't be gone long. Before you know it, I'll be back." She widened her smile, but her mother only nodded somberly.

"We have to go," another voice said, and Corre turned to Hermes, who was leading the group to the River Styx on his own horse—the fastest and finest on Olympus.

"Okay. Bye, everyone. I'll be fine." She waved and smiled at the small group seeing her off, and when she met Phineas's gaze, she narrowed her eyes and added, "And don't do anything stupid."

He rolled his eyes but didn't say anything. He knew better by now.

Then Hermes let out a 'Hiya', and his horse was off, and before Corre could process it, so was she.

The journey to Styx couldn't have been long, but it felt like an eternity. Corre couldn't hear anything other than her heart pounding in her ears, and she couldn't stop thinking about Markus. She feared for his safety, as well as her own. Thanatos might decide to make an example of him in front of her, just for fun. Or maybe the other way around. Or both.

But there were also moments when her heart flitted at the thought of seeing Markus again, even if all they shared was a single glance. She hoped seeing him would heal her of the constant aching she'd felt since she last saw him. That constant pain that ran from her chest into the pit of her stomach, rooted in the fear of not knowing where he was or what he was going through. Or what he thought. How much pain he was in.

Finally, they made it. This time, she let one of the guards of the small group help her off the horse. She was almost too weak to stand, and her hands had turned cold. She stared at the cave's mouth, her eyes falling and finding the black water. She'd never drifted over any waters in Tartarus. But the one she'd touched that day . . . That blinding, green pool . . .

She nervously gathered her skirt in her hands. Hopefully, this river wasn't like that one. She knew the journey wouldn't be joyful regardless, though. She was about to travel the river that escorted the dead to the Underworld. And she was alive.

The hooded ferryman appeared from the tunnel, guiding his boat to the mouth of the river. When he stopped, his shadowed face turned to hers. A chill scuttled down her back. He lifted his arm and revealed a skeletal hand, palm facing up. "Payment?"

Corre blanched. "Um, I don't—"

"I have it," Hermes said, handing a peculiar, brassy coin to Charon.

The cloaked figure turned slowly to face her, and despite her inability to see what lay beyond his drooping hood, she made out a smirk. "Come in," he said, his gravely voice lined with something sadistic.

Corre looked back at the party of four gods and two goddesses on horseback behind her. None of them were faces she recognized, other than Hermes, and that was only because of his fame on Olympus. Maybe Zeus didn't want her to feel at ease today, because even Athena wasn't among the appointed group. Punishment for her irresponsibility—for getting herself into this mess in the first place. She wouldn't put it past him.

Since no one was there to truly see her off, she stepped inside the rickety boat, her stomach flopping at the unsteadiness of the wobbly water beneath her feet. No more words were exchanged, and before she could ready herself for whatever lay ahead, Charon moved the boat forward, and she was swallowed by darkness.

For an agonizing lifetime, it seemed, Corre couldn't see anything. Her bearings were lost. She sat in her impractical dress, shivering either from fear or the cold rising from the chilly, unpredictable water and feeling the slight waves ebbing from beneath. Only a thin board kept her body from the abyss below. With no way out or light to guide her, she'd inevitably drown, and since she wasn't mortal, she'd likely drown forever, lost to everyone who knew her. Even to herself.

She swallowed and sat as still as she could, begging her legs to stop shaking. The creaks of the boat were the only sounds other than the sporadic rush of water whenever Charon's staff pushed them farther along the river. Relief washed through her when a light appeared in the distance. It was small at first, but she watched in anxious anticipation as it grew.

The relief vanished in an instant when she heard the chorus of moaning at the site of that light. The closer they got to it, the harder it was to ignore. Screams, cries, and sorrow so palpable Corre could feel it in her soul. One terrifying element was swapped with another.

The boat glided forward, and the moaning intensified. Her body curled in on itself, her hands pressed tightly against her ears so her eardrums wouldn't burst, but even so, she couldn't stop the aching. As the sounds grew unbearable, they were bathed in that light, leaving the tunnel behind.

For the briefest moment, Corre looked up, straitening her back to see where they were.

Big mistake.

The moaning turned to fierce growls and snaps as the souls leapt at her from the water. They were everywhere. Illuminated and bright, but the thing of nightmares. She could see right through their gaunt faces, but their transparent mouths were deformed and falling apart, their bony hands much like Charon's, but twisted and bent in unnatural ways. One crooked hand grazed her back, singeing it with something white-hot, but she managed to scoot to the middle of the boat before it pulled her in.

As her back hit the other side of the small boat, another hand grabbed hold of her wrist. When she shrieked, Charon turned around and slapped the soul's hand from her skin. Its withered spirit melted away, but even after she was safely back in the middle of the boat, she could feel its clammy grasp on her skin, seeping into her bones.

She rubbed the spot over and over, trying to erase the eerie sensation, but a new chorus of moaning erupted. She looked up and saw an enormous field of souls that looked just like the ones in the river, but these ones were walking aimlessly on a wide patch of dead grass. As they got closer, Corre's eyes started to burn. The air was putrid, smelling of sulfur and burnt hair, and there was a feeling of death in the air. The jarring absence of life was so tangible that it soaked Corre in a blanket of melancholy until her stinging eyes gushed with tears.

Charon continued sailing them along as if nothing was amiss.

She was still crying when the noises ceased, and they glided into an empty grotto.

Then, finally, they docked.

The boat bobbed as the ferryman guided it onto the land. His long, spindly body stood at the bow. It seemed like he was going to speak when, instead, he stilled. His body almost twitched before he spoke to whoever was standing opposite him on the shore. "Where is General Nikias?"

"He got tied up with something," the voice said and, instantly, Corre recognized it. She suppressed a gasp and waited behind the hooded being.

"Do I know you?" Charon crowed.

"Of course," the man said, somehow both gruffly and nonchalantly. "I live here. I work here. I'm sure you've seen me."

"I was instructed to stay with the girl until the general arrived."

"Things change sometimes, and I was commanded to retrieve her instead."

The hooded figure was still for another moment, standing there without saying another word, until he finally turned around and faced the goddess at his feet. Pointing to the shore, he said, "Go with this man to the general. Do not wander."

Corre nodded swiftly and stood to see her escort. Her heart soared at the face of the familiar old man—the familiar *mortal* man. The one who'd helped her when she snuck down here over three months ago. She never thought she'd be so happy to see this scruffy man again, but as he took her hand and helped her out of the water, she beamed. Because something wasn't right, but in the best way. It took all she had in her not to smile and give the old man away.

She turned to Charon and said, in her best fake-somber, faux, meek voice, "Thank you, sir." The figure let out a groan and pushed his boat back into the water, leaving the way he'd come.

"Follow me, miss," the old man said authoritatively, and Corre did as she was told. She didn't dare utter a word until she knew they were safe, and since she wouldn't know when that'd be, she waited for the old man to speak first.

But the silence between them lengthened, and as they walked deeper into the tunnels of Tartarus, her stomach turned. What was once relief at the prospect of being rescued was now uneasy uncertainty. Maybe she'd gotten the wrong idea. She had no idea who this man was. For all she knew, he worked for Thanatos.

But . . .

She thought back on their conversation all those weeks ago.

"Thanatos is a monster. He should have never been given the throne. Even as a placeholder. Zeus just agreed to the Titans' demands. He didn't care."

The man didn't seem to like Thanatos, and what he'd said lined up with what her mother told her about that night her birth mother died. She studied the back of the man's head as she followed him. He'd helped her before. He had to be helping her now. But they were getting deeper into the heart of the Underworld, and still, he said nothing. Something was wrong.

Without thinking, Corre blurted out, "Who are you? Where are you taking me?" She didn't mean for the words to come out so loudly. She suppressed a yelp, lips curling inward, wincing at the words now echoing across the cavern. The man froze, and Corre studied the gray hairs on the back of his head.

There was something familiar about this man. The way he stood. The way he spoke. It wasn't from when she'd met him. It was like she'd seen him in another life.

He turned around and, with a stern expression, looked her in the eyes and lowered his voice. "You listen to me. Keep quiet and remember every-thing I say. You hear me?"

She stared at the man in shock, still trying to place where she'd seen him. "Who are you?"

His stern expression didn't change, but he took a moment before re-sponding. "My name is Thomas. I'm Markus's father. And I finally know how he can take down Thanatos."

CHAPTER THIRTY-SEVEN

Corre

I t all clicked into place.

"You're Markus's what?" Corre asked, but he was already walking down the corridor.

"You heard me. Now, let's go. We don't have much time. The general will realize you're missing, and Tartarus will be in a frenzy until they find you."

She hurried along as he wound into the complex labyrinth. "I have so many questions," she said, but the man only grunted and kept moving. "Are you going to tell me how we'll take down Thanatos?"

"We'll need to find Markus first."

Her heart soared. "Really?" She couldn't help the smile that spread across her face.

"Really." He took a sharp right, hurrying along, but she didn't miss the warm chuckle that accompanied his reply. Corre tripped, almost falling as she hurried to stay close behind him. His shoulders fell slightly, and he paused before answering. "The night Markus was taken," he started, his voice low, almost reverent, "I was terrified. My wife was inconsolable, and I was furious. We had no say in Markus's ugly fate." He took another sharp turn, and Corre had to follow him even closer to hear what he was saying. "I did what I could. I begged Zeus, but he wouldn't listen. There were no other candidates, he'd said, so I did what I had to. I followed my son down here."

"Markus has no idea, though. He thinks you don't care about him. He thinks his parents abandoned him."

Thomas sighed. "Well . . . I'm sad to hear that, but I can't say I'm surprised. Thanatos is a master manipulator, and he's been with him a long time."

Pain flickered in Corre's chest. "You've loved him all this time. And—wait. How did any of that make you mortal? I know Zeus took your immortality, but how did he justify it?"

"I was caught. Zeus has spies everywhere. When he found out I went against his wishes and was trying to find a way to bring Markus back, he banished me from Mt. Olympus and made a point to paint me as a traitor. My powers and immortality were taken from me, and I had to stay here, mortal and alone."

She fell silent, wishing she knew what to say, but the next thought that came to her was of the man's wife, and how Zeus had wanted her for himself. "Your wife stayed on Olympus," she said quietly, though she wasn't sure how much she should reveal of what she knew.

"I'm afraid so. Lily almost came with me, but I convinced her to stay. One of us had to stay on Olympus. If we were both cast out, there would be no way we could bring Markus home. She reluctantly agreed, but I was

racked with guilt. She lost her family that day. Her son *and* her husband."
He was silent for a beat. "I still feel terrible, but we both agreed it had to be
done."

Corre weighed her words before deciding to finally ask him. "Do you
know what happened to her?" She didn't want to be the one to tell him
what Lily's fate had been, but she needed to understand everything, and so
did he.

"I do, and by the sound of it, you do, too."

Her cheeks flushed. "She married Zeus . . . but why did he want to marry
her so badly? He already had Hera."

He gave her a sidelong glance. "Do you know Zeus? I swear he has more
wives than followers these days."

Corre's eyes fell, but she kept her feet steady so she wouldn't trip again.
It was still hard to believe that someone she'd thought was a good person—someone adored both on Earth and Olympus—was such a pig. A pig
who was also her father.

"And she had a daughter with him," he added. "That's how I found out
the truth of how to give Markus the throne so his life as a slave could finally
end."

The man stopped abruptly, and Corre bumped into him. He didn't
seem to mind, though. He stood there, standing at a set of enormous metal
doors. The mysterious entrance was as black as night, with handles of gold
that curled in the shape of two serpents facing each other. Those small
glimmers of gold were the only indicators that the blackness wasn't made
of shadow; they were the only reason Corre could tell this large space was
a set of doors.

She looked at the man's stoic expression. Quietly, she spoke. "Why did
Zeus's daughter help you?"

He chuckled. "That kid loves mischief. It's probably one of the reasons
she led you here to begin with."

Corre thought about the silver-haired girl in the forest. "Tyche knows everything, too?"

Thomas nodded and stepped to the door. "Despite all her antics, she has a good heart. She's been helping me for years. She loves Markus, and somehow, she's been able to slip between Tartarus and back undetected. And through her constant wandering, as well as her curiosity and Zeus's leniency with her—and his gross underestimation of her—she was able to find out just enough to give me a lead."

Corre watched with bated breath as the man grabbed hold of the gold handles, but as soon as his flesh touched the surface, he made a sound of pain and jumped back. "What's wrong?"

Thomas inspected his hands. "I can't go in.". It sounded like he was talking more to himself than to her, and the sorrow in his voice nearly broke her heart.

"Why not?"

He dropped his arms and threw his head back, swiping a hand down his face in frustration. "I assume it's because I'm mortal."

Corre bit her lip and thought for a moment. She tried not to lose hope, but all those hopes were crashing down at lightning speed. "What are we going to do?" she said quietly.

"You'll have to go alone," he said. "But you don't know these tunnels," he added with a sigh.

"How do *you*?" she asked, not meaning to sound as rude as she did. "I mean, because you're mortal, it seems you can't enter."

"I've lived down here for years. I just apparently can't make it into this part of the labyrinth—the one leading to Hades' domain. But I know where you and Markus must go. If Tyche is right, and my hunches are correct—the knowledge I've gathered over the years, rather—then you'll need to go deep below Tartarus. To a place Markus probably doesn't even know about."

Corre's mouth dried up, but she squared her shoulders. "Tell me everything I need to know, and I'll relay it to him. I promise."

The man gave her a half-smile. "I know you will, but it's important you don't forget any of this. Especially, the incantations you must recite once you get there."

Her heart raced. "I'll do my best."

"No," he said curtly. "You have to succeed. This is his only chance."

Her skin went cold. "But what if I can't do this?"

The man put his hands on her shoulders and lowered his gaze to hers. "You *can*. Just listen carefully and find Markus. He should know these incantations. He learned them once before. He simply needs to remember, and it's important he knows to use them. The right ones at the right times." He leaned back and let go of her shoulders. "It'll be okay. Just listen closely and be quick. Remember, they're looking for you. Nikias probably already knows you're gone."

"Okay." She took a deep breath. "Tell me everything.

Markus

Markus swung the sword at the thirty-headed beast, trying his best to sharpen his focus. He hadn't been given a difficult opponent for the last week, until now. There was a small part of him that hoped it was Thanatos's way of letting him heal before facing such a vicious creature. Up until the last few months, he would have let himself believe that, but he knew better now.

His master could care less about him, so that week-long rest period made him suspicious. Thanatos was hiding something. He had to be.

The creature lunged forward, but Markus slid out of the way, moving with quick precision, and slicing off another one of its heads. The next hour went just like that—him dodging the beast's blows before striking—and soon, he realized that this creature wasn't as difficult as he'd thought. Maybe all his extra training—and punishments—these last three months had paid off.

He could hope, anyway.

When the last of the heads dropped to the dungeon floor, Markus let himself slump onto the rocky surface along with it. His head fell back against the wall as he caught his breath. He rested his eyes and thought back on the last time he'd approached Thanatos, just a few weeks before.

He'd just slain one of the creatures that had plagued the Underworld for centuries, from the beginning of the first Titan's creation. He'd been so sure this would finally earn him the throne, but his master only laughed and said that tale was only that—a legend to make him feel mighty once he defeated the beast.

It was all part of his training, Thanatos had said. "You're a long way from the throne," he'd mocked, cackling as Markus left, the young god's blood boiling and the last few strands of hope tearing inside him.

He opened his eyes. Correlia would be here any day if she wasn't here already, and Thanatos would home in on her next. What kind of punishments did he have lined up for her? Maybe that was why he'd given Markus this rest period. He was trying to soften Markus and distract him while Thanatos tormented Correlia.

Fear tightened his chest, and Nikias's words echoed in his mind. *"I'll touch her enough for both of us."* His blood turned to fire, and he jumped to his feet. He couldn't let that weasel of a man get a hold of her.

If he hadn't already.

No. He would've heard Nikias's gloats by now. There was no way his rival would give up the chance to taunt him. Markus had to act now. He had to find Nikias and warn him of what lay in store for him if he so much as placed a finger on Correlia. If there was one thing the gangly blonde was, it was cowardly. When he didn't have half an army to back him up, he wouldn't attempt to fight back. Nikias knew who the stronger of the two was, and Markus intended to show him just how strong he'd become.

He swung the dungeon door open and strode into the hall. His fists tightened as he thought of Nikias. Of his stupid, smug grin. Of his nerve. He'd regret his threats, and he wouldn't live if he'd already followed through with them.

Markus swept his dark hair from his face and focused on the path to Nikias's room, but just as he passed his chambers, he heard someone's footsteps bounding toward him. He would have thought it was Nikias, but the echoes were too light. Too hurried. The general walked in careful strides as if he had something to prove.

He slowed his pace and waited for whomever it was to approach him. The footsteps quickened, making the young god curious. It almost sounded like whoever it was was running from something, but there were no scratches from the claws of demons, and it wasn't Nikias. Who was this creature?

He didn't realize he'd stopped walking until he saw who it was. Because as soon as he saw her, he couldn't breathe, let alone move.

His eyes were playing a cruel trick on him. There was no way Correlia was standing there in front of him, having rounded the corner before meeting his gaze and freezing in place just a few feet away.

He didn't move, as if any movement would make her disappear. She stared back at him long enough for him to realize that this wasn't a dream or a mirage. She was even more beautiful than he remembered, and she was wearing a gown that fell from her delicate shoulders and fluttered like the flowers outside of her house.

She was radiant.

And she was real.

Excitement surged through him, and that same excitement lit on Correlia's face, too, and they ran to each other. His heart nearly burst from his chest as he grabbed her and kissed her with every ounce of strength he had left inside him. He threaded one of his hands through her hair, the other cradling her face.

She kissed him back, throwing her arms around him, and the world around them was gone. Tears stung his closed eyes as he kissed her and kissed her, that familiar fire blasting through his blood. It tore through him in such beautiful bursts. Kissing her again, touching her, feeling her against him, healed every broken part of him. Every shattered bone and bruise.

And she tasted even sweeter than he remembered. He wished he could put the taste in a bottle and drink it, feeling it warm his body as it slid down his throat. He kissed her deeper, sliding a hand to the small of her back and pressing her tightly against him.

He couldn't think. He couldn't feel anything but her. The way her arms wound around the back of his neck. The way her chest fluttered against him in quick, flurried breaths. Her lips against his, every nerve shocking him to life, awakening more and more with every urgent press of her full lips.

A tear escaped his closed eyes, and he wished he could save this moment in time. If only he could cut them out of reality so this kiss could last forever.

He'd missed her. So much.

It had driven him mad. Utterly insane. She could do anything she wanted to him, and he'd love it. He wanted all of her, now and always. He needed her, and he was finally okay admitting it.

He would do anything for her. Destroy Tartarus. Create a new world. Anything. Whatever she wanted, he would do it without a second thought. He longed to keep her in his arms forever, never forgetting any part of this sensation. And that would keep him going one day at a time.

Finally, she leaned back, her heels falling to the floor. She looked up at him, and his heart flitted in his chest. Her lips were ruddy from their kiss, and she smiled, her nose scrunching, causing her freckles to dance along the bridge of her nose. Her cheeks dimpled, and he forgot to breathe all over again.

"Markus," she whispered, and another tear fell down his face.

He closed his eyes and started to cry. He let his head fall to her shoulder, then he fell to his knees, and she wrapped her arms around him and held him against her. "I missed you so much," he whispered, and she kissed the top of his head. He looked up at her, and she smiled, a tear skating down her face and falling onto the tip of his nose.

"I missed you, too," she said. "And I have something important to tell you."

"What is it?" he said, still marveling that she was really in front of him.

She gently grabbed his face, and he eclipsed her hands with his. "I know how you can take the throne."

His heart stopped. "What?"

She nodded excitedly. "Your father told me."

His brows pulled together as he got to his feet. "My father?'

"Yes. He's . . . He's been caring for you from afar this whole time. I can explain more later, but we have to go now."

He frowned. "Correlia, you must be mistaken. My father doesn't care about me. I haven't seen him since—"

"He *does* care about you. And he told me how to save you. How to dethrone Thanatos."

He studied her gaze. She was telling the truth. But . . .

His head spun.

He needed to breathe.

"It's okay," she said softly, stroking his cheek with her thumb, and all his fears and muddled thoughts melted away. "This will all make sense. I promise. Just listen, please. I know how to help you."

He smiled and let his face rest in her palm. Then he kissed it and said, "Go on." She smiled, and his knees were weak. He couldn't help leaning down and kissing her one more time. "Tell me how we can take the throne." He let his forehead rest against hers. Her breath was warm against his lips, and his own breath snagged in his throat before he added one more promise before whatever came next. "I want to give you everything," he said, "and I'll do whatever it takes to do it."

CHAPTER
THIRTY-EIGHT

Corre

C orre stroked his face, combing her fingers through his wavy hair. She couldn't look away from his tender gaze, those dark eyes she never stopped thinking about. Her heart turned to goo, and emotion swelled in her chest. She didn't have much time to tell him everything, but there was something she had to say before anything else.

"Markus." Her voice shuddered as she sucked in a breath. Her eyes filled with tears. "I'm so sorry." The words came out in a whisper. His gentle gaze deepened.

He shook his head and held her face in his hands. "You have nothing to be sorry for."

"I do. When I left, I trusted Thanatos over my own judgment. I betrayed you." Tears spilled from her eyes, and that heavy weight that had been stuck in her stomach ever since she'd left Tartarus continued sinking, pressing deeper into her until she could barely move. "You've had so many people stop believing in you. I shouldn't have been one of them." She couldn't tell what he was thinking, and fear pricked up her neck. Maybe she shouldn't have said anything. "But it was only a moment," she added quickly. "I'm so sorry."

He smiled softly and traced her jawline with the back of his hand. "I never blamed you for a second."

"You should have, though. I'm so sorry."

"Stop apologizing," he said, his voice soft. "Really. I understand everything was confusing. My master is devious. I'm just sorry I couldn't remember what happened that day." His face fell. "I still don't know. So you shouldn't feel bad. For all we know, I did . . ." He paused before saying, "Kill your parents."

"No, Markus. You didn't. I know that now. I know what happened that day, but I can't explain now. We have to hurry. Before anyone finds us."

He sighed with a nod. "Okay. What are we supposed to do?"

Corre nervously twisted her dress in her hands. "Well . . . I don't know exactly. Your father only told me what we had to do. There's . . . um . . ." She fumbled to get the words out. It was a lot more complicated to explain than she thought it would be. Thomas explained it so effortlessly. "There's someone in a . . . a room or something. Down below Tartarus."

"Below Tartarus?"

"Yeah. Apparently, Thomas was told that there's been a strange energy sensed by some of the spirits down here. Tyche has heard whisperings, over time, I think, that something is going on in a cave down there, guarded by the deity Hypnos. It's his grotto, but it's almost impossible to get to because one must go over the river Lethe. Tyche hasn't been able to investigate because of this, but your father thinks incantations can get us through long enough not to get our souls sucked out."

Markus's eyebrows shot up. "Wonderful."

Corre lowered her voice. "Did you know you have a sister?"

Markus didn't say anything at first, but then he nodded. "I know Tyche is my sister. She's visited me a couple of times, but she always tries to stir trouble. I don't know how reliable her word is."

Corre shifted her weight. "Well, Thomas seems certain she cares about you. She's just a little rough around the edges, I think." She shot him a grin. "Like someone else I know."

Markus let out a half-chuckle. "Fair enough. I guess we don't have any other leads." Corre wanted to tell him more. She wanted to explain that on Tyche's other side, she was *her* half-sister, too. But now wasn't the time. She'd tell him sometime in the future, but first, they needed to secure that they'd *have* a future. They needed to hurry.

"Right. Apparently, she heard about some of this through gods on Olympus, too."

"What did she hear exactly?"

"Just whisperings about the same sort of thing. She heard them talking about how the humans' sleep has been disrupted for a while. More and more. They think Hypnos might be behind it somehow. It makes sense. He's the only one with power over sleep."

Markus nodded, but he still didn't look convinced.

"It's the only lead we have, and it seems promising. Your father has been trying to figure this out for a while now. He told me, when I first came here a few months ago, that Thanatos shouldn't still be on the throne and that something isn't right."

"You saw my father before, too?"

"I didn't know who he was at the time. I only found out before meeting you here today." He stared off, his expression heavy. She wasn't sure what was going through his mind, but she did know they didn't have time to think. They needed to act. "Which way to the river Lethe?"

He ran his hands through his hair and looked the opposite way down the corridor he'd just come from. "It's quite a way from here. There are rivers all over Tartarus."

"Then we better get going," she said, grabbing his hand.

His lips flickered into a smile. "Okay. This way."

Nikias

The river was unnervingly empty. Where were Charon and that girl? Thanatos had given him very specific instructions. He was to fetch her and bring her to him. And she needed to be watched. Carefully.

The general's face tightened. "Charon!" he screamed, but he didn't let his composure slip as he waited for the ferryman to appear.

After no more than a second, the hooded figure skated over the water with his long staff. Nikias couldn't help but notice the boat was very girl-less. When the ferryman was close enough to respond, Nikias glared straight at him. "Where is she?" he hissed.

The boat docked. "The girl?" the ferryman croaked.

"Yes, the girl!"

"I was told you had urgent business to tend to. Someone else fetched her in your place."

The blood drained from the general's already pale face. "And you believed that nonsense?"

Charon didn't answer. He even looked bored.

Nikias ground his teeth, vibrating with fury. "Who took her?"

"A mortal."

His eyebrow flickered. "A *mortal*?"

The figure nodded.

"Where did he take her?"

Charon pushed his boat back into the water. "I wasn't told. Somewhere in the labyrinth."

"Where are you going?" Nikias wailed, but the ferryman kept rowing back down the river toward Olympus.

"Back."

"Back?"

"This is your problem, general. Not mine."

Nikias seethed and let out an angry yell before wheeling around and running to Thanatos's palace.

Corre

"I don't think Hypnos guards this river. I actually remember coming down here as a young boy," Markus said, stepping down into a gravelly ditch, carefully helping Corre down with him. "I don't remember much, but I remember searching for answers. Strangely, it felt familiar at that time, too, but I was sure I'd never been there before." He helped her over another short rocky wall. "But I do know that this is his grotto, and the river is tied to him. This whole place is Hypnos's domain. But, as far as I've been told, Lethe doesn't suck out your soul. It just wipes out your memory."

He led her over a hump of jagged rocks. The air in this pocket of Tartarus was thick and extremely damp, and the farther they crawled into the narrowing tunnel, the darker it became. She could barely see him by the time he led her down the last dip of rock before an unnerving ledge. She had to trust him. If she let herself be scared, she wouldn't be able to do whatever it was they had to for Markus to take the throne. So she kept her hand in his and kept going.

"That's just as frightening," she said, wobbling over a slick bed of stone. "I don't want to forget my life. After all this, after all we've been through, forgetting would be worse than death."

She didn't see him turn around and wouldn't have known he had if she hadn't felt his lips brush against her knuckles. He pressed a kiss into the back of her hand, and her heart flipped.

"I agree," he said, "So let's be careful."

"But what about the incantations? Your father said we have to recite them."

"Incantations," Markus mused. "I don't know. Maybe he didn't get the story right. I guess I don't know if the river or grotto could suck our souls out for certain. We'll be careful. Just stay with me. I won't let anything hurt you."

Warmth filled Corre's chest. She squeezed his hand. "Okay. I trust you."

He led her down another path, and finally, a light appeared—a shocking, flashing light emanating from the end of the long, rocky tunnel. She wasn't sure what she was expecting, but she might have been half-expecting a horrific dungeon at the mouth of such a river. But that's not what she saw when she stepped out of that tunnel.

The sight was beautiful. There were poppies so expertly crafted that she wondered if her mother could even make flowers so alluring, and who had possibly made them. They spread across the opening of a large grotto. At one end was an ebony nest of some sort, and Corre couldn't help being drawn to it. The dark wood it consisted of was perfectly rounded, as if it had been formed by a giant tool, smoothed to perfection by the Titans, ready for a giant fowl to rest in it. It looked like an enormous bowl set in a field of lush grass and beautiful flowers. The deep red of the poppies spread before the mouth of the river like a tongue crowning the entrance to the incredibly lethal body of water.

"How do we get across?" she asked. There was no way around the river and into the depths of whatever lay beyond the grotto other than to sail through it.

"I guess we have to recite those incantations," Markus said, turning to face her, his fingers still threaded in hers. "What did you say they were?"

She grimaced. "I didn't. Um . . ." She thought hard about what Thomas had told her, but he'd poured so much information into her. It was hard to remember it all. But this was the most important of all of it. She groaned and rubbed her temple. "I think it was something like, 'You raise the dead from slumber, wake from . . . underwater?'" She winced.

Markus scanned the water, then looked up at the nest. "I don't think that's it, but I do think that's a proper incantation, or at least most of one. It rings a bell . . . though I can't place from where . . ." He trailed off before smiling at her reassuringly. "Still, that doesn't seem like one we need right now. Didn't you say you learned multiple incantations?"

"There was another one. I think maybe this one could help." They had no choice. She might as well place hope in it. "'Where the magic flows, power swells, we reach inside to skate this well.'" As soon as she uttered the last word, a large crash roared from the river.

They staggered back, and Corre gasped as a large wall of water burst from the river's murky surface. When the surface calmed, a small rowboat was revealed. A smile stretched across her face, and she swung to her left to face Markus. "We did it!" She took his hands in hers and jumped as she led him to the boat. But there was a hesitance in his steps that made her stop just before placing her foot inside the ebony craft. "What's wrong?"

"This doesn't seem right." His eyes darted to the large bowl-like nest at the far end of the grotto. "Doesn't this look an awful lot like that thing over there?"

"Yeah . . . So?"

"I don't know. Something feels off."

Corre's shoulders fell. "Markus, we don't have any other choice right now. I think someone is looking for us."

"Who?"

"I think your father said he was a general."

"Nikias. Right. Why didn't I think he'd be on our tail? I'm sure he won't stop until he's caught us." He sighed. "And I'm sure Thanatos gave him an army to fulfill the task." He sighed again, an even longer, louder one. "Okay. I guess we have no other choice. Let's go."

Without further ado, Corre stepped toward the boat, but before she could get inside, Markus said, "Wait!" She swiveled around to see him narrow his eyes on the boat and walk closer to it. "Let me get in first, so I can help you in. I don't think I could live with myself if something went wrong and you weren't safe. If you fell in the river . . . and . . ." His eyes were distant before he looked back at her. "Something could happen to you. Let me help you in."

"Okay." She suppressed a smile. Why did it feel so good to be loved so much? She watched as he carefully stepped into the boat. He stood still, examining the structure with his arms out like he was waiting for something ominous to happen. When moments passed and nothing so much as stirred, he offered her his hand.

She took it, and off they went.

As they floated out of the grotto, Corre smiled at Markus. "You're doing this so effortlessly."

He looked back at her with baffled eyes. "Doing what?"

"Pulling the boat?"

"I'm not pulling the boat," he said, and something eerie fell against her shoulders. A pounding pulsed in her ears, crawling into her mind. The veins in her temples throbbed uncontrollably. She let out a cry and toppled over. It was loud. A muffled ringing in her head. Words were trying to reach her through water, but she couldn't make them out.

"Markus?" she thought she said, but she couldn't hear her voice. Her body was paralyzed, and a force unlike anything she'd ever felt was crushing her. An unseen weight, making it hard to breathe and impossible to move.

Finally, she managed to look at Markus, but he wasn't sitting at the bow of the boat anymore. He'd fallen to the floor of the small vessel, his hand on his forehead, also racked with whatever power this was. But he appeared to be withstanding it a lot better than she was. He turned to face her, and, at the sight of her struggle, he crawled over to her. "Correlia," he mouthed, but she couldn't hear him. His eyes widened in panic, and he looked around as if searching the walls for what to do.

She couldn't keep her eyes open anymore, but as soon as she closed them, the pain left her mind. It was sucked from her head, and when she opened her eyes again, she saw Markus's hand positioned close to her face, turning slightly and then pulling back. All the pain was extinguished, and she felt completely clear. Like she'd never been racked with pain at all.

As soon as relief eased her shoulders and spread through her body, she couldn't help but feel a surge of attraction to him. His strength and focus. His devotion. If they weren't in such a precarious position, she'd definitely be on top of him right now.

His eyes were closed, but his face was tight, his body rigid. He was concentrating. Meditating, or something similar. Then his features relaxed, and he opened his eyes.

"How did you do that?" she asked, unable to hide a smile.

"A lot of discipline and years of training," he replied. "But I've never felt a sensation like that before. I was afraid I wouldn't be able to fight it off."

His eyes fell to his hands, and her heart ached for him. She wished she could help, but this was far from any knowledge or abilities she possessed.

She tried to think of something to say, but the boat jerked to an abrupt stop, and she almost fell out of it. Markus caught her before she toppled out. She let herself rest against his chest before he stood up and helped her out of the water.

She looked past him and spotted an ominous door, but before she could take another step, her body constricted in pain. Another wave of that horrid sensation thrust into her head. Her temples throbbed, and she could barely stand.

Markus quickly made his way in front of her and pushed the magic radiating from the massive steel doors away from them, throwing it out to his sides. The thick, oozing, translucent material dissipated, and the doors swung open.

There was a moment of silence after the doors slammed against the grotto walls, sending echoes skipping across the water. Markus turned to her. "Are you okay?" He held her close to him, and she nodded. "Good. We're here," he said, and the blood drained from her face.

"How do you know?"

"I'm not sure, exactly," he said, his voice low, "but something tells me this is where it all ends."

Her mouth dried up. She couldn't speak, as if there was anything she could say to that.

"There's a lot of power here. Whatever we need to find, I think we're in the right place." He took her hand and led her forward, and she followed him into the dark.

CHAPTER
THIRTY-NINE

Nikias

"What?!" The deity howled, tossing his hand to the side and sending five of his men clattering to the floor.

Nikias winced. "She wasn't there," he repeated, swallowing his fear and hoping Thanatos wouldn't notice the tremor in his voice.

The colossal god stumbled off the throne. "Where is Theron?" he shouted.

"I-I didn't check, sir. I came straight to you when the girl was missin—"

Thanatos threw the general across the room before he could finish. His back cracked against the wall, and a flash of pain skittered up his spine.

"You're useless!" Thanatos growled, and Nikias wiped the blood from the gash on the back of his neck. His master looked to the demons who guarded the labyrinth. "Bring me every soldier and meet me at Theron's chambers at once!" The room quaked with the thunderous roar of the deity's commands, and every demon did as it was told.

The general hopped to his feet and ran to his master, bowing the whole time. "I am so sorry, Master. I won't disappoint you again."

Thanatos snorted. "I highly doubt that. But you may come."

Nikias kept his head down, but he could hardly contain his excitement, and as soon as Thanatos turned his back, the general smiled and followed close behind.

They walked down the winding labyrinth until they made it to Nikias's least favorite god's chambers. One of the demons swung the door open and much of the army flooded in, including Nikias's master. There was a pause, then a great clattering. Thanatos growled with rage. "Where is he?!" The deity ran out of the room, stumbling every few steps from his giant form, and likely because he wasn't used to being so mobile.

The giant deity whipped around and bounded toward him. Nikias froze. He clutched his underling's shoulders with his long, yellowed talons. "Are you certain they didn't leave for Olympus?"

"I-I don't know. The ferryman simply said a mortal took him and—"

Thanatos's eyes went black, and he released his hold on Nikias. The blonde finally let himself breathe a little, but the terror in his master's face was unsettling enough that it was still hard to exhale. "A *mortal*?" Thanatos said in a dry, quiet hiss. This wasn't usual for him, and Nikias almost preferred his master's screams.

"Yes, a mortal," he said again, but the deity was frozen in place.

Thanatos's chest quickened, and panic widened his eyes. "Nooo!" he roared, and the labyrinth shook. Bits of rock and ceiling fell in crumbles atop their heads. Thanatos fled down the tunnels, and Nikias knew better than to wait for a command. He turned to his soldiers. He didn't know what to say to them, but his look must have been enough because, almost at once, they all straightened and moved into formation.

The general looked back to Thanatos, who was quickly disappearing from sight. "Move ahead!" Nikias called as he ran to catch up. His soldiers followed in two long, neat rows of about seventy-five.

Seventy-five demons. This was the most men he'd ever commanded.

His mouth curled into a smile.

When Thanatos saw him pull this off, there would be no more Theron of Tartarus. There would be only one option for Hades.

Him.

Corre

As they crept into the tomb-like cavern, Corre couldn't stop thinking of that strange, powerful force that had twisted her mind, fogging it up and rendering her immobile. *What* was *that?*

She looked around the cavern. It was a surprisingly pristine dome made of the same stone as the labyrinth above. It was so smooth and well-structured that it looked hand-crafted. Like the bowl-like nest at the mouth of the river.

Before she got too deep in, a glimmer of something on the walls caught her eye. She couldn't help following it. She crept closer and closer, and it glinted again. It was magnetic—*mesmerizing*—but it wasn't coming from the wall itself. It was a shimmer of some sort of magical substance seeped into the walls. Like a semi-translucent coating.

It really was beautiful. When she moved, the blackness reflected dark hues of blue, purple, and red. Deep shades she'd never seen in anything other than carefully, expertly crafted paintings.

She leaned in closer.

It was fascinating.

She reached out to touch it.

As soon as her fingertips brushed the surface, that same mind-numbing power forced its way into her head. She let out a cry and fell to the ground.

"Correlia!" Markus ran to her. He skidded to the ground and pulled her onto his lap, deep lines of worry creased along his forehead. But the feeling passed the moment her fingertips left the wall. She adjusted to her knees and rose to her feet.

"I'm okay," she said, taking his hands, but something at the back of the cave caught her attention. "Markus. Look." She pointed to a large, curved lump nestled against the back wall. "What is that?"

They walked closer. It wasn't until they were past a long shadow in front of the shape that they realized what it was.

"It's a woman," she said.

Markus took a step forward. "It is . . ." He walked closer, and Corre laced one of her hands in his, holding onto his arm with the other. The closer they got, the clearer it became that this figure was a gloriously beautiful, unusually large goddess. And she was fast asleep.

She had long, thick waves of sapphire hair—a slightly darker tint than her sky-blue skin that sparkled like the clear waters of Olympus. She was curled within her hair, sleeping in the soft bed of loose ringlets. Corre would have thought she was sleeping peacefully in such a comfortable position if it weren't for her strained expression.

"Who is that?" she asked.

"I don't know."

They walked closer, and before she realized what she was doing, Corre found herself reaching out to touch her. She probably shouldn't have followed such an impulse, but something was pulling her to the goddess.

"What are you doing?" Markus whispered, but she couldn't help it.

She touched the goddess's shoulder.

And everything went black.

That same mind-numbing force blasted through her. She jolted back and fell to the ground, hitting her head against the stones below. She heard Markus call her name, but it was muffled and warped. She couldn't hear past the ringing, and everything sounded like she was underwater.

She couldn't keep her eyes or mind open. Unlike touching the wall, releasing her fingers from the goddess's skin didn't stop the horrific sensation.

A nightmare flashed in her mind, but it wasn't her own.

Corre was somewhere else entirely.

When she could open her eyes again, she was in a field of grass, the blades moving gently by a subtle breeze. She didn't recognize this place, despite all the locations her mother had dragged her to for work throughout her adolescence. It was serene. It had to be somewhere on Olympus, but the sky was dark and there were no other signs of life other than the blue goddess and two others—cloaked figures Corre couldn't make out. Their faces were hidden, but they were facing the goddess.

"Why are you doing this?" the goddess said, and that's when Corre realized the goddess was crying. She didn't look scared, but the other giant beings were rigid and staring up at her. They were enormous, but she was over a head taller, her shoulders a little broader.

"You know why," one of the voices said, and instantly, Corre recognized who it belonged to. She could never forget that raspy voice. That evil, taunting, malicious voice. "You've left us with no choice."

The goddess sobbed, chains appearing on her wrists, sprouting from deep within the earth. The storm clouds twirled faster, thundering and flashing with a bright light before transporting Corre to a new scene.

A dungeon. A small, dingy room. A makeshift prison cell. There was a palpable feeling of dread in the air, and it left her with a sense of melancholy that left her body weak. She trembled violently as anxiety rattled through her, rising by the second.

Her greatest fears flickered across the wall in dark shadows until they changed shape and turned their attention to a young boy in the corner. The feeling of despair was so great that it was difficult to focus on anything going on around her, but in a brief moment of clarity and focus, Corre saw the boy more clearly.

It was Markus.

He was about thirteen or fourteen years old, and he was huddled in the corner, his knees pressed tightly against his face. She only realized who it was by the way he cried and the familiar waves of black hair atop his head. But when he looked up in terror, screaming at the shadows, there was no denying his identity.

Her heart splintered into a thousand broken pieces. This poor boy was in a room of nightmares.

"I'll help you! Get up! I'll help you out!" she yelled. She desperately wanted to snatch him from this den of fear, but he couldn't hear her, and the door was sealed shut.

Wake up, a voice said. A female voice. *Wake up.*

She looked around but saw no one but young Markus.

There was nothing Corre could do. She was helpless. Useless.

"Why am I seeing this?" she whispered, tears streaming down her face. "Why do I have to see this?"

Then everything went black again.

And she heard that voice one more time. *Wake up!*

She whipped around but was still shrouded in darkness, until a flash of light blinded her, and she was thrown back into the present. That powerful force that had immobilized her body left her cold and shaking on the floor, then fled like a passing whisper. But it didn't leave without taking most of her energy along with it.

"Correlia! What happened?" Markus cried. He was bent over her, his hands cradling her face. Her eyes focused. Air. She needed air. She sprang forward and gasped for breath. "Correlia!"

She couldn't speak. There was no time to think. She worked her way to her feet, keeping her eyes fixed on the sleeping goddess a few feet away. She coughed and croaked, finally finding her voice, and turned to face him. "I think I know what we have to do," she said. He frowned, baffled, but followed her as she walked to the sleeping goddess. "She's under a spell. We need to wake her up."

"The incantation," Markus said, and Corre nodded.

"How did it start again?" She strained to remember the words, but the ordeal she'd gone through left her with little ability to focus or do much of anything.

"It started with, 'You raise the dead from slumber, wake from . . .'" Markus said. "But the last word wasn't right. I remember learning it at some point, but I don't remember what the last part was."

"'You raise the dead from slumber . . . wake from . . .'" Corre's head throbbed. *What did he say?*

"Was it—" Markus started, but a terrible roaring cut him off. The whole grotto shook. They turned toward the sound. There was a shadow—a troll-like shape lengthening on the wall. The darkness grew until it revealed a being almost as large as the sleeping goddess.

Right away, Corre knew who it was. There was no denying it; the power radiating from his body as he approached was impossible to ignore.

"Hypnos," Markus said.

Hypnos.

The terrifying creature was enveloped in shadow as it trudged toward them. Markus whipped around and grabbed her shoulders. "Recite the incantation! Hurry! I'll fight him off!"

The creature hurriedly bounded over and smacked him, sending him plummeting to the wall. "Markus!" Corre screamed, but the being towered over her, and she got a good look at his face.

She gasped.

He looked like . . .

"Thanatos!" she yelled. He looked exactly like Markus's master, only his skin wasn't pale and grayed. It was a dark, mossy green, like the gunk beneath a swampy rock.

"It's not Thanatos," Markus said, his voice tight as he staggered forward. The deity turned to face him, and the shock manifested on the young god's face as well. "But why do you look like him?"

The creature laughed like he had told a joke, but Markus was horrified, mystified. *I have to hurry.* Corre ran toward the sleeping goddess and tried remembering the incantation. "'You raise the dead from slumber, wake from—'" The creature wailed and barrelled toward her. She held her hands out to block it, but Markus used his power to knock him over at the last second.

"Keep trying!" Markus shouted, racing to Hypnos and using his powers to get into the deity's mind. It wailed. "Can't you handle your own tricks?" Markus snapped, twisting his hand and pushing it out at the giant god.

It grabbed its head and screeched—a dual wail, like two voices came from the being, one deep and one shrill.

Corre searched her mind again. "'You raise the dead from slumber, wake from . . .'" A lump formed in her throat. She was too weak now, and the word . . . what was that last word? "'You raise the dead from slumber, wake from—'"

"This curse and collapse asunder!" Markus finished.

Hypnos bellowed and lunged at him, but it was too late.

Light burst from the slumbering goddess—a blinding, sublime, sapphire-infused light. The grotto shook even more violently than before.

"Nooo!" a raspy voice cried, followed by a thundering trail of footsteps. The real Thanatos entered the room in a fury, Nikias and his army rushing in close behind.

The light grew. No one dared to move.

As the grotto's rumbling settled, the enormous, ethereal goddess rose from her slumbering place and opened her eyes.

"Noooo!" Thanatos roared again, but Hypnos bowed his head and fell to his knees.

"It's over," Hypnos said to Markus's master. When Thanatos didn't move, Hypnos growled. "Get down," he said. "And bow to our mother."

CHAPTER FORTY

Corre

The goddess's hair fell around her, pouring over her shoulders and onto the ground in great, graceful waves. She was breathtaking, her beauty surreal. She looked like she'd been molded from the ocean. When her icy eyes fell upon Markus, she frowned, and they darted to the two evil deities bowing at her feet.

"Rise," she said, her voice smoky and commanding. She waved her hand up, beckoning them to stand. "Hypnos." She fixed her heavy gaze on the Deity of Sleep, then shifted to the other. "Thanatos." As the two deities got to their feet, her gaze settled back upon Markus. "Markus, son of Thomas and Lily?"

He nodded slowly. The tension in the room was thick. Suffocating. Corre looked from Thanatos to the goddess, and then to the still bowing Deity of Sleep. She stifled a gasp and looked up at the goddess. "You're Nyx," she said, and the goddess smiled.

"That's right." Her alluring voice was somehow both loud and smooth as it rippled across the cave. "I take it I have been asleep much longer than a few hours." She looked to Hypnos, and her expression immediately changed. "Explain yourself." Her hair shuttered, coming alive as fury sparked in her eyes.

Hypnos continued to bow. "I'm sorry, Mother. Forgive me."

"I didn't ask you to apologize. I asked you to explain." But the god said nothing. Nyx growled and then shot a look at his twin brother. "What have you two done?"

"Nothing, Mother. We were only fulfilling our callings—"

"Lies! You were told to train the boy. You are the Deity of Death, not the God of the Underworld. You were to train the boy until he was of age. But it seems you and your brother have done something devious, considering during Hades' entire upbringing, I've been lying dormant in this place." She looked around at the dreary cavern. "You kept me down here," she said it as if only now realizing it. "You two have plotted something."

"I'm so sorry, Mother," Hypnos quickly spouted. "Thanatos beguiled me with an influx of power. I was intoxicated by it as it came."

"You pathetic—" Thanatos started, raising his hand to smack his brother, but Nyx rose hers instead and, with a flick of her wrist, secured the evil god's arm behind his back.

"Let your brother speak," she said, then looked back at Hypnos.

"He had a plan that would allow us access to the entire world. We could rule it however we pleased. He said we could become more powerful than even the Titans. And he was right. He gave me power."

"How?" Nyx narrowed her eyes.

"Through the dreams of the gods."

The air was sucked from Corre's lungs.

"You're only to be over the humans' sleep. How did you toy with the gods like that?"

"With Thanatos's help—"

"Stop dragging me—" Thanatos's mouth was clamped shut by another flick of his mother's wrist.

Hypnos continued without skipping a beat. "I was able to create a room of nightmares for the young Hades, and it gave me power as he was trained. Thanatos told me it would help shape Theron into Hades while also giving me power."

Corre's heart pulled in her chest. She glanced over at Markus, but he showed no emotion as he watched the peculiar exchange.

"If you thought you two would rule the world, why would you need the boy?" Nyx asked.

"That was what he'd first told me, but after a few months of the boy's training—" *Torture*, Corre wanted to correct, but she didn't dare speak. "—I became stronger, and through his fears in that room, I was able to do more than I ever thought possible."

"Including placing your mother in a cursed sleep," Nyx hissed, and Hypnos cowered, bowing his head again.

"I apologize greatly, Mother."

"That doesn't cut it," the goddess snapped.

Hypnos fell to his knees again, trembling as he stared fixedly at the damp floor.

"Is that what the power I felt was?" Corre finally piped up. "All that mind-numbing power? And the strange feelings the gods on Olympus have been feeling?"

Hypnos didn't respond, but then Nyx said, "I'd like to know, too. Speak."

"Yes."

Corre laughed bitterly, but her mind was whirring at lightning speed trying to keep up. She knew she'd been blind and naïve about the affairs on Olympus, but just how much was she unaware of?

"If you've been taking a portion of Markus's power his whole life," Corre started, "why are the gods only now feeling ill, or strange, or whatever it is?"

"I never took his power," Hypnos said. The words were stiff as they came out. Like Corre was beneath speaking to. "I only received power through his fears, but the more powerful he became, the more power seeped into those fears, unguarded, in that room. And then into me. He hadn't returned to it for years, until recently." The Deity of Sleep looked up, dreamily, staring off into the leaky grotto. "It was the most power I'd ever felt. It was glorious. So much power . . . I could start working toward the world Thanatos had planned—" Hypnos grunted in pain as his brother struck him across the face.

Markus's master looked to the goddess Nyx. "He doesn't know what he's saying. I wasn't trying to rule anything. I was only trying to reach my potential and show my brothers how to do the same."

"That's not—" Hypnos started, but Thanatos glared at him.

"You've spoken to your other brothers, then?" Nyx said, and Thanatos's features twisted. "I'll take that as a 'no'." She sighed heavily and stroked her forehead. "You chose the easiest to beguile first. You wanted to show them the start of your devious plan. What exactly were you expecting to accomplish?"

"Just as I said, to reach—"

"Do not lie to me!" Her voice bellowed higher and higher until it was a piercing screech, like the sound of a hydra. Thanatos stood his ground and didn't so much as shake. Hypnos, on the other hand, collapsed onto his face, quaking with fear. "You meddled with the divine," she said, scowling in disgust. "Who do you think you are to believe you can interfere with the affairs of Olympus? To take Hades' fate from him and torment him for your own selfish, disgusting purposes? Who do you think you are?"

Thanatos's eyes were black with fury. "I am the Great Deity of Death!" he howled. "The *true* God of Death! The deity of death itself! The throne of the Underworld shouldn't go to some sniveling boy who didn't even want it!"

"That's not up for you to decide!" Nyx shouted. "You were to *train* the boy as a god of death! To *train* him! That is all! And now you have made a grave mistake. *Many* grave mistakes." She turned to Hypnos. "As did you. You both will suffer for what you've done. I'll get to the bottom of every last part of it. With the new, true reining head of Tartarus." She turned to Markus, her scowl quickly, jarringly, turning into a smile. "Are you ready, young Hades?" she asked gently. "To take the throne that is rightfully yours?"

Corre's face lit up, her spirit soaring; she smiled so hard her cheeks hurt as she grabbed Markus's arm and looked into his lost eyes. "Markus! Did you hear her?" But he didn't move, and her smile fell. "Markus?"

"See?" Thanatos scoffed. "The boy's soft. He doesn't have the stomach to rule as God of the Underworld."

"Do you believe you're above all other gods?" Nyx snapped at her son. "That you know better than the Titans and the prophecies?"

"So, there *are* prophecies," Corre muttered to herself, but the goddess heard her.

"Yes, child. A great many."

Her gaze fell. "Oh." If they were all prophesied of their places on Olympus, or below, then where did that leave her?

"But that doesn't mean you can't make your own destiny," Nyx added, and Corre looked up. The goddess smiled down at her, then once again shifted her focus to Markus. "Young Markus, what say you? Are you ready to take the throne?"

Markus continued staring off, frozen.

"Markus?" Corre asked softly, threading her fingers in his. "What's wrong?"

Finally, he met her gaze, curling his hand over Corre's and taking a breath. "Nothing," he said quietly. "This is all so much, but," He looked up at Nyx, "I'm ready to take the throne."

A smile stretched across Corre's face again, but there was still a weight heavy in her chest. She'd hoped there were no prophecies. That the tale that spoke of them was just another story she got wrong.

At least Markus would finally be free.

She pressed her face against his side. "You did it, Markus. You're free." She lifted her hands and tenderly grabbed his face. They looked into each other's eyes, tears filling Corre's. "You're okay now. It's all over."

He didn't smile back. He wiped a tear from her face and said, "What about Correlia?" He looked up at Nyx.

"What about her?" the goddess asked with that same melodious hum in her voice.

"Can she stay?"

Nyx laughed. "That's for the two of you to decide. You're the ruler here now. Not me."

The weight lifted from Corre's chest. "Markus!" she gasped, so gloriously relieved, and he wrapped his arms around her.

"It's over," he said, emotion welling in his voice.

"It's over," she confirmed, rubbing his back.

"This is a mistake!" Thanatos screamed. "You don't know what you're doing! He doesn't have the strength to be Hades. He—"

Nyx lifted a hand and scowled. "Enough," she said, throwing the giant god to the ground.

Corre's jaw dropped, but when she looked over at Markus, she couldn't help but love the glimpse of satisfaction on his face. The retribution.

"You have caused enough trouble," Nyx continued, walking closer to Thanatos, who was forced to his knees by his mother's power. "You will suffer for what you have done." She shook her head slowly. "You're no Great Deity."

"Zeus won't let you—" he started, but Nyx burst into laughter.

"Please! Zeus fears me. He wouldn't dare go against anything I say."

Just as Thanatos's eyes widened, he was thrown onto his back, and a burst of light sprung from his crooked frame. A powerful, blasting light. With every second, it grew. It was like a giant rush of glowing fire was being sucked from his body and into his mother's outstretched fingers.

Nyx watched, expressionless, as Thanatos yelled and writhed, the glow around his body thunderous and blinding. Then, almost suddenly, Thanatos's body began to shrivel, and the power turned into a flash of light.

Corre covered her eyes, squeezing them shut behind her hand. When she opened them again, there were spots in her vision, but there was no denying what the blinding light had left behind. A shrunken shell of a former Thanatos, now the size of a regular god. Thin, wilted, and far smaller than his former apprentice.

At first, no one said anything. No one dared to move. But then Nyx spoke. "His powers have been stripped from him." She shifted her gaze to Markus. "And now you decide his fate."

"No!" A quiet, scratchy voice croaked. Thanatos's withered form limped forward. "He doesn't deserve the throne."

"You're wrong!" Corre squeaked. At first, she didn't realize the words had come from her, but when everyone turned to face her—even Markus, whose eyes were wide and hopeful—she didn't let herself back down. "You're wrong," she said again, more boldly. She looked straight at Thanatos. "Markus has been training harder than anyone ever could. He's the strongest god I know." Her eyes met the young Hades; tears were forming in his dark brown eyes. She smiled and slid her hand into his. "It's true," she said softly. "You're worthy of everything you desire."

A tear skated down Markus's face, and he smiled before leaning forward and placing a gentle kiss on her lips.

"See?! Do you think a god of—" Thanatos started, but Markus whipped around and cut him off.

"You have no more power here!" he said, and his voice boomed across the room. Corre's heart flipped.

The withered god looked at Markus, aghast. "How dare you speak to me like that?" The young Hades walked forward, letting go of Corre's hand as he looked down at his former master. He got mere inches away from his face and peered into the god's tiny yellow-black eyes. Thanatos lifted a skinny arm and tried to strike him, but Markus caught it effortlessly and smacked it away.

"You hold no more power over me," he said. "Not anymore."

"You—" Thanatos started, but Markus interrupted him again, turning his face to his new guards. His new army. Everyone he now ruled over. Including Nikias.

"Take him to the throne room," he commanded. "I'll deal with him there."

The demons stood at attention, bowed, and, almost unanimously, said, "Yes, sire." Quickly, they all flocked out, two of them locking Thanatos's small wrists behind him with chains before pulling him back out of the grotto.

Nikias was the last one to leave.

"General? Did you hear me?" Markus shouted.

Nikias flinched, then muttered something under his breath. "Yes . . . Sire . . ." He grumbled, then turned on his heel to leave.

When no one was in the grotto but Markus, Corre, Nyx, and a bowing Hypnos, the young Hades turned to Corre and grabbed hold of her hand.

"Are you ready to go?" She nodded, unable to hold back the tears now spilling from her eyes.

"Of course," she said.

"I shall speak with my husband, Erebus," Nyx said. "And I will speak to Zeus. None of this will go without consequence." Then she smiled. "But we can discuss all of that later. I believe Thanatos's punishment awaits. As does your crown."

CHAPTER FORTY-ONE

Corre

It was surreal watching Markus enter the throne room so resolved, his hand guiding hers. A thousand and one thoughts were probably pounding in his head, and she desperately wanted to know each and every one of them. Was he scared? Was he excited? What was he going to do next?

When they reached the steps to the throne, he stopped and turned around. His shoulders were back, and his face was set in a stoic, unreadable expression. His eyes locked fixedly on Thanatos as the husk of his former master was brought before him. A role reversal that Markus had probably waited much of his life to experience, at least to some extent. If he'd ever believed it would come.

The wicked god was tossed to his knees by his former guards, his hands still chained behind his back. Thanatos chuckled dryly. "You have no idea what you're doing."

Markus's expression didn't change. "You don't know anything about me."

Thanatos let out another dry laugh. "Oh, boy, you have no idea."

Corre's eyes swiveled to Markus's, her hands wringing, hoping Thanatos wasn't wriggling his way into his pupil's mind. Her heart raced, but then the corner of Markus's mouth turned up.

"You don't know when to quit, do you?" His deep voice resounded through the chamber. "You're nothing now. Beneath everything and everyone you've ever pushed around. You can't take it. Can you?" Markus smirked, which made Thanatos growl and stagger to his feet.

"You think you can rule this place, *boy*?" He turned to Corre and pointed one gnarled finger at her. "And what about her? You're okay damning her to this place?"

"I make my own choices," Corre spat, and Thanatos gawked at her, as if not realizing she had the ability to speak.

After an uncomfortable amount of staring and silence, the withered god burst into rickety laughter and looked back at Markus. "You have her fooled for now, but she'll eventually see what you are." His laughing faded, but an evil grin stretched across his face. "She'll leave you once she sees your true worth. Or rather, your lack of it."

Her blood boiled, and she stepped forward, opening her mouth to say something, but Markus grabbed her hand. "It's okay." He smiled softly at her. "Really."

She nodded and let her hand fall to her side.

He took an even breath and walked closer to his former master. The closer he got, the more twisted Thanatos's features became, until fury shot from his hollow eyes. "Do you truly think she cares for you? No one could ever care for you. You know that."

"You can't hurt me anymore," Markus said, and Thanatos let out an ear-splitting yell and dove forward, but Markus took him by the chains and threw him to the ground. Thanatos toppled over in a heap of resounding clanks from the chains binding him to his former servants.

"Take him to the dungeon," Markus said, shifting his gaze to the guards. "And prepare him for his fate."

Thanatos heaved shallow breaths, growling with his face pressed against the floor. "And what fate is that?"

"With no power and no strength, there's not much you can do for yourself. Is there?"

Pride was all Thanatos had left, and it was quickly slipping away. The realization was written all over his face. Markus smirked. "Sentence him to the underbelly of Tartarus. In those deep trenches, only the beasts wander. Give him a task impossible to reach. Something he almost attains but forever cannot grasp." He shot a look at Thanatos. "Give him a taste of his own cruel games."

The miserable god's face lit with fury, but the guards took him by the chains and led him out. "You won't be able to detain me for long! You need me!" Markus scoffed, but the monster continued, perhaps seeing a glimmer of hope. A crack in a door. "You'll need advice. My guidance. I've been running this place since its beginning. You'll need me. You've always needed me."

Markus folded his arms and narrowed his eyes on his malicious former mentor. "I'll manage," he spat.

The last thing they saw on Thanatos's face as he was dragged from his former domain was the look of defeat when he realized he no longer had a hold on his victim.

That he had lost.

When only a handful of guards remained, Corre grabbed Markus's hand and rested her head against his arm. "I'm so proud of you."

"I couldn't have done it without you," he said, gently trailing the back of his hand down her cheek as she looked up at him.

"No. You did this all on your own," she said, and his eyes softened. The warmth of his gaze spread through her chest, but then something out of the corner of her eye snagged her attention away.

She frowned as she focused her eyes on the general. The one Markus despised. The one she just now realized she'd never really looked too closely at before.

Something shivered in her mind.

"Wait . . ." She walked toward him, and Nikias's eyes latched onto her. Markus instinctively grabbed her wrist, but she turned back to him and said, "It's okay. I'm okay." But she was in a daze. She looked back at the general. "I . . . I know you. Where do I know you from?"

"You probably saw his pompous ass walking around this place—"

"No . . ." she said, and it was like she was slipping into a dream. An unsettling, familiar dream. "It was . . ." The space between her eyebrows creased. "Before . . ." A horrible pain split through her head, and a scene from a memory flashed across her mind. One that had been locked tight, but its bolts and pieces were now breaking apart.

She saw a terrible fire burning a familiar cottage. She winced.

"Correlia, are you okay?" Markus asked, but when she turned to look for him, she couldn't see him.

All she saw was that moment. The moment her home had been destroyed and a familiar cackle had broken through the crackling flames. She tried to blink herself back to the present, but her mind wouldn't let her go. There were children everywhere, their parents holding onto them, desperate to save them. Except for one. A boy, with hair as bright as the moonlight spilling over his burning home.

And then she was released from it. The memory came back to her, every detail solidifying in her mind. Retrieved. She looked at Nikias. "You were taken that night, too. Weren't you?" Her head was throbbing. Maybe some of Hypnos's powers had stuck around, or maybe a part of them had lifted.

Maybe something had been sleeping within her this whole time, only now awakening. A part of her that had remained dormant since that horrific night.

"Don't look at me like that," he spat. "Don't you pity me."

"I'm not. I'm just trying to remember."

Nikias's face pinched. He opened his mouth to say something else, but Markus stepped forward, giving him a death glare so fierce the general practically shook in his black leather boots.

Corre couldn't help but smile, but the blonde still shot her a glare. Despite everything, she couldn't help but feel sorry for him—at least a little—at the memory of his mother pushing him toward Thanatos in juxtaposition with her mother desperately clinging onto her until her last breath. She couldn't bring herself to ask him about it, but she knew what had happened that night. It gave a little bit of humanity to someone devious enough to hurt, for all these years, the man she loved.

She wouldn't forgive Nikias for that, but somewhere inside that cold heart was a boy. A boy thrust into this life in the worst possible way. "You were there," she whispered, looking down at him from the steps of the throne. More memories were unlocking. She knew him. As a child, she'd known him. "You were my neighbor."

"I don't know what you're talking about," Nikias said, turning away from her. "And you don't belong here. You're not worthy to walk these halls." The words didn't hurt her, but the memories sinking into her mind left a hollow feeling in her chest that she couldn't reconcile.

"She belongs here as much as I do," Markus said. "You're the one who shouldn't be here."

Nikias stared at her like she was an insect, and as she got closer to him, she could feel Markus's unease, but then she stopped, her stare heavy on the general's. "You're a vile monster," she said. "I understand why you might have become one, but it doesn't excuse what you've done."

"How dare you speak to me like that!" He stood up and lifted his hand, ready to strike her, but was immediately propelled backward.

Corre looked back at Markus. His hand was raised, and his eyes were on Nikias. The move was effortless. When Nikias got back to his feet, the young Hades pulled him forward through the powers surrounding them until the front of the general's uniform was in Markus's hand.

"Do *not* touch her," he hissed and threw Nikias to the ground.

Nikias leapt to his feet, refusing to back down. "You're not fit to run this place! Everything Thanatos said is true! You shouldn't have been deemed Hades! You're not worthy to be the ruler here."

"What would you know of that?" Corre challenged, and Nikias looked at her like he'd already forgotten she was there.

"You—"

"You could have found a friend in Markus," she said, her voice shaking. "But you chose to hurt him instead. You spent a lifetime tormenting him."

Nikias barked out a laugh. "A friend in *him*? This worthless creature?" He pointed to Markus and laughed again. "Please. He's always been a weak, sniveling child. Just as our master always claimed." Markus's hands tightened into fists at his side. Nikias grinned wickedly. "See? So easily combustible. He's always been weak. It's why he was never given the throne. He doesn't deserve it."

Markus didn't move, but his face was lit in anger.

"He *does* deserve it," Corre said, "and that's what makes you furious. It's so easy to see."

Nikias's mouth formed a tight line on his renewed scowl, but he didn't respond. Instead, he turned to Markus. "You'll ruin this place, and then you'll go crawling back to our master, like the pathetic worm you are."

"Don't talk to him li—" Corre started, but Nikias shot her a look and screamed back at her.

"This doesn't concern you!" He looked her up and down. "You little brat! You b—"

Markus yanked the general into the air, his hand outstretched. "Be careful what you say next," he hissed. "We won't ruin anything." Something zipped through Corre when he'd said 'we'. "But you *will* have to follow my orders now." Markus stepped closer, a triumphant smile flickering across his face. "So, you will leave this room at once and you'll get ready for the next stage of your life. With your *new* leader." He cocked a brow. "Okay?"

He threw Nikias to the ground, and the blonde quickly shot to his feet, straightening himself. He narrowed his eyes and sucked on his teeth until he reluctantly grumbled. "Yes."

"Yes, *what*?"

Nikias rolled his eyes back to the new leader of the Underworld. "Yes, *sire.*"

Markus's smile widened. "Good. Now, take the guards with you and leave us be."

The general threw one more nasty look at him before striding out of the room, the rest of the guards trailing behind him.

As Corre watched them leave, she wondered what had made him hate Markus so much. She'd known vaguely of his cruelty. Markus never said much about it, but she knew he'd gotten under his skin and that the general had been a great source of pain in his life and that he had been instrumental in separating them and getting Markus tortured mercilessly.

If only Nikias had chosen differently. What could have been done about all of this—about Thanatos and Hypnos and the throne—years ago if Nikias had found a comrade in Markus instead of an opponent?

"What is it, my love?" Markus's hand found her chin, and he lifted her face to his.

Warmth pooled through her, and her mind went hazy. She would never grow tired of the way he looked at her, or the way her body turned to water when he gazed at her like this. Like she was all that mattered. Like she was a precious pearl taken from the sea.

"Nothing," she said breathlessly. "I just . . . I wish your life could have been different." Her chest tightened, but when he smiled softly and stroked her face, that familiar warmth took its place.

"I don't care about anything that happened before I met you."

She looked into his dark eyes, and the world around them disappeared. He leaned forward and kissed her, and she let her body fall against his. He took her face in his hands and kissed her over and over, and she hungrily accepted each one and matched it with equal fervor.

"Are you ready?" he whispered.

"For what?"

He took a step back and moved his hand in one swiping motion at the seat of the throne. Branches and materials from across the room pulled together, weaving into two solid-black crowns. One with tall, spire-like branches fit for the God of the Underworld, and then a smaller one. Fit for his queen.

He looked at her and kissed her again. "For our coronation."

Her lips parted slightly. "*Our* coronation?"

His smile faded. "Well, that is, if you . . . want to . . . be my queen . . ." Panic flooded his face, and Corre couldn't help but think it was adorable.

She lifted her hand to his cheek and leaned closer. "Of course I do." She scrunched her nose in a smile, and relief washed over his features. His shoulders relaxed.

"Oh good," he said with a laugh. "So . . ." He took the hand she'd placed on his cheek and led her to the crowns. "How shall we do this?"

She pursed her lips, then picked up his crown and lifted it to him. "You are an exceptional god, with the strength and capacity to rule the Underworld in a way no one else can." She smiled at the pink dust creeping up his face. "I hereby name you the official ruler of Tartarus." She went up on her toes and planted a kiss on his lips, then, stretching her arms above his head, she placed the crown on his inky waves of black hair. Her arms fell to his shoulders. "My Hades," she whispered, a smile dimpling her cheeks. She kissed him again.

She leaned back, and he smiled down at her with tears forming in his eyes. His eyes didn't leave hers as he reached out toward the throne and fetched her crown with the power in his fingers. The warmth inside of her grew until it felt like sunshine was spilling from her fingertips as she lifted them to her lips. She suppressed an excited giggle as Markus raised the thin crown over her head.

"May I?" he asked, and her legs weakened at the deep richness of his voice. She nodded giddily. "Then, with this, you are my queen. Do you agree to this? To be Persephone, Queen of Tartarus and wife to Hades?"

Wife.

Her heart fluttered. "Yes," she said, barely managing the word as she looked into her groom's eyes.

He smiled. "Then you are hereby declared Goddess of the Underworld. And you are mine." Her body heated at the deep rumble of his voice and the seductiveness of his tone.

He placed the thin black crown on her head, and a rush of magic coursed through her. A gasp escaped her throat as she watched the silk of her dress turn black. Her rose-like gown no longer reflected the gardens of Olympus. It mirrored the shadows of her new world. She now looked like a flower plucked from the sky on a low-lit night. And something in her clicked. Like a piece of her had been loose all her life until this very moment, when it fell into place.

For the first time in her life, everything felt as it should.

Everything fit perfectly.

When she looked back up at Markus, she noticed his eyes flick up to her crown. Before she could ask him what he was looking at, the answer fell like fairy dust from the top of her head. Blood-red roses had bloomed on the sharp curves of her crown, their soft petals falling around them.

He tipped her face to his, pure adoration reflected in his eyes. "I love you," he whispered. "So very much."

"I love you, too," she breathed, pressing into him. Something shimmered in the darkness of his eyes. "I am yours."

"Forever?" he asked softly.

"Forever," she whispered, and he kissed her.

The sweet intoxication that followed was overwhelming. Her hands trailed up his back, her fingers pulling at the fabric of his shirt, as he sunk deeper into their kiss.

And she let everything else slip away.

She was his wife. Persephone, Queen of the Underworld.

At last.

CHAPTER FORTY-TWO

Corre

"Shall we inspect our palace now, my queen?" His lips grazed hers before pulling away. Corre's heart fluttered.

"I'd love that," she managed to say, then smiled coyly. "My king."

He pulled her out of the room, and they made the ascent to the castle. It was wild to Corre that Markus had never been allowed to live there until now. As the giant, gold-encrusted doors were pulled open for them by two of about fifty guards, her jaw nearly hit the floor.

The wide marble staircase was so intricately carved she could hardly believe it was real. She reached out and touched the smooth banister, letting her fingers trail up the long, winding body as Markus led her to the top of the stairs. She marveled at the deep red of the rug lining the floor and the shimmering silver of the walls around them. As they walked deeper into one of the halls, Corre realized it looked like they were within an urn. A beautiful, exciting, story-filled urn. So alive in a place that was supposed to be dead.

"I've never been up here before," he said, and Corre tore her eyes from their surroundings to look at him.

"You've never been to this palace at all?"

"No, I've been to the palace. Just not down these halls. This was Thanatos's dwelling." He stopped in front of a room with a silver lock chaining the handles to its doors tightly closed. "But I heard he wasn't able to get into Hades' chambers. Which are here."

"Only you can?"

He nodded and raised his hand to the door. Closing his eyes, he took a deep breath and concentrated until the lock shimmied and broke apart. Its shattered pieces fell like glittering confetti across the scarlet floor.

Corre looked up at him excitedly. "Let's go in!" He nodded, but there was something holding him back. "What's wrong?"

"What do you mean?"

"Something's off about you. I can tell."

He paused, then looked back at the door. "I just . . . This all happened so fast. It's hard to believe it's real. I'm almost . . . I'm almost too scared to believe it. Just in case . . ."

She placed her hands on his face and looked into his eyes. "This is real, Markus," she said, and he studied her like he wasn't sure. "I'm real. This place is real." Her hands fell to his chest, but her gaze didn't stray from his. "You can let yourself enjoy it." She smiled gently. "I understand if it's hard. Don't feel rushed. But . . ." She slid her hand back into his. "Just know that this is all real, and you deserve every bit of it." Finally, he nodded, the hint of a smile on his lips, which made her beam. "Do you want to open it or shall I?"

"How about we both do it?"

"Okay." She placed her hands on the shimmering doors, feeling the grooves of each embellishment against her palms before, together, they opened the doors into their new quarters. The room they now shared.

It was magnificent. Corre practically skipped inside. The room was pristine and looked clean and brand new, having never been used. The walls in the hallway had been lined with silver, but here, they were decorated with swirls of gold and emerald. The carpet looked like magic, with its lustrous shine and changing colors. It shifted with each step Corre took around the circular room.

She twirled in the center, and Markus laughed. "You were made to be the queen here."

"Was I?" she said playfully, and her eyes fell on a creamy door on the other side of the room. Prancing over to it, she didn't try to resist the sudden urge that beckoned her to find out what was behind it. She took hold of its handles and pushed it open.

What unveiled itself through the ivory doors was breathtaking. Almost overwhelming. As soon as her eyes took in the view, Corre was hit with a powerful force.

"Wow," she whispered, walking onto the rounded balcony. She hadn't realized how high up they were. She could see nearly all of Tartarus from here. And an empty field.

She looked down and watched as the yellow field stretched to the rest of the Underworld. It appeared half-dead but, still, it was theirs, so to her, it was beautiful. Even more beautiful than the bright gardens by her old cottage. Maybe she could bring life to it one day and make it even grander.

She leaned over the marble balcony and inspected the earth-like atmosphere. From here, they could see the entrance to the Elysium field, where souls could be happy and free after death. She couldn't help but wonder what her place would be here—what her duties could be. Would she help those souls? Would she tend to the various fields as Persephone?

She was so wrapped up in her thoughts that she jumped when Markus's hand slid around her waist. "It's just me," he whispered. The warmth that always accompanied his touch spread through her, and she let her head rest against his chest. But she was still caught up in her thoughts.

"What will I do here?" she finally asked, sighing as her eyes followed the horizon. "It's clear what your place is in this story, but I don't know what mine is." She watched the murky sky turn gray and wondered what made it shift. There was so much about this place she didn't understand.

Markus wrapped his arms around her from behind and rested his face on her shoulder. "This kingdom is yours." The bass of his voice made her knees weak. She closed her eyes and listened. "You can do anything you want here. It's just as much meant to be yours as it is to be mine." He kissed her neck, and her face warmed.

She looked up into his eyes, and that warmth skated across her skin. He looked at her so adoringly—in that way she could never get enough of. Suddenly, she was at a loss for words. She was pressed against him and enveloped in his stare. His hand stroked her face and then fell down her back, and she was breathless.

Her eyes fluttered closed, and he pressed his lips against hers. Her arms draped over his shoulders as he kissed her more deeply. One of his hands trailed down her leg, and her breath dissolved in her lungs. His fingers wrapped behind her knee, and he scooped her up, carrying her back into the room.

She didn't open her eyes. She just kept kissing him, the evening air cool against her bare shoulders. She didn't see anything at all until she felt herself fall onto the large bed at the back of the room. A surge of excitement sparked through her blood as she looked up at him.

The hungry look in his eyes made her ache, and she let herself fall defenseless beneath him. His lips fell onto hers with a flurry of sparks, the impact rippling down her body in dozens of light, shocking waves. Warmth pooled through her, and her arms sprawled out onto the plush bed. He pressed against her, kissing her madly, his tongue trailing against hers. She surrendered herself to him, letting her mind shut off and live by feeling. His hand roamed through the gaps in her dress, and their kissing intensified. They let themselves go, kissing wildly. Urgent. Hungry. Chaotic. Free.

His hands found their way to her neck. Each finger slowly trailed down her exposed skin, and when his grasp reached the material of her dress, he pulled it lower. A spark of heat rushed down her legs, and she helped him tug off the top of her gown. He pulled it lower until nothing was left on her body but him.

She opened her eyes to see the way he looked at her. The way he touched her body and drank in every inch of it. The urge to be one with him was too great for her to stand any longer. She reached forward and gathered the material of his shirt, and he helped her take it off as she clawed herself closer to him. They kissed feverishly until nothing existed between them but the warmth their bodies made together. His mouth left hers, and he kissed down her chest, and her nails scratched up his back.

His tongue formed a map up her body until he was back at her lips, and a tempestuous rush of blood pulsed through her. He grabbed hold of her hips, pressing into the hollow of her bones as he removed any ounce of space left between them. The heat between them rose until she gasped, and they finally became one.

Her shoulders rolled back, and her mind went blank. It was explosive. A beautiful sensation that woke every nerve in her body. Every ounce of blood and starved emotion. Every frenzied craving was ravenous as she moved with him, their bodies finally fully tied. She reveled in the intangible bliss and let herself succumb to every passionate motion.

She wanted to feel every part of him. Every breath. Every movement. She wanted to know every thought, every emotion—everything that passed through him. She wanted all of it. This gave her a piece of that. This passionate act she had longed for so desperately.

They were fire and ice in a raging storm, thunder crashing around them, lightning fizzing through their veins.

Then there was an explosion of color. A powerful blooming deep within her. And starlight.

She opened her eyes.

He leaned down and placed his forehead on hers as he caught his breath. She swallowed and tried to breathe, but it was hard when he was on her like this. So vulnerable and bare and completely hers.

He smiled an infectious grin that left her laughing, though she wasn't sure why. He fell beside her and joined in her light laughter, gathering her in his arms. She nestled herself against his chest as he pulled a blanket around them. Her face was hot against his skin, but everything else was so perfectly warm. She sighed in dewy peace, closing her eyes and enjoying the balmy sensation settling in her blood like warm water.

She smiled in her half-conscious state as she felt his fingers trail up and down her arm. Her senses were quieting, but her mind was still too fuzzy to function.

"Mmm . . . I liked that," she said mindlessly.

"Which part?"

"All of it." She opened her eyes to cast him a flirtatious look. She stretched her arms above her head, then let them flop on the pillow above her, coyly scrunching her nose. "I like you."

He ran his hand through her hair, studying the blush-tinted strands as they pooled over his fingers. His dark eyes were gentle and serene as they met hers. "I love you, Correlia," he said. Sincerely. Absolute.

"I love you, too," she whispered back, the beginning of tears stinging her eyes. He smiled, continuing to brush his fingers through her hair.

"I enjoyed it, too, by the way," he said with a wink. "Very much." He cast her a playful smile, and she felt the warmth creep up her cheekbones. She squealed and buried her face in her hands. She forced herself to ignore how bashful she felt and looked up at him, but when she saw his eyes widen at something across the room, she paused. "Correlia . . . Look."

She sat up and followed his gaze, but she didn't need to. They were everywhere. Filling the room with a soothing fragrance.

Flowers. The most beautiful assortment of blossoming roses and lilies she'd ever seen. And there were many others—plants that didn't have names yet, in every color she could possibly imagine.

"Did I make those?" she asked in awe. He raked a hand through his hair, and she watched the muscles on his arm flex slightly. Her gaze followed his movements, and she bit her bottom lip.

"You did," he said, finally taking his eyes off the flowers and looking back at her. He grabbed her hands and squeezed them. "You made all of these. I'm so proud of you."

A smile stretched across her face. She didn't know what was more pleasing—seeing what she'd created or witnessing the incredible cuteness of his face after making such an adorable statement.

"I knew you had it in you."

She couldn't help but giggle again. "This is insane," she said, falling onto her back. "I can't believe I made all of these." She couldn't process it. She couldn't process *anything*. Her mind was liquid.

He leaned over her and trailed his fingers down her chest and onto her stomach. His eyes followed the movement of his hand, and she followed the movement of his eyes.

She wanted him again.

Without taking so much as another breath, Corre leaned forward and kissed him, and he grabbed onto her and kissed her back. She let herself become his again. Until the room was so filled with flowers it was impossible to move. They laughed and spent the rest of the night playfully enjoying each other's company, wrapped up in the comfort of their new home.

The crystals hanging from the chandelier above them were like rain-drops frozen in time. That's exactly how they felt—what they had always wanted to be—suspended in time, together.

It was magical. This whole palace was. Everything from the marble floors to the balcony that showed her the fields she could roam and rule forever. And this bedroom. Their brand new haven in this glorious castle made just for them.

And of course, seeing Markus let himself go and finally be happy and at peace was the best part. She could get used to this life. To this seemingly impossible happiness.

Eventually, they fell asleep, drunk on love and bliss. And strenuous exercise.

CHAPTER
FORTY-THREE

Markus

M arkus smiled as he watched the even movements of Correlia's chest rising and falling in her sleep like the flutterings of a bird. He loved seeing her in such a tranquil state. He moved a strand of light hair from her face and let his hand fall down the curve of her neck. When she made a small noise and moved slightly, still fast asleep, his heart swelled.

How had he gotten so lucky?

His gaze lingered on every feature of her face. On the freckles dotting her nose and the way she held her lips. The daintiness of her chin and the curves of her cheeks. And when she'd finally awaken, he'd be able to see the light in her eyes. And whatever else was in that gaze of hers when she looked up at him so unabashedly. With such honest adoration. Like he deserved to be loved so much.

But the swelling in his chest soon vanished, and Thanatos's words resounded in his mind, swapping that joy he'd finally let himself grab onto with a sharp, stabbing pain.

You're pathetic.

You're weak.

No wonder your parents didn't love you.

Do you truly think she cares for you?

No one could ever care for you. You know that.

The words cut through him, splicing his mind and bleeding into his chest.

No matter how happy he wanted to be, he just couldn't.

Thanatos still had a hold on him, squeezing his heart from his place in the shadows. Not allowing him to be happy, even after he was gone.

Maybe Markus didn't deserve such a luxury as being happy and carefree. No matter how much he wanted it.

He didn't deserve it.

He *wanted* to deserve it.

He wanted to embrace it.

Correlia thinks I'm worthy of love, he begged his mind to accept, but Thanatos responded in its stead.

You're pathetic. You worthless child.

He curled his hand into a tight fist on his lap, his nails digging into his skin. The pain of everything else was too overwhelming. The darkness was rushing in like a violent wave. It was as if he was trying to escape that room of nightmares with no way out.

But then his way out spoke.

"Markus? What's wrong?"

He looked at her. His new wife, sleepy-eyed with a voice full of worry.

How can you make her happy? the voice in his mind chided. *She's going to regret tying herself to you.*

"Markus?" She leaned forward, and those beautiful eyes stared up at him.

The muscles in his chest clenched, and tears flooded his eyes. "Why can't it all just go away?" he whispered.

Her eyebrows pulled together. "Why can't what go away?"

His breaths shuddered, and the pain in his chest intensified. Those muscles cranked tighter and tighter like a key turning in the back of a clock. His whole body trembled. "I can't . . . I can't." How could he tell her that he couldn't be happy? That he was so defective that his mind wouldn't allow the emotion to linger longer than an hour or two, if that? How could he explain that as soon as he let himself feel joy, pain or guilt or whatever it was flooded through him, and he heard Thanatos's voice in his head?

"I don't know how to explain it," he finally said, and her frown deepened. The guilt in his gut worsened. "I don't want to hurt you."

"What do you mean? You could never hurt me."

His gaze fell to the risen skin on his palms—the half-moons of pink from the pressure of his nails. "There's something wrong with me." He didn't look up. He couldn't. "I want to be happy, but . . . I can't." The tears burned in his eyes, and he had to swallow hard to keep going. "There's so much pain in me." He stared at his hands until he caught his breath enough to speak again. To stop the quaking of his limbs. The cranking in his chest.

"Correlia, when I'm with you, I'm so happy." He swallowed, trying to figure out how to put this strange horror into words. "But I have so much pain. It's smaller now because of you, and less frequent when I'm with you. But it's still there. I don't know . . . I guess I thought it wouldn't be there anymore." It was strenuous getting the words out, but he owed her the truth. A part of him hoped she'd be able to help him decipher what it all meant. Her eyes searched his. He tried to read her expression, but when she still didn't reply after more and more seconds ticked by, he panicked. "But it has nothing to do with you!" he said quickly. "I love you. So much."

Please don't leave me, he wanted to add.

But instead of getting upset or hurt, like he thought she would, she reached out and hugged him, squeezing him tight, holding him until he remembered again—that he *was* worthy of love. That someone *did* love him and that she was the one worth sacrificing everything for. He wrapped his arms tightly around her and buried his face in her neck. He was so glad he'd risked everything to see her that day and that every day since he had let her walk deeper and deeper into his heart until she'd filled it completely, sealing all the gaps and rounding all the crooked edges. She even lit up the darkness when the pain crept in.

And she did it effortlessly. In an embrace. In a kiss. In the glimmer of her eyes and the dimples in her cheeks.

"Maybe it won't be easy at first," she whispered, still clinging to him. "But every day, it will get a little easier. And some days, you won't hurt at all." She leaned back and looked at him. Those beautiful eyes stared up at him with all the sunshine they always possessed. "And some days you may *really want* to punch Nikias in the face." A laugh burst from his mouth, and she giggled, trying to continue. "But! *But*. It will be okay." She stroked her fingers down the side of his face. "I promise. I'll always be here for you. Through all of it. The good and the bad."

The emotion swelled in his chest again, and he tried not to wonder what she saw in him and just let himself be loved. He didn't want to cry, but at this point, she probably wasn't surprised when the tears streamed down his face. He couldn't speak, so he nodded and wrapped his arms around her, holding onto her like she was a raft keeping him safe at sea. Little did she know that keeping her safe kept him together, too.

Maybe there was something to the whole soulmate idea. Because he wasn't sure how much of him had ever existed without her. He needed her. And he'd admit that fact if she ever asked—that he needed to feel her love in the moments he wanted to die or disappear. In the moments he felt like falling apart. He could finally admit that needing help wasn't a weakness. He needed her in the darkness just as much as in the light—in their beautifully carefree moments of laughter and passion. He needed her. Like a tonic to cure the most vicious pain.

And he wanted her. Always. In every way.

She was the sun to every broken star in his sky. The warm day to his bitter night. He hoped that, some days, she'd let him be her sun, too. Because loving her came with that desire. To take care of her like she took care of him.

He would never let anything happen to her. She was everything. He loved her beyond comprehension. So, for her, he would try.

Tears were still falling down his face, but he managed to speak. "I'll work on it. I'll fight these demons. I'll find a way." He held her face in his hands; it looked so small and delicate in his large palms.

"I know you will, and I'll help you," she said softly. "You don't have to do it alone."

The love and relief that washed through him was striking. He whimpered and broke into another quiet sob, letting his forehead rest against hers. In complete opposition to every time Thanatos had told him that it wasn't masculine to cry or be cared for, he let himself cry and be cared for. She rubbed his back, and he sobbed. He sobbed until they were lying on the bed and he was all out of tears.

When he could finally speak, he pulled her into him and kissed her. "I'd do anything for you." He brushed the rosy hair from her face and watched it fall onto the pillow like a strawberry waterfall. He kissed the tip of her nose, and he loved how she scrunched it and smiled when his lips left her skin. An invisible arrow dove right into his heart.

"I know," she said. "I feel the same way."

Her long lashes fluttered as she looked up at him, and his gaze fell to her lips. He touched them, and they parted slightly. All the love pulsing through his body amplified and melted into desire. It was hard to ignore that the only thing she was wearing was a blanket.

The heat in his blood rose, and his eyes fell down her body, his fingers following their lead. When she let out a small noise, he looked up and saw the yearning in her eyes, and he couldn't hold back anymore.

He dove deeply into the fullness of her lips and fell on top of her, draping the blanket over them. Her legs wrapped around his waist. Her skin was warm against his. His blood turned to fire, and his hands found every part of her.

He wanted to swallow her whole as he sucked on her bottom lip and tasted her tongue against his teeth. His mind lost all function as she scratched up his back and grabbed onto the hair at the base of his skull. She held onto him so desperately it drove him crazy. He sucked on her collarbone, biting it gently as she let out another feminine sound. His teeth trailed against her skin. Excitement surged through him at the way she surrendered to his every whim. His every touch, kiss, and bite. He needed to make her his. To make her a part of him both in soul and body.

He let himself go, and she gave herself to him, begging him to take control of her. He loved that she fell apart when he touched her and that she wanted him to take over. He loved that he could touch her and move with her and give her every beautiful spark and delicious sensation—that the primal instincts within him found hers and gave her everything she desired. That he could show her what it felt like to be in existential bliss.

After everything had peaked and thundered, and the blinding passion had calmed into a pool of serenity, he looked down at her. Nothing was sexier than how she looked in this moment. The muscles on her face relaxed, the color hot on her cheeks. The smile on her lips completely unguarded.

He couldn't help but kiss her one more time, and she accepted it breathlessly before he fell beside her and wrapped her back up in him.

Closing his eyes, he let out a long breath. Every anxious thought was gone, purged from their passion and the unbridled love between them. He hummed, absentmindedly stroking her hair, slightly damp with sweat, and his skin went warm at the touch of her fingers on his chest.

"I love you," she whispered before kissing the spot her hand had just touched.

"I love you too. I'm not sure why you do, though." He tried to give her a playful look, but something about it seemed to bother her.

"Do you really not know why I love you?"

Oh, no. Did I screw this up?

"It's okay! I'm sorry," he said quickly.

She sat up and looked at him. "Don't apologize. I just want to know."

"Oh." He wasn't sure what else to say.

A slight smile returned to her lips. "I love you for so many reasons." She trailed a finger across his chest. "A lot of it is hard to explain. It's almost intangible and indescribable. You just . . . You make me feel so . . ." She let out a long, content sigh, and looked into his eyes. "You make me feel like I'm not alone. You see the good in me. You're a part of me I recognized the moment I fell for you." She laughed. "I'm not sure which part happened first. I guess, at some point, I just knew you and I were made from the same soul, and everything else made sense."

"I feel the same way," he said, stroking her hand. "I feel you so deep within me I sometimes don't know which parts are me and which parts are you."

She leaned forward and fell on top of him. He was so much bigger than her; her entire body could rest comfortably on his. She placed her chin on her hands and looked up at him.

She was so beautiful. This radiant, magnificent goddess.

How could she believe she was anything less than perfect?

"I don't know how I could possibly find any fault in you," he said, his arms wrapping around her. He kissed her again.

"Believe me. I have plenty of faults."

"I don't believe that."

She laughed. "That's precisely why one of the reasons I love you is that you see the best in me."

"Well, if there are any faults in you, you do a good job at hiding them."

"You're silly."

"What?" he laughed.

She leaned up and rested her cheek against her fist. "You are so wonderful."

He blinked, staring at her in shock. "What are you talking about?"

Her nose scrunched when she smiled, and he nearly died. "Something you probably don't know about me, my love," she said, "is that I simply do a very good job at hiding the darkness."

He frowned. "What darkness?"

Her smile faded. "I'm not as happy as I seem sometimes. I have that darkness in me, too. The kind that makes it hard to think or sleep. The kind that brings back memories you wish you could forget. I'm just very good at hiding it when it comes barging in."

He watched her carefully as she spoke. It killed him that she ever had to suffer, and he had no idea it was something she struggled with often, too. "I would take it all from you if I could," he said.

"I know you would, but you have enough on your shoulders. I can handle this much."

Her gaze fell away, and her smile turned forced. She was already doing it again. Putting on that mask. He tilted her face toward his. "Correlia, I'm your husband now. It's my job to help you carry this. Just like you want to help me with mine." He smiled. "I guess, *you're* the silly one."

She laughed. "Why am I the silly one?"

"Because you want to help me but don't want me to help you. That's silly."

She rested her face on her hands, still lying contently on top of him. "I guess you're right," she said. "I guess that is a little silly."

He ran his hand down her back and then squeezed her tight. "Don't worry. I still think you're perfect."

She giggled and looked back up at him. "Well, then. I guess I should keep telling you why I think *you're* perfect."

He raised a skeptical brow. "How the hell am *I* perfect?"

"You're strong," she said, and the conviction in her voice was startling. "You're brave. So ridiculously brave. You make me want to be more courageous—to stand up for things more. And whether you realize it or not, you've taught me so much about the world. About how humanity and the gods really work."

"What do you mean?"

She moved off of him, sitting beside him to look at him more directly.

"Before I met you, I thought things were pretty simple. I thought the gods I knew were good and the ones down here were bad. And Zeus . . . People love him." She sighed and leaned against the headboard. "People respect him. He's charismatic and friendly, and he seems to be everybody's friend, but he was one of the worst monsters all along." She looked back into Markus's eyes. "Everyone had always told me that you were the monster, but you're the kindest, most sincere god I've ever met. I've never felt so un-alone in my life now that I have you."

With her face so close to his, he could see how much she meant every word, and though her lips were turned up into a gentle smile, tears were forming in her beautiful, emerald-honey eyes.

"You're not alone," he whispered, pulling her closer. "Not at all." He kissed her softly, then quietly added, "And I'll make sure you never feel alone again."

"Thank you," she said, and he kissed her. They kissed until they were all tangled up in each other between the sheets. And soon, he found himself peacefully resting against the top of her head, mindlessly playing with her hair again.

Her face turned up to look at him. "There is so much to love about you, Markus," she said, and in those earnest eyes, he saw absolute sincerity, and he decided to believe it.

"Okay," he said. "I'll believe you."

Her face lit up. "Good. Because I'm right."

He chuckled, physically unable to take his eyes off hers. "But only if I'm allowed to hold onto my belief—my *knowledge*—that *you* are the perfect one in this relationship."

She narrowed her eyes, but she still smiled. "That I cannot agree to."

"You can't deny the truth, Correlia."

She let out a playful growl and hit him with a pillow.

"Hey! What was that for?" he said with a laugh.

"For being silly again!" Her face was so unbelievably adorable he couldn't stop himself from grabbing her and tackling her.

She fell in a fit of laughter.

He wrestled with her, laughing and feeling so very un-alone as he tried to pin her against the mattress, but she launched herself on top of him instead. His stomach cramped with laughter, and he wasn't sure if he'd ever laughed this much in his entire life, even if he added up every time he had ever done so.

He basked in it—in the sheer joy in the air and the melody of her voice as she giggled and squealed his name. He finally realized that being happy was possible. And that this was just the beginning.

EPILOGUE

Corre

C orre watched Markus pull his shirt over his broad shoulders and admired every muscle on his back. Her mind floated back to their moments of passion. The heat of his body and the feelings of ecstasy. Her brain had turned to syrup, and her body was so light it was hard to tell she was still confined to its physicality.

She sighed and ran her hand over the bedding, feeling its silky, creamy texture on her fingertips. "What are you going to do today?" she asked.

"I haven't really thought about it." He turned to smile at her. "I've been a little too preoccupied."

"Fair," she said coyly, and he fell next to her, bouncing her gently as he leaned into her. He kissed up her neck, and she let her eyes close again. "I'm going to forget how to think if you keep doing that."

"Then I'll know I've done my job properly."

"Is that so?" She laughed, but when he got back up again, she couldn't help but remember the day before. Before all the beauty and bliss. She thought about Nikias and that flash of memory, and about everything that had happened that should have left her fully exhausted if she hadn't ended the night feeling absolutely euphoric.

"Are you going to—" She started, but she wasn't sure if she wanted to finish the sentence. Maybe she should have thought before starting it, though, because now he was looking at her expectantly, and she knew she had to finish it. "Are you going to address your new subjects . . . and . . ." She stared up at the ceiling, counting every crystal dripping from the chandelier and watching the light fracture off each one.

"What is it you're not telling me?" he asked.

She picked at the material on the blanket wrapped around her, wishing it was at least a little imperfect so she had a loose thread to focus on. But there was no such thread, so she was forced to look into Markus's eyes and possibly ruin the moment. He was so happy and peaceful. She didn't want to take that away.

When she smiled half-heartedly, he frowned and placed a hand on her arm. "What is it?"

She chewed on the inside of her cheek, but she couldn't stop thinking about it. She could almost feel the fire from the cottages that day. She remembered the sorrow on her mother's face, and the moments before her death. She remembered the boy whose parents had willingly done the opposite of what her mother had done, their hands begging Thanatos to take the boy and spare them instead, despite the child's desperate cries as he clung to his mother's apron.

A lump formed in her throat, and she had to stare at the light above her to stop tears from falling. She wished she could forget that day and erase the memory of her mother's death. She hadn't remembered it for so long. She wished it had never resurfaced, but she also knew it was important to remember.

She thought carefully before responding. "Markus, I knew the general before he came here." She winced as his face fell. "I know he's a horrid, wretched man, but I think you should talk to him. I think you should maybe still let him work with the soldiers here. As long as he behaves himself. Maybe that validation could bring him peace. And maybe . . ." She slid her hand into his black, wavy hair. "Maybe that could give you peace, too. Maybe he will finally respect you the way you deserve, and even if he doesn't, at least you set him free in a way Thanatos never did for you. For either of you. Who knows what he told Nikias about you—what lies he might have spun to pit you two against each other."

He wasn't looking at her anymore. His face was tense, his jaw clenched. But his hand still softly held onto her arm. "I don't know if I'm ready for that."

"That's okay!" she said quickly, running her hand through his hair again, then holding onto the back of his neck, moving to face him. "Just something to think about."

He nodded and, to her surprise, he smiled. "Thank you," he said softly, leaning forward and kissing her on the forehead.

"Of course. I'll be right there beside you whenever you want to do anything. Whatever you're ready for, whatever you want to do—about anything—I'll be with you." She kissed him on the cheek, and his face fell gently onto hers.

He wrapped her up in him and held her. Her heart warmed again, her mind going hazy. The clenching in her chest stopped, those memories fleeing, unable to compete with the peace Markus brought her.

"There *is* something I'm ready for," he finally said.

"Mm?" Her mind was still mush, and the rich deepness of his voice didn't help.

"I want to see my parents."

She pushed herself up to look at him. "Really?"

He nodded. "I think I'm ready." He grabbed her hand, first eclipsing it in his enormous one, and then threading his fingers in hers. "If you come with me. I think I'd be ready to hear them out." His dark eyes flickered to hers, and she smiled.

"Of course." She placed her hand on his face, and he leaned into it. "Are you ready to go?"

"Now?"

"I mean, we don't have to, but nothing is on our agenda today."

He stared off for a moment, then nodded. "Okay." He let out a long, heavy breath. "I guess now is as good a time as any."

"Let's get ready to go then." Corre kept her voice light, hoping it would ease his nerves. She whipped off the blanket and started sliding off the bed. "I'll just get ready and—"

Markus grabbed her by the arm and pulled her back to him.

She blinked up into his eyes and instantly knew what he was thinking. A sly smile crept up his face.

"Maybe we can wait just a little longer." He moved the back of his hand down the side of her neck and off her shoulder, his eyes following it before slowly making their way back to her gaze.

Heat flooded her face. "Okay," she said, but she was already breathless. How was it possible that he still made her feel this way after all their activities the night before? A smile formed on her lips. "We have time." She barely let the last word out before he kissed her, and she fell back onto the bed.

Markus

"Are you sure we're going the right way?" Markus asked. He'd roamed these labyrinths hundreds of times over the years, but his brain hadn't functioned properly in over twenty-four hours thanks to his new queen. He stole another glance of her in her black gown, unable to stop looking at her exposed shoulders and the way the dress fell in perfect folds against the curves of her body. The determination on her flawless face as she guided him through Tartarus was enchanting, and he was convinced she was the only deity worthy of ruling this place. She was the only being, alive or dead, who deserved to rule this place, Olympus, or the Earth itself.

She deserved everything, and he would do everything he could to give her as much of it as possible. He could handle not being able to think anymore if it meant he could be loved by her and be one with her in flesh, bone, and soul.

It was a small price to pay.

Correlia shrugged. "I think so." She turned to look at him. When she caught him studying her body, he quickly shot his gaze forward. His face instantly went red. She laughed. "We were *just* intimate. How are you still looking at me like that?"

"I will never stop looking at you like this." He smiled at her, and the coy look on her adorably scrunching face made his shoulders relax. It was hard to believe he was married to her. Bound to her. She was so perfect. The embodiment of life itself.

To him, she was everything.

"Ah. I think we're almost here." She walked in front of him, holding tightly onto one of his hands as she stepped through a dank opening in one of the rocky walls outside the more well-kept labyrinth he was used to roaming.

"Um . . . Are you sure?"

"Yes, I'm sure!" She shot him a playful glare. "Don't you question me."

He lifted his free hand. "I'm sorry, my queen. How could I ever doubt you?"

She started to laugh but was cut short when they rounded the corner and he saw someone at the end of the hall. It looked like an old man stoking a fire. "There he is!" she said, and he couldn't believe it. Her voice bounced across the rocky walls, and the man turned in their direction.

As soon as Markus saw him, the young Hades froze. He never thought he'd see that face again. Even though they'd gone searching for him, part of him hadn't believed they'd actually find him. "Father?" he said, and the old man at the end of the corridor dropped the long stick he was using to keep his fire alive.

He walked toward them slowly, with just as much surprise and disbelief as his son. Correlia released Markus's hand and stepped back. The young god was in a daze, and as he took one final step toward his father, he felt the old man's hand reach up to touch his face.

"Markus? Is that really you?"

"Yes," he said in a whisper. A knot formed in his throat, and his chin quivered. The next thing he felt before the tears fell from his eyes was his father bringing him in and holding him tightly against his chest.

"Son. I've missed you so much." Markus let himself cry as he held onto his father. "I thought I'd lost you."

He tried to compose himself long enough to reply. "I thought you didn't love me."

His father pulled back and looked straight into his eyes, his arms gripping Markus's shoulders. "I have always loved you."

There was a hole that had always been gaping open in Markus's heart, and though Correlia was healing him one shattered piece at a time, this filled something she could not fill alone. He was so grateful she'd led him here. That he could reunite with someone he hadn't known loved him and actually feel loved by a parent. To have someone to properly guide him. Someone far from the treacherously evil god that had raised him with cruelty. Someone who looked to have sacrificed something for him that no other god would. This scruffy-looking man with grayed hair and something in his eyes he'd only seen in Correlia's. Kindness.

"Father," he said again, but his voice was shaky. "You're mortal."

One side of his father's lips turned up into a smile, and he grunted out a laugh. "It's a long story, but I can tell you on the way up to your mother's."

Markus froze. "My mother's?"

His father cocked a brow. "Don't you want to see her?"

"Yes, of course—"

"Then, let's go."

The sun was bright, and that damp scent of Tartarus was gone. Markus had forgotten how warm and sweet it was on Olympus. It reminded him of Correlia, who was squeezing his arm with an unrivaled tightness.

"Why do you seem so nervous?" he asked.

"Do I?"

He laughed. "Just ask my arm."

"Oh." She loosened her grip, and he laughed again.

"It's okay, really, but what are you worried about?"

Markus felt even lighter than he had that morning, which was saying something. His father told him what had happened the day he'd been taken, and memories were slowly finding their way back to him, though they were still muddled. When he heard his father's words, he half-expected to get the sort of revelations Correlia had—those moments of clarity and remembrance—but he didn't.

It was okay for now, though, because he felt the realness of his father's words. He knew in his heart that they were true. One day, he might remember, but for now, hearing the story had been enough. He'd been loved all this time, as Correlia had assured him, and now, he'd finally see his mother's face after all this time. The woman he sometimes dreamt about, who had held him and sang to him when he was just a child.

"Mother?"

Markus looked up, confused as Correlia uttered the word before running toward a small woman cradling a basket of fruit just a few trees away from them. They were almost out of the woods on their way to one of the peaks of Mt. Olympus. What were the odds that they'd run into Correlia's mother on the way to see his? It almost seemed like fate, especially for the slight woman whose hands flew to her mouth.

She dropped the basket of fruit she'd been holding as she ran toward Markus's new wife. He watched the two come together as an armful of fruit rolled down the slight bump in the ground and hit his boot. He couldn't take his eyes off Correlia as she squeezed the now weeping goddess in her arms.

"Correlia, I thought I'd lost you." The woman squeezed tighter.

Markus froze at the familiar words, and guilt pinched at his gut. Would Correlia's mother have gone through what his father had if Markus had never come up here to see his own mother?

He rushed to Correlia's side. She was already releasing her embrace with her mother when she turned to introduce him. "Mother, this is Markus. My husband." The pinching in his stomach released. He would never tire of being reminded that he was hers.

He smiled and pulled off one of his gloves to offer his hand to the goddess. "It's nice to meet you," he said, wondering if that was how people usually introduced themselves. "I'm sorry if I worried you," he quickly added. "It was not my intent to—"

"Oh hush," the woman said, waving her hand in the air, and he blinked. "Wha—"

"Just come here," she said, now waving both her hands toward herself.

He hesitantly stepped forward, and Correlia laughed. "It's just a hug, Markus. She's not going to eat you."

He chuckled nervously, but he still couldn't help feeling guilty. He bent down and tried his best to hug this stranger, but she was so small he worried she might break if he embraced her with even a quarter of his usual strength.

She patted his back heartily when he finally did give her an awkward partial hug. She was stronger than she looked.

"I'm sorry I didn't bring her to see you sooner."

"Sooner?" Correlia asked. "Markus, we just woke up less than three hours ago." He straightened his back, and Correlia reached forward to take his hand. Her voice softened. "It's okay. No one is upset with you. We would have come to see her soon. I would have asked, and you would have listened." She looked up at him with those beautiful eyes, and he had to swallow a lump in his throat. "Okay?"

"Okay." He returned the smile dimpling her cheeks.

"How about you all come to my place? I'll whip you up something to eat," Correlia's mother said.

He opened his mouth to agree. He'd never had Olympus food before, but Correlia shook her head. "We're a little busy today. Maybe tomorrow?" She looked up at him with a smile, and his heart skipped.

"Tomorrow would be great," he agreed.

"I'd love that," the small goddess said, and Correlia gave her one more hug before they started back toward the mountain peak.

"I'll tell you everything," she said as she waved to her mother. "Well, almost everything." She winked at Markus, and his face burned.

He couldn't bear looking at her mother after that, so he just yelled a quick, "See you tomorrow," as they headed up to his mother's cottage. When they got far enough away, he shot Correlia an unamused look. "You're wicked," he said, and she smiled mischievously.

"You love it." She scrunched her nose at him, which gave him the sudden urge to push her against a tree and kiss her ravenously. But his father was still present, and he wanted to stay focused on the matter at hand, so he resisted. He hadn't seen his mother since he was a child. Now, he would finally have his chance to. It was best to stay focused.

The trek was much longer than Markus had anticipated, and it seemed like their destination would never appear. It didn't help that his heart was pounding nearly out of his chest the closer the moment approached. When he saw his mother, what would he say? Would she still look the same? What if they ran into Zeus?

"This way," his father said. "We're just about there."

They were higher up than Markus had ever been before. It was a little unnerving as he glanced down the steep side of the mountain. The trees they'd weaved through earlier looked like little vegetables from here. It would be beyond painful if he slipped.

His stomach leapt up his throat.

"Now, who's nervous?" Correlia teased, and he realized his grip on her hand was tighter than it should have been.

He quickly let go. "Oh, I'm sorry."

She took it again and reached up to kiss his cheek. "Don't worry about it." When she looked ahead again, she pointed. "Look." He followed her gaze to the small, rectangular cottage, similar in size and color to Correlia's old home.

He swallowed hard, his skin turning cold. The world was moving slowly around him, and each step was harder to take. What if his mother didn't want to see him? What if she was disappointed in what he'd become?

"Maybe this was a mistake," he said.

"What? Markus, no!" Correlia looked up at him frantically.

Thomas stopped and turned to Markus. The wind whipped against his silvery hair as he looked his son in the eyes. There was a gentleness in his voice as he spoke. "It's all right. She will be happy to see you. Happy is an understatement." He nodded toward the cottage. "Come on."

Markus reluctantly continued on. Breathing was difficult, but he kept moving. They stopped at a set of beautifully carved wooden doors. His father knocked on them with a shaky fist. And then it hit him. This was likely the first time Thomas had seen his wife after all these years, too.

But before he could think too much about it, the doors swung open, and a goddess almost as small as Correlia's mother stood gaping at his father in shock. "Thomas?" she said in disbelief, leaning forward as if to make sure her eyes weren't playing tricks on her.

"It's me." He took a step back. "And I brought our son home."

She looked past her husband at the tall, no-longer-thirteen-year-old standing behind him. Tears formed in her eyes. "Markus?" She said his name in a whisper. She took one hesitant step before rushing to him. There was a desperation in her eyes as she looked up at him. "Is it really you?" Tears spilled down her cheeks, and she grabbed hold of his arms, causing that lump to reform in his throat.

"Mother . . ."

She let out a half-sob. "You're all grown up." She laughed shakily, and tears fell like rain down her face. "You're so handsome." She buried her face in his tunic, and he held her, trying to reconcile this moment with every lie Thanatos had ever told him. In the end, everything his former master had told him was a lie.

Markus *was* loved. He hadn't been abandoned.

Maybe he wasn't a monster after all.

After a long embrace, his mother sniffed back tears and said, "Come in, come in!" She was smiling now, her youthful face glowing. He couldn't help but notice that her dark brown eyes matched his own. They were locked on his eyes in disbelief. Then she squeezed his cheek like he was a child again. Right now, it felt like a part of him still was, as he felt his mother's love and remembered how it felt when she said his name and squeezed his cheek. He couldn't stop the tears that fell as she led him into the cottage.

There wasn't a dry eye among them. They embraced that fact as they spent the rest of the day in each other's company, laughing and eating and learning from each other. Correlia was a delight, as to be expected, and she had Markus and his parents enraptured in her stories and liveliness. She was equally enraptured in the stories they told of when Markus was a child. He loved every minute of it.

When the sky outside turned into a ruddy mixture of orange and red, and Correlia started to yawn, Markus reluctantly decided to call it a day.

"I think we have to go for today," he said, and his mother frowned.

"What? So soon?"

"Lily, he's been here for nearly nine hours," his father said, and Markus couldn't help but laugh at this slice of a normal life. A life that was now his. He was witnessing bickering parents with his very own eyes.

"We'll be back," Correlia said, her voice as light and cheerful as it often was. One of the things he loved about her. "And thank you sooo much for the food. It was wonderful meeting you."

"You too, dear," Markus's mother said as she gave her new daughter-in-law a hug. Her eyes once again met her son's, and she ran over to embrace him. "I can't believe you're really here," she whispered, and he wrapped her into one last embrace before leaving.

"I can't believe it, either," he said, and when he pulled away, he looked up at his father. "Don't feel like you have to leave. We can make it back on our own."

Thomas lifted a mug of cider. "Don't worry. I won't." He gave him his signature half-smile but then got up and gave him a hug, too, before the new leaders of the Underworld left the cottage and headed back home.

"Your parents sure are lovely," Correlia said, and despite his cheeks hurting from smiling so much today, he grinned.

"They are, aren't they?" He took hold of her hand as they walked down Mt. Olympus, but Markus was in a daze. So much had happened in such a short period of time. His mind was shifting from one thought to another every few seconds. He thought about his parents. About Thanatos. About Nikias. He wondered how much Thanatos had wedged between the two boys. What might the former ruler have said to make the general hate Markus so much?

A flurry of conflicting thoughts and emotions tossed through Markus's head. He still couldn't get himself to see Nikias with anything but disdain, but maybe Correlia was right. He needed to give Nikias that one moment of mercy. He needed to talk to him, and maybe he'd get some answers as to how their master had played into their feud.

Thinking about Thanatos still plucked at his nerves, but his thoughts were thankfully interrupted by the beautiful beam of starlight holding his hand.

"Are you okay?" Correlia asked.

Markus's face had fallen at some point, his features held tightly in a scowl, but when he looked at her, the muscles relaxed, and he was able to smile again. He couldn't fully explain why, but when he looked at her—and when she looked at him the way she was now—he knew that everything would be okay.

"Yeah. I will be, anyway." Her face brightened and she threw her arms around him, catching him off guard. "Well, hello," he said, laughing.

The smile stayed on her lips, and there was a sort of dewy gleam in her eyes. "Will you carry me home?" she asked, the rosy sunset bringing out the golden speckles in her eyes. The warm breeze fluttered through her hair, and he kissed her, tasting the citrus bread they'd eaten before leaving his mother's cottage.

"I'd love that," he said, and he pulled her into his arms. She let out an uninhibited giggle as he did it, which made it all the sweeter. It was a miracle they didn't go tumbling down any hills on the way back to Tartarus because he couldn't take his eyes off of her the whole way there. She was magnificent. And she was his.

When they finally made it into Tartarus and her feet touched the stone floor, he couldn't help but notice that despite their dark, gloomy surroundings, a light radiated wherever she walked. Color followed her wherever she went, and he stared at her, sometimes smiling but always in awe, as she twirled her way to their palace. He was so enamored by her. Intoxicated. Utterly, unabashedly in love.

He chased her up the stairs and into the room as she squealed. His arms looped around her as they fell onto the bed, accompanied by her peels of laughter. He traced his finger over her nose, outlining her profile and letting his finger fall to her lips. When she kissed it, he jumped on top of her, and she giggled again. But he didn't go in to kiss her. Not yet. First, he wanted to look at her, and her full lips turned up into a smile.

 Right now, everything he had ever worried about, been sad about, or any conflicting feeling at all, fell away, ceasing to exist. All he saw and felt was her.

"I love you," he whispered.

She leaned up partway and kissed him. "I love you, too, my king."

He laughed. "Are we always going to address each other like that?"

She shrugged. "Probably." A smile broke across his face, and he fell on top of her, showering her with kisses as she laughed and tried kissing him back.

He had never been this happy in his entire life. It almost didn't seem right to be this happy, but he knew he needed to learn that it was okay. And he would. He'd learn how to accept it. He'd learn how to get used to walking on air.

And it would be glorious.

ACKNOWLEDGEMENTS

I would first like to thank my husband, who is extremely supportive and my biggest believer. I couldn't do this without his help manning the fort while I hid away to work on my craft. Writing is like breathing to me, and I'm so glad I have someone who does everything in his power to make sure I have time to devote myself to it. Thank you, Alex. I love you more than I could ever express.

I would also like to thank my parents for always helping me and believing in me as well. And I am thankful to all those who have loved my work and to all those who have given me a chance by reading this book. Thank you all for reading, and I hope you enjoyed this little story about Hades and Persephone. There is more to come, and I am so excited to share it with you all.

ABOUT THE AUTHOR

Elise Nelson is an author of romance, poetry, comics, and more. She has a Bachelor of Arts degree from Boise State University, where she studied English literature, creative writing, and multimedia storytelling. She is also a therapeutic writing teacher and a passionate mental health advocate. When she isn't busy writing, she loves reading, laughing, and making memories with her family.

You can visit her website at www.elisenelsonauthor.com

Milton Keynes UK
Ingram Content Group UK Ltd.
UKHW032047180324
439698UK00004B/347